Books by Catherine Gaskin

EDGE OF GLASS

THE FILE ON DEVLIN

THE TILSIT INHERITANCE

I KNOW MY LOVE

CORPORATION WIFE

BLAKE'S REACH

SARA DANE

DAUGHTER OF THE HOUSE

ALL ELSE IS FOLLY

DUST IN SUNLIGHT

WITH EVERY YEAR

THIS OTHER EDEN

EDGE OF GLASS

Edge of Glass

CATHERINE GASKIN

DOUBLEDAY & COMPANY, INC., GARDEN CITY, NEW YORK

1967

*All of the characters in this book are
fictitious, and any resemblance to
actual persons, living or dead, is
purely coincidental.*

Library of Congress Catalog Card Number 67–13784

For Joxer and Jem-Jem,
for Kay and for Al
—and the memory of the
year of the Enclave

EDGE OF GLASS

CHAPTER 1

I

Sometimes when I see a scrap of paper blown before the wind I am reminded of the way he seemed to come into the shop that morning—almost soundlessly, with only the stirring of the draft from the door causing me to look around. His stance there had that tenuous quality, as if in a second the wind might blow again and he would be gone, elusive, whimsical. I had looked at him, and with the unreasoning instinct women are forever denying and always using, I knew I didn't want him to go.

So I hurried toward him down the long narrow shop, past the game tables and writing tables, the rococo ornamented commodes, the Staffordshire dogs and the silver trays, indifferently polished now that Blanche was not there to see that they were done properly, or to do them herself. As I walked, it seemed as if I walked into one of those gilt-framed convex mirrors we sold, though I had never noticed this effect before. Perhaps it was because the man at the other end of the shop seemed to loom suddenly so largely—everything else, at the edges, diminishing. The figure was tall, and the face instantly striking—too beautiful, perhaps, for a man, though there was nothing feminine in those features, the planes sharp, the mouth a straight deep line. Perhaps my reaction to him showed in my own face, making him uneasy. He appeared about to open the door again and go; it seemed the gesture of a shy man, someone who is unsure of his acceptance.

"Can I help you?" I said.

The half-glance became a full stare, and I knew I was mistaken about the shyness. The eyes were deeply set, of that hard, brilliant blue sometimes encountered in a man, sensual in the way that the hard, straight lips also were sensual. Then he offered me a smile that softened all the lines of that arresting face, and that seemed for me to melt the gloom of that rainy Friday morning.

"Oh—I'll not be troubling you. If I could just look about for a wee while . . . ?"

"Of course," I said. I would have liked to have shown him about myself, just for the pleasure of it, but I stepped back and allowed him to get past me. His smile still lingered, as if I had done him a personal favor.

"That's very kind," he answered. His voice was deep and yet soft, an Irish voice, the accent a little thicker than I would have expected from the way he was dressed—the good tweed suit carelessly worn, the buff raincoat just fashionably soiled. Perhaps he did not quite carry off those clothes, because when I had first looked at him I had thought of an actor, but an actor would long ago have polished that accent out of existence. He continued on down the shop, pausing here and there, moving with a grace and lightness that pleased me, and I also rejected the idea that he might be a prosperous farmer, a farmer on holiday in London. And then I realized I had been tricked into the game I had vowed I would never play—becoming interested in the personalities of customers, guessing about them, acting as if I would be in this business, this shop, for the rest of my life, as Blanche had been. So I turned my back on him, stared out the window, and tried to remember that this was only a morning's work.

The name, BLANCHE D'ARCY, was still lettered in gold on a long black board above the shop, although Blanche had been dead for four months, and I could see, backward, the distorted reflection of those letters in the window of the shop across the King's Road. The traffic flowed by, the cabs and the red buses, and when the pace slowed I could see in their sides the reflection of the lighted chandeliers that hung down the length of the shop, and that reflection in turn was thrown back on the rain-slick surfaces of the pavement. Blanche's name was still high above the King's Road, as it had been for almost twenty years, and the chandeliers were lighted, as she had always lighted them to attract the customers. Blanche's customers still came, out of loyalty and affection, but we knew it was all over. The lease of the shop still had six years to run, but I knew I wouldn't stay here six years. If Mary Hughes, the woman who had worked with Blanche, didn't want it, I would sell it. It would become another coffee shop, I supposed; something that would make quick money. It was a rainy morning of a cold spring day in London, and my spirits were dampened; I remember I stood there watching the traffic and thinking of other places in which there was always sun, the kind of places I hoped to find next week when I took my holiday in France, the kind of place described in Lloyd Justin's letter from California that had arrived that morning. I wondered why, in England, we always talked as if sun was the answer to all our unhappiness.

The sound came in one of the rare moments when there was no traffic, so that it seemed louder than it need have been—the sharp tinkle of glass breaking. I swung around, but he was looking, not at the splatter of crystal fragments on the floor, but directly at me, waiting for me to turn, knowing that the glass would break and I would turn and come toward him.

"I'm very sorry," he said. "It was very clumsy of me."

Clumsy was almost the last word I would have used of him. He met my eyes and we both knew that he had lied; he knew that I knew he had lied, and he didn't care. For some reason the little crystal vase had to be broken.

"Of course I'll pay for the damage," he said. "Was it valuable?"

I bent and picked up a triangular piece of the base; he bent at the same time to forestall me, and again our eyes met. I wondered why I should be the one to look away, discomfited. Blanche's handwriting stared back at me from the little sticker on the fragment.

"Sheridan," I said. "Three guineas."

He nodded, as if the question of the money was not the most pressing on his mind. "Irish," he said. "It's Irish glass."

"Yes," I answered. He waited, and at the same time his hand went out and he took the fragment from me, not to check the price, because he didn't even glance at it, but as if he sought to make the contact. He waited, still saying nothing, and I felt compelled to add the information, as if he had the right to it. "My mother always bought Irish glass when she could. She came from Ireland."

"Your mother . . . ? Then your mother would be Blanche D'Arcy?"

The hurt was still there, as if the jagged glass had suddenly pierced my flesh. "She was Blanche D'Arcy. She's dead."

"Ah . . ." The sound was regretful. "I'm sorry. Was it long ago it happened, then?"

"Four months. Look . . . I don't . . ." I wanted to tell him to stop asking his questions, but he knew what I meant.

"Ah, well, it comes, finally, doesn't it?" He turned the fragment over and over in his fingers, still not looking at it. "Would you ever, then, have any more Irish glass? Antique pieces . . . Something to send back to Ireland. Any more Sheridan, perhaps?"

When I hesitated, he pressed again. "You know—it would be a joke, wouldn't it, to send back something Irish from London. Ireland's been a poor country so long, people forget we ever made anything good."

Perhaps it was the way he said it, as if he cared more than the casual tone would have had me believe. Which made his smashing of the Sheridan vase all the more strange. In my experience of the trade, young men looking for antique glass were rare enough, but a young man like this one, who might seem to be more at home in some masculine Irish world of pubs and race courses, was an oddity. And I was of the generation to which oddities are attractive. I had seen his hands as we had exchanged the broken fragment of glass; they were heavy and too blunt for the rest of his build, reddish, as if they had been mercilessly scrubbed. The shock was in the seams and calluses, the multiple scars of what looked like cuts or burns. They were strangely at variance with the face.

"Perhaps there's something," I answered finally, compelled by his stare. "Down here at the back."

He followed me closely, and I wondered if I had gone mad. He had deliberately broken a Sheridan piece—both of us knew it had been deliberate—and here I was calmly offering to show him more of it. But that was the trouble; I wasn't calm at all. And I had thought, until this moment, that I was at last past the stage of being swayed and moved by a mere face, a presence; a couple of years of hard-won sophistication seemed to vanish with this man. This irritated me, and I was curt as I motioned him to where Blanche had her desk, where she had done her accounts, surrounded by the clutter of little *objets*. This was in the little alcove formed by the space left over from the hall, with its separate street entrance, and the stairs that led to the flat above.

There were about a dozen pieces which I remembered Blanche had said were Sheridan in a glass-fronted cabinet that hung on the wall beside the desk. There wasn't room to display them properly, and I couldn't recall that Blanche had ever made any particular fuss about them, but I couldn't recall, either, that she had ever shown them to customers, even those whose interest was antique glass. As I searched for the right key from those on the ring, I was uncomfortably aware that I was poaching in a preserve that had been Blanche's own; I hadn't any special knowledge of the things we sold in the shop; until Blanche had become seriously ill I had lent only occasional help on Saturdays. But without being able to pinpoint the arrival of any particular piece, I remembered that any time Blanche had acquired a good example of a Sheridan goblet or glass or plate, it had never been allowed to mingle with the general items in the shop, but had sat with its fellows on the dusty shelves of the cabinet. Obviously she had not considered the little vase which had been broken good enough to join this select group. It wasn't odd that Blanche had this small collection; most dealers in antiques played favorites. What was odd, now that I thought about it, was that if Sheridan glass had been Blanche's favorite, she had somehow failed to say so.

As I fitted the key in the lock I glanced back at the man behind me. He was looking, not at the glass, as a prospective buyer would have been, but directly at me. His stare, instead of warming me, made me feel the chill of the morning once more. I looked away, and my fingers fumbled.

No one had washed the Sheridan pieces for a long time; their brilliance had given up to the greasy dust that is London's air. But even to my comparatively inexperienced, and until now indifferent, eye nothing could ever detract from their fine lines, the sureness of the execution, the ingenuity of the craftsmen who had spun them. I selected the plainest piece I could see, a dessert plate with a design of flowers engraved on its center, the omnipresent grime lodged in every cut of the engraving. I turned to give it to him.

But I heard the quick, sharp, intake of his breath, and his hand was already reaching past me. It went unerringly to the finest, the most intricate piece, a two-handled goblet on an air-twist stem, the handles a marvelous interweaving of blown glass, culminating, where the drinker's fingers would grip, in sprays of flowers and leaves. It was heavily engraved, with a portrait head and lettering—some kind of commemorative glass. The man looked at it closely, turned it upside down to see the engraver's mark. His hands were enormously sure as he touched it; now, as it rested between those scarred fingers, I had not the slightest fear that this also would lie in fragments on the floor.

He murmured, without looking at me, "Sheridan . . ."

"Yes."

"What's it worth?"

I didn't know. I didn't know the value of half the things Blanche had in the shop. She had tried to label all the small oddments of glass and china so that I wouldn't have to ask her constantly on Saturday afternoons when the shop was filled with King's Road strollers. But the important pieces had been Blanche's business, hers and Mary Hughes.

"It isn't for sale."

He looked up. "But you showed it to me."

I had done that, and I couldn't explain why. I shrugged. "I thought you might like to see some good Irish glass. You said . . ."

Now it was his turn to shrug. "Looking is for museums. But still, if you won't sell . . ."

I didn't want him to make the whole matter so personal. "It isn't that I won't sell. It just happens not to be for sale."

"But if it were for sale—just supposing it were for sale—about what would it cost?"

I was backed into a corner; I was ignorant, and he probably guessed it. So I put the price as high as I dared, perhaps ridiculously high—I couldn't tell. "Fif—seventy guineas."

"You're daft!" He uttered the words without passion, simply as a statement of fact.

"It's a very fine piece of glass," I said defensively.

Now he smiled again, a slow smile that mocked and pitied my ignorance.

"Let me tell you—just let me tell you about this." He flicked one of his nails against the goblet, and I heard the sweet ring of crystal. "This is not just a very fine piece of glass—though it is that, indeed. This is a unique piece. If you were ever interested enough to look, you'd find the original of this pictured in every history of English glassmaking."

"English?" I was glad he had made the slip; it gave me back some self-esteem.

"English," he repeated. "The original of this is known to glass-fanciers as the Culloden Cup. It and its two copies were the main reason why the Sheridan family of glassmakers were forced to leave England and resettle in Ireland—and lucky to be allowed to do that without a charge of treason."

"Treason?" I wondered how I had even imagined that this man might be a farmer. His expression, as he scrutinized the glass, was intent, absorbed; he was talking of something he knew and loved intimately, and I could not have stopped him talking even if I had wanted to.

"You see this?" He pointed to the engraved portrait. "Charles Edward Stuart—Bonnie Prince Charlie—the Young Pretender. Then these flowers on the handles—the thistle and the rose— the crowns of England and Scotland. And here, twined about the portrait of the Prince, the stricken oak, the Jacobite symbol. Of course there are a lot of these glasses about, but this must be among the finest and the most famous. The Sheridan family were for the Pretender, and Thomas Sheridan himself—the great Sheridan—made two copies of his original and sent them to the Prince as he and his army entered Liverpool on the way south— 1745, was it?—you'd know English history better than I do. Then the luck ran out—those Stuarts were a very unlucky family, I'm thinking—and the Prince was chased north again. I suppose you could say the Battle of Culloden Moor was the end of the Jacobite dream. After Culloden one goblet was found among the Prince's abandoned baggage. The maker was easily identified, of course. The goblet was destroyed, the story goes, by the Duke of Cumberland himself, the victor of Culloden. Sheridan and his family ran to Ireland. But somewhere between Liverpool and Culloden, the second goblet vanished, either broken it was thought, or given to some loyal supporter of the cause."

"And the other?"

"With the Sheridan family still—in Ireland."

I looked with awe, nervously, at the piece in his hands. "Then this one has to be . . ."

"The one lost since Culloden."

He turned it reverently, his finger tracing the lines of the engraving, following the interweaving of handles, stroking the smoothness of stem and foot. The sensuous quality that I had read in his eyes was revealed again in these movements, the hands of a lover on the body of the beloved. His tone was almost dreamy as he murmured softly, "Lost for two-hundred-odd years . . . where has it been? Put away in some cupboard, too dangerous to display until everyone had forgotten the Pretender's cause, then itself forgotten, sold at auction with the contents of a house. Where did she find it, I wonder? God, what incredible chance! What luck . . . and for her of all people . . ."

Without asking my leave, once again he stretched past me and carefully replaced the goblet on the shelf, closing the cabinet door. "So you see," he continued, his tone normal now, "it doesn't have a price. It belongs in a millionaire's collection —or with the Sheridan family. Or perhaps," he added, with a touch of malice, as if he wanted to deny the former dreaminess, "you should be patriotic and give it to the Victoria and Albert, on the grounds that it really is English."

"*You* almost had it—for seventy guineas."

He shook his head. "Sure, there'd be no sport in a thing like that—it would have been too easy to all but steal it from you."

"And if there had been some sport in it?"

He smiled again, mockingly, and with a deliberate air of faint wickedness. "Oh, I'm always ready to take a chance on a horse —or a woman."

"Lucky for them, isn't it? It's nice of you to give them a sporting chance."

"I think," he said, "that you're after making fun of a poor country boy from the bogs." With those words his accent had thickened into a caricature of itself; he carried a kind of half-covered bitterness with him as well as those scarred hands.

"I'm here to help customers, not make fun of them."

"Aye . . ." His expression had seemed to darken. "I was forgetting that I was a customer, and you're Blanche D'Arcy's daughter."

"And what's that supposed to mean?"

"Nothing—nothing at all. Now, I believe I owe you three guineas. And since I'm not a millionaire collector, I'd better clear out of here and stop taking up your time." He was rapidly counting out the money on the desk, making up the exact amount—three pounds, a half-crown and a sixpence—so that, I thought, I wouldn't have to make change for him. I left it where he put it.

"Did you *know* my mother?"

"No, I never knew your mother. And now . . . good-day to you."

He turned and walked down the length of the shop. "Good-bye . . ." I said, but I didn't know whether or not he heard me. The glass fragments crunched under his feet, followed by the click of the door. Then he halted, and faced back to me. I took a few steps toward him expectantly.

"Oh—another thing. Your father—he'd be dead too, would he?"

I gave a little gasp at the question. I called down the length of the shop to him angrily, "Is that some concern of yours?"

He seemed to consider the question for a moment. "No—I suppose you'd hardly say it was."

The door snapped shut, and I could see his tall figure darting across the road to the bus stop. I moved at a half-run down to the front of the shop and was just in time to glimpse the flying tails of the raincoat as he leaped and lightly gained the back platform of the number eleven bus as it moved off.

The rest of the morning I was depressed and restless. One of Blanche's old customers came in and bought a Spode tureen. But I was absent-minded with her, and must have seemed off-hand. I knew that she hadn't enjoyed the buying very much; probably she wouldn't come any more. But I had two things on my mind; Lloyd Justin's letter and the man who had told me about the Culloden Cup.

✦   ✦   ✦   ✦

I spent the afternoon pretending to smoke a cigarette before a camera—which was my real job. It was a long, tiring afternoon; we went through the motions over and over again, so difficult to attain is that look of sheer spontaneous enjoyment that makes the cigarette advertisement—or any other kind. It was through at last, though, and I was about to leave when the telephone rang and Rudi's secretary said it was Claude, my agent.

"Maura?" Claude never wasted his time on unimportant things like "how are you?" "Listen, I want to see you right away. I'll meet you at the White Hart at half-past five. Something's come up."

He hung up without waiting to find out if the arrangement suited me; that also was typical of Claude.

II

The White Hart was one of those Chelsea pubs currently in fashion—one could always trust Claude never to be seen anywhere that was passé. It was just opening time, and it was almost empty; he made a faint motion that passed for standing up as I came to his table. Women weren't Claude's line; he tolerated the models whose lives he controlled because that was the way he made a living. He was very polite to fashion editors and film directors and handsome young men. There wasn't much left over for the rest of us.

"Two things, actually," he said as I sat down. "First there's—"

"Claude—do you mind? First I'd like to order a drink. It's been a long afternoon."

He clicked with impatience, and signaled to the bartender. I asked for Scotch, and I knew I would have to pay my share; Claude didn't take his models out on his expense account.

"Well—" he took up again. "First I've got a job for you. A walk-on part's become available in a film Peter Hatch is making in Spain—you know that one there's been all the publicity about. There's nothing to it, really—the part's only a couple of lines. But the girl wears some fabulous clothes. He particularly asked his people to see if you were available."

"Me? Why *me?*"

Claude shrugged, as if he couldn't see why either. "Didn't you meet him at the Thompson party? After all, you're not going to star. It's just to wear clothes."

I had, of course, met him at the Thompson party. I thought of that aging, clever face, the watchful eyes, the few drawled words he had spoken to me. Film directors as famous as Peter Hatch rarely had much to say to models; they were always surrounded by beautiful women who were also actresses. It surprised me that he had remembered my person, much less my name.

My drink came. After I took the first sip I said, "When?"

"Well, that's it. He wants you right away—end of next week at latest. The part's just been written in, and it belongs with the location shots. It fits very well, since you're going on holiday on Sunday."

"Well, it doesn't fit, does it? I mean—I was going on holiday, not to work." I had meant to take my car and let myself wander on down through the spring sunshine of France, sit warm by lakes and look at the snow on the mountains, taste the spring cherries, sip the wine, slip on through to the Mediterranean if that was where my whim finally took me. It would be the first time away from London since Blanche had died, the first break in the grayness. I wanted it very badly.

Claude's mouth dropped open slightly. He blinked behind his heavy glasses. For once I had shattered his preoccupation with his own affairs.

"You can't mean to refuse! Maura, this man is a *star-maker!* And he's asked for you. Believe me, you won't get this chance twice."

"I didn't say I was going to refuse. But it *is* my holiday."

He shrugged. "Well, of course if you're going to look at it *that* way . . . I'm sorry Hatch even bothered about you—I'm sorry *I* bother about you. My girls always take my advice. They *never* let anyone down."

"Claude, I'm tired," I suddenly snapped at him. "I suppose

I'll go and do the job, and wear Mr. Hatch's clothes, and do as I'm told. But don't expect me to be delighted about having to do it right now. After all, I'm a model, not an actress. And Mr. Hatch hasn't promised to make a star out of *me*."

"Who knows, baby, who knows?" Claude said, sparing a frosty smile for me. "You can never tell about these things. Now, what you need is another drink," he added, prepared to pamper me a little now that I was looking at things his way.

"I'm not finished this one," I pointed out.

He didn't pay any attention, but signaled the bartender again. The place was beginning to fill up, and the bar was getting busy. Claude had to go to the bar himself and get it, which meant he had to pay. That he didn't seem to mind should have warned me that something else was coming.

"That was the first thing," he continued, sipping at his vermouth. Claude never drank hard liquor. "And I'm very pleased about it because it should do you a lot of good where it counts if you make the right impression. But the *real* thing came up this afternoon too. Never rains but it pours, as my old mum used to say."

I was warned finally; he was being too nice. "What is it?" I wondered why I sounded wary.

"Well—I suppose you heard about Rosemary Parks being in that car smash? Poor thing, they say she won't be able to work for at least six months." I could tell he wasn't sorry; somehow Rosemary's loss was going to be Claude's gain. "Well, of course, this leaves the Wild campaign dead. She'd got the contract, you know, to be the Wild girl."

I nodded. It was one of the more exciting plums that had come to a young model that season—being chosen as the only model for a new line of cosmetics, a line designed exclusively for the young, and for the money that was tumbling out of their pockets. It literally had meant, until Rosemary had been involved in her accident, that for a whole year she could be certain of seeing her own face almost wherever she looked. "Yes?" I said.

He twirled his glass in triumph. "Uncle Claude," he said, "has been busy, and now *you* are going to be the Wild girl. Fabulous, isn't it?"

My face stretched in an aching smile. "Fabulous," I echoed. "How did you do it?" It was Claude's accomplishment, not mine; he would expect to be invited to tell it all.

"Oh—I keep my ear to the ground," he answered, letting me know how hard he worked for his clients. "I knew they had already shot the photos for the first series in the campaign. It was due to start in the autumn. And then came this thing with Rosemary, and I knew they would be way off schedule. So I just went along and hit them with those photos Max Arnott took of you, and they couldn't resist."

"Max's photos . . . ?"

"Well, of course, they were a natural. They were exactly what they wanted—the girl-in-the-autumn-woods thing. Better than the ones they already had of Rosemary. And ready for them. No time lost."

"You mean they're going to use . . ."

He wouldn't let me finish. "Of course, Max had to be part of the deal. And he's agreed to do it because it will mean so much to you. A big concession from Max, since he's stopped doing that girlie stuff years ago. Of course, the Morton agency is tickled pink that the great Max Arnott will do the whole series—a real feather in their caps. Marvelous, isn't it?"

This time I couldn't quite bring out the dutiful echo. I wasn't thinking of the Wild campaign, or of what it was going to do for me; I was thinking of the photos. Of all the hundreds of photos of myself I had seen in the three years I had worked as a model, of all I ever would see, these were burned in my memory. They had been taken on a Sunday of last autumn by Max Arnott; he had rung Blanche in the morning to say that he and Susie were taking a picnic into the country, and Blanche and I were to come. By then we had known, all of us, because Max and Susie were Blanche's closest friends, that Blanche was going to die, probably quite soon. The morning had been rainy, and so beyond London there hadn't been much traffic, and the woods where we had picnicked had been empty of people. In the afternoon the sun had appeared and the golds and reds of the autumn had come out strongly. It had been hard to keep our eyes off Blanche's face as we had walked, with the wet leaves underfoot; she was looking with the intensity of a person whose looking was to last the rest of a lifetime. Suddenly she said, "Take some photos of her for me, Max? I want to remember . . ."

We knew what it was she meant, but it was we who would do the remembering. I had shaken off my grieving because I had not wanted to give her sad pictures to look at in what time remained to her. So I had thrown myself into a mood of zany humor, had pranced and postured beneath the tall trees where the shafts of sunlight had struck. The wind had come and blown my loose hair and my skirt; I had thrown back my head and laughed, so that she would see no grief in those pictures. And Max had struck the mood himself, urging me on, so that between us we had found a puckish madness.

It was the first really professional piece of acting I had done, and of course, when he had seen the pictures, Claude had recognized it at once. The colors of the day had prompted Max to use color film, although he preferred black-and-white. Claude's eyes had widened at the accidental harmony of my russet skirt, the thick, knee-length socks, the orange sweater and the tangle of my dark-blond hair; he had begged a set of prints, much enlarged, from Max. And now, all these months later, with Blanche dead and the original purpose of the pictures fulfilled, he had used them to pluck this plum for me.

"Max has really agreed?" I asked finally.

Claude grew cautious; we both knew that Max was too great a photographer, too big a name, too tough a man to tolerate Claude's little stratagems; he didn't dare to lie outright about him. "Well—he's agreed, as long as you do. As I said, he's willing to do this just to help you along. Damned generous of him, I think."

2

I was remembering the photos again; it all came back, the golden colors of the autumn day, the borrowed mood of dizzy youthfulness, the grieving that had sharpened my senses and made me responsive to every half-expressed command from Max. It wasn't so much that I doubted I could do it again; what I doubted was that I even wanted to try.

"Do they have to use those—those particular ones? I mean, wouldn't it do if they started with the first of a new series Max shoots?"

An irritated note came into Claude's voice. "Of course they've got to use them. How do you think I sold *you* to them? Without pictures for the autumn campaign ready at this stage, they're in a mess. They're buying Max's pictures, that's what it amounts to. Naturally they want to have the same girl through the first year's series." He looked at me sharply. "It really doesn't have to be *you*, sweetie. Max could photograph any girl and make her look great. So count yourself lucky. For a year you'll be the Wild girl. At the end of that year you'll be able to name your own price. So just do as you're told and leave everything to me."

He leaned back in his chair, satisfied; he had got it all settled, all in order. For a year I was going to be the Wild girl, with my pictures on vast hoardings, staring at people from along railroad tracks, from superbly colored showcards in chemists' windows, and from every magazine and newspaper a young woman might read. The thought of it should have elated me, but oddly, it didn't. I had heard of models who had started out as a something-girl, and hadn't known how to stop. And besides, they were going to use Blanche's pictures, the pictures that had been private, not meant for chemists' shop windows.

Claude got himself another vermouth, and then took out his pad and began to write down what I was to do about contacting Peter Hatch's film company in Spain. "The main office is in Madrid, but they're shooting north of there . . . you'll save yourself time by . . ."

I was only half-listening; part of myself was standing off and

watching me being committed to something I wasn't even
sure I wanted completely. It was, as Claude said, fabulous
luck—two strokes of fabulous luck in a single day; it would
push me a long way toward the place which all models were
supposed to covet—the top place. I looked around the room
that was now crowded, every seat taken, and people packed
three deep around the bar. I fidgeted with my glass while
Claude wrote, wishing I felt happier about the thought of going
to Spain to play my bit part for Mr. Hatch, wishing I felt happier about being the Wild girl. I tried to draw some excitement
from the seeking, restless faces of the crowd about me, but they
gave me nothing—nothing but the assurance that to be a
clothes horse for Mr. Hatch, to be the Wild girl spelled a kind
of success that was understood and applauded here, in this
world, and what right had I to ask for anything else? I would
be envied and admired, and that would be enough. The babble
of the voices, rising every minute as the room grew more
crowded, seemed to shriek at me that I was mad to want to be
happy when I could be successful. Perhaps Lloyd Justin's letter
lying on Blanche's desk promised me something—a fixed way of
life, a certain security, a shining new-pin house complete with
swimming pool and the endless sun of California. But who
could promise me happiness? At least Claude was honest; he
only offered me success. So I put Claude's piece of paper into
my bag, and turned once more to look at the people about me,
feeling as bright and restless and discontented as any of them
could be.

Then I saw him, the man who had been in the shop early
that morning, the Sheridan man, I called him—he with the
too-beautiful face and the work-seamed hands.

I sat and watched him, feeling the same sense both of ex-
hilaration and disquiet I had experienced that morning. Our
second meeting in a day, wasn't, I suppose, too strange; the pub
wasn't far from Blanche's shop, and he probably was staying
somewhere in the neighborhood. The White Hart was men-
tioned often in the newspapers, and most likely he had come

to see what the Chelsea set looked like, how they behaved. But this time, I thought, I wouldn't let him go, not let him disappear as he had done that morning. This time I would answer any question he asked—about my father or anything else. I suddenly knew what had seemed so shocking in what he had said to me; he had asked a personal question, and in London that was rarely done, at least not on a chance meeting; no one had the time, and no one cared enough. So I sat and waited, expectant, knowing he would turn and see me, knowing he would come.

He was standing at the bar, on the fringe of a group of young people, but he did not belong with them. He listened openly to their talk, and they knew he was listening, the way a man alone in a pub might do, hoping to be drawn in. Then I saw one of the men of the group speak to him—ask for a match—because he at once produced a lighter. It wouldn't be long, I knew, before they allowed him to buy them all a round of drinks; I had seen it done so often, when they knew the stranger was an outsider. It happened quite soon, and he seemed complaisant about being allowed to pay. I saw him take up his own glass, nod and half-smile to the only one of the group who raised a glass to him in brief thanks—it was a girl, of course—but almost at once he was closed out again, on the fringe, his attempts at conversation practically ignored. For a few minutes he persisted in his effort to participate, but he was completely an outsider, with only the price of a round of drinks to commend him. The knowledge grew on him; I watched his expression darken with anger and a return of that swift bitterness he had shown briefly to me that morning. He stepped back, and I prepared myself, ready to smile whenever he turned his head and saw me. Eventually, staring over the heads of the group because of his height, his gaze locked on mine.

The reaction was quicker than I had expected. He stared for a few seconds, as if to make sure it was I; then he slammed down his glass on the bar, and pushed through the group, jostling them rudely, paying no attention to the protests, offering no apology. But instead of coming toward me, as I expected, he headed for the door. With the welcoming smile still fixed on my face, I watched in utter disbelief as the outer door swung open and closed again, giving a glimpse of the rainy street.

I was on my feet at once, clumsily jolting the table so that Claude's attention was forced back to me.

"Maura . . . ?"

I snatched up my coat and handbag. "I'll ring you tomorrow —all right?" I was shouldering myself through the crowd, and then I was out on the street, searching for him.

He wasn't anywhere in sight. I was standing there, foolish and empty, not knowing why I had run after him. I buttoned my coat and started to walk home.

III

Before I went to sleep that night I reread the letter from Lloyd Justin—the California letter that had come that morning, the sun-bright letter, the new house and swimming-pool letter, the young research engineer letter, trying not to be too smug about the good life, trying not to be too pleased because he had left another kind of life and another kind of climate behind in England. Last summer Lloyd Justin had wanted me to marry him and come with him when he took up his job with one of the giant aircraft manufacturers in Southern California. I had hesitated, and had not given an answer, feeling that the basis of a marriage had to be something much more compelling than what I felt about Lloyd, or, up to this moment, about any other man. My lack of an answer had made him angry, but that was the time when I found out the nature and the future of Blanche's illness. Everything had seemed to come to a standstill; I had told Lloyd that the lack of an answer did not matter, because I would not leave Blanche. It had been a tactless, perhaps a stupid way to tell him; he had gone away hurt as well as angry, and I had heard nothing from him. I missed him, and

I might have regretted the sharpness of the break, but for the fact that concern over Blanche and a rash of jobs that Claude had promoted for me gave me little time for what might have been pondering. Now, through a mutual friend he had learned of Blanche's death, and this morning's letter had arrived asking me to come, offering me the life in the sun. I found that I was no more sure than I had been last summer.

Once I had talked with Blanche about marriage—before I had known Lloyd. I remembered the careful way she had felt for her words. "I think the marriage worth making won't be something you have to decide about. You won't be able to imagine doing anything else." That was where my doubting lay; it was still quite possible to go on imagining myself not married to Lloyd.

My thoughts were of Lloyd and Blanche as I drifted into sleep, but when I dreamed, it was a dream in which once again I twirled and pirouetted in the autumn woods, but now I wore the fantasy clothes designed for Peter Hatch's girl in the film. And suddenly the Sheridan man was there also, holding the Culloden Cup, extended toward me so that the slanting shaft of sun struck it, lighting it to radiance. Then a wind blew, and my wispy clothes streamed behind me like banners; the sun was gone; I shivered; the man and the Cup both were gone, lost in the wet woods.

When I woke the Saturday dawn was chill and damp and the eiderdown lay on the floor.

CHAPTER 2

I

It was later than I had intended on that Saturday evening when I got back to the shop in King's Road, my mind full of the things yet to do before I got the air-ferry from Lydd to France early the next morning. Mary Hughes had said she would wait for me, though; we would eat supper together and go through the bills and anything else that might need a decision while I was away. There wouldn't be very much; Mary had always been very efficient. Blanche had said she was the businesswoman of the two, but they both knew that Blanche's eye for furniture had been finer and truer. There never had been any worry in leaving the shop in Mary's hands; I expected none now. The fact that all the lights were still on, even though it was after seven o'clock, didn't worry me either. Like Blanche, I wasn't of a particularly economical turn of mind.

It was only when I walked up to the door and saw the uniformed policeman standing inside as if on guard that I realized that the squad car at the curb had business there—business that concerned me.

The constable opened the door in response to my gesture.

"I'm Maura D'Arcy. Is there something wrong?"

"You'd better speak to the Sergeant, miss."

The sound of our voices had reached the back of the shop. Mary was there, talking with two men. They turned as I approached.

"Oh—Maura!" Mary looked distracted. She had a streak of dust across the front of her dress, and her wiry gray hair stood about her face in an untidy fuzz. "This is Detective-Sergeant Kerr."

"How do you do, Miss D'Arcy—my assistant, Constable Saunders."

I acknowledged the introductions with a nod, but spoke to Mary. "What's wrong?"

Mary gestured helplessly; she was seldom helpless or distracted. "Oh, some unpleasantness. I think something's been stolen—but I don't know what."

As I frowned, she gestured. "Back here—come and look. Perhaps you'll know if there's anything missing. Goodness knows, I *should* know, but I've never handled anything from this cabinet, and I can't remember exactly what was there. I've explained to the Sergeant about the way Blanche and I worked . . ." As she spoke she was leading us all to the back of the shop. I guessed where we would end, and we did.

"Look . . ." she pointed to the cabinet on the wall beside Blanche's desk.

The cut in the glass was so neat it wasn't immediately obvious. Both doors of the cabinet were closed; only the lack of reflection of a small area around the latch on the right-hand door would make one look closer. A semicircle of glass, just big enough to permit the passage of a hand had been cut and lifted away; with the glass gone the latch could be easily opened, and it had been. Even my first quick check of the pieces crammed on the dusty shelves told me what was missing.

"Who did it?"

Mary repeated her gesture of bewilderment. "I don't know. It could have been any number of people. The shop was crowded all afternoon, with people all over the place." Her voice faltered. "I'm awfully sorry, Maura. But you know how it is . . . Saturday afternoons . . . There were dozens of people all asking me questions and prices . . . and it's so easy for someone to come back here while I'm at the front of the shop, and you know you just can't *see* if someone's back here."

I nodded. "I know . . . it's really my fault for not being here. You shouldn't have to cope alone on Saturdays . . ."

Sergeant Kerr grew impatient of our exchange. "Could *you* tell us, Miss D'Arcy, what is missing, if anything?"

Like Mary, I shrugged helplessly. "Antiques really aren't my business, Sergeant. It was my mother . . ."

"Yes, yes," he said. "Mrs. Hughes has explained that. What we'd like to know is if you can identify any objects as definitely being missing from the cabinet—or any other place in the shop." Now it was his turn to look rather helplessly at the hundreds of items spread down the length of the room. "Mrs. Hughes," he added, "says she isn't familiar with the contents of the cabinet."

Mary went quickly to her own defense. "Well, I've told you, Sergeant, that the things in the cabinet weren't for sale. Blanche—Mrs. D'Arcy—just had her own little collection of old glass. But she never made any particular fuss about it, so I can't tick off each piece she had. Well, I mean . . ."

"Quite so, Mrs. Hughes. And you, Miss D'Arcy?"

I had been looking at the shelves again. There was no reason not to tell him. I wondered why I felt so reluctant.

"I remember one piece that should be here that isn't here now."

"What was that?"

"An eighteenth-century goblet—Sheridan, engraved, air-twist stem and two handles, rather elaborate." Saunders was writing down what I said; perhaps it was the sight of the words being recorded that stopped me. I didn't say anything more about the glass, nothing about the particular kind of engraving, or what the intertwined flowers of the handles had represented. Let Mary add that, if she knew.

It seemed she didn't; no other information was offered beyond her saying quickly, "Well, *all* the glass in there is Sheridan. It was Blanche's hobby. I thought I *told* you that, Sergeant."

"No," he said patiently. "No, you didn't, Mrs. Hughes. Anything else, Miss D'Arcy?"

"Nothing that I can remember now." I pointed to the empty semicircle. "Wouldn't this be rather difficult to do, Sergeant, in a shop crowded with people?"

"Not necessarily. The pane is simply gripped with a rubber suction-cap and held while the glass is cut. A routine operation for a certain kind of burglar, I'm afraid."

Mary gave a loud snort. "Not very routine to come into a crowded shop and do it."

"No," the Sergeant admitted, as if he didn't like to admit anything. "It is not routine, Mrs. Hughes. This thief seems to have been very selective. Could you put a value on this—er—goblet, Miss D'Arcy?"

I appealed to Mary, and she answered for me, making certain that Blanche's collection wasn't underrated. "I'm quite sure that the least of the pieces wouldn't have gone for less than twenty guineas—many of them are worth considerably more than that, I'd say. Good eighteenth-century glass is getting quite rare. But this piece . . ." She shook her head. "None of them were for sale, so we had never priced them."

I half-turned away, as if examining the rest of the pieces in the cabinet, and I said nothing. I said nothing at all about what I knew of the Culloden Cup, nothing of its rarity, nothing about its being unique. I knew who had it, of course—or who had caused it to be taken. I also knew that he wasn't a thief. If he had insisted, I might have sold him the Cup for seventy guineas; he hadn't had to tell me what its real value might be. I stared at the neat, empty circle; it seemed provocative in a way, mocking me, tantalizing me, compelling my attention the way the smashing of the little vase had done. He was mad, of course, and the goblet should be taken away from him, but for some reason he didn't expect it to be taken away. He didn't expect me to act as I should act; he didn't expect me to turn to the Sergeant and tell him what I remembered of a strange man, tall, with an Irish accent, very good-looking, a man whom I believed had deliberately destroyed a little Sheridan vase. I didn't fear the same fate for the Culloden Cup. I could recall those hands as he had examined it, careful, knowing, almost reverent. I did not think he would destroy it, but if he had meant to do that, the deed was done already. I remembered also those odd questions he had asked me about Blanche and about my father. He meant to say something to me through the taking of Blanche's goblet. The act was not completed; the conviction was growing in me that I would hear from him again.

Then why, if this were so, had he not merely cut me in the White Hart yesterday evening, but had actually fled from me? It was too much for me; I was confused and unhappy, wondering what Blanche would have done about this strange man with the face of an angel, and the scarred hands.

I hung back while Mary did a slow tour of the shop with Sergeant Kerr, trying to determine if any other items were missing. It didn't surprise me that she found none. Saunders was at my elbow, still with his notebook out, but his attention wasn't entirely on his superior. I sensed him hovering, the way one does, and I turned to look at him, the first time I had really looked at him.

I met at once a sheepish smile. He was young, he didn't seem much older than I was. "Thought I recognized you," he said.

"Recognized me?" Why did I feel guilty because an officer of the law recognized me?—what had I done?

"You're the girl in the Marsh's chocolate ad, aren't you?" I nodded, relieved.

"Smashing, I thought," he added. I wondered if Saunders meant the chocolates. "I thought you looked smashing—but they didn't do you justice."

Absurdly, I felt myself blush. Funny how this unsought compliment from an unexpected source reassured me. It was so normal. I was the girl in a chocolate ad, and to him I looked as wholesome as the chocolates I helped to sell. It was all very far from the world of Claude and Wild and Peter Hatch; it was a simpler world where a young man would snatch a minute from being an officer of the law to say what he felt in an absolutely straightforward way. It couldn't last, but it was wonderful.

Mary and Sergeant Kerr had finally reached the door. Saunders made to move toward them; he half-turned back to me. "Perhaps I'll see you again . . . ?"

I hoped my smile didn't encourage him too much; it wasn't going to happen, and we both knew it. For him I would go on being the girl in the chocolate ad; for myself, I had gone too far in the world where a girl's smile was simply something with which to sell chocolates. But it was nice that it had happened.

The Sergeant was telling Mary that if she discovered any other items missing, she was to telephone; they would be in touch, he said, if they turned anything up. He didn't sound very hopeful. It was a minor crime, the theft of one eighteenth-century goblet, whose value might have been between twenty and thirty guineas. The only thing to give the crime interest was the manner of its execution, the single-mindedness of the thief's objective, his indifference to any other thing in the shop. "Sounds like a collector to me," the Sergeant observed, a little more unbending now that the routine was dispensed with. "We do get this kind of thing from time to time, you know—cranks who have a mania for a particular thing, and who just have to have it whether they can afford it or not. Awfully difficult to find them, though. You see, they never steal for profit, just for the joy of possession. They never attempt to get rid of it to a fence—just lock it away and gloat over it in private. Our usual channels are useless when we are up against a type like that." He seemed now to be appealing for some understanding, as if his job was much harder than people believed. "We're much better equipped for dealing with the professional than the amateur, you see."

"But all the same," Mary said, after I had poured two Scotches in the kitchen upstairs and began the preparations for the meal, "I think that's rather feeble. Of course, when they couldn't find two million pounds after the Great Train Robbery, I don't know what we can expect them to do about a single goblet. They'll put out a description and that will be that! But it's still a valuable piece of glass, and I think it's a shame someone can just walk into a shop and do what he did . . . Blanche would be furious . . ."

I made murmured inconsequential replies as I assembled the things I needed for poached eggs with cheese fondue—the mushrooms on which they would sit prepared for grilling, the marvelous smell of minced shallot and garlic making me pleasantly hungry, giving the Swiss cheese to Mary to grate, measuring the vermouth. I did all this with my eyes going frequently to Blanche's recipe book, and my mind still pondering the problem of the Culloden Cup. I very much doubted, as Mary had said, that Blanche would have been furious; I thought her feelings might have been much less simple that that. I was beginning to sense that some relationship existed, or had existed between Blanche and the young man, and its key lay in the Culloden Cup—or perhaps in Sheridan glass. I began to add the wine and stock to the mixture, wondering why, then, the man had said he had never known Blanche. As the cream and the cornflour went in I thought that he wasn't old enough to have known Blanche well when she lived in Ireland—he would have been a young child at that time. I grew impatient as I realized that I very likely never would have the answers to these questions unless the man reappeared and volunteered them; at the same time I grew reckless with the cream and cheese.

"How do you do it?" Mary said, watching the process.

"Blanche showed me. Well, I don't have to tell you—she was a far better cook than I'll ever be."

"No—I mean how do you eat such things and still not get too fat for modeling? Now me . . ."

"I eat lean all week so that I can have two fat meals." I set the mushrooms to grill, and began to poach the eggs. "I expect I'll have to stop when I'm twenty-five—they say that's when you start to put on weight."

"Blanche didn't."

"No—but then I'll never *look* like Blanche, either. She was . . ." I didn't know what words to use for Blanche. The lines of her fine, lean body had been indestructible; she had been beautiful.

We ate the eggs almost in silence, appreciatively, and then I brought out the brie which had come to the precise stage of ripeness. With it was the freshly ground Blue Mountain coffee which was an extravagance I had inherited from Blanche. I needed courage, so I poured two brandies. Mary's eyebrows lifted a little, but she said nothing, just produced her cigarettes.

"Mary, can you remember a certain man in the shop this afternoon . . . ?"

I didn't make a very good job of the description, but he wasn't someone easy to overlook or to forget. She began nodding her head almost at once. "He was there, all right. He bought an ivory letter-opener. Big, fantastically good-looking, Irish . . . I remember the accent. Why?"

I told her about the Culloden Cup and watched the incredulity and dismay grow on her face.

"But, my God, Maura, it must be worth *thousands!*"

"So much?" I asked weakly, afraid she was right.

"Easily. You don't understand how cracked some of these collectors are. And lots of them are very rich. If he's right about there only ever being three cups made, and they have that kind of historical association, then some of these old boys could go demented about it. Oh, yes, it could fetch a price, all right . . . What I don't understand is why Blanche . . . she knew a good deal more about glass than I'll ever know. Maura, you were *mad* not to have told Sergeant Kerr. It was exactly the kind of information he was looking for. It *has* to have been that Irishman!—it all fits. Oh, the gall of the man!—fancy having the nerve to stand there and pay for a letter-opener and all the time probably having the goblet in one of his raincoat pockets. And I thought how charming he was! He told me he was buying it as a present . . . Where's that extension number the Sergeant gave you?"

I went so far as to lay my hand on the telephone, and then I withdrew it. "Mary, I don't think he meant to steal it."

"What kind of nonsense is that? Stealing is stealing."

"I don't think it's stolen. I think he means to return it—or tell me where it is . . . or something," I added helplessly.

"You *can't* mean to do nothing then? Just sit here and wait for him to make a move. I don't believe you'll ever see him again, *or* the goblet. Stealing is stealing," she repeated.

I twisted the brandy glass nervously in my fingers, trying to find the words to explain something I wasn't sure of myself.

"But you see, if he'd wanted it so badly, he could have had it for seventy guineas—and made a huge profit on it. He didn't *have* to tell me the value of the thing. Why should he? All's fair between dealers, isn't it?—and between dealers and customers. *You* don't go into a shop or auction room and tell them that something they've got is worth a lot more than they're asking for it. It would have been too easy for him to have taken the Cup from me legitimately, don't you see?"

"But it wasn't for sale! That's why he had to steal it."

"I put a price on it. He didn't know till afterward that it wasn't for sale."

"But you wouldn't have sold it. Not Blanche's glass!"

"He didn't know that. And I don't know it either. One day the shop will have to go, won't it, Mary? I mean, I can't keep it on, can I?—and if you don't . . . Every antique dealer along the King's Road must know that the shop won't last—he could have heard it from any one of them. Why wouldn't I be just selling off things as the offers are made. Yes, it's quite possible I would have sold Blanche's glass."

Mary was upset; I could tell from the way she, usually a fastidious and moderate drinker, sloshed another heavy jog of brandy into her glass. Perhaps it was the thought of the shop going that upset her, or the feeling that she had let something rare and valuable that had belonged to Blanche get away from her. The bottle rattled agitatedly against the glass.

"Then you tell me why he did it?" she said loudly. "You tell me *why!*"

I took a sip of the brandy, and said carefully, "I think he meant me to know it was he who took it. I don't know why. That will come—very soon now. I think he'll tell me himself."

"Well then, he's a crackpot! Though why any man as good-looking as that would have to do such an extreme thing to make a girl remember him . . . well! All right—granted that. Now, what do you mean to *do* about it?"

"Think about it," I said. "There's some connection to Blanche . . . there's some explanation. I just have to think. It's odd really, how little I know about Blanche and my father. I just wasn't very curious. Like Blanche's collection of glass. Why didn't *we* ask her about it, Mary? Why didn't we?"

She ignored my question. "And if you don't think of the explanation . . . what then?"

"On Monday I'll get back to the police."

"By Monday you'll be halfway to Spain."

"So I will." I had forgotten that; the journey and even the need for the journey had faded from my mind. "Then you'll get on to the police. Tell him I only just remembered about the man."

"The Sergeant won't believe it. They're not quite fools, you know, in spite of the Great Train Robbery. You could be in trouble for withholding evidence."

"He can hardly put me in jail when it's my own goblet that's been stolen."

I had meant it to be flippant, but she choked on her drink and looked at me strangely. I began quickly to gather up the dishes to take them to the kitchen. She wasn't in a hurry to follow me. It was the first time, I believe, that she had finally realized that all that had been Blanche's property was now mine. It was one of the hundred small deaths of Blanche that I had had to witness.

Presently she came to join me, her face composed, but stiff. She looked as if perhaps she had shed some tears. She took up the towel to dry the dishes. "You're mad, you know," she said. "You're as mad as that man is—whoever he is. It's just wishful thinking to expect him to tell you . . ."

"I know," I cut in. "But all I'm asking is one day. Just one day to try to remember anything that Blanche might ever have said . . . just anything that might give me a clue before we put the police onto him."

She shrugged, and polished the glasses fiercely. "Maura, why didn't you tell me about the Cup as soon as you knew?—just assuming this man was right in what he said about it? I wouldn't have let it out of my sight—it's probably far more valuable than anything we've ever had in the shop."

I sighed. "What was I to do?—there wasn't time to have it verified before I left. There's been so much to see to. To tell you the truth, I really didn't know whether to believe him or not, but I knew if I told you you'd worry about it. After all, it's been in the shop—how long?—Years? When did Blanche find it?"

"I don't know," she answered slowly. "I don't ever remember her saying a word about it. It could have been here before I came. I wonder where she found it . . . of course she couldn't have known anything about its history. But still, she was something of an expert on Sheridan glass. I wonder . . ."

The same doubts that assailed me had clutched at her. She was unusually silent as we finished the dishes, her practical nature and loyalty to Blanche visibly doing battle with the strange aura, the inexplicable circumstances that surrounded the Culloden Cup. Hers was a nature not given to doubts or to questionings; she was strongly affected by the thought that Blanche might have withheld knowledge of something of this importance right into death. She was preoccupied as we went through the few business details that needed attention, and her eyes questioned me again as she said good-night and wished me a good journey, and success with the filming in Spain. I went downstairs with her to the street entrance of the flat, beside the shop. She walked across the road to the bus stop, and I waited there at the door until she was on the bus. It revived the memory of the man running across the road yesterday morning, and swinging up on the back platform. Possibly that, and the glimpse of him in the pub, would be the only times I ever saw or heard of him, and possibly I was as mad as Mary said I was.

II

The telephone began ringing as I went back up the stairs; when I lifted the receiver I heard the voice I had been half-expecting to hear.

"Miss D'Arcy?"

"Yes."

"I have the Culloden Cup."

"I know."

"I'm taking it back to Ireland with me."

"It's not yours to take anywhere."

"It belongs with the Sheridan family."

"It belonged to my mother."

"Your mother *was* a Sheridan, Miss D'Arcy."

The words hit me and they hurt as if they were physical blows. Like Mary Hughes, I couldn't quite accept the fact that Blanche could have withheld something of this importance from me, that she could have left it to the whimsy of chance. I had always accepted without question her own statement that there was no family belonging either to herself or my father left in Ireland; I remembered, too, that she had said her name, before she married Eugene D'Arcy, had been Findlay.

So I said to the man on the phone, "You're mistaken—or lying."

"I promise you there's no mistake and no lie. But there's also no reason why you should take my word for it. Why don't you come and find out for yourself? The Sheridans are there, Miss D'Arcy—all that's left of them. I can't say they're waiting for you, but I do say that they need you, whether they know it or not. And I'd make a guess that possibly you need them—now."

And then, unbelievingly, I heard the click of the receiver.

"No!—wait!" I jangled the button, and the dial tone answered me. Then I let the receiver drop back into its cradle. I was still standing there, staring at it, trying to sort out what he had said, when it rang again, a minute or so later.

"Now wait a minute," I said quickly, knowing who it was. "What about—"

He cut in. "I neglected to tell you that I didn't steal the Culloden Cup. I took it—yes. But I left a check in the drawer of the desk. It's not as much as the Culloden would have brought at auction, but it's about as much as my bank account holds. The rest I'll have to owe you."

"You're taking an awful chance—you could go to jail."

There was a shrug in his tone as he answered. "Sure, what's one more chance?—aren't I taking a hell of a one right now? I'm going back to Ireland with the Culloden. I swore I'd never set foot in Ireland again, Miss D'Arcy—but you and the Culloden changed that."

"Why?—*why?*"

"Good-bye, Miss D'Arcy. I hope I see you again—in Ireland." And then once again came the dial tone.

This time I didn't stand by the telephone, but went downstairs to the shop. There, right on top of the papers in the narrow first drawer, was the blue check slip. I knew the importance, if not the substance, of what the man had been hinting at when I saw the sum it was made out for—fifteen hundred pounds. It took me much longer, sitting there at Blanche's desk, beneath the little cabinet of Sheridan glass, to decipher the scrawled signature. But at last I had it—*Brendan Carroll.*

III

I made fresh coffee, a large pot of it, and broke into a new pack of cigarettes; then I took them and the hatbox to the sofa in front of the fire. The hatbox was the family safe—I suppose no better and not much worse than the places most people store their papers—Blanche had told me that she didn't trust safe-deposit vaults since the time she had seen a bank blown to bits during the blitz. In any case, ours was a big Lock & Co. box, and for the first time, as I poured a mug of coffee, I wondered where it had come from. I had been about nine years old when my father had been killed in a jeep crash in Korea; from Blanche's talk of him, and what I remembered, he hadn't been a Lock & Co. kind of man. He had had a host of friends who had filled the flat above the shop, most of them journalists, like himself; he had worn rather crumpled tweeds, and so had they. Thinking of that time, I remembered the gift of laughter he had had, the gift of ease and gentleness. I remembered the thick brown-red hair, the freckled skin, and the smile wrinkles about his eyes. I could remember also, seeing it then with a child's eyes, the desolation in Blanche when he had gone from our lives. He had been a much-loved man, my father. I took the lid off the hatbox gently, feeling glad, somehow, that he hadn't been a Lock & Co. man.

The hatbox had had to come down for two reasons. The first and obvious one was that I had to get out my passport for the journey to Spain; but that wouldn't have needed the pot of coffee and the cigarettes. The more compelling reason now was to find out if the box contained anything that would lend weight to what Brendan Carroll had told me about Blanche.

I hadn't been near the hatbox since Blanche had died except to thrust in the death certificate, the simple will she had made, and the small insurance policies of which I had been the beneficiary. In my mind the hatbox still had the association of the horror and shock I had felt on the day when I had come home two hours late from a modeling session and found Blanche unconscious in the easy chair in her room, the hatbox open on the floor beside her. That was the period when the pain had been gaining on her quickly; a nurse was coming three times a day to give her injections, and we both knew that very soon she would have to make the move to a nursing home. We kept putting it off, both of us, and the disease made enormous and uncheckable progress. She had been taken unconscious to the nursing home that night, and there had followed two weeks when she had rare and brief periods of lucidity. If she had meant me to do anything about the papers in the hatbox she had never been able to say so; it had been pushed hurriedly into the cupboard in her room and left there, until now. I put my hand reluctantly on those top papers, knowing that if any evidence existed of Blanche's family, it would be here.

It took much longer than I thought, and the coffee grew low in the pot. Business papers were jumbled with personal things—the lease of the shop, an insurance policy my father had taken out before going on his assignment to Korea, and then, heartbreakingly, his letters to Blanche from Korea. I glanced at only a few of them, feeling an intruder into a relationship and a passion that came startlingly to life in my father's large, impatient script on the faded paper. Of course they had loved—even a child would have known that; what I did not know was how they had loved.

I thrust the letters back into their package, feeling that they should be destroyed because their special intimacy was a private thing, yet knowing that I would never be the one to snuff out this last and final proof of it.

There were some pictures of my father, ones that Blanche had shown me years before; I was struck again by my own resemblance to him. There was the picture of them both on the steps at Caxton Hall, he in RAF uniform; Blanche had told me they had been married there, but I had never seen this photo. There was the picture Gene D'Arcy had taken of Blanche out-

side the shop on the day it had opened, with the big sign above
her and only one small writing table to display in the window.
That would have been in 1946. What struck me as odd now
was that their personal history seemed all to have begun
abruptly in this period of the forties. There were no papers, no
photographs from childhood, no photographs of parents, or
young people who might have been brothers or sisters. Blanche
had told me there was no family belonging to either of them
left in Ireland; my father had cousins in Boston whom he had
never met, she said. Before this, the fact of their both being so
barren in family connections hadn't appeared strange to me;
there had always been so many friends, I hadn't missed a family.

Finally, there was the large manila envelope marked, in
Blanche's hand, *Lawrence*. I broke the seal without any thought
of violating privacy; it was time to know. I flicked through its
contents and found there the reason why Blanche and Eugene
D'Arcy's history had seemed to begin from nothing in the early
forties; it was clear, and, I suppose unless it happens to be
one's own story, fairly commonplace. There was the registry
certificate of the marriage of Blanche Sheridan to Lawrence
Findlay in 1939 at Fermoyle, County Tyrell, Ireland; Blanche
would have been barely nineteen at that time. Then a record of
Army allotment payments to Blanche in London. These ended
with the letter from a firm of Dublin solicitors informing
Blanche that Major Findlay had now designated his mother as
his next-of-kin, and future payments would be made to her.
The last document relating to Lawrence Findlay was a telegram
from Ireland: LAWRENCE HAS BEEN KILLED IN ACTION. It was
signed GERALDINE FINDLAY.

Strangely, here in this envelope, as if the two events were
forever linked in Blanche's consciousness, was the certificate
of her marriage to Eugene D'Arcy. It had taken place about a
month after the arrival of the telegram from Geraldine Findlay.
On it, Blanche's name was given as Findlay, née Sheridan, and
her marital status as "widow."

I had never seen the certificate before, and I knew why. The date of the marriage was about a year after I had been born.

I sat there with the papers spread about me, and wondered if Blanche had ever intended me to see them. It would never be possible to know now if, on the day she slipped into the final coma, the day I had found her with the open hatbox, she had intended to show them to me, or to destroy them. Of course the proof existed in other places—at Caxton Hall and at Somerset House; but would I ever have been likely to check those files unless something like Brendan Carroll's telephone call had not prompted it? She had waited—how many years?—to tell me. Too long. I wondered why she could seriously have doubted that I would be glad to be my father's daughter, rather than the legal and perhaps routine child of someone I had never known. All that mattered was to have been loved; perhaps the fact of legitimacy by date mattered more to Blanche's generation than mine, or mattered in particular family circumstances. I guessed that I found some of the reason for her silence in a letter written about a month after I was born. It bore the heading of another firm of solicitors in Dublin, Swift & O'Neill. It was addressed to Mrs. Lawrence Findlay.

> *Dear Madam. Our client, Lady Maude Sheridan, has instructed us to inform you that she is in receipt of your communication regarding the birth of a child to you and Eugene D'Arcy. She further wishes you informed that any other communications received from you will be returned unread.*

✓ ✓ ✓ ✓

The coffeepot was drained, the cigarettes were all smoked, and I was aware, for the first time since the telephone call from Brendan Carroll, of Blanche's little clock chiming on the mantel. It was three o'clock, and in a few hours it would be time to go. So I returned the papers to the hatbox. I didn't need any of them with me; everything they contained was now burned upon my memory. I put the Lock & Co. box back in Blanche's cupboard, and then I went to pack. But I left hanging the things I had prepared to take to France and Spain, the gay, bright-colored things to wear in places where the sun always shone; instead I put in my bags the clothes I would need for a rainy spring in Ireland; and when I got into the car I didn't head south for Lydd and the air-ferry to France, but north to Liverpool and the steamer to Dublin.

CHAPTER 3

I

I gentled the battered MG to a halt; my hands fell from the wheel, my shoulders eased themselves into the curve of the bucket seat. The top was down; I sat and listened to the quiet of the countryside, the absence of noise that is a sound in itself. Then I began to hear the beat of my own heart, a pounding that was no part of the quiet. Ahead lay Cloncath, the town of the Sheridans. It had been easy to find them. Lady Maude Sheridan was listed in the directory that served the whole of Ireland, with the town address of Cloncath; and in Cloncath also was the Sheridan glassworks.

It was Monday afternoon, and now, here in Ireland, with Cloncath hardly three miles away, the resolution of that Sunday morning decision in London had seeped from me. I looked down at the bread and cheese and the bottle of Guinness on the seat beside me, and knew that I had bought them not because I wanted to picnic, but because to stop along the way would be a postponement of the time when I had to translate impulse into purpose. Until this moment the fact of the journey had sustained and distracted me; I had enjoyed the sense of independence, moving in my own way instead of at Claude's direction. Now the momentum had run itself out, and I had to deal with what I had chosen to put ahead of me, as well as what I had left behind. The telegram sent from Dublin that morning would probably bewilder Mary, but at least reassure her that something was being done about the Culloden Cup; the telegram to Claude would infuriate him. Of course I had lost the part in the Peter Hatch film, the walk-on part for the clothes horse; I had earned Claude's wrath, both for missing my chance and for daring to disobey when everyone knew that Claude's models always did as they were told; I might have caused a mild annoyance to Peter Hatch himself because he would have to find someone else for the part, and certainly he would not ask for my services again. I had done the unforgivable by offering a snub to that world of agents and directors and star-makers. And for what? An impulse born in the small hours of the morning, fattened on coffee and cigarettes and fatigue, given weight by the discovery of a family that was my own, and a man who had said I was needed. But here I was near to the end of my doubtful journey, and if I had to say in words why I had come, I could not have found them.

For some miles the road had followed a stream, swift-running, steeply banked, flowing toward Cloncath and the sea. Where I had stopped the car the road widened a little to give a sweep in to a stone bridge. The bridge led to tall iron gates, breaking the line of the high stone wall which had marched beside the stream for the last mile or so, and which stretched ahead and out of sight on the Cloncath road; next to the gates was a lattice-windowed lodge, one of its walls formed by the estate wall itself, its small garden a tide of purple and yellow iris. From the gates an avenue ran straight and wide between two lines of oaks, budding with the new green of spring; the avenue narrowed to nothing in the distance, without sign of a house. Sleek cattle grazed the land on either side. The oaks were old, like the ivy which clung to the lodge and clambered on and embraced the walls. It was a scene of eighteenth-century peace and beauty disfigured by the ugly practicality of the heavy wooden barriers that guarded the road side of the stream, and by the serpentine coil of chain and padlock on the closed iron gates. The bridge, whose pillars bore a weather-worn crest, had given way to the force of the stream in flood—fairly recently, I guessed, from the absence of weeds and moss on the great blocks of stone its collapse had hurled into the bed of the stream; white water swirled and thrust against them now. I gathered up my raincoat and lunch packages from the car, and walked a little downstream, seeking a place away from turbulence of the water, away from the windows of the lodge. Around the next bend a new wooden footbridge had been thrown across the stream; it was marked by muddy footprints and many bicycle tracks. I crossed it and walked downstream on the other bank where the high wall continued to follow the curve of the stream; where it grew broader and the banks gentler, I spread my raincoat.

It was, I supposed, one of the thousands of trout streams of Ireland that one heard about—clear, swift-running, deeper than I had expected, with odd pools of stillness formed by its bends and the jutting brown boulders. It was stunningly cold to the touch, but when I cupped my hands and drank, I had never tasted water like it, with a zest and a lift to it, like a champagne. After that I didn't need the Guinness, but I drank it, anyhow, to give myself courage. Then I lay back on the raincoat and lit a cigarette. Everything was peaceful; the sound of the water on the stones was gentle, calming, a murmur of no hurry and endless time. Time was what I, momentarily, had seemed to have left behind; time was the rush of the week before, the rush to get my jobs done, to be ready and gone to Spain, time was the night without sleep over Blanche's papers, the sudden, hurried drive to Liverpool to catch the Dublin ferry. Time was the tiredness and tension that now began to ease itself from my limbs and brain; I felt rocked and lulled in the cavern of the stream and the arch of the spring green leaves above my head, and beyond that, the softness of the Irish sky.

*   *   *   *

"Lotti . . . !"
Probably I heard the first cry as part of a dream, for I seemed to hear it twice. "Lotti . . . ?" I sat up, pulling myself with difficulty out of sleep. It had been a sound of shocking intensity

and pain, and it had come from along the bank near the footbridge; the trees hung low, and for a second or two I didn't
see the figure of the man whose brownish tweed suit seemed
to blur against the mossy stone. But when he began to move
toward me, I saw two things—that he was not young, and that
the tweed was the only thing about him that suggested a coun-
tryman; he moved awkwardly along the bank, less, I thought,
because of the stick on which he leaned, than because he would
be more at home on city pavements. He was a short, heavy-set
man whose face was screwed up in the effort to keep his footing;
distinctive about him was his thatch of iron-gray hair, beautifully
barbered, but worn more than usually long; the hand gripping
the silver-tipped stick was pudgy and white. For the first time
it occurred to me that this side of the stream might be private
property; I got to my feet and prepared to explain myself.

But he had halted a little distance away, gesturing vaguely
and erratically with his stick; his thick body seemed to sway,
and he uttered a word or two that I didn't understand. Then
he moved, bent, as if he had been struck and wounded, to where
an outcropping of rock on the bank offered a level surface for
him to sit. He lowered himself carefully, his hands clasped together over the head of the cane; his face was gray, and I could
see the perspiration on his forehead and upper lip. I came
close; momentarily he closed his eyes, clenching the cane as if
to win back control. It was the face and posture of a man in
a kind of agony.

"Can I . . . can I help you?"

He shook his head, but did not speak. His lids still were
lowered.

"Could I . . . get you some water? There's that cottage back
there . . ."

Again he shook his head. "No . . . no, thank you. It is not
necessary." He had opened his eyes, but the tone was weak.
He took long breaths now, and gradually the fierce grip on the
cane began to relax, to slacken. I waited, wanting to run to the
lodge I had passed, but afraid to leave him. I bent over him,

and he seemed aware of my concern, because he raised his head to look at me, and tried to erase the expression of anguish that still lingered.

"I am sorry," he said. When he let go of the cane to take the handkerchief from his breast pocket I saw that his hand trembled. "I am sorry," he said again. He was dabbing his face now, and some color was returning.

"Are you sure I can't do something? If it's all right to leave you now I could go to the cottage . . ."

He shook his head. "There's no one there. And no help is necessary." His English was excellent, but his accent belonged to middle Europe. "You are kind . . . I am sorry if I frightened you. You were asleep . . . yes?"

"It doesn't matter."

"I thought—for a moment I thought you were someone . . . The hair—for an instant it looked . . . Not possible, of course. Foolish of me." The remnant of pain was still in his tone, the plaintive hope. I warmed to this stricken little man and wished that whoever it was he had called to might have been there in my place, or that I could offer some substitute. There had been such longing in that cry, such need released in that brief explosion of hope, and now smothered under this blanket of polite disclaimers. I wanted to touch his shoulder and tell him to rest; that I would stay with him for whatever comfort my presence offered. Without the words, though, he seemed to know it.

"You are kind," he said again, and this time it wasn't for the sake of politeness.

"I'm sorry, though, that my being here startled you. I hope I'm not trespassing. I didn't think about it—and there were no signs about its being private property. Should I have stayed on the road side?"

He shook his head, and his hand waved off the notion. Again he wiped his face with his handkerchief, and I was relieved to see that the action was stronger and firmer. "You are welcome. When one is a guest in a country one does not put up 'No Trespassing' signs. The stream is for everyone to enjoy, and I did not think you had come to steal my cattle. Finish your lunch, please."

"I'm finished." A thought suddenly came to me. "Look, I've got some Guinness left in the bottle. If you wouldn't mind drinking from it . . . ?"

He hesitated just seconds, then nodded. "Thank you . . . yes." I ran to bring it to him, wiping the neck of the bottle carefully with Kleenex before handing it to him. I thought that again he hesitated before he tilted it to drink; but then it was gone in a few gulps.

He said, yet again, "You are kind." I wondered why he expected so little. He continued to sit there, but he looked as if he had recovered from the shock he had had. I didn't know what to do, so I went back to my lunch packet and raincoat and gathered them up. When I came abreast of him I picked up the empty Guinness bottle. "I think I'd better go—if you're all right now. I'm sorry, again . . ."

He almost let me go. I walked up the bank and had reached the footpath at the base of the wall before he spoke. "Do you live near here?" I was sure he knew I didn't.

"No." I looked back. Did he seem lonely, somehow forsaken, perched there on his rock? Was he waiting for me to say something else? Suddenly I sensed that he was indeed alone in this country, alone with the prize cattle and his beautiful park, his broad avenue and chained gate. "No—I'm just on holiday. Just driving. I was . . ." I went on because he seemed to want to listen. "I was planning to stay at Cloncath."

"You're from England—from London?"

I nodded. He said, "There's not a great deal for you in Cloncath. Just one hotel and a few guest houses. There's the harbor, of course, and a little strand. The Irish go there—in summer."

"Well, I . . ." Why, I wondered, was I attracted to the odd little man?—because he hadn't seemed to care about my trespass?—because he was so unpossessive of the beauty he owned? Because he had needed my help, had accepted it from me? He looked gnomish, seated on the rock, with the springing gray mane of hair and the brown suit, a stout gnome. I felt I could trust him. I was tempted to ask my questions of him, rather than the hotelkeeper in Cloncath. After all, he himself must once have been a stranger here, and would remember what it was like to have to ask questions in a small town, to feel one's way. He would be more sophisticated than he looked, of course, and he would be shrewd, because he was rich. Somehow I knew that he had made his own money; he had the kind of held-in energy that characterizes the rich who work. Since he was a foreigner, he had to have bought this place, not inherited it. A shrewd, rich, stout little gnome; he might be full of malice as well, but I did not think so. Of all the unknown qualities that faced me, I would take my chance on him.

"I also have a call to pay in the district."

I saw his gray eyes light with curiosity, and was thankful that he wasn't an Englishman who would politely mind his own business. "So?" he said, frankly inviting me to tell him the rest of it.

I tried to sound casual. "Yes—on the Sheridans. Lady Maude Sheridan. Do you know her?" I waited; it seemed a long time. Then slowly he began to nod his head.

"I do. But you do not know Lady Maude yourself, young lady." It was said with certainty, and I knew that once again my face had revealed everything I was thinking; it was what had always marked me as an outsider in the cool world of Claude and the London we both inhabited. I was aware, too, that this little man had had long experience in reading people much more profound than myself. Inwardly I shrugged, and gave myself into his hands.

"No, not yet. I thought I would telephone from Cloncath."

He was shaking his head. "Not good. I doubt she will see you."

"Why not?"

He cocked an eyebrow. "She is a little mad, you know. Daft, the Irish say. Harmless, but a little mad. She does not go into society. No one goes to Meremount any more. I should not call if I were you. You will probably not be received. It is an odd household."

Without knowing it he seemed to be holding the door open to me to back out of what I had committed myself to. It would be so easy to accept what he said, and head back to Dublin. I could treat it all as an impulsive mistake, and try to forget about it. Why had I been foolish enough to go against the pattern of disengagement that Blanche had established over these twenty years and more?—why should I assume that time would soften the stern dismissal of that reply to Blanche through the Dublin solicitors? If I went now I would be on my way and in Spain by Wednesday; it was possible that the job in Peter Hatch's film was still open. Sometime it might even make an amusing story around a dinner table—how I went to Ireland to see my mad relations and never made it. But Blanche was not for sporting with, not for making an amusing story of. And there was the Culloden Cup.

But the gnome's expression was not as unconcerned as it should have been. He was anxious, and he pressed his point too hard.

"Look," he said, "why give yourself any unpleasantness? She is a daft old lady. She can be—touchy."

"Why should there be any unpleasantness?" I was enjoying his discomfort a little as he realized that he had said too much —was he not so shrewd after all? "It's a perfectly normal thing to do, isn't it? The Sheridans are a family connection."

"Family?" His tone was disbelieving. "There is no family."

I decided to get it over with; if this was the usual small country town—if Brendan Carroll had a tongue in his head—half the population would probably know of my presence tomorrow. "My mother was a Sheridan."

"Your mother?" He tapped the ground with his stick. "Who is your mother?"

"She's dead now. Her name was Blanche D'Arcy."

For a moment he struggled with his memory, and then I saw the recognition begin; he blinked rapidly. "Blanche . . ."

he repeated. "Yes . . . I remember . . . I remember. It happened a long time ago. Before I came here."

"I suppose so. I . . . I really don't know anything about it."

"You don't know?" He was shaking his head. "Then why have you come?"

I gestured helplessly, feeling irritated and confused, wondering how much of his business all this was, wondering why I had decided to confide in him. "There's something that belongs to me—I want it back." It was useless to try to explain that I had come for more than the Culloden Cup; I couldn't explain it.

"Then," he said, "I think you had better come back to my house, young lady. I myself will contact Lady Maude."

"That won't be necessary, thank you. I can do it from the hotel in Cloncath."

"I think . . ." He gestured with the stick. "No, I will be frank with you. I am *sure* it will be better if your arrival is announced in a less public manner than by the hotel telephone. It will be sensation enough in the district when it becomes known that you have come, but less if it seems that you have come by invitation. The old lady is mad and misguided, but she has had enough trouble in her life." He paused, and his tone was quieter. "Heaven knows why I am so gentle with her, since she does not trouble to be gentle with me—but then, why add to the blows?" He sighed. "We will try to disturb her as little as possible."

"Will my being here disturb her?" He was taking too much on himself, I thought.

"I would think it likely. If I was told the story rightly—if I remember it rightly—Blanche was Lady Maude's daughter. I doubt that many people around here would know there was a granddaughter."

Suddenly I was cold and tired. I had come too far on this journey; farther than I had thought I would go. I had not envisaged where it would end. Using the lure of the Culloden

Cup, playing on the loneliness he had sensed in me, a man called Brendan Carroll—still the only thing I knew of him was his name—had led me a long way back into Blanche's past.

"Granddaughter." I repeated the word helplessly. How awkward it sounded. The term was strange and unfamiliar; I didn't know myself in this role. But it was the truth, of course. Only a relationship as close as mother and daughter could have been terminated with such violence, only close flesh and blood offered such cruelty, such unforgiveness.

The gnome's face puckered—with compassion, perhaps, or simply curiosity satisfied. I didn't care; I put myself in his hands. He knew at once I had capitulated. "You had better do as I say, young lady. We will go to my house. That is your car parked along there?"

I nodded. He got carefully to his feet and we walked then in silence back along the footpath under the wall, across the narrow bridge. I threw my raincoat into the back, and waited while he squeezed his bulk down into the passenger's seat. He directed me where to go—back the way I had come, a turn off the Cloncath road, another turn east, all the time following the wall of the park. At last he motioned me to slow, and we were at another set of gates, standing open this time, another lodge where the gnome waved to two small children playing in the garden, another broad avenue lined with oaks.

II

"What is your name?" the gnome said.

I told him, and he nodded. "I am Otto Praeger." It was the first time we had spoken during the journey. He tilted his head back in an awkward, unaccustomed movement, and stared up at the trees overhead, the way one does in an open car.

"Your ancestors, Miss D'Arcy, planted these trees. They built the house I live in—Castle Tyrell. I bought it and what remained of the estate a little more than ten years ago." He glanced sideways at me. "You wonder why I bother you with all this when you have more important things on your mind? It is to prepare you for what you will be told when you see Lady Maude—if you see Lady Maude. She will undoubtedly tell you all this, and much more. Her madness is her family—the lack of it, and the past—too much of it. She is obsessed with the way things used to be. She lives, I think, only for the day when she will repossess the house she sold to me, when she will live again in the place where she was born. In the nature of things it can never happen, of course."

"This is the Sheridan family . . ." I was sorting my way through the relationships.

"Not the Sheridans. Lady Maude was a Tyrell. She married beneath her rank, and while the world has forgotten about such things, she never can. Charles Sheridan was in trade—I don't think it ever occurred to her that he was the descendant of a famous glassmaker. I wonder if she has ever forgiven him—he's been dead many years—for so far overreaching himself as to ask her to marry him. Or herself, either, for the necessity of having to accept him."

He had been right to discourage me, and Blanche had been right in that long-ago decision to keep me away from this. "The rest of the family?" I asked faintly.

"As I told you—no one. Not a Tyrell, and not a close Sheridan. There's a Sheridan running the glassworks, but he's the son of a distant cousin—Connor Sheridan."

I had been waiting for the other name, but it had not come. So I asked. "Do you know someone called Brendan Carroll?"

I felt, rather than heard, the intake of breath; the bulk in the seat beside me seemed to quiver.

"I do," he said, and that was all. I saw the pudgy hand clasping and unclasping the stick; he didn't any longer look up into the trees.

Finally the avenue ceased to run on into the distance; I could see the glint of calm water. We crossed another stone bridge over the stream that fed a small, artificial lake to which sloped brilliant green turf and banks of azaleas. On a low rise was the house, a long pile of stone, battlemented, turreted, towered, the odd result of many generations of building fever—not beautiful, but unalterably impressive. At the far end the house joined, but did not blend into, an ancient square tower, which rose high above it, a fortress tower from the days when bowmen watched from the slit windows for the invader who came from the sea mists.

Involuntarily I had slowed the car as I stared.

"They burned it during the Troubles," Otto Praeger said. "The family could no longer live there, and there was no money to put it back in order. It stayed roofless until I found it, a shelter for the small animals of the wood that grew up within its walls. It might have been," he added, "less expensive to have razed the whole thing and begun again—but in those days I was in no mood to tear anything down. By 1945 I had seen too much of the world blasted out of existence."

I wondered what he himself had lost by the end of the war to make him cherish this pile—and where he had lost it. Oddly, with the exception of the ancient tower, the house itself had little real effect on me; it was as if I looked at a cardboard cutout, a toy thing made for play. Otto Praeger said my ancestors had built it, but my experience of my ancestors stopped with Blanche. I should have left it that way, I thought. I was not of the time or the generation that could venerate family or buildings or a special plot of earth; Lady Maude would feel that the rejection of her only direct descendant all those years ago had been prophetic and justified. Tomorrow, probably, I would leave for Spain.

The drive led past the house and round to the other side. I parked the car on the graveled space below a terrace. This end of the house was mid-Victorian Gothic, all the windows and doors elaborately and heavily arched. An attempt to lighten the effect had been made by placing tubs planted with pansies on the flight of steps that led to the main door, but they were dwarfed by the scale of the house itself. As we got out the door opened and a youngish man wearing a dark gray servant's jacket and a bow tie, wildly askew, ran down the steps.

"It's himself," he called back over his shoulder to someone unseen in the hall.

"I am," Otto Praeger said in a low voice, "chaotically but affectionately served. I tried it another way, with an English butler and housekeeper, but the house went to pieces in a month. So now we do it their way, and we almost manage."

"Mr. Praeger, sir," the man said, hurrying toward me. "Wasn't I about to send out after you. It's gone half-two, and you've no lunch in you yet."

"Well, then, we'd better have tea, hadn't we, O'Keefe."

"Tea?" Consternation showed in O'Keefe's face. "At this hour? I'll see what herself has to say about that."

"Yes—tell her I'm hungry."

"I will that, sir. And what will I be doing with the baggage, sir?"

"Baggage?"

O'Keefe was staring at the bags piled in the space behind the seats. "Oh, that . . . well, I'll give you instructions later."

I waited until O'Keefe had gone ahead of us, calling again to whoever was in the hall, "Himself will be wanting tea. He's hungry. Tell Mrs. Sullivan."

"You should have told him to leave the bags where they are," I said. "I'm not staying. The hotel in Cloncath seems the best bet—at least it's neutral ground."

"There's no such thing as neutral ground in Ireland, Miss D'Arcy—as you will learn. If Lady Maude refuses to see you, you will, of course, spend the night here. And no one will know that that was not what we intended all along."

"Whatever happens," I said, "tomorrow I'll go."

"We'll see," he answered. "We'll see."

III

"I have sent Lady Maude a note," Otto Praeger said.

"A note? Wouldn't a telephone call have done?"

"She rarely consents to talk on the telephone, I understand. I myself have never tried to telephone her. And if I did now, half of Cloncath would know it within the hour. But we will have tea, and wait. The reply will be here soon. It is no distance to Meremount."

We were seated in a room which overlooked the lake at the farthest end of the building from the old tower, a handsome room that served as Otto Praeger's study. It opened off the central hall, which had surprised me by being plain and modern, when I had expected heavy Victorian paneling; then I recalled his talk of the roofless walls where a young forest had begun to grow up. It had been restored in rough white stucco and un-carved wood, its plainness serving to emphasize the brilliance of the collection of Chinese rugs and ceramics. The hall had opened out onto a long gallery of connecting rooms facing the lake, their walls hung with paintings. I had wanted to linger, but Praeger had bustled me into his study.

"Later," he said. "You will come later. Everything I will show you later. Now we will have tea."

Before O'Keefe had arrived with the trays and teapots, a heavy, middle-aged woman, wearing what seemed almost an uncon-scious caricature of an Irish countrywoman's dress of thick tweeds and brogues, presented herself at the door. She carried a notebook and pencil, and a sheaf of papers.

Immediately Praeger waved her away. "Later, Fräulein, please. Did O'Keefe not tell you I had a guest?—and I have not had my lunch."

The woman nodded. "Yes, Herr Praeger. And do not forget your pills."

When she had closed the door Praeger observed sadly. "The

young ones are pleasanter to look at, but if one travels with a young secretary, people make stupid remarks, and the press is snide. Also the young ones are not so efficient, and they never remember the pills."

"Do you travel much, Mr. Praeger?" I was confused about what all these strangers were doing in Ireland.

He blinked, as if I should have known. "My offices are in Frankfurt," he said. "Yes—I travel a good deal."

"Frankfurt? But you live here!"

"I live here a few days a week."

I spread my hands, indicating the house. "But all this for so little time . . . ?"

He eased himself down into an armchair opposite me. "I saw Europe destroyed, Miss D'Arcy. I promised myself that if I should survive I would find myself a place that war hadn't touched." He shrugged. "When I found this, it also bore scars of a long war—but it was an honorable and just fight. And remember, in those days there weren't many places a German was accepted. But these people were decent and kind, and if they disliked me, they kept it to themselves. Only Lady Maude— she, of course, being an aristocrat, and Anglo-Irish, felt it her duty to despise me, as she took my money for her house—oh, excuse me, I should not have said those things. There is nothing so boring to the young as a self-pitying old man. And she is your grandmother . . ."

"She is my mother's mother," I said. "Whether she is anything to me personally, we'll have to find out." His expression was doubtful, and I gave vent to the resentment and dismay that was growing in me. "Mr. Praeger—my car's out there. I'm free to go any time I want. I don't owe Lady Maude anything —not anything at all."

O'Keefe was entering then with the tea things, and Praeger made only one slight comment. "You will excuse me—but things are never quite as simple as that."

Then he busied himself with pouring for me, and trying to get me to eat. "You are thin," he said. "But a lot of girls are

thin these days, even the German girls. They all look as if they
are trying to be models."

I let it go. I was becoming more nervous as we waited, and
I didn't want to eat; I felt as if I had a race to run, and it should
be on an empty stomach. I regretted the Guinness by the
stream; I regretted almost everything I had done since Brendan
Carroll's telephone call. Mrs. Sullivan seemed to have decided
to throw lunch and tea into one meal, and there were plates
of smoked salmon, a potato salad, ham, cheese, as well as the
obligatory silver tray of tiny sandwiches and cakes. Otto Praeger
gave up urging me to eat, and settled to it himself; he ate
silently and with relish. I smoked a cigarette and drank tea, and
when the telephone rang in the silence I started, and some of
the liquid spilled into the saucer.

"Yes, Fräulein," Otto Praeger said. "Yes, put him through
. . . Yes, she is. Yes . . . yes, I will direct her. I think she is
able to find her way. Good-day."

He turned to me. "That was Connor Sheridan. I also sent a
message to him at the glassworks. He and Lady Maude are expecting you."

I put the cup down slowly; my knees didn't seem to want to
bear my weight when I stood up.

IV

I found Meremount easily, and too quickly. Fräulein
Schmidt's typed directions were painfully explicit, but I didn't
need them. Otto Praeger had told me to return to the North
Lodge where I had parked the car to eat lunch, and to continue
on the Cloncath road. Meremount's gate was about a mile farther. When I saw it I forgot my nervousness for a moment in
the sheer pleasure of looking at it. It was a perfect Queen Anne
house, exquisite in every proportion and line and detail, as
symmetrical, as straightforward, as pleasing as a child's drawing
of a house. It was surrounded by the pasture land of its farm,

an orchard on each side of its gently curving avenue where sheep cropped the long grass. The lodge was a small cottage of the same period where washing hung out to dry; here the iron gates stood open. They looked as if they had rusted that way and would never close again. There was no real garden that I could see—just a rough lawn surrounded by the sheep fence, a few scraggly rhododendrons under the windows, a circular bed of unpruned roses into which the weeds had encroached, and some geraniums in pots at the bottom of the steps. A high brick wall continuous to the front façade cut off the view of the outbuildings and might have concealed another garden; rampaging ivy and wisteria almost hid it. After the groomed massiveness of Otto Praeger's castle, Meremount was reassuring.

The big front door stood open, and on the steps and down on the weedy gravel circle before the house were scattered pieces of furniture, obviously taken from a battered lorry that stood to one side. There was a fine little writing table, a Victorian washstand, numbers of unmatched chairs, some of them very good—and all set about haphazardly as if they had dropped out of the sky. From the hall I could hear the sound of voices raised in altercation; one voice, thin and aging, was always dominant and imperative.

"No—you idiot! There! Turn it *there!*"

I moved toward the steps. There were mumbled objections, and the voices of two men giving each other instructions. Then there was a cry, and the sound of shattering glass. It was instantly followed by recriminations from the high thin voice. "And how, Michael Sweeney, am I to replace that? That sconce was nearly two hundred years old. For all you know your great-great-great grandfather made it for Sheridan . . ."

"Whist!—don't fuss yourself, Lady Maude! Haven't we the exact same thing hanging in our hall? Sure we never use the thing since we got the electricity, so you're welcome to it."

I had reached the top of the stairs. A thin, gray old woman wearing a blue-green tweed skirt and jacket stood half-turned to the open door. With their backs to me, hands on hips, two men surveyed the frame of a high fourposter bed, and scattered on the floor about it, the crystal from the pendants of a small sconce. They had obviously been trying to maneuver the bed along a narrow passage through a collection of furniture greater than any Blanche had even had at one time in the shop. It was the weirdest assortment of things I had ever seen, good, and less than good—pieces to furnish a mansion and a dozen cottages, chairs, tables, desks, sofas, bric-a-brac—the rubbish and gems of a whole lifetime. It all stood there, without even the order of an auction gallery, waiting for something, for some place to go. It completely obscured the magnificence of the hall, the slim columns which divided its lofty spaces. Above the sea of furniture I could glimpse the delicate tracery of two Adam mantels, and just the beginning of a wonderfully carved staircase which opened from the hall at the right. The dust lay thick on the mantels and the chandeliers, on all the furniture but that nearest to the small aisles that had been left for the people who had to inhabit this storehouse.

The old lady sensed my shadow at the doorway, and turned fully toward me. She said nothing, just stood looking, and I felt right into my limbs the merciless scrutiny of the faded blue eyes; a slight working of the lips was the only sign of emotion she betrayed. I stood rooted, unable to move or speak.

The two men now became aware of her gaze fixed on something beyond them. They turned—they were dressed in somewhat similar fashion in odd working trousers tucked into gumboots, and roughly cut jackets of the same tweed as the old lady wore. I guessed that they were farm laborers called in to help move the furniture off the truck. Their mouths fell open a little as they took me in.

Her voice came again, thinner, shriller, forced; there was some emotion, after all. "Well, leave it now. Leave it and go and bring in the other things before a shower destroys them. Michael Sweeney, don't stand there gaping. Don't you see my granddaughter has arrived?"

And then to me. "Well, come along. I've been expecting you."

V

"How do you take it?"

"Without milk or sugar, please." She shot me a sharp glance, as if I had been guilty of affectation, but said nothing as she handed across the dark tepid liquid in the Crown Derby cup. She indicated the plates on the small table between us. "Bread and butter?—a scone?" I was afraid to refuse, so I tried to nibble at one of the rock-hard scones, with its butter not spread, but stabbed in an extravagant lump on its unyielding surface. The dry crumbs caught in my throat, and I coughed.

Again the sharp look. "You're not ill, are you? You're too thin . . ."

I shook my head, unable to answer. While I struggled with the crumb, she didn't take her eyes off me, and I could feel all the criticism she didn't bother to express—didn't she know this was the era of the short skirt and the straight long hair?—and that I didn't wear either one extraordinarily short or long, and they both were clean, and one well combed? I knew I got no good marks for that, though; her own hair was worn in magnificent high silver plaits above a face of translucent skin, crossed by hundreds of tiny fine lines, and stretched on bones that reminded me of what Blanche's bones had been. She had beautiful hands, uncared for, and she managed the thick slabs of bread and butter, and then a scone, as if they had been the delicate kind put before Otto Praeger; but then she must have known what to expect because she spread it all thickly with strawberry jam from a smeared crystal pot.

We were seated in what she termed the drawing room, a large high room with a beautifully ornamented ceiling and paneling. Not much of the paneling was visible for the furniture that stood about the walls—the high mahogany bookcases, empty of books, but crammed with silver and china, the library tables thrust up against the bookcases, the big rococo commodes, the

side tables, the round tilt tables on their delicate tripods. We
sat on Chippendale chairs with frayed tapestry seats and backs
in a relatively clear space before the carved marble mantel. I
could see the rest of the room forlornly reflected in the gilt-
framed mirror above it, the long curtains whose silk had gone
to shreds along their stiff folds, the rain-streaked French windows that led out to a garden that had almost vanished under
a tangle of briars and vines. Here the furniture was not the
catch-bag variety of the hall; it was all of extraordinary quality
and carefully selected, as if this had once presented the appearance of an ordinary drawing room. But somewhere along the
line it had all gotten out of hand; it was now a sad storage
room full of furniture that no one ever used. As I took it all in
I was reminded of the shop in King's Road—of the years when
I had absorbed without knowing it the basic styles of the
great cabinet makers—Chippendale, Sheraton, Hepplewhite,
Adam. I could not have put names to every style and period I
saw, but Blanche could, and now I knew where she had learned
them.

There had been no greeting between myself and Lady Maude.
After the first moments in the hall, witnessed by the two men
whom she had dismissed, she had led me here directly.

"Sit down," she had said, "I'll tell them there'll be one extra
to tea," for all the world as if one or a dozen extra made no
difference. And then she had left me alone until the moment
she had preceded the woman who had struggled in with the
huge silver tray set with the Georgian service and the Crown
Derby—a tall, bony woman in her fifties, with faded red hair
caught into a sagging bun, wearing an apron, blouse and cardigan
that flopped over a baggy skirt of the now-familiar tweed. I
had the impression, though, that the silver and china were commonplace items to her; she made wickedly strong tea in this
pot, and rattled and chipped this china every day, and had no
idea how precious they were. She had threaded her way clumsily
through the furniture to the door, with many backward glances
at me.

"More tea?"

I was cold, and the room was cold, and the tea had at least a little warmth left in it. The cup rattled on the saucer as I passed it over, and spoiled the aura of calm I had tried to convey.

"I don't know why you've come," Lady Maude said as she handed it back. "We've managed very nicely without you all these years."

She included both Blanche and myself in that statement; by myself I could never have earned such vehemence. "I imagined so," I said, and did not permit my eyes to slide once more over the chaos of that room.

"Did she send you?"

"She?"

"Your mother."

"My mother is dead."

"I know she is dead." She spoke as if Blanche had died twenty years ago. "The solicitors informed me. But did she *send* you? Did she tell you to try to make amends? After all these years did she think she could send you here to do her work?"

I couldn't stand it any longer; the thin fabric of politeness broke. "Send me?—no one sent me! I never *heard* of you before last Saturday night. I never would have heard of you if it hadn't been for . . ."

She didn't allow me to finish. "You are saying that Blanche never told you about her family?—actually that she never told you about the Tyrells?"

"She didn't tell me about the Sheridans, either."

"The Sheridans . . ." The old woman waved her hand in dismissal. "Didn't she tell you that her grandfather was Lord Fermoyle?" I looked at her blankly, and in a kind of frenzy of disbelief, she swept on. "*His* grandfather was the Fermoyle of Waterloo. His uncle was First Sea Lord . . . She didn't tell you?"

I shook my head, and didn't try to explain to her that that world was as dead as these names were, and that Blanche had been one of those who early had known it, and had never bur-

dened me with such a past. It would have been useless to say
to this old woman that the present lords of the earth were the
Otto Praegers, whomever he turned out to be. Perhaps what
I felt showed, because her features lost their momentary ani-
mation; they hardened and the lips grew tight.

"Then why have you come?" Never could there have been
less welcome in a voice.

Indeed, why had I come? Impossible to tell her of the impulse
that had sent me, the sudden knowledge, the sense of searching; impossible to look into that cold, wounded face and say
that I had come to discover something of myself. Inwardly I
shrugged; it had all been a mistake, as any half-wit might have
predicted. I would get it over with, and go. I had my small excuse
ready to buffer my pride, and now I presented it.

"I've come to collect a piece of my property which I believe
you may know something about."

"Property? There's no property for you! Whatever put that
into your head? I owed Blanche nothing—she chose to go and
leave it behind. Nothing was ever hers—and her going cost me
more than property!"

I took a long breath. "Lady Maude, may I finish? I've come
because a man called Brendan Carroll has something that belonged to Blanche, and which now belongs to me. I've simply
come to get it, nothing more."

I wouldn't have believed that her face could grow even stonier.
"Brendan Carroll is nothing to me. Why have you come both-
ering me about what he does?"

"It was Brendan Carroll who told me that my mother was
a Sheridan. It was Brendan Carroll who took the Culloden Cup.
He implied that I could have it back if I came here."

Her hand sketched a gesture of dismissal, of impatience.
"What has Brendan Carroll to do with this? And why have you
come from Otto Praeger? Of all people, these two! Why don't
you come in a decent civilized manner? Better not to have come.
Better to have left me in peace. I didn't ask you to come."

"I *know* I wasn't asked to come. And I'll go at once. All I want is to have the Cup back. It doesn't belong to Brendan Carroll, or you, or the Sheridans. Blanche found it, and now it belongs to me. I would like to have it back."

"*What* Cup?" the Lady Maude burst out, suddenly seeming older and bewildered, in the way the old are. "I don't know anything about it. I don't understand all this talk about the Sheridans and Brendan Carroll. What has it to do with me? You are my only grandchild—the only Tyrell left. Why do you come here and talk about something that doesn't interest me?"

I had to beware of pity. I couldn't deal with her; whatever had happened between her and Blanche was all too long past and gone. There was no link left between this old woman and myself. I began to edge forward on my chair, getting ready to rise.

"Then I must find Brendan Carroll," I said. "I had assumed you would know about the Culloden Cup. I'm sorry I troubled you." I picked up my handbag and stood up. "Thank you for tea . . ." It sounded incredible. I couldn't be saying this to Blanche's mother, and yet I was. What else was there to say?

"You're going?" Her tone was disbelieving, childish.

"I don't want to bother you any longer . . ."

"You can't go," she said calmly, flatly. "You have only just come back."

"Come back?" Now it was I who was bewildered.

"I have been, of course, expecting you for a long time. Waiting. Waiting to see, if, in the end, being a Tyrell would count. And now you have come—"

"But I didn't know—"

She swept on. "—it is not possible that you could leave so soon. I was prepared for this day never to arrive, but now that it has, we must make of it what we can."

I didn't know what to do. She was a little mad, as Otto Praeger had told me. I stood there, uncomfortable under her steady gaze, wondering how I could get out with a little grace and a little kindness, when the noises began—noises as if someone had collided with a pile of furniture in the hall, the slam of a door, the kind of chaotic noises that would go with this household. And a man's voice. "Annie—where are they, Annie?" A woman's voice, faintly, in reply. Then the drawing-room door was opened quickly and crashed back against a delicate little rosewood side table.

"Oh, damn the thing! I beg your pardon. I'm Connor Sheridan. Otto Praeger sent a message to the works but I was delayed in leaving. You're . . ." He fumbled for a second for the name; it was strange on his tongue. "You're Maura D'Arcy."

"Yes." There was relief in his coming, a sense of normalcy. He talked as if he belonged to the world of everyday experience, not the shadow world of Lady Maude. His age helped to bring back a feeling of reality; he was older than I—ten years or so— but still of my era. He would understand how little all this would mean. I began to hope that I might now complete the business of the Culloden Cup, forget about the unspoken things that had brought me here, and take my leave.

I wondered why he scowled, and did he know that he did it? Was it at me, or Lady Maude, or simply at the unoffending rosewood table. He was, I suppose, one of what they would call the "black Irish." With his pale skin the black hair and hooking black eyebrows were startling; at this distance I couldn't tell the color of his eyes; they were so deeply set they gave only the impression of darkness.

"Well, Brendan has been—" he began.

"One moment, Connor." Lady Maude had cut him short. She had twisted in her chair and fixed her awesome stare on him. "It is customary to observe some manners in this house, if you please—whatever you may have learned elsewhere. This is Connor Sheridan. My granddaughter, Miss Maura D'Arcy."

He acknowledged the introduction and his opinion of such niceties by closing the door behind him with what amounted to another slam. "How d'y'do? I suppose you've come about the Culloden Cup?"

His action and the kind of bluntness of the words amply

conveyed the impression that he would see that I had the Cup and was on my way as quickly as possible.

"Well, I have it. Carroll brought it to me this morning. He said he believed you might let it stay here, but I told him naturally we'd have to return it. I don't know whatever gave him the impression that we'd want to keep it. It was a daft thing to do—"

"Brendan Carroll has gone," Lady Maude said. "You told me he had gone."

"Well, he's come back."

"Why?"

"God knows. Some damn-fool notion of bringing the Cup back to Sheridan Glass."

"Cup? What Cup?" Lady Maude's voice had grown querulous. "Why does everyone keep talking of a Cup?"

"The Culloden Cup, Lady Maude. One of the two copies of the famous Culloden Cup has been found. Brendan Carroll found it in . . ." For the first time he lacked words.

"My mother found it," I said. "Brendan Carroll saw it among her personal collection of Sheridan Glass. He decided to bring it back here . . ."

"The Culloden Cup?" She seemed to dismiss it. "You mean the one my husband set such store by? I never could remember the story that went with it—there were always stories. I had enough of my own to remember."

"Yes." Connor could not keep the bitter sarcasm from his tone. "Then I won't trouble you with any more. Let's just say it is a valuable piece, with historical associations, particularly for the Sheridans. It belonged to Miss D'Arcy's mother and now to her. She has come to take it back. I brought it from the works and I have it in the office." He spoke directly to me. "It's quite safe, I assure you. You can take it as you leave . . ." I sensed that he wanted the second Culloden Cup very much, but not enough to hold back my going for the sake of it.

"She will have what is hers certainly. But she will not be leaving, Connor."

"Indeed? We are to have a visit then? A lost granddaughter restored—it's quite a fairy tale, isn't it?"

"No fairy tale!" The beautiful worn hands clenched the carved arms of the chair. "What was always meant to happen has happened. The last of my bloodline has come back. Blood always tells in the end . . ."

I was appalled by what was being taken for granted. "I have to leave, Lady Maude," I said quickly. "I have to go back to London. I have to go to Spain. I have a job."

She stared at me, and the stare was quite terrible. "Yes, you have a job—a task, let us say. Like your mother—like everyone these days—you will try to avoid it. But you sought the task, it did not seek you. You came—I didn't ask you to come. You must stay to finish what you have begun."

I didn't know what she was talking about. My instinct was to run from the mad obsession betrayed in the words, but instinct held me, an instinct to preserve dignity and the fear of betraying to her that Blanche's daughter—and the daughter of Eugene D'Arcy—had turned out to be a coward. I looked over at Connor Sheridan, half-hoping that some objection would come from him, but he said nothing. But he was not cool, this man; just standing there I sensed a power and a kind of violence of emotion in him that would not permit him not to care. He tried to play it indifferently, but indifference did not live in him. I think he wanted very much for me to go, but he said nothing.

Helplessly I looked back at Lady Maude and was once again caught in the spell of her unshifting gaze. I had told myself that I was winning independence, that I would never again be commanded, but here I stood before this formidable woman, who had no weapon but the force of her obsession, and I was unwillingly compelled. One night, I told myself; just one night I would stay. Perhaps I owed her that, but certainly no more. Having come this far, perhaps I also owed myself these extra hours of discovery. In the morning I would be free to go.

It was Connor who broke the silence. The hostility seemed

to have left him. "You would like to see the Cup, Miss D'Arcy? Just to reassure yourself that it is safe . . . my office is just across the hall." He opened the door smoothly; I felt that I was being led into something I didn't understand. I nodded, and it was an acquiescence both to him and to Lady Maude. In some way they had both won something from me, but I didn't know what.

She knew she had won; there was no uncertainty in the way she spoke. "I shall have your baggage sent up."

She ended the interview by rising and going before me from the room. There was no emotion to disturb that stately tread; she acted as if she had been expecting me for twenty years—and perhaps she had. I followed, but she paid no further attention to me; she seemed to glide through the maze of furniture and was gone.

As I came close to Connor at the doorway I learned the color of his eyes—the color of dark gray mud, they were, and I had been wrong, because the hostility was not gone, but only masked and held in check. The gray eyes seemed to be filled with an unexpressed, as yet unshaped, threat. It was the first time in that house that I experienced physical fear.

CHAPTER 4

I

Connor led me across the hall to the room he called the office —it had served Lady Maude's husband in that way, and he had taken it over he said. It was a high, handsome room, as all the rooms at Meremount were, its windows looking out over the avenue. It was crowded, of course—no room at Meremount could escape that fate, but it was not chaotic. Mahogany bookcases lined the walls, their shelves filled with files; there were two library tables, and a big, double-fronted carved desk, a sofa before the fireplace, too many chairs, too many vases, too much of everything, but still a sense of order. It was possible to know the function of the room, to move within it, to sense from it what Connor might have made of the whole house if it had been permitted him.

From a bed of shavings in a shipping box he drew out the Culloden Cup, dusting it carefully with a clean handkerchief, and set it between us on the desk. He gazed at it for a moment, and then he said slowly, "Well, there it is—marvelous, isn't it? —and sad. I never thought I'd see this one—the mate. Let's have a drink on it." He reached down and opened the bottom drawer of the desk. "I wonder where your mother found it. I wonder where it's been for two hundred years. I wish she'd told you."

"She probably didn't know herself. She probably found it in some sale, or some antique shop somewhere. If she'd inquired about its history, someone would have discovered what it was.

She could never have afforded to buy the Culloden Cup once the owner knew what it was worth."

"I suppose not. Pity, though." He was pulling a collection of bottles from the drawer and looking at the labels. "I suppose you're used only to eight-year-old Scotch, are you? Well, you're just going to have to settle for good old John Jamieson. Won't hurt you. Part of the national heritage."

"I think I can stand it."

He poured the whisky. "Without water?—certainly without ice. A baptism of fire, no less." He pushed a glass, which he had also dusted with his handkerchief, toward me, and took up his own. "So, here's to you, Maura D'Arcy. Welcome to your ancestral home—or homes, since you've already been at Castle Tyrell."

I choked slightly on the whisky, and recovered myself. "And you and I, Connor Sheridan, know that ancestral homes are things to be got rid of these days."

"So you don't go for ancestors and bloodlines and all that kind of thing that the old lady talks about? Not heroes of Waterloo and all that?—she must have told you about Fermoyle of Waterloo. She tells me every week."

I shrugged. "Heroes in their own time are all right. I just think it takes a different kind of man to be a hero now."

"What's your idea of a hero—someone who goes to jail to protest the Bomb?"

"Are you drunk?" I said. "Or just nasty?"

He sat down heavily. His face, which had worn its mocking, hostile expression, abruptly relaxed and fell into lines of weariness; just then he seemed oddly tired and vulnerable for a man of his strength and age. "Drunk? No. I'm seldom drunk. And when I do get drunk, I do it deliberately, in a congenial atmosphere, with good friends, who wish me no harm. Or rather, I should say, with good companions—I'm not certain I have a good friend. Nasty? I suppose so. I suppose I'm nasty in many ways. It's nasty, for instance, to prefer to drink a whisky or two here by myself, selfishly, than to sit and sip cheap sherry in that impossible place she calls a drawing room with a crazy old woman. But then, since she considers me her social inferior —to be fair, she considers most people her social inferiors—I'm not very often invited to do even that."

"If it's so bad, why are you here? *Who* are you, in fact?"

Again he mocked me. "Do you really want to hear? It's a long story for someone who's only here on a one-night stand to have to bear."

I sipped my drink. "Suit yourself. We're both Sheridans, aren't we? I begin to understand there aren't too many of them."

"Too few for Lady Maude. She had to scrape the bottom of the barrel for me. My father was about a third cousin of her husband, Charles Sheridan. I doubted they'd even met—my father died when I was quite young. After Charles died Lady Maude carried on the glassworks with the manager she had— or didn't carry it on, because it did even less business than it did before—and I can tell you, Irish glassmaking hasn't been exactly a growth industry. By the time the manager—Fogarty was his name—died a few years ago, there almost wasn't a Sheridan Glassworks left. The Sheridans have been great and, in my opinion, they've been damn good fighters, too. But Ireland and the times have been against them. I don't know how much of the history of your mother's country you know, but I can tell you doing any kind of business in Ireland until about ten years ago was more than a small battle. That Sheridan Glass continued to exist in Ireland for more than two hundred years—even Waterford Glass disappeared you know, and was only revived ten or so years ago—says a great deal for the men of the family. They just never let go—that's their history."

He swirled the liquid in his glass slowly; he had a thick, powerful body, with a look of strength, but now the broad shoulders seemed to hunch beneath the heavy tweed jacket.

"I hope," he said, "that I am not the Sheridan with whom their history ends."

"Is it likely to end—now?"

He shrugged. "Something has to happen, soon. It has either

to come to an end, or it has to have fresh capital. It needs
fresh everything—and the money for fresh ideas. It needs re-
building. Glassmaking's one of the arts that hardly has changed
much over the centuries—only a certain degree of mechanization
is possible with a hand craft. But you still need glassworks
that don't let the rain in—and furnaces don't last forever. The
men grow old, and new ones don't come in to train. They get
better wages in England. Sheridan Glass is moribund, and it
will soon die. Everything is worn out." He raised his head and
made a visible effort to shake off the depression that had fallen
on him. "For God's sake, in the accounting department they're
still on high stools and they've never heard of an adding ma-
chine."

"And what are you? Accountant or glassblower?"

"Neither. The only qualification I have for being here is that
my name is Sheridan. Lady Maude is a traditionalist, even when
it comes to the traditions of lesser people like the Sheridans.
I'd never even visited the glassworks when I was growing up—
I knew about them, of course, but they weren't a very important
concern, and there wasn't much interest in them. Then the revival of Waterford stole what little glory they had—Waterford
is the only name people know in Irish glass. I grew up within
an easy drive of Cloncath—my father was a solicitor in Bray—
but I'd never seen the glassworks until the old lady roped me
in four years ago."

"How?" I had fished out cigarettes from my bag and extended
them to him; after exploring his own empty pack he accepted
mine, and then nodded his thanks. He lighted it and began to
talk again, eagerly, as if he had forgotten his hostility in the
sheer need of a listener.

"I dropped out of Trinity—lack of ambition and lack of
money. There was nothing for me in Ireland except a widowed
mother, and we didn't get along. So when Lady Maude contacted me I was in Canada. Gone to make a fortune, of course,
and when the letter arrived what was I? I was the assistant
manager of a medium-sized hardware store in Calgary, with four

of the boss's sons growing up and stepping on my heels. And there wasn't any fortune to be made there. A letter came first from my mother, who's a snob, and who was no end impressed with a visit from one of the Tyrells. And then a letter came from the old lady telling me it was my duty to come and run the glassworks and the farm. I knew there had to be a snag, because she had left it so late to come looking for a Sheridan, and I had no qualifications whatever. But in the middle of a Calgary winter, and after two years in a hardware store, anything seemed an improvement. She had sent the money for the fare—canny old woman to know that when you're under thirty, the fare to anywhere is irresistible. And—well, I suppose I was homesick, though as soon as I got back I wondered what there was to be homesick for in this rain-soaked backwater. Then I came to the glassworks, and to Meremount, and I knew I should have gone anywhere in the world instead of coming here. I should have taken that fare money and gone as far from all this as I could go."

Somehow the sense of shock he must have known then was still in his voice, the frustration of a young man who is suddenly made older because a bright dream is gone. He shifted in his chair, and then rose and went to the window; momentarily I was forgotten and shut out as he seemed to live again the sickness of that long-ago disappointment.

"The glassworks," he said, "were so run down you could smell them rotting. Everyone in the place seemed to be about a hundred years old. I didn't know what I was doing—what I was supposed to do. Lady Maude just threw me in and let me learn the best way I could, quite confident, of course, that because my name was Sheridan I would know it all by instinct. The day I arrived she was off at an auction, and I knew what I was stuck with. Well, Meremount you can see for yourself. It's uncomfortable and damn cold. It's dirty and it needs every kind of repair done to it. Meremount is a nightmare, and the farm is a laugh—a few cows and sheep and some badly drained land, a few rotting fruit trees. It hasn't had a penny spent on it in fifty years. In Lady Maude's eyes the farm is simply the land that surrounds Meremount, and Meremount in its turn is just a storage place for the furniture that crazy old woman collects against the day when she is going to get Castle Tyrell back again and furnish it."

He turned to look at me. "That's what she expects to do. That's what the piles of junk are for."

"Most of it is a long way from being junk."

"Wait until you've got a dozen bruises on you from bumping into it in the dark—most of the lights don't work, either, you'll find out."

I sat thinking about it, the woman alone through the years, husband and child gone, family inheritance gone, hardly attempting to cope with a decaying glassworks and a run-down farm, her only passion the acquisition of furniture for a castle she would never live in. I saw it, the mountains of furniture slowly piling up, while the floors sagged with the weight of it, and the windows were darkened by its bulk, while her mind grew more baffled and confused as the years piled on her also. I began to understand, finally, what kind her madness was.

"Why did you stay?" My voice seemed a whisper in the quiet.

He came back to the desk, rested his hands on it and leaned toward me.

"What should I have done? Where was I to go—and what better was offered to a man who had nothing? She promised me—no, to give the old devil her due, she never made a formal promise. She gave me to understand, she let me believe that there was no one else to inherit. She had disowned her daughter —a lot of people around here think Blanche was killed during the London blitz. There was no one else but me. So I stayed . . . and sweated my guts out, and kept Sheridan Glass going for another few years . . . for whatever little was there, for some hope for the future." He added, "That's all changed now."

"What has changed?" But I knew the answer; sickeningly, I knew it.

"You—you have happened. She never told me there was a child."

"I make no difference. I'm leaving in the morning. I want nothing that's here."

He straightened. "You must think me naïve. You have come to see what's worth having, to establish your claim. And with that mad old woman the single fact of being the granddaughter of a Tyrell counts more than all the sweat I've put into Sheridan Glass. You heard her—'the last of my bloodline,' and all that nonsense."

"But I'm not staying, I keep telling you. Tomorrow I'll be gone."

"That's what you keep telling me." The smile that cracked his face had no humor, just the self-mocking irony of a shrug. "Well, I always was an unlucky bastard. Always too late or too early. You've come, that's what makes the difference. Even if you go, she'll count on you coming back. And there's the will. No one knows what the old she-devil has put in the will. Now that you've come, she could change it."

"She won't change it."

"Perhaps it doesn't need to be changed. She's probably always believed in her addled mind that you'd come. Perhaps you're in it already."

"Now *you're* talking nonsense. I'm leaving first thing in the morning. My coming this once can't have made any difference."

He picked up the whisky. "I hope you do leave first thing in the morning. For both our sakes I hope you do just that. Now, let's have another drink and act as if you hadn't just wrecked everything I've worked for in the last four years. I don't know which is worse—to drink alone or to drink with an enemy."

We sat and sipped the strong liquid, and a pale evening sun struggled through the grime of the window, and touched the Culloden Cup with marvelous grace. I thought of what had happened to me since the moment that Brendan Carroll had first reached past me and plucked Blanche's great find from its shelf. He had brought the Cup home, but he had meant me to follow it, to know this house of madness and despair. Well, I was here, and no one believed that I would leave in the morning.

II

Dinner was served in a room whose curved alcove of long windows overlooking the ruined garden would have been a thing of serene beauty if the eye had not been distracted by every-thing else that the room contained—the four sideboards of vari-ous periods, one delicate Regency piece stacked on a sturdy oak, the assortment of chairs that seemed common to every room in the house, the walls full of spotted mirrors and pictures dark with smoke and age—good or bad I couldn't tell. We ate at a table placed somewhere roughly in the middle of all this, and were served by the red-haired woman, whose name was Annie, still in the tweed skirt and blouse, her face flushed with exertion and some embarrassment as she lugged the tarnished trays in and out the service door. Connor hacked at the tough, over-cooked leg of lamb, and Annie carried around the shriveled po-tatoes and watery cauliflower. Lady Maude ate calmly, without looking to see how anyone else fared—as if the food at Mere-mount must always be beyond reproach. Her eyes, though, fell sharply on the label of the wine that Connor poured into the unmatched Sheridan glasses.

"Nuit St. Georges? Where did that come from?"

"I drove into Cloncath and got it—your cellar's been empty a long time, Lady Maude."

"Not from the—"

Connor filled her glass. "Not from the housekeeping money. My own contribution to Miss D'Arcy's pleasure."

"Young girls don't need strong drink."

There was no time to feel surprise at Connor's gesture of hospitality, the knowledge that he had taken trouble over this one thing he could do to make the food palatable. As I took the first sip I said to Lady Maude, "I'm twenty-three."

Her fork clattered against the plate as she jerked her head around to see if Annie was still at the littered sideboard. But the service door was closed.

"I did not think it would be necessary to point out to you that these people thrive on scandal and gossip."

Surprised, Connor put down his glass. "What in the world is that supposed to mean?"

"Lady Maude," I said, looking at her and not at Connor, "is referring to the fact that anyone who wants to calculate will know that I was born before my mother was married to Eugene D'Arcy—before Major Findlay was killed."

He leaned back. "I see—oh, I see it now." The hooded eyebrows were raised high, and then gradually settled. He also spoke to Lady Maude. "What an evil-minded, unforgiving old woman you are to care about such a thing! So, what if the last of the Tyrells was born out of wedlock? It's only in this blasted country that children of love are matters for shame or regret—and in minds like yours, Lady Maude. So that's why your granddaughter has never been spoken of, why no one ever got an answer to a question about Blanche. You've sat here alone, lonely, all these years . . . what a waste! What an unbelievable waste!"

"Be quiet, Connor Sheridan. What do you know of what is behind all these years? You didn't live them—none of you young, stupid, heedless things had to live them. How do you know what harm Blanche did me? I should have had my grandchildren about me here—born as they should have been born, growing up here, learning the things they would have learned. Instead of which I have—"

Connor broke in. "I think," he said, "that you owe Maura an apology."

"What apology did I ever get from her mother?" Then she ended it; her long arm, clad in its dusty black velvet, shot out and she rang the bell violently. Almost instantly, as if she had been waiting on the other side of the baize door, Annie appeared to clear off the plates that were still half-full. In silence we were served a fruit pie whose crust was a close match in hardness to the scones of teatime. Annie still hovered at the sideboard, and bumped her way in and out of the service door, breathing heavily, trying to handle the plates without noise, but never succeeding. My throat was tight, and it became harder to swallow. I sat between two enemies; I didn't even feel grateful that one had chosen to champion me in this case. He had done it only to taunt Lady Maude. I pressed too hard on the unyielding pie crust and it skidded off the plate and down into my lap. Lady Maude looked across at me as if she might have expected no less.

As I scrubbed at the fruit stain with the limp grayish napkin, I was aware again of the dress itself. It was a Mary Quant design, one of the long-sleeved, collared, deceptively demure dresses that were currently the height of young fashion. I wore it with white lace stockings, and I cursed myself for being such a fool as to have had the idea of pleasing the old woman, even superficially with the quaintly old-fashioned look the costume achieved. I despised myself now for the half-hour I had spent ripping the two-inch hem and hurriedly replacing it with a tiny turn-back to give the dress extra length. It seemed now such a craven thing to have done, a denial of myself.

The scraping of Lady Maude's chair ended my thoughts, and the dreadful silence. She rose, her body looking leaner and slighter than before in its long ancient gown collared in yellowed Limerick lace. She seemed more frail and worn than she had done that afternoon, as if the hours and their happenings had taken their toll.

"You may tell Annie I will not require coffee."

Connor held the door open for her, and closed it after he had watched her progress across the crowded hall; in the semidarkness I could hear the two minor collisions she had with the piles of furniture. Connor returned to his seat.

"You saw that? She didn't want to stay, but she made herself sit there until a respectable amount of this wretched pie was eaten so that Annie wouldn't run to tell the countryside that we had a disagreement at table on your first night here. You'll find that the Irish have as great a sense of face-saving as any Oriental. And the sad part of it is that she can't conceive of any servant having the intelligence to keep her mouth shut out of loyalty. She demands loyalty from Annie as her due, and she hasn't the faintest appreciation of what she's getting from that poor woman."

"Lady Maude looks ill," I said.

"She always looks ill. She's getting on—in her seventies—and she eats nothing. Not that that proves anything. The food in this house would set anyone against eating for life."

"Why do you stay then? There must be other places you could live."

He shrugged and went and brought the wine bottle and a board with Cheddar and stale biscuits to the table. "Because it's cheap. Because I can keep my eye on her and try to stop the worst of the follies if I'm in time. Because she is, after all, rather old and mad."

He looked at me closely and we both knew what he had not said—because he had believed that this house also was to be his. He poured more wine, and his manner didn't try to deny the thought.

Annie came clattering through again. "Put the things here, Annie. Lady Maude has gone up—she won't have coffee."

"Then I'll not be givin' meself the trouble of takin' it up to her. Will that be all ye'll be wantin' now?"

"It will. Good-night, Annie."

"Good-night, Mr. Connor. Good-night, Miss Maura."

"Good-night, Annie." The words seemed to linger even after the baize door had finally, reluctantly, swung to behind that tweed skirt. I savored them, commonplace as they were; for the first time in my mother's house I had been addressed ordinary words in an ordinary way. I watched as Connor reached into his pocket and brought out matches. Slowly, softly the candles in the two prism-hung candelabra came to life. The chaos of the crowded room slipped back into the shadows; what was left was the height and grace of its proportions, the long slender rectangles of twilight at the windows, and the two of us, facing each other, washed with the glow of the candles. Connor's hand motioned toward the coffeepot.

"It's undrinkable," he said, "but you can give it a try."

It was undrinkable. So he refilled my glass and I nibbled cheese with the wine, leaving the damp biscuits on the board. A quiet closed over us, a small interlude more serene than anything I had known since I entered this house. I stretched a finger and gently touched the hanging prisms, creating the sweet ring of crystal against crystal.

"Sheridan?" I said.

He nodded. "They must date from about the 1750s—possibly from the hand of the master himself. There wasn't a very big volume of production those first years in Ireland, so a lot of the quality work was Thomas Sheridan's own."

"And this house? He didn't build this house, did he?—it's earlier than the time he came to Ireland."

"Build this house? There was never a time in Ireland when Sheridan Glass was prosperous enough to build this house. It belonged to a lady called Anne Grant, the spinster daughter of an English landowner. She was plain as a pikestaff—there's a portrait of her somewhere around the house—twenty-nine years old, and in spite of being an heiress in a small way, no one wanted to marry her. Thomas Sheridan's son was twenty years old, and a golden youth. He had all the family's hard-headedness, though, and plain little Miss Grant didn't mind at all that he married her, and used her money for Sheridan Glass, and moved his family into Meremount. I suppose the alliance of an English heiress to a common glassmaker raised eyebrows, but probably she was past caring—and he *was* very handsome. It's been the farm land belonging to Meremount that's saved Sheridan Glass —they didn't start to sell that off until the Troubles, were forced to sell it off. I suppose."

He cut squares of cheese methodically, evenly. "Over the

years England has clamped all kind of restrictions on Irish industry and farming—duties, tariffs, outright prohibition of exports. The descendants of Thomas Sheridan have made just about every kind of glass there is just to keep the furnaces alight—though sometimes they were down to one furnace with the senior Sheridan as gaffer and his own sons as his team. You can see it all in the order books at the works—young Sheridans riding all over Ireland trying to get orders for anything that would bring in money—bottles and crown glass for windows, as well as chandeliers for the mansions of the English. They hadn't had the energy ground out of them as most of the Irish had by that time—and they had the good luck not to be Catholic, although they had supported the Jacobite cause. If they had been Catholic the penal laws would have finished them. But they hung on, and their own energy saved them—and the Meremount land. But glassmakers they stayed, even when it was hardly worth the trouble. Sheridan Glass still exists."

Now it was Connor who touched the prisms. "It doesn't all have to be like this," he said. "It doesn't all have to be handblown and shaped, it doesn't have to be only for the rich. You can make glass by assembly line, pressed glass, inexpensive—glass for housewives and factories and hospitals. There's money in glass. The world can't get along without it now—test tubes and television tubes and all the rest. Sheridan Glass ought to make both kinds. The old kind by the old methods for those who can pay for tradition, pressed glass for those who need it —and that's everyone. But that needs capital, and capital we don't have. So Sheridan Glass still exists but unless something happens soon to save it—it will disappear."

Then with a single quick gesture he brushed his hand across all the prisms, their violent collisions loud and strident in the gentle darkness, as if an angry wind had swept them. I started, and at this moment a light-colored shape suddenly appeared at the end of the table, and padded silently toward the light from the candles. It was the most extraordinary cat I had ever seen—long, awkward Siamese limbs and brilliant blue eyes, its

pointed face, ears, the paws and tail all a smoky lavender-blue.
It greeted Connor in a thin, plaintive voice, and waited while
he cut a piece of cheese and extended it on his fingers.

"I hope you don't mind cats," he said to me.

"No, I don't mind them. This is your cat?" It couldn't be,
I thought. Two creatures had never less belonged to each other
—the feline quality was no part of his rock-hard masculinity.

"Her name is Sapphire. No, she isn't my cat. I don't much
care for cats."

"But you feed her."

"I feel sorry for the poor devil."

She couldn't be Lady Maude's cat, either, I thought. The old
lady needed no companionship of this kind; cats were too in-
dependent for her autocratic nature to tolerate. I watched as
Connor cut another sliver of the Cheddar and Sapphire nibbled
at it delicately. The brilliant blue and creamy beauty of the cat,
and what I thought of as the darkness of Connor—the hair, the
brows, the smudges of dark lashes were a potent foil for each
other. During this time over the wine and cheese, linked with
this new aspect of him revealed in his gesture to the cat he did
not particularly like, something had begun to grow between us
—not friendliness, because he did not want me there, but,
strangely, a kind of trust because he had not pretended anything
different. I could ask my questions and he would answer them
or not, just as he pleased. I thought he would not lie.

"Who is Otto Praeger?" I said. "Why doesn't Lady Maude
like him?"

"Otto Praeger?" He seemed for a moment reluctant, as if he
were trying to make up his mind about something. "Yes, you
met him, didn't you? Just like him to manage to meet you before anyone else knew you were here. With all the other things
I'd forgotten about him meeting you. He didn't forget, though.
With typical German efficiency he sent a message to me at the
works as well as to Lady Maude that you'd arrived—didn't trust
the way she'd behave, I suppose. And it was a good guess—she

might well have decided not to see you. But then he usually guesses right, that man. He went to a lot of trouble . . ."

"I was impressed with him. Who is he?"

"Before the war he was Praeger Optics—Bergen cameras are a small part of Praeger Optics. Since the war—well, I suppose he's the kind of man you think of when someone mentions the German economic miracle. Since the war he's built a whole empire in light industry—plastics, small appliances, that kind of thing. He's in everything that has a mass consumer market."

I felt let down; Otto Praeger had talked of survival, and I had sensed something more heroic in that stout little gnome. "And the war," I said. "What did he do during the war—make gunsights and binoculars?" It sickened me a little to think of Castle Tyrell bought with such things. "Was he a . . ."

"A Nazi? No. And he didn't keep quiet about the Nazis, either. He spoke out, and they took his business away from him. One of the leading manufacturers in Germany couldn't publicly disagree with Hitler's policies and still be allowed to stay around. They sent him to a concentration camp, even though he had powerful friends to plead for him, as well as the Church. In this Irish climate you'll never see Otto Praeger without sleeves, but *I* have seen the numbers tattooed on his forearm."

"He stayed alive, though."

"He stayed alive, and went back and fought them for what remained of Praeger Optics. It was almost nothing—factories bombed, no trained staff left. But he's a man gifted with energy, and very persuasive. The Americans were desperately anxious to restore Germany as a buffer against Communism. So he got his loans, and that was all he needed. The man has a genius for money, of course. He knows where to use his strength. He knows how to borrow. It's one thing to have survived—another to make the survival count."

I thought of Praeger, and the green, peaceful acres in a country unblasted by war that he had craved; I thought of him alone in the hugeness of his turreted house.

"It was Lady Maude who sold him Castle Tyrell? Is that why she doesn't like him?"

"She wouldn't like anyone to whom she had been obliged to sell. Praeger gave her a pretty generous price for an uninhabitable ruin and some grazing land, but by the time the debts and interest were settled, there was almost nothing left. She keeps blaming everything on the burning of Tyrell and on Praeger for paying her so little, but the fact is that it would have gone that way whatever happened. Her father didn't start the rot, he just kept it rolling. The Tyrells have all been a bit weak in the head for generations—they had all the traditional talents of the aristocracy—horses, women, and gambling. But when the IRA burned the place during the Troubles, the old boy really went off his head. Maude's only brother, you see, was killed in the fire. So Maude married poor Charles Sheridan because he was willing to take both her and her crazy father and by that time, they say, she'd turned down a dozen much better suitors as being beneath her. After the fire, when the whole sorry state of the Tyrells was let out in the open, it was a case of beggars can't be choosers. So Charles Sheridan had the bad luck to be accepted. Then, of course, the Sheridan land adjoined the Tyrell land, and she was always expecting to move back."

"Why did they burn it?"

He shrugged. "Why did they burn anything in Ireland? To make a point. The Tyrells were landlords—that was enough. The Tyrells were opportunists. They fought for Elizabeth, and after the conquest of Ireland was completed, their land was their reward—land and a title. When Cromwell was finished with Ireland, the Tyrells owned half the county—why do you think it's called County Tyrell?"

My mouth dropped open a little. "I *didn't* think of it."

"Then think of it, and remember it, and don't be surprised that the name of Tyrell isn't exactly loved around these parts even to this day. So, they murdered Maude's brother—accidentally or not. But they'll tell you to go count the peasants lying dead in Tyrell ditches after they'd been thrown off their land and the roofs ripped off their cottages. Ask what the Tyrells did for their tenants during the Famine—nothing. And don't be surprised if Otto Praeger's more popular than you'd expect a German to be. True, he spends money, and that's always popular. He's built a plastics factory near Wexford that employs a lot of people. Good reason to be popular. But always remember that Ireland for a long time has been hospitable to the enemies of England."

I had sought another world as an antidote to the cool world of Claude's London and found this pool of violence and madness and remembered grudges. Of course I didn't belong here either; I clung to the thought of Otto Praeger as a symbol of something more understandable, whose life, though holding horror and hardship, seemed more commonplace than this.

I said, "Who is Lotti?"

His head jerked back. "What do you know about Lotti?" I wasn't sure which was first in his tone, anger or pain; why did it seem to echo the anguish that had been in Otto Praeger's voice when he had called that name?

"Nothing. I don't know anything about Lotti. Just the name. It was what Otto Praeger called to me—Lotti."

"When—when was this?"

"This afternoon. I had lunch by a stream on the road in to Cloncath—where the bridge is collapsed. I went along the bank a little on the wall side. I lay down for a few minutes and I fell asleep. He woke me by calling that name—Lotti."

He was a long time in replying; I wondered if he ever would. I saw his fingers grip the edge of the table as if he were going to rise. "Lotti . . . yes, I can see. The hair—she wore it in the way you do, straight, long, though yours is darker. She was one of those bright Nordic blondes."

"She's dead?"

"Dead, yes. She was killed at that bridge last November. Lotti was Otto Praeger's daughter."

He drained the last of his wine, and finally did get to his feet. The movement was heavy. "Lotti was my wife," he said.

I sat and watched as he moved away, retreating from the light of the candles until the darkness engulfed him. I listened to the sound of the door opening and closing softly, the sound, muffled, of him moving through the hall; distantly I heard the closing of the heavy front door and after a minute came the noise of a car engine, the crunch of loose gravel under tires, the uneven rhythm as they hit the ruts on the drive. It was not driven fast; this was no sudden flight. It was like the way he had left the dining room, deliberately, patiently, heavily, as if acceptance of a young wife's death had been achieved hardly, and he was afraid to shatter it by too violent protest. I wished that I had never heard of Lotti Praeger. I would never have asked my question, would have left in the morning without having to witness this muffled grief.

I blew out one set of candles, and took up the other candelabrum. The cat still crouched motionless on the table, her glazing eyes never leaving me. I knew now that she had been Lotti's cat, and the same kind of pity that Connor confessed to also stirred in me. "Come on, then," I whispered. I didn't know why I whispered. The cat stretched and uttered the low little cry with which she had greeted Connor. She jumped down from the table and I felt her brush my legs. She was at the door as I opened it, and with me as I threaded my way through the maze of furniture in the hall and mounted the beautiful wide carved staircase. She ran ahead of me, and kept returning, moving with the agility of her kind through the small objects that were piled on every tread of the stair and on the landing—lanterns, Chinese vases, warming pans, firedogs, footstools. One large window at the landing gave the slim outline of a crescent moon and a faint glow to touch the dark shapes of the chests and folded rugs and tapestries. I shielded the candle flame and leaned close to the window, searching for another light in the darkness of the countryside, but there was none. There was not a wind to stir a tree, not a dog to bark. It felt as if, in the whole world, no other human soul was left alive; I was strangely grateful for the warm brush of the cat once more against me. I moved on up the staircase to my room.

Someone—Annie, I supposed—had turned back my bed and put two hot-water bottles with hand-knitted covers on them between the sheets, and drawn the frayed damask curtains against the darkness and the emptiness of the night. A small electric fire attempted to warm the great spaces of the room, a lamp was lighted by the bed. On a big Georgian silver tray stood an exquisite Dresden cup and saucer and a battered, leaky Thermos containing hot chocolate. I blew out the candles and the acrid scent of the smoke lingered.

In one of the three writing tables I found age-spotted paper stamped *Meremount, County Tyrell, Ireland*. I wondered how it would strike Lloyd Justin when he opened it, perhaps on one of those sun-filled California patios they showed in films and magazines. The cat perched beside me as I wrote; when it had cooled she delicately lapped the chocolate I had poured into the saucer. She stayed there while I slowly covered the pages with words of finality, the end of the California dream. I couldn't begin to understand yet fully what the hours of this day had done to me, or why I now was sure when before I had not been. But I had glimpsed the legacy of passion and toughness and frailty that was mine from the Tyrells as well as the Sheridans, and I knew why the bland comfort of the life in the sun with a man like Lloyd was not to be. I had nothing and no one then to put in Lloyd's place; but I would take my chance, suddenly knowing that the certainties were no more certain than the wildest leap into an unknown future. This though, was not what I said to Lloyd; I made the words as gentle as possible, and I told him that I was not coming.

CHAPTER 5

I

I was awakened by the voices—the high, old voice, shrill now, too loud, and the lower, deeper tones of a man speaking; I could distinguish no words. The cadence was angry, staccato, rising and falling. But under the eiderdown, with the hot-water bottles held close, I was warm, and the day had been one of unusual length and complexity. I let myself fall back into sleep, the cat curled at my feet, leaving to them whatever it was they shouted at each other about.

I didn't hear him, though, when he entered the room. A scream froze on my lips as I felt his hand.

"Maura! Wake up—oh, for God's sake, wake up!" The bedlamp snapped on full in my face. Connor was shaking me roughly. "Maura . . . Maura!" Behind him the door to the room was wide open, and the lights in the hall switched on.

I struggled out of sleep. "What is it? What's all . . ."

"It's Lady Maude—she's had some kind of attack. Heart—stroke. I don't know. She's unconscious. Do you know anything about what to do?"

"Nothing." I fumbled for my dressing gown and slippers. "Have you rung a doctor?"

"I was going down to do that. Would you stay with her? See if there's anything you can do, will you?"

I was following him along the hall, running. "What about Annie?"

"Useless," he said. "She'll have hysterics. There . . ." He

thrust me toward an open door on the opposite side of the passage from my room, but did not come with me into the room. "Will I bring up some brandy?"

"*Ring the doctor*," I said fiercely, but softly. "And spirits are the worst thing to give anyone. *Hurry!*"

The old woman lay on the bed sprawled sideways across a mound of pillows as if Connor had lifted her and put her there. She was wrapped in a faded purple dressing gown, and the silver hair was bound into a single thick braid. In her unconscious state she seemed terribly shrunken, the colorless skin cleaving to the bones of the face, the lips tinged with blue. My inexpert fingers could find only the faintest flutter of a pulse; the breath was so slight I wasn't certain it was there at all. I could almost feel her slipping away from me as the seconds passed, and in a final, despairing moment I pulled the pillows out from beneath her head, turned it sideways so that the tongue would not slip back, and then bent and placed my own lips on hers. Never before this had we touched each other; now we were locked in this most intimate, desperate act. In what I thought might be the last minutes of her life I forced the breath from my lungs steadily into hers, withdrawing my lips to let it escape, going back each time to my task, breathing the smell of her age and decay, seeming to die a little myself with each breath.

Then I felt and heard the return of her own breath, faint, but growing stronger. The thin-veined eyelids flickered open; there was an instant of recognition. I didn't know that I had won anything; she might have come to this point on her own. But she knew that a battle had been fought for her, and we were joined by the bond of the struggle as well as by blood. Very slowly I straightened.

From the doorway came a long, wailing cry. Annie stood there as if she were afraid to come nearer, the dressing gown clutched about her.

"Mother of God, is she dead, then! Has he killed her after all?"

II

The doctor slowly ladled three spoonfuls of sugar into the tea Annie had made and brought to Connor's office. "It was a warning," he said as he stirred. "But Maude Sheridan never pays attention to warnings. After that slight attack she had two years ago—you remember that, Connor?—I told her there could be others, and what she had to do to try to avoid them. She told me she'd die in her own time and her own way—as if she had any say in the matter. But that's the Tyrells for you!" He gave a derisive, affectionate snort. "Well, I wish I could get her into hospital—but she's flatly refused to go. There ought to be tests to determine the damage to the heart. Ah, well—we must do the best we can here. She must have complete rest. I will insist on that. And she must have a nurse. If I can ever get anyone to stay with her." He seemed to doubt it.

He ate with relish the thick bread with the butter stabbed on it in Annie's own style. "How," he said, "did it start? Was she alone? Did she call?"

I waited for Connor. He thrust his hands into his pockets and turned back from the window, where he had been peering into the darkness as if he were waiting for the first of the dawn to outline the mass of trees against the sky, for the first twitter of a bird.

"I had just come in," he said. "I was passing her door and I heard her cry out. She was out of bed. She had collapsed when I reached her."

It was very smooth lying. He had shaken me out of sleep, so he had assumed I had never woken, never heard their voices raised in argument. And he could trust Lady Maude's pride not to admit a quarrel to an outsider, even her doctor. I wondered how often he lied in this accomplished style; I wondered why he lied. I wondered why Annie had said "Has he killed her after all?"

The doctor was nodding his head. "Well, it's to be understood. If it was going to happen, this would have been the time."

"What do you mean?" I said.

"You, Miss D'Arcy—you. Maude Sheridan has been without close family for so long, and then, suddenly, out of the blue, here you are. To say the least of it, it would have been a shock."

How did he know it had been out of the blue? How did he know the visit hadn't been planned? But Otto Praeger had told me that it would be this way; that in a small place like this, people would know more than I could believe possible for them to know. I would have to remember it.

He continued to eat the bread and butter, folding it over on itself, and between bites he wrote prescriptions and special sickroom articles that were to be got. "Annie can stay with her for now," he said, "but of course she'll have to be spelled. I'll have to get someone competent who can bathe her, and so on." He looked up from the pad at me. "You'll be staying, of course. You could be a help—there's a special diet she'll have to follow and you'll have to see that she gets it."

I didn't say anything. Connor's eyes were on me closely as I nodded agreement. It didn't have to bind me; I could go any time I really wanted to go. That was what I told myself.

The first light was coming strongly when we went with the doctor to the front door. It had rained a little, and the morning was chill. "I'll be back about eleven," the doctor said as he put on his hat. As he was about to start down the steps he suddenly stopped and turned back to me.

"It's a good thing you've come back—even if it is late. I used to know Mrs.—your mother." He had almost said Mrs. Findlay.

I watched as he and Connor went down to the car, and Connor opened the door for him, and stowed his bag. He was the only one who had given me even half a welcome to this house, who had spoken of Blanche as if she had had some identity; and I couldn't even remember what his name was.

✓   ✓   ✓   ✓

Connor came up the stairs slowly; he looked disheveled and bone weary. "Well, that's that," he said. It was not indifferently or callously spoken, but just as if he were too tired to feel any reaction. And then, "I'm starved. Do you think there's anything fit to eat in the house?"

"We could try." I didn't know quite how to take it—as a gesture of friendliness, as recognition that I would be staying a while, or simply the need of a man for food and someone to talk to as a release from strain. I began to make my way back toward the dining room.

"Just a moment—I'll get that brandy Lady Maude didn't need. If she couldn't use it, I can. I expect you could, too." He came back from his office waving the bottle. "Half-full," he said, "and five star." On his way through the dining room he collected two glasses from one of the sideboards; I picked up the board with the cheese and biscuits still on it. The signs of mice were around it. Connor pushed open the baize door with his shoulder and held it while I passed. "Switch is there on your right—can you manage it?"

The light revealed a strange sight. The room, which on one side of the door could once have been a large butler's pantry, and on the other perhaps a storage room, had been ripped apart, revealing the bare brick walls and dangling electrical connections. In the empty space in the middle were a number of large crates marked with manufacturers' names—a refrigerator, stove, dishwasher; a double stainless steel sink lay on its side; the floor was strewn with copper pipe.

"What . . . ?"

"What was once to be," Connor said, shrugging. "And never will be. This way."

He thrust open another door and once again directed me to the switch. This time it was the kitchen I had expected, enormous, flagstoned, grimly old-fashioned save for the startling newness of a gas cooker and an Ascot water heater above a battered sink and draining board that would have been installed before the turn of the century. There was also an Aga cooker which was lighted, making this the most comfortable room I had been in at Meremount. A steep staircase rose against the far wall; high wooden dressers were stacked with china; a single light over the sink thrust the corners into deep shadow. Connor put the glasses and bottle on the big bare table. "The food's kept out in the scullery—natural refrigeration, Lady Maude says. It's also a picnic ground for the mice. I advise you to have a nip for courage before we try our luck."

He held a beautifully cut brandy goblet toward me, a third full. The light caught the rich amber of the liquid, the facets of the glass refracted it. My hand closed over it gratefully. "It looks good—it tastes better," I said.

He took a second drink. "It's about the only thing that will be good for a long time, I'm afraid." He lowered the glass. "It's impossible, isn't it?"

"What is?"

"All of this. This whole bloody situation—the old lady being ill, this terrible house—you're being caught here like this." His gesture, expansive, despairing, included it all. "It isn't fair to expect you to stay and even try to cope. It isn't your problem. It never was. But still . . ." He took another sip and didn't seem likely to finish what he had begun.

"Still what?"

"Nothing. I won't try to persuade you. We'll get extra help—they'll always come if you pay them enough, and this time we just have to have it. Dr. Donnelly will find a nurse. Someone will do it for his sake, if not for Lady Maude's—Jim's a very decent sort. We'll manage . . ."

Was he trying to let me out easily?—to make me feel that I could escape all this with no blame attached to me? Last evening, in the office, he had said that he hoped for both our sakes I would go; he had been direct and blunt, and I had believed him honest. I had trusted him, then, but I didn't any longer. I was riding the seesaw of his alternating friendliness and hostility, the disarming honesty, then the smooth lies. I turned away from the appeal of his masculinity, from the kind of weary sadness that urged me to help him, to ease the burden for him. But he was also saying that he would not blame me if I refused this task. If it was feigned, it was a devilishly subtle performance. So I turned away quickly from the folly of allowing myself to like, to be attracted, where I could not trust.

"We'll see," was all I said.

The scullery was what the kitchen had foretold—damp, with splintered wooden shelves where dishes and crocks of food were sparsely arranged. The sinks obviously were no longer used. There were rows of heavy iron and copper pots stacked on the high shelves, unused also, I guessed, in the last twenty years. The selection at hand was cheap aluminum and enamel, battered and chipped.

"Annie does her best, to give her her due," Connor said, as if he knew my thoughts. "But she was never trained as a cook. She just sort of fell into that when no other help would stay. We try to get help from Cloncath and Fermoyle to do some cleaning, but they never last. Meremount has a bad name. Lady Maude, of course, never notices what's put in front of her, or the state of things in the house. To her, Meremount has always been temporary. Nothing matters here. After a while, everyone who comes into the house feels the same—no one gives a damn."

I was checking the contents of the shelves—ham, dark and dried, eggs, bread, butter, cream, sausages. Last night's leg of lamb sat there in its congealed fat; the sight of it reminded me of that meal, almost untasted, and my stomach was suddenly in an uproar of protest.

"Quickly," I said. "Let's do some eggs and sausage before I get too weak from hunger to lift the pan. And look, these thin pans are no good. Will you reach me down some of those up there—yes, that size."

"It's full of dust," he said, surprised, but bringing it down all the same. "No one ever uses them."

"More's the pity. They'll clean—and that one too, the copper one." I gloated over the array. "There's a chef's treasure in copper pans here. My mother would have loved . . ." I didn't need to finish.

We carried what I had selected into the kitchen and laid it out on the table. Connor slipped off his coat. "I'll clean the pans," he said. I nodded, and began the search for whisk and bowls and chopping knives; they were all found eventually, most of them with the appearance of not having been used for a long time. I began to sense what had happened over the years of serving one old woman who didn't care what she ate, of cooking in a house where the horizons shrank constantly, where no sign of appreciation or satisfaction from beyond the baize door helped those on this side of it to fight the crumbling kitchen. The menus had eroded down to the same few dishes, endlessly, carelessly repeated; the simple, good, abundant food was extravagantly misused to create no taste other than the taste of defeat.

I looked across at Connor, who was wiping the pans with a torn gray cloth. "Is there a kitchen garden? Would there be a scrap of parsley . . . ?"

"I'll look. There used to be a wonderful herb garden out there, but it's—" He gestured. "It's like everything else at Meremount."

He returned, his jacket and hair beaded with rain, clutching a mixed bunch of herbs he had cut at random with a kitchen knife. They were the product of wild overgrowth, coarse, run to seed—parsley, mint, rosemary, thyme. He offered them to me like a bouquet. "I don't know how they've survived, but here they are." He seemed touchingly anxious that I should be pleased with his garnering.

They smelled of rain and damp earth and the country in springtime. I held them under my nose and thought of how Blanche had loved the smell of herbs—the shallots and garlic that seasoned her dishes, the parsley and thyme and chives that grew in pots on the windowsill of the flat above the traffic of the King's Road, not fragrant of the country and a rainy morning as this was, but still something to which she must have clung as part of this vanished scene.

"You know," he said, "you're a very unexpected girl, Maura."

I raised my head from the herbs. "What do you mean?"

"A contradiction. As modern as your short skirts and yet full of little grace notes as old-fashioned as those herbs and the copper pots."

I laid down the bouquet. "Will you do the toast? I'm almost ready to do the eggs."

He had a dangerous charm, on the surface so ingenuous that one thought he couldn't be aware of it, and yet used so skillfully that it had to be calculated. I had to keep remembering that he had been married to Otto Praeger's daughter, and the daughter of such a man could never have been a simpleton, could never have succumbed to mere good looks. Connor Sheridan troubled and fascinated me—and I would find out what Annie's words had meant. Over and over I heard those words: "Has he killed her after all?"

Cognac at five o'clock in the morning is very potent; Irish cream is rich, eggs are abundant, and Irish sausages are stuffed with real meat. Connor pushed back his chair, stretched, and sighed luxuriously. "I don't think I've ever really tasted scrambled eggs before—or you've some kind of magic in your hands."

"Let's just say it's magic, and leave it at that," I answered sleepily. Even the coffee hadn't tasted too bad, considering the state of the coffeepot and the doubtful age of the grounds. Or maybe it was the brandy—I had let my mistrust of him slip, had put it aside, had left examination of it for another time when my senses would be sharper. I had let myself talk—haphazardly, a bit here and a bit there, about modeling and Claude, about the King's Road, Blanche's cooking, even, foolishly, I suppose, a little about Lloyd Justin. What one says over cognac and scrambled eggs in the first hour of the dawn may be too much, but I managed to close my lips on the confession of the letter written in those far-off hours before sleep.

"Do you think you'll like California then? All that sun and those swimming pools and the smog?" He was only half-joking; I had to remember that he had once responded to the lure of the break from all that was old and stale in Europe; it had not been what he hoped, but he did know the pull, the nagging discontent that sometimes attacked.

"I didn't say I was going."

"You haven't said you're in love with him either."

"Love?—no, I didn't say that, did I?"

"Is it love ye're after discussing, then?"

Annie had come down by the back stairs, and she paused midway, the long clumsy robe and wild red hair standing out from her head fashioning her into some sort of untidy recording angel to remind us of what we had momentarily slipped away from, to remind us of the old woman upstairs and the hostility and unhappiness of the night before. Her eyes swept the table with the beautiful Sheridan goblets, the cognac, the cracked kitchen china. I was at once aware of what she saw beyond that—that I wasn't dressed and that Connor was a man of powerful and unusual charm.

"Well, then," she said. "Mr. Connor's the man to be discussin' it with. He'll be something of a past-master at it, won't you now, Mr. Connor?"

The morning fell flat upon us, gray, rain-laden. I rose. "I'll do the dishes before I go up, Annie."

CHAPTER 6

I

All day it rained, a sodden, sad rain that had no wildness in it, no fury; all day I listened to it, listened as an occasional gust of wind sent it splattering lightly against the window panes, listened to the mournful, steady drip from the eaves. It was the only thing that was constant in that day. The house thrummed with an unaccustomed movement and the sound of voices, voices that strove to keep themselves low, but kept breaking into excited orders and counterorders; there was the confusion of a house stirring and peopled after a long silence.

First there came Annie's second cousin, Bridget, from Cloncath. "She'll stay and help for a bit, Mr. Connor. Her legs are young and she can carry trays and answer the nurse's bell." Bridget was a plump young girl, red-cheeked, her fine-complexioned face innocent of make-up; red hair ran in the family.

Then there was the nurse. "I'm Mrs. O'Shea, and I'm only doing this for Dr. Donnelly. Everyone knows what it's like to work for the auld lady."

"She's ill, Mrs. O'Shea," I answered, as gently as I could. "There's not much she can do except what she's told."

"And haven't I had plenty that were ill and still wouldn't take a sup or a bite but what *they* fancied?—and wound up dead for their trouble? But still, she's a patient, and not many of them have got the better of Molly O'Shea yet." She talked all the way up the stairs as Michael Sweeney carried her bag, his ears wide for her comments and my answers.

"Mother of God, will you look at all the stuff that's here? And all of it auld things you wouldn't be caught dead with. Enough to furnish a hotel they always say in town . . ."

"Aye, or a castle," Michael put in. "And most of it too grand for a cottage, Molly O'Shea." He bristled with a kind of defensive pride in what, until this moment, he had regarded in the same light as the nurse did; it had been something that he and Jim Duffy, the other farm worker, had to move about the house at Lady Maude's whim, to make room for more. Now it was something that belonged to the family, suddenly his family. I sensed in him the fear that had struck everyone in the house when the news of the old lady's illness had reached them, the fear and nostalgia that the end of an era had come; they didn't like what they had now, but they liked the thought of change even less.

In her room Mrs. O'Shea looked about her with open scorn. "Well, I never thought I'd see the day I'd be sleeping in an auction room." Her competent, managing hands touched the dusty lace bedspread that was slowly falling into tatters. "And I never thought I'd see on a bed that belonged to a Tyrell a thing that Molly O'Shea would have thrown out donkey's years ago. Well, I'll see my patient now."

She lingered, though, in the big, old-fashioned bathroom that must once have been a dressing room and which connected both with her room and Lady Maude's. "Well, it's close at hand, though I'd not give it marks for comfort. At least there's a fire—that's something." The gas fire was new, and it had been a hasty addition; there were crude holes torn in the paneling to permit the gas pipe to come through.

Mrs. O'Shea touched my arm, a gesture of inquisitive sympathy I didn't like. "I hear your poor mother's dead—God rest her soul. Sure none of us ever expected to hear of her again— someone said she died years ago. Not that anyone would ever know from Lady Maude. So close-lipped no one ever knew even the name of the man . . . Ah, well, you're back, and I'm sure it's a grand thing for the auld lady to be having her own kin about her now, though I'd take a bet on it it was a terrible shock for Mr. Sheridan, and he expecting . . ."

I ended it by opening the door to Lady Maude's room. Connor was there, having been summoned from the office by Annie to meet Mrs. O'Shea. As we entered—Mrs. O'Shea commanding in her starched uniform and broad belt—Lady Maude's hand was raised feebly in a gesture of protest. She said something, and Connor bent over her to hear it.

"Quite unnecessary." The whisper reached across the room. Mrs. O'Shea flushed, and her chest went out.

"Dr. Donnelly will be the judge of that. And it's not here for the joy of it I am." She looked about her briskly, dismissing any opposition. "Now, Mr. Sheridan, there'll be some changes here. Would you ever call back Michael Sweeney, and you'd best send for Jim Duffy, as well."

"What kind of changes, Mrs. O'Shea?"

"This furniture, Mr. Sheridan—this furniture. I can't nurse in a room like this. If, God save us, there should be an emergency, a doctor couldn't move in this room. If we should need an oxygen tank . . ."

Despite another protest from the figure in the bed, what Mrs. O'Shea wanted was done. For the moment she had power; she knew it and enjoyed it. But I couldn't help thinking that she would have used it less if the patient had not been Lady Maude Sheridan. The old woman lay in the bed, gray-skinned and exhausted-looking; the lids fluttered closed on her eyes when Michael and Jim arrived to carry away what Mrs. O'Shea said must go. I felt that I should reach out and take her hand to ease the agony of seeing her beloved things go, but I knew that the act would have been furiously resented. For a brief time, in her moments of struggle during the night, we had joined forces in the common battle, had been united. But I knew I must never presume on that moment. No one must ever feel sorry for Lady Maude Sheridan; respect and not pity was what she demanded. When some clear spaces began to show along the walls, there came again the fierce whisper from the bed.

"That will do."

"Lady Maude, I am in charge in this room," Mrs. O'Shea said.

"Enough."

The habit of respect and obedience would die hard. The men put down the table they had lifted, took their caps, and left. Mrs. O'Shea turned her back and began to fuss over the contents of her nursing bag to cover her defeat. She jerked her head in its starched veil at Bridget, who had been carrying out small objects. "You can go now, Bridget. And be back sharp at half-twelve so that I can have my lunch." Her tone had the crack of anger. I was dismissed along with Bridget. It didn't seem right to leave Lady Maude alone with Mrs. O'Shea's resentment, but I guessed that the old lady would, even in her weakened state, hold her own in any battle of wills.

Outside, Annie waited. "Mr. Connor said to tell you he's gone to the works for a few hours. If there's anything you need, he said, you're to give him a ring."

I should have expected no different. He'd left me to all this, as if to say "I told you you didn't have to stay—but since you have stayed, don't think it's going to be easy."

"Very well," I said shortly, and turned to Michael and Jim, who stood, interested spectators beside the furniture that they had carried from Lady Maude's room, waiting instructions. They looked as if they enjoyed being on hand to see if I would manage or would flounder under what I had taken on. What devastating people the Irish are, I thought—on the surface concerned and sympathetic, underneath just a little cruel.

"Now, we'll have to find somewhere in one of these other rooms to put these things. She'll want them back just as soon as she's well . . ."

I moved swiftly along the passage, but I should have waited for Annie, should have taken my prompting from her. But I didn't; I charged on, splashing about an uncertain authority.

"What about here?" Almost at random I selected the room next to the one that Mrs. O'Shea would occupy. I threw open the door with a show of confidence, expecting the usual crowding, the usual scene of neglect and disorder, the moldering air of a closed room. In the first shock of seeing what was actually there, the handle slipped from my grasp and the door crashed back against the inside wall.

It was dim; the curtains were drawn tightly. What I was first aware of was the hyacinth-like perfume that lingered. I could see very little except the shine of many mirrored surfaces in the darkness, the watery sheen of silken curtains and carpet. But the vision was already being cut off; Annie had reached past me, and was closing the door.

"We'll find some other place, Miss Maura. I'm thinkin' Mr. Connor would not be too happy to have these rooms disarranged. Aren't they Mrs. Sheridan's rooms?—an' no one is allowed in them."

I was bewildered. There were too many new things to remember. "Mrs. Sheridan?" I repeated stupidly.

"Miss Lotti—Mr. Connor's wife."

✓   ✓   ✓   ✓

The day wound on, the very thrust of it, the trivia of what needed attention giving me no time for thought. When we came downstairs after the furniture finally had been disposed of at the end of the bedroom corridor, there was the telephone call from Otto Praeger. The telephone was in Connor's office.

"This is Otto Praeger here, Miss D'Arcy." Precise, exact, a businessman; hard to imagine the gnome.

"Yes, Mr. Praeger."

"I was sorry to hear of Lady Maude's attack." Was he sorry, or did those of a certain age always hate to hear of anyone stricken?

"The doctor said it was mild. But she must rest. It's hard to make her do that. She refuses to go to hospital, but we have managed to get a nurse . . ."

"Ah, so. You are staying then. I thought you would stay."

"I'm staying for a while. I didn't mean to."

"What one means to do and what one does rarely coincide. Now I must ask you what I can do to help you."

I did not take it as I would have taken such a platitude from anyone else; it was not a conventional inquiry, a way to end up a conventional phone call. For a moment I held the receiver and thought of what Otto Praeger could do. I thought of the choked chaos of this house, its poverty, the stubborn refusal of an old woman to admit change, the ancient routine, the services that had almost ground to a halt. Then I thought that his daughter had lived here, his daughter, Lotti, whose money and youth had not won out against Lady Maude. I thought of Castle Tyrell, geared to the service of one man, smooth, clean, efficient, though an efficiency that had an Irish twist to it, given through affection, not because it was possible to command it. I thought of the one thing that Otto Praeger could do immediately.

"Yes, there is something."

"I am glad. What is it?"

"It's going to sound funny—but we need food. The food here is—well, it's not good, and we have more people to feed. I'll get the kitchen better organized and then I'll be able to cope. But just for the beginning, it would be a help."

"Yes, I understand. I know about the food at Meremount, and the kitchen. I understand perfectly. It will be attended to. Is there some other thing?"

"Just one other thing."

"Yes?"

"When there's time—when things settle down here, I would like to come and see you."

"Ah, so—yes, of course, you would like to see Castle Tyrell?"

"Castle Tyrell doesn't mean very much to me, Mr. Praeger—it hasn't until now. I would just like to come and see you." I wondered why suddenly I wanted so much to see him; if, in him, I was seeking a refuge of sanity and common sense from this house of unease.

There was only a fractional delay. "It would be the greatest pleasure, Miss D'Arcy. Yes, come! If I am in Frankfurt when you come, come the next day. I will be back."

I left Connor's office feeling as if I had established some sort of line of retreat; I felt better. I was even able to take calmly Annie's wail of protest.

"The cheek of some people! Molly O'Shea, if you please, will have two lamb chops for lunch. Just a little underdone, she says. And here's me with nothing in the house. It was the day to order, but with all that's been going on . . ." She sounded indignant, but she was more worried; the forlorn routine of the house had fallen apart, and she was not able to handle the new.

"Well, Mrs. O'Shea will just have to settle for an omelet, won't she? Don't worry, Annie—I'll make it. We'll chop some of that ham . . ."

I watched her face carefully. It was a crucial moment; if she let me take over the kitchen from her, we might survive. If she held on, refused to let me in, I might as well pack and go this moment, for all the use I would be here.

She sagged into dependence, showing her relief in a wide smile that revealed yellow false teeth. "Aren't you the one now, Miss Maura? Whoever would be thinkin' to look at you that you could do the like of it?"

Then I borrowed her raincoat from its hook in the scullery and went out into the garden. When I had asked about the herbs she had looked blankly at me for a moment and then offered that I would find "a few lavender bushes and some auld plants down at the end." It was an ancient garden, older than the present house, perhaps—high walls festooned with thick wisteria vines, beautiful, intricate brick paths, an arbor collapsing under the weight of tangled honeysuckle. Near the house work had been done recently; the beds had been cleared and spaded, the paths scraped free of mud and gravel; but this late in the season no vegetables had been set out, and fresh weeds were sprouting. Farther from the house the old state of neglect persisted—paths disappearing under soil and weeds, and the rampant, rank growth of plants gone out of control. At the far end, where the afternoon sun would strike, where an old stone bench invited the leisure hours of the lady of the house, I found the herbs. It was sad to see their neglect—unpruned, gone to seed, choking on themselves. I recognized the lavender, untrimmed of last year's flower heads, the monstrous growth of geraniums. Strangely, I recognized others too, not just the parsley and thyme of the windowsill above the King's Road, but others—borage, rosemary, sweet marjoram, savory, and sage. Once Blanche had brought back from an auction a set of eighteenth-century prints of herbs, and hung them on the stairs leading up from the street door to the flat. Part of my learning to read had been those names, chanted over and over, my fingers tracing the outline of stalk and leaf and flower. Now, for the first time I saw them as living things, and in the garden where Blanche herself must first have learned their names.

II

We had used the last of the ham on Mrs. O'Shea's omelet, so I made one for Annie and myself with the herbs. Annie didn't care for it; she nibbled the edges tentatively, poked about in the runny center, and then settled for bread and cheese, her faith in me considerably shaken. We ate at the kitchen table, and all the time her stream of talk flowed on; a listener was not someone to let go lightly. I didn't discourage her.

"Sure Lady Maude couldn't tell the difference between a cabbage and a carrot," Annie sniffed when I asked her about the replanting of the vegetable garden. "'Twas all Mrs. Sheridan's doing. She had some gardening big-wigs down from Dublin. The whole place—kitchen-garden as well as the big garden—was to be done over to look the way it used to look in the old days. 'Tis my private opinion, mind you, that they were going to carry it a bit far—in the auld days people just planted things where they wanted them without havin' to be told where. But they had these auld prints and charts and 'twas to be a showplace. They made a start on the kitchen-garden—'twas all cleared out ready to be planted this spring. They didn't get as far back as that stretch where the lavender is. Then Mrs. Sheridan . . . had the accident. And that was the end of it. Everyone just packed up and went away. Everything stopped. I'll tell you, 'twas a sad thing."

"Yes," I said. I wasn't sure, then, whether she meant Lotti Sheridan's death, or the cessation of the work. We were washing the dishes by then, and Annie paused with the dishcloth held in suspension and gave a sigh that was sheer exaggeration.

"Oh, there were to be grand doin's, I'm tellin' you, Miss Maura. Wasn't the place crawlin'? with the experts tellin' Mrs. Sheridan what was to be done. We were to have central heating, mind you. And water and bathrooms everywhere, and new curtains and carpets, all the paneling stripped down and repaired, and the floors all seen to." She said it like some litany she had repeated to herself many times. "A new kitchen—an American kitchen. Mrs. Sheridan was going to bring a chef from London or some place to help me, and sure with all the fixin' there was to be done about the place, wouldn't half of Cloncath have been knockin' down the doors to work for me."

She pointed to the new gas cooker and the Ascot heater over the sink. "'Twas as far as we got. Mrs. Sheridan insisted that the Aga was too hard to cook on, and put this one in just for the time being—that and the gas heaters in the bathrooms upstairs. There was an unholy row about that, I do remember. Mrs. Sheridan ordered it put in in the bathroom Lady Maude uses as a surprise to her. Herself was off at an auction when they did it—in a hurry-like, because Mrs. Sheridan had her doubts about Lady Maude being too pleased with it, atall. Well, when Lady Maude saw the holes chopped in the wall for the pipe wasn't there the devil of a row. And she never would use the heater even though Mrs. Sheridan had a whole line of gas tanks delivered from the Lord knows where at terrible cost.

They're down in the cellar now, and I do try to be economical with the gas, because when it's gone, there'll be no more."

"Lady Maude didn't care for the changes?"

"Well now, Lady Maude was a wee bit slow to agree with all the plans—didn't want her things disturbed, and didn't like the men from Dublin. After the day when they put in the gas heater behind her back she never would leave the place for fear of what would be done without her knowing. But she would have come round, no doubt of that at all. Mrs. Sheridan had the knack of getting her own way, and she was very attached to the house."

"She was?"

"Proud of it, she was. She once showed me a picture of it in some auld book she found in Dublin about Irish houses. They do say in it that Meremount is something special, though you could never tell it to be lookin' at it, could you now? But she was going to do it all over, and make it a showplace, and all the magazines were going to come to take pictures of it. Of course, some day she would have had Castle Tyrell, but she liked Meremount better. It was like a hobby, you might say. And her so happy with it all—flitting about from one thing to another like some beautiful bird. Mad for everything Irish, she was. Of course, there were big plans for the glassworks, but she had some schemes all her own—a weaving factory in Cloncath, for one. Irish tweeds and the like, and special laces. And wasn't she mad about horses, so there was to be a racing stable. All the drawings and things are still up there in the rooms she and Mr. Connor had. He won't let anyone touch them. All her clothes are still there, dresses and fur coats, and things you've never dreamed of. Lady Maude wasn't able to stop her fixing her own rooms, you see. She turned a dressing room into a bathroom, and I never saw the like of it in me life—all mirrors and such. Like something in the pictures. Well, it's done for now, and so is she, poor lady. All the beautiful plans are ruined. We're stuck back the way we always were at Meremount."

She smoothed her apron with her big rough hands. She

seemed to brood over something that had been briefly glimpsed and then whisked away.

"I suppose she . . . I suppose Mrs. Sheridan was pretty?" I wondered why it mattered to me what Lotti Sheridan had looked like; it was not a question I could ever ask Connor.

Annie's head came up. "Lovely, she was. One of those faces you want to keep lookin' at. Great eyes, she had, with hair about the color of the stubble in the fields after haying. Everything she did was beautiful. Oh, Mr. Connor was mad for her! Only a few weeks they knew each other before they were married, and then eight months she was here, and that was the finish of it."

"You all miss her then. . ."

"Miss her? We do, yes. But you'll never hear her name spoken between Mr. Connor and Lady Maude. Since she went he spends a lot of time in that office of his, just sittin' there. Never goes near Mrs. Sheridan's father, either. Can't bear to talk about her. But it isn't as if she never was, if you know what I mean. Things changed at Meremount while she was here, and we're missin' the thought of them ever since. There'll be no money put into the glassworks now, and none of the things she planned to do will ever be done. Things get a wee bit slower every day. It's hard to think how it was—how it was goin' to be. Nothin' happens any more."

She put the damp dishcloth across the back of a chair. "You're the only thing that's happened at Meremount since Mrs. Sheridan went. And who can be tellin' what will come of it, atall?" She said the last in a low tone, as if it were her own private rumination, not meant for my ears, but surely something I must already know.

III

At midafternoon the shooting-brake came from Castle Tyrell, driven by O'Keefe, who greeted me as if I had been a long-time fixture at Meremount, and strove to give the impression to

Michael Sweeney that he knew a great deal more about my arrival than it would have been possible for him to know.

"And how are you today, Miss D'Arcy? Himself was very concerned about you. Sure, it's a terrible thing that happened to Lady Maude. Whoever would have thought it, with you just come?—be careful, will you now, with those dishes." This last to Michael, who had opened up the stiffly hinged gates to the kitchen garden to permit the big car to back up near the scullery door. "Sure it's behind the plow you still should be, Michael Sweeney, with the big hands on you."

Together we brought the food in and laid it on the scullery shelves. Somehow its richness made that grim, sad room seem worse. There was a whole smoked salmon, there were game pies and fruit pies, there was lean moist ham, four kinds of sausage, smoked trout, a roasted joint of beef, basket of fruit, baskets of vegetables, fruit cake and soda bread. There was a box of tinned delicacies—caviar and artichoke hearts, Portuguese sardines and smoked oysters, hearts of palm, preserved ginger, anchovies. I lost track of it all, and I knew I had made a mistake.

I could feel O'Keefe's enjoyment as he and Michael made their many trips from car to scullery, feel his kindly but definite patronage. "There—I'm thinkin' you'll not starve at Meremount now, Miss D'Arcy."

But it needed Annie to say it for me. She stood staring at the loaded shelves after O'Keefe had gone, twisting her hands. "Oh, the shame of it! Just to be thinkin' of what will be said in Cloncath when the story gets out, as Kevin O'Keefe will make sure that it does."

"But, Annie, there's no shame—people often send food to help out when there's an illness in the house, and everyone knows there's extra work and no time for cooking."

"That isn't it, Miss Maura. Look you here—there's eggs and butter and bacon. Bread, too. Things no decent house would be without, no matter what. Sure, the story will be around we're beggars here at Meremount. And I wouldn't put it past O'Keefe to have put them in himself, just for the sake of what he'd have to tell in the pub. That he brought bread to Meremount. Oh, I'm tellin' you, I'll be goin' to early Mass of a Sunday from this on so as not to be meetin' the winks and the nods."

And I felt her shame also; it was silly, it was unreasonable, but I felt it. That was the first time I identified myself with Meremount.

But we had smoked salmon sandwiches and fruit cake when the vicar called at teatime to inquire after Lady Maude. The Reverend Patrick Stanton was a threadbare young man who ate what was put before him as if he needed it.

"Lady Maude won't want to see me, of course," he said. "She's not religious." And that part of his duty done, he went on to talk as though he were also starved for a listener. He told me that he was not married, that he had just come from four years as minister to a poor parish in Connemara where he had spent his time taking care of the physical needs of the Catholics because there were so few Protestants, and they didn't seem to have spiritual needs for him to minister to.

"Before the Treaty—before Independence," he said, "it would have been unthinkable to have given someone like myself"— with a single gesture he indicated the youth, his poverty, his garrulousness—"the parish church of the seat of the Tyrells. But things have changed. The Protestant Church in Southern Ireland," he said morosely, "is withering away. Look, I have an enormous church, built in the days of the Protestant Ascendancy, very expensive to keep up. My permanent parishioners number no more than forty, and many of them don't come except at Christmas and Easter. Sometimes I don't blame them. The bellows of the organ are broken, the roof leaks, and the church is miserably cold. All my flock is so *old* . . ." He said it with a kind of anguish, all the time eating as if those good things, too, might suddenly wither away. "I stand in the pulpit on Sundays and wonder if they understand a word I say—or care to understand it. I talk about the world's hungry, the world's dispossessed, the Bomb—and it's not their concern. A lot of them are English living in Ireland for cheapness, and their greatest worry is whether inflation will erode their savings or pension to less than the break-even point before they die. I tell you, Miss D'Arcy, it's discouraging. Will you come on Sunday? Sometimes a young face . . . And you're a Tyrell. The name still counts with them, a reminder of the better days. Even if they come just out of curiosity . . ." He reached for more cake before I could extend the plate. "But that's no good, is it? I never thought in my student days that I'd ever hear myself urging someone to come to church for what it might do to other people. Religion has become a form, and I'm talking to myself. But will you come on Sunday?"

"I don't think I'll be here on Sunday. Lady Maude isn't seriously ill, and there is a nurse. There's not much reason to stay."

He looked dismayed. "You can't go so soon," he said. "You're needed. I don't mean for nursing."

I shrugged, and because he was young and truthful and despairing, I said what was on my mind. "I'm not needed in any case. My mother left here more than twenty-three years ago, and she never came back. Now that I know this place and know Lady Maude, I understand why. She was married then, Mr. Stanton—but she met my father in London. Ever since that time Lady Maude has behaved as if she had died. I suppose you already know that?"

"Yes, I know. People have long memories, and the Irish still enjoy retelling a good story. You suddenly appearing here, when no one even knew you existed, makes it all the better, don't you see? Rounds it out for them. But you're needed for yourself, don't you see?"

"No, I don't see. I've upset Lady Maude by coming, and Dr. Donnelly as good as said I caused her heart attack. And I haven't changed anything, except to make it all a little harder, perhaps."

"But you must see." His cup rattled agitatedly in the saucer. "This house has need of something young and fresh and beautiful. Someone with some enthusiasm—some hope—left in them."

"But surely Mrs. Sheridan was young and . . . ?" I couldn't finish. His face had assumed an expression of utter distaste. It was all the more startling for his not being able to control it. He put his cup down and rose.

"I didn't know Mrs. Sheridan very well. I must go now."

"You don't know me either."

"I know the difference," he said. "Call on me if you need me. I mean it. God knows, few enough people seem to need a minister these days."

He picked up the few remaining sandwiches from the plate and munched on them gloomily as we threaded our way through the furniture in the hall and out to his dilapidated car.

IV

After Mr. Stanton had gone I went upstairs to relieve Mrs. O'Shea in Lady Maude's room. All day I had known that at four-thirty I was to take over while Mrs. O'Shea had her tea and a rest, and I had dreaded it. As I opened the door I wondered again, as I had done countless times that day, why I came into the presence of this old woman as if I were going to punishment; the only answer I could find, a faint answer and not very convincing, was that the world of non-involvement, the cool world, was what I had sought escape from. But need this involvement have been so total? Did it demand that I be the scapegoat for Blanche? To that I had no answer.

It was worse than I had expected. The door had barely closed after Mrs. O'Shea when Lady Maude turned fiercely in the bed— much too quickly for a woman who was ill—so that she faced directly the chair in which I sat.

"Why did you permit it? It's a disgrace!"

"What is, Lady Maude?" I knew what she was going to say.

"Otto Praeger sending food *here!* How does he dare? See, I am laid up only a single day, and already everything is falling to pieces about me. He would never have dared offer this insult if I had been at the door to meet it."

"You're mistaken. He asked if he could help, and I said he could. I explained about all the extra people in the house—and Mrs. O'Shea likes her food, you know—and the callers, and I asked if he would send over some things. I didn't expect so much—a ham, perhaps, and some fruit. Mr. Praeger is very generous."

"The man is a scoundrel! He's just like all the other foreigners who have flocked into this country stealing what isn't theirs. For years Praeger has been waiting for just such an opportunity. And to think it came at *your* invitation!" Her voice rose dangerously. I heard in it the shrill cadence of the night before when Connor, not I, had been with her in this room. It frightened me.

"Please, Lady Maude . . . If you excite yourself you may . . ."

She half-turned her face, as if she could not bear the sight of me. "Why do you pretend to care? It is too late to care. The caring should have come from my daughter. She should have been here to guard the inheritance that was hers, to rebuild it—"

"She tried!" I broke in, knowing that I shouldn't even begin to engage her in this argument, but unable to dismiss the memory of the letter that had forbidden further communication from Blanche. "You know she tried after I was born—"

"When it was too late! When the damage was done. She knew she could never return here. She deserted me. She left me to be surrounded by fools and liars and cheats. I married a fool, and he gave me nothing. My only child deserted and betrayed me. My inheritance was stolen from me—yes, *stolen!* You don't suppose I don't know that Otto Praeger was behind all the people who wouldn't wait any longer for some trifling sums of money owed to them? So he got Tyrell almost for nothing, and he refused to return the carpets and pictures and silver—all our beautiful things that he found in the cellars."

"Tyrell was burned," I said. "Nothing could have remained after all those years."

"Lies and treachery," she cried, as if I had not spoken. She was wandering, I told myself; her mind, already shadowed by phantoms from a tragic past, was magnifying imagined wrongs. But there was no stopping her; the stream of her words washed over me, scouring, abrasive, corroding.

"And not content with having Tyrell, he sent his daughter to take Meremount. She seduced that fool Connor whom I brought from nothing, and there she is in my household, taking it from me, taking this, taking that, pushing me aside . . ."

"She was *giving*," I said quickly, defending Connor rather than his wife. "You can't say she wasn't paying for what she did here. And the money that was going to be put into the glass-works . . . ? What about that?"

"Another lie. A worthless promise. I had heard it before. Blanche had used it to cover her corruption, her faithlessness. I had made for her the best match in the whole of Ireland— the Findlays had money, *English* money, and they were going to invest in the glassworks. And what came of it?—only desertion and betrayal and scandal. If Blanche had done what was expected of her, if she had been the daughter I was entitled to, the wife that the Findlays had the right to expect, the glassworks would have prospered. There would have been money —and Tyrell need not have been lost. But she wanted only what her own selfishness demanded. She was greedy and lustful, and I was the one to suffer for it. And then this other one came, and there were the same promises. And they came to nothing. And now you have come—too late. Just to torment me. Is it any wonder I have no peace? Everything is gone."

Her tone dropped down into a barely audible muttering. I saw her fists clenched on the bedcovers. She seemed to have forgotten that I was there, or did not care; I was of no consequence. She had forgotten why this stream of talk had begun. Her wrongs, brooded over day after day for many years, were now completely dominant, and not I, nor anyone else, would ever right them. They were her only reality. I sat and watched the thin tense figure in the bed, myself shaking a little, my hands pressed together, conscious of my longing for a cigarette. The minutes dragged by; she said nothing more. Gradually the rigid frame relaxed back into the pillows, the muttered words had ceased, the hands were still. Incredibly, she had dropped into sleep; she was older than one thought. I went close to check, and her breathing was even and free.

When I went back to the chair I noticed that the rain had stopped. There would be a sunset.

Bridget's tap on the door delivered me. I put my finger to my lips, and she came close and whispered to me. "There's a man on the telephone for you, Miss Maura. Annie says I'm to sit with Lady Maude for a spell."

I nodded, and as I rose to go, she whispered again, her eyes bright with curiosity and excitement. "It's Mr. Carroll, that's who it is!"

v

All day I had waited either for him to come to the house or to telephone; I had begun to think that he would disappear as he had done that night at the White Hart. I was angry with him, and wretched from the last scene with Lady Maude, and at the same time I wanted desperately to see him.

My palms were sweating but I hoped my tone was cool. "Hello?"

The remembered voice answered me, the siren voice that had lured me into this bog. "Well, it seems," he said, "I brought you into more than either of us bargained for. How are you?"

"How do you think I am? So confused I don't know which side is up. For Heaven's sake, why didn't you leave me where I was?" It was easier to blame him than to reason why I didn't just leave all this myself.

"Ah—wasn't I always the one to be stickin' my nose in where

it wasn't wanted?" It was said with a teasing regret; he had slipped back into that caricature brogue. "I'll have to be beggin' your forgiveness. Where can I see you?"

"What for?" Why should I make it easy for him?

He sighed. "Nothing like good old English bluntness, is there? It's a fair question, but I don't happen to have an answer. Perhaps I should apologize. Perhaps I could set you right side up about a few things. Perhaps I just should come right out and say I'd like to be seeing you, *allanah*. Will any of these answers do? Or do I have to be completely logical and English?"

"Oh, what the hell!" I was tired and fumbling, and I couldn't fence with him. "Where do I meet you? Anywhere but here."

"Anywhere but Meremount is right. I'm not exactly welcome there. And better leave out any of the pubs for twenty miles about—I'm what might be called a well-known character in such places, and of course all Cloncath knows that Blanche Sheridan's daughter has suddenly appeared."

"Where then?"

"Here—my cottage. Do you mind?"

I brushed the question aside. "How do I get there?"

"Not too difficult. But you have to take the long way round. I hear you've already been to Castle Tyrell, so you know how to get that far. Well, just don't cross the bridge leading up to the Castle—the avenue continues on along the other side of the lake. Just follow it straight through. It comes to the North Lodge. That's where I live. The gates are closed, though. There's a stream and the remains of—"

"—a bridge," I finished for him.

"How do you know?"

I felt a kind of coldness engulf me, the premonition that the knowledge I had sought might turn out to be more than I wanted to know. I said quietly, "I've been there before," and put down the receiver.

There were lights on already in Castle Tyrell as I drove by on the far side of the lake, although the dusk had hardly begun to settle—so many lights burning just for one man; I wondered if the black nights of the concentration camp gave him now the urge to hold back the darkness, or if it was merely an extravagance, like the overabundant food. I remembered that I had not telephoned him to thank him for the food sent to Meremount; I didn't know how to tell him that it had been too much.

Lights and an open door greeted me at the lodge. There was a stab of recognition as I saw the tall figure lounging in the doorway; he straightened as the headlights of the car swept over the cottage. He had his hand on the door before I had fully come to a halt.

"I'm glad you've come." Now there was no mockery in his voice; the accent was natural, soft. He peered into my face closely as I got out of the car. "You've not been having an easy time of it, I see."

It betrayed an awareness, a concern I hadn't expected. "Do I look that much older?" It was an attempt to shrug it off.

He answered me seriously. "You do that . . . you look older. Come on in."

I paused in the cottage door, Brendan behind me, and I think it was a sight and a feeling my senses had been craving since I had come to Meremount. The first thing was that it was warm; a fire burned brightly in the white-painted brick fireplace, and its spirit and cheerfulness seemed to reach out to embrace me at once. It was a very small house—when it had been built in the eighteenth century the perfect proportions had mattered more than the comfort of the lodgekeeper's family. This defect now had been overcome by taking down the interior walls, leaving just the brick chimney column and the narrow staircase, white and uncarpeted, to the second floor. Standing in the doorway I could see beyond the chimneypiece to the new kitchen fittings along the back wall. There was very little furniture—two chairs, a sofa, a wall fitted with shelves for books, a radio and record-player. There was a large orange rug on the floor and golden tweed curtains at the tiny leaded windows. It was plain and bare, and, after Meremount, an incredible refreshment.

"I can't believe it," I said.

"Sure it's just a humble wee bit of a place. Hardly fit for a Tyrell atall, atall."

"There you go again! Did you ask me here just to laugh at me?"

"I did not." He closed the door. "'Tis me shyness, Miss D'Arcy, that takes aholt of me tongue, and I find it saying a devil of a lot of things I never meant it to."

"Shy! You don't know what the word means!"

"You're right," he said. He took my raincoat and laid it across the back of the sofa. "How is it that Lady Maude hasn't got you wearing the Tyrell tweed?"

"The *what* tweed?"

"You must have noticed it. It's that bluish tweed that everyone around Meremount wears. All the Tyrell servants used to wear it in the old days, they say—a sort of everyday livery, it was. They say there was an enormous order for it on the looms up North at the time Castle Tyrell was burned. The Tyrells couldn't pay for it, but the mill couldn't sell it, either, because no one wanted a servant's tweed. So there are whole bales of it up in the Meremount attics, and Lady Maude doles it out to Annie and the farm hands. I don't suppose they mind—it saves their own clothes, but none of them would be caught dead going into town in it. What will you have to drink?"

"Do you have Irish whisky?"

"I do. But who's been teaching you to drink that?"

"Who else but Connor? Not Lady Maude."

"Ah, yes—Connor. Well, he's need of it from time to time in that house, I'm sure. Will you have ice with it? You see I'm able to offer you all the amenities."

"Yes, please. How did you get this cottage?"

He brought the drinks from the kitchen area where he had prepared them. "You mean, how did I get Otto Praeger to let me have it? Well, obviously, he didn't need the money. I have it rented—he wouldn't sell. It happened to be vacant, and I needed a place to live. The family that was in it he moved to the new estate cottages he built—they had seven kids, and this place was an elegant slum. Sure you must have noticed that Otto Praeger's a bit daft about the Irish—about their letting him be here and all. So he's after giving the estate workers all kinds of fancy frills—a bit of a benevolent despot, you might say, but so far, he's harmless. Of course, there's method in his madness; they'll not leave him to go and work elsewhere that they don't get his pretty cottages and the bus to take them to Mass on a Sunday, and the Christmas party and the August picnic races, and all the little bits of feudal paraphernalia he surrounds himself with. He loves it all, of course. Calls the lot of them his family. It amuses him to spend his money on this make-believe family, but then he doesn't have to put up with the screaming kids one minute longer than he wants to."

He raised his glass. "Cheers—and welcome to the land of your fathers."

"Right now I'm looking for a way out of the land of my fathers."

"True," he said. "It's been a pretty strange welcome. I didn't know how the old lady would take it, but I never expected it to nearly carry her off entirely."

"She knew I existed. It shouldn't have been such a shock."

He said thoughtfully, "You haven't had any official existence in these parts, you know. There were rumors—no one seemed to be sure. It was as if, after Blanche Sheridan—Blanche Findlay—left here to volunteer for some kind of war work in England after her husband went overseas, there was sort of an agreement between Lady Maude and Mrs. Findlay to bury everything about her. Both of them refused to talk about her. You'd think it would be easy to know what was happening to someone—London's no distance. But it was wartime, and people around here were sticking close to home. Perhaps some of your mother's Dublin friends knew the whole story, but they didn't pass it on if they did know. There were rumors of a man she became involved with, and some talk that she wouldn't be coming back here. Then her husband was killed, and no one ever heard anything about her after that. At least that's the way it's remembered around here. No one knew the name of the man concerned—or whether she'd married him or not. So when people made trips to London anyone with curiosity to satisfy had no place to start."

"How did *you* know?"

"I wasn't being snoopy, mind you. There seemed good reason to know. I asked Annie."

"Annie? *Annie!* She knew—and she told you?"

"She knew because she knows as much about Lady Maude as anyone will ever know. She told me because I think she understood what I had in mind to try to do. It was her hope, too . . . Well, she knew the name of the man. She knew there had been a child. After that it was simple. I simply looked in the London telephone book. What was harder was to walk into that shop. I didn't know what to do or what to say."

"So you had to break a vase and steal the Culloden Cup?"

He sprawled on the sofa, and at the recollection of that episode in the shop, a broad grin cut his face. The blond good looks that had so impressed me that morning when he had walked into Blanche's shop had not been exaggerated in my mind. But he didn't look like an actor any more; he was wearing a worn jersey and flannel pants with mud on the cuffs, and a streak of paint at one knee. In this glowing, warm room he seemed to be what was rare in a young man—or at least in any young man that I knew—complete, whole in himself, not fragmented and striving to be six other men than the one he was. It was oddly reassuring.

"You'll not hold that against me forever, will you now? Didn't I pay you—for both? And didn't I restore you to the bosom of your family?"

I sighed. "I wish you'd left me where I was. *Why* did you have to do such a thing?"

The lightness went from his face. His shoulders seemed to hunch and the long frame bent inward upon itself.

"You might say I believed I owed the Sheridan family a debt —what kind of debt I'd rather not say. It was nothing that money could repay. To restore the Culloden Cup to them would have been only a token. To bring you back to them might have been everything. It was all I could think of to do. If I've failed completely—if I've brought a lot of trouble on your shoulders, and done them no good, then I'm sorry. I apologize to them and to you. But if you could find it in you to be patient a while —if you could bear to stay at Meremount a little longer to give Lady Maude time to get used to you—I think at least a part of what I hoped to accomplish might be done."

"Good for her, perhaps, but what about me?"

"Yes . . . there's you, isn't there? It's all for them and nothing for you."

"Connor doesn't think that. Connor thinks I've come—like this, at the last minute almost, with the thought that I can inherit all the things that he's worked like a dog to hold together."

Brendan gave a low, dismayed whistle. "Does he now? Stupid, I am, not to have thought of it. It's nonsense, of course. Everyone knows that Lady Maude intended the lot to go to him. That was why she was able to entice him into a pretty thankless job in the first place."

"Was it thankless?"

"Until the arrival of the Praeger money—yes, I would say it was thankless. The glassworks needed modernizing, and there was no capital for that. Lady Maude would never consent to letting any part of it go to try to raise money. Connor has spent years flogging what is practically a dead horse. Then he married Lotti Praeger, and everything changed. There was going to be a whole revival of the Sheridan tradition—and a lot that was new, as well. He had the Sheridan name, and then he had the money for a new works and equipment. There was going to be a training program for apprentices, and gradual expansion as the trained labor became ready—it takes five years to train a boy fully in glassblowing, engraving, and cutting. He would have done all of it, Connor would. He's a man who knows how to go after a thing and stick with it. He knows how to hold on. But he couldn't hold the Praeger money. When Lotti went, the money went, too."

"Why? He was her husband. There must have been some claim . . ."

"It turned out that Lotti owned nothing in her own right. Who knows why? Perhaps it was Papa's way of making sure that she paid him some attention. Perhaps Praeger did it so that anyone she married wouldn't automatically assume rights to it. She *spent* plenty of money, but it was Papa's money. It was Papa, not Lotti, who would provide the new capital for the glassworks. Lotti dabbled with her allowance—the money for the renovation of Meremount, which Lady Maude had never consented to, the racing stable, the weaving factory she was going to start in Cloncath. Probably she could have financed them all herself—or Papa had promised her extra money. But, you see, nothing was concrete. There were only plans. There was no cash in the till. When she was killed, there was nothing there—not for anyone."

I understood better the quality and depth of the despair that had settled on Meremount, the hopes raised and dashed. Connor would have been less than human if he did not grieve a little for the future his blonde love had taken with her when she went.

Brendan seemed to know my thoughts; he nodded toward me, as if affirming them. "All that's left is the memory of her. To the people around here she was like some bright comet flashing by. They hardly knew her, and then she was gone, but there's a kind of afterglow. They talk about her—how beautiful she was, the clothes she wore, the car she drove—all the things she was going to do. Heaven knows if she would have done half of them. But they credit her with them, and that's what counts. She was full of life and intelligence, and far more sophisticated and knowing than they ever guessed."

"Why did they hardly know her? Didn't she live here?"

His eyebrows shot up. "Didn't you know? Lotti only came once with her father to see the place just after he bought it more than ten years ago—she was still at school in Switzerland, I think. The next time she came it was with a German film company who made a dreadful film with Castle Tyrell as a background about five years ago . . . I wasn't here then. Last year she showed up again—a holiday, she said, just to rest. A few weeks later she was married to Connor. It set the county on its ears, I'm telling you. But when the fuss and feathers settled down, there was general rejoicing to think of all that beautiful Praeger money that was going to stay right at home in County Tyrell. Lotti was the most popular bride in a long time."

"But why did she marry Connor?"

He smiled. "Are you denying there's such a thing as love? Couldn't she have been swept off her feet?"

"By Connor, in some other place—yes! But Connor at Meremount, weighted down with the glassworks and the farm . . . I don't know."

"Don't underestimate Connor—he's quite a boy-oh. And who will ever know the why of such things? But what you mean is that for all his charm and good looks he's still Irish provincial, and for a girl like Lotti Praeger . . ."

"Did you know girls like Lotti Praeger?"

Now he laughed openly. "You mean I'm Irish provincial, too? Well, not completely. I've done my stint on the Continent— Murano, Kosta, Elgberg. Yes, I've known a few that you might say were girls like Lotti Praeger. Not rich, like Lotti—perhaps all of them weren't as beautiful as Lotti. But sleek like her— girls who seemed to know everything." He smiled down at his drink. "They taught me a few things, at any rate."

"You liked it—the blonde girls, and all the new things?"

"Yes, I liked it. I was free of myself, for one thing. I didn't keep meeting little Bren Carroll clumping down the lane to school in his brother's gumboots. Ireland's a hard place to break

the mold in—it moves slowly. Perhaps that's why Otto Praeger
likes it so much."

"Then what are you doing back here?"

"I'll have to have another drink before I can begin on that."
He reached out and took my glass. While he poured them, I
sat and savored the peace and serenity of the room, the bright
fire, the warmth the whisky had left in me. On his way in to
refill the glasses, Brendan had drawn the curtains across the
windows. There was no reminder now of the world outside, of
what I would have to go back to.

He placed the glass in my hand. "I was part of the whole wonderful future that everyone talked of for Sheridan Glass—that's
why I came back. I was brought back. I was at the Eide works
in Denmark—on the design staff. Connor Sheridan showed up
one day and practically handed the whole thing to me—bright
future, Praeger money and all. Not even a letter before he came
—that's what I mean about Connor, he knows how to go out
after something he wants. He was just there outside the works
one evening, took me to dinner, filled me with good wine, and
after that I could hardly wait to tell them I was leaving."

He slapped his palm down on his thigh. "It all sounded so
bloody marvelous! The revered Sheridan name, but they were
going to break new ground. They would continue to use
Thomas Sheridan's designs, because they're steady sellers, but
try some new things—modern designs, and begin to build up a
new market. I was to have all the facilities I wanted to do
things on my own—and be encouraged to do them. Connor
wanted to exhibit wherever he could to put the Sheridan name
in as many places as possible. I was going to be their first, and
their chief, designer."

"How did he know where to find you?"

"My mother still lives a dozen miles from here, and my five
brothers and two sisters are scattered around the countryside.
I hadn't been backward about letting them know about how I
was doing out in the big world—and the word spreads around.
My father was a farm laborer. He had a couple of acres and he

ran a cow and a few hens to help keep us all fed. He was a decent man, but I just didn't fancy doing what he did all my life. So I went to Sheridan to learn glassblowing. But Waterford was coming up as the big concern, with all the export orders, so I moved over there to finish my training. It got me away from the family, too, and at least I had a bed to myself. But I got tired of cutting and engraving the same designs all the time, and seeing the same shapes go by. At Waterford, you know, everything's handblown, even the ordinary domestic glass —but they blow into molds. Which is fine, unless you have a notion to do something by yourself. So I saved a bit of money and took off for Venice. Well, that was where I saw what I hadn't learned at Waterford, and never would. It was a terrible thing, the way I wanted to try some of the shapes they were doing, but of course I wasn't an Italian, and my great-grandfather hadn't been a Murano glassblower, so I didn't have a chance. But I hung around Venice for a while, getting odd-jobs, and whenever I could I went and watched them working in the glass houses, and I learned what I could. In Sweden I had a couple of jobs, and then I had an offer from Eide in Denmark. You know, in Scandanavia they like to practice their English, and someone was always asking me if I had an Oxford accent. They were only partly satisfied when I told them I spoke with the tongue of George Bernard Shaw. But they taught me a lot, too, and they were hospitable people. I enjoyed life there, and I thought I was never coming back. I thought I had broken the mold of Ireland for good.

"Then Connor showed up. He knew all about me—he'd tracked down a few exhibition pieces I'd made, he knew the kind of thing Eide turned out, and that was what he wanted to make a start on at Sheridan. He said Waterford already had the world market for traditional eighteenth-century Irish glass sewn up. Our chance was to break into something new, but using a great name. I went for it all, and who wouldn't? I was to advise on the design on the new works; I was to have a free hand to hire anyone I wanted—I was to go out after more designers with Continental experience. But you see, I was the local boy, so the men would take orders from me when they wouldn't from someone speaking Swedish-English. Directorship, shares, everything . . . it was worth coming back to Ireland for.

"I remember the night after Connor first contacted me I went into Copenhagen to have dinner with him and Lotti. That was last spring—it was cold, there'd been a late snowstorm, and when it cleared the stars were as big as your fist and jumping out of the heavens at you. I remember saying some damn fool thing about how grand it would be if you could ever make crystal that came to life like those stars, and I actually gathered up a handful of snow and we all stood around like children under a street light, looking at the individual prisms of it. Oh, we talked! The best thing of all was that night. We were going to remake Sheridan's name. I was going to be the world's greatest artist in glass. I could see it all—palaces of glass, cathedrals of glass—all the world aglow with light and brilliance. I was drunk on champagne and the beauty of it all—and the three of us, we were beautiful too. I remember Lotti wore a leopardskin coat and boots that matched it. I had never been that close to real leopardskin before. The fur was pale, like her hair. That night, if I was the greatest artist in the world, Lotti was surely the most beautiful girl."

"And you fell in love with her," I said.

The lids drooped over the burning blue of his eyes as he looked at me. "I suppose it shows, doesn't it? And I suppose it did happen that first night. I suppose it shows, too, that I don't know as much about beautiful girls as I've been making out, because I didn't know until later that that was what had happened to me."

Then he tipped back his glass and drained it, a kind of salutation, I thought, to that night.

I finished my own drink more slowly, but in the ten minutes or so it took, Brendan didn't speak again. He seemed to have forgotten me, but I did not feel slighted. It was as if he had already admitted me to his most cherished dream, and having shared it, I could never again be on the outside.

I put down my glass gently and reached for my raincoat.

"I think I'll have to go back now."

He turned quickly and looked at me as if I had emerged from some mist of his conjuring. He blinked rapidly. "Go back? Why?"

"I think they expect . . ."

"They have no right to expect anything. They've got along without you until now."

"That isn't what you said to me in London. You as much as said I needed to have someone expect something from me."

"Is that how it sounded? Or did you only hear it that way because you wanted to? Well, they don't need you right this minute. Stay, and we'll find something to eat. I'd like to take you to a grand dinner, but Cloncath doesn't have much to offer in that way. Anywhere else is too far for the kind of day you've had. Will you stay?"

I nodded, feeling weak and passive. "They know I'm with you."

"I thought Annie would guess. I didn't give my name—but then she didn't ask it."

"I wonder what's so bad about being Brendan Carroll? If I mention your name—to Connor, to Lady Maude, even to Otto Praeger—they all freeze up. What have you done to them?"

He shrugged off the question. "Perhaps I haven't done anything to them. They knew, of course, that I couldn't stay on long after we found out that the money wasn't there after all to rebuild Sheridan Glass. I've stayed out my year and tried to teach the experienced men what I could, and just hope they'll pass it along. But there can't be a program now of opening up a line of modern glass—they don't have the facilities or the trained men. Sheridan will just have to trail behind Waterford as it's done in the past. There's nothing else for it. But they don't need me for that—they can't afford me, and I can't afford to stay here to do nothing."

The thought that had troubled me ever since Connor had

first spoken of Sheridan's need for capital occurred again. "Wouldn't Otto Praeger be the obvious backer for Sheridan Glass? After all, he began in optics—and he was going to invest in it through Lotti."

Brendan shrugged again, seeming uncomfortable for the first time. "Who knows. Maybe he's gone cold on the idea. Maybe he was only interested because Lotti was. It's his business—and Connor's. Not mine. Let's go and see what's to eat."

He rose and went into the kitchen as though to end the subject. I followed him. "Then you're not staying here now? You haven't come back for good?" The idea of his not being here as long as I was at Meremount was oddly disquieting, as if a refuge had abruptly been withdrawn.

"No—I thought I was gone for good when I went to London. And then I had that daft notion that I could perform one last service to Sheridan Glass and the family. I thought if Blanche Sheridan could be persuaded to come over and see her mother . . . well, Blanche Sheridan was dead, and there was only you. I didn't see how you were to be induced to interest yourself in a broken-down old glassworks and an almost equally broken-down old lady. So I took the Culloden Cup. I had to make it serious, or you wouldn't have paid any attention to me. Coming back here was just to deliver it safely—and perhaps to steer you a little if you did decide to come. I felt responsible for you, you see. Now look, will we stop the cackle and do something about food?"

He had opened the small refrigerator and squatted to survey its contents. "There's the easy stuff—eggs."

"Not eggs," I said quickly.

"Well then, sausages, best Irish pork. There's sole, fresh off the quay at Cloncath today. And Dublin Bay prawns. You know, the rivers and lakes of Ireland, and the seas around it teem with the best fish you've ever put into your mouth, and the Irish won't eat it except as penance on Fridays. There's some new potatoes. Cherries—from the Rhône Valley, the green-grocer swears. And a bit of Camembert . . ."

I smiled down at him. "You do yourself well. Do you have any white wine?"

"I do."

"Then we'll have poached sole. And if you'll peel the prawns, we'll have those too."

"Would it be possible you're a cook, then?"

"I am," I answered, dropping into the lilt of his speech, using the affirmative that is a characteristic of the Gaelic tongue.

"And whoever would think it to be looking at you," he said, unconsciously echoing the words that Annie had used. "Sure it's a pleasure to turn me kitchen over to you. And it's not to every female I'd be doing it, either. Sure wasn't it one of the things I learned when I got out of Ireland that the greatest cooks are men. And when I tasted what could be done with food didn't it annoy me to think of all the good things we had at home that no one took much notice of except to dish up in the same old way. I was taught to cook spaghetti sauce from an Italian glassblower who had eight kids. There was a restaurant owner in Stockholm who was persuaded to let me hang about the kitchen and watch how they did it in return for a collection of glass animals I blew for him to represent the fish and game and meat he served in the restaurant—friggers, those kind of pieces are called in the trade. He put them on display, and people in Stockholm began to call the place the Glass Menagerie. As long as I ate in the kitchen, I could get a free meal whenever I wanted it. Well, it taught me that I didn't have to take indifferent food for granted, or wait for someone else to prepare better for me. I could do it myself. But mind you, I didn't say a word about this when I came back to Ireland—anyone who heard me talk about cooking like this would seriously doubt I was a man at all."

"Not if it was a woman you were talking to," I answered, and then busied myself among the bottles of his small wine stock.

He did as he promised—he gave the kitchen to me, only doing the things I asked him to do, and the rest of the time leaning against the chimney wall, drink in hand, watching me with a kind of amused satisfaction. He lighted a second fire in the hearth that faced into the kitchen, and we ate at a table placed before it. There was a Rhine wine, and cherries for dessert, and Grand Marnier with the coffee he brewed himself. At the end of the meal he stretched luxuriously and leaned back in the chair, pouring more brandy for himself when I refused the proffered bottle.

"Might as well enjoy it," he said. "In a few weeks there's going to be no money for things like Grand Marnier and cherries from the Rhône Valley. No money, and even less time to enjoy such things."

"Why?" I was growing drowsy, the warmth of the fire and the liqueur reaching to me. It had been the longest, the strangest day, begun in the rainy dawn with eggs and brandy and another man.

"I'm starting a new glassworks with an Englishman I met in Sweden—Tim Henderson's his name, a real artist in glass—almost," he grinned, "as good as I am. No Praeger money this time. Just the wee bit of capital we both put in, and a one-furnace glasshouse in an old warehouse his family owns in Bristol. There'll be just the two of us, and a couple of boys who want to learn. It will never be an assembly line, and we'll never be rich. In fact, for a few years we'll probably be bloody poor."

"Will you live in a garret above the glasshouse?" I said teasingly.

"You need to learn something about glassmaking, don't you, *allanah?* No one lives above a glasshouse, not unless you expect to be roasted in your bed. Warm in winter, but highly dangerous."

"Why should I learn about glassmaking? I've managed so far without it."

"Why, indeed? And you a Sheridan! The old man must be

turning in his grave. Connor will probably take you over the works and it's something you should see. You should do it for the sake of the men working there too. It could mean quite a lot to some of the older ones to have the most direct descendant of Thomas Sheridan there. Connor will tell you all the technical stuff—how hot the furnace, the proportion of soda, lime, and silica. He'll show you the glassmaker's tools, and you'll see several chairs at work—a chair, you'd better know, is the team that works under the master glassblower, who's called a gaffer. You'll hear so much your head will spin—"

"It's spinning now."

He ignored the interruption. "Connor's good on all these things. He's learned it all, and thoroughly. Sheridan Glass is well served, and if he ever got another chance with some money he'd know how to use it. But Connor knows it all with his head, not with his hands or his imagination."

"Imagination?" I wondered if I were drunk, or merely tired. His voice fell smooth as silk on my ears, soft, evocative. There was only the firelight in the room, the red heart of it, and the leaping shadows on the walls.

"Think of it," he said. "Pliny tells a tale of some merchants a few thousand years B.C. who camped on the sands of the River Belus, and how they placed their hot cooking pots on some cakes of natron they were carrying, and in the morning found that the heat of the pots had fused the sand and the soda, forming glass. It's a nice story, but I'm thinking they must have had a very overcooked dinner for the pots to have been that hot. That's man-made glass. Then there's the glass that comes in nature, black obsidian—whole mountains of it. The ancient Mexican tribes shaved themselves with it, and sacrificed their victims to the gods with knives of it. But the Egyptians made the first glass we know of. They had what glass needs—sand, soda, and fuel from the acacia groves—and people rich enough to pay for such an expensive item. In the beginning they made their bowls and bottles by forming a liquid fusion of silica and soda about a molded core of clay or sand that could be poured away when the fusion had cooled to hardness, leaving a hollow shaped vessel of opaque glass. They went on for a long time that way, and then someone discovered that the liquid fusion could be gathered on the end of a hollow iron rod and blown into a bubble, and that it could be blown into molds so that identical shapes could be made. This was a kind of mass-production, and glass became relatively inexpensive. By reheating the molten bubble every time it began to cool and harden they found that you could keep it in a workable state, and do almost anything you liked with it—stretch it, squeeze it, flatten, cut, tear it. You see . . ."

He reached and took up his empty wineglass. "If you were making this by the 'offhand' method—that's entirely by hand —you'd start with heating your batch. That would be silica, soda and lime, or soda and lead, depending on the type of glass you wanted. You'd add to the batch any bits and pieces of glass of the same type and color you had—this is called the cullet and it helps speed up the fusion of the raw ingredients. When it's white hot we go to work—me, the gaffer, and my team. We work around a reheating furnace called a 'glory hole' —in glasshouse humor it's supposed to be a vision of the future after death. The gatherer starts the whole process by taking up molten glass on the blowing iron, and blows out the first shape. He can elongate this by swinging the blow rod, but all the time it has to be kept rotating so that it won't sag out of shape. Now it's given to the gaffer who's sitting at his chair with big level arms that let him continue to rotate the blowing iron with one hand while the other works on shaping the glass with tongs and shears and measuring for size with calipers. The piece goes back into the glory hole just as many times as it needs to keep it soft and workable. When the stem and foot are shaped the whole thing is transferred to a solid rod called a pontil by pushing the pontil into the base and cracking off the blowing iron. That leaves what's going to be the drinking edge free. Back it goes into the glory hole and when it's workable I rotate it, flare it out and shape it back in, trim it to the height I want it with shears, measure for size, smooth it and trim it, and never stop rotating because gravity will pull it out of shape if I do. The whole art of the glassblower is judging where and how the glass will fall, and when you first see it, the operation will seem faster than the eye. If it's to have handles the gatherer will bring me long pulls of glass and they will be curved and stuck on, then the heat of the glory hole again fuses one to the other. When it's done it's held between tongs while I give it a sharp tap to break it free of the pontil at the base—that's why all handblown glasses have that hollow under their foot. Then it goes into the annealing oven so that it cools very slowly, otherwise it will be too brittle—the outside surface will cool more quickly than the inner core. When it's cool, it's ground for smoothness and then I can paint, enamel, engrave, cut—do anything my skill and taste allows for decoration. And if I want to be seditious, to the symbolic handles of thistle and rose intertwined, I add an engraving of Bonnie Prince Charlie. And you have the Culloden Cup."

I stared at the wineglass still in his hand. Before my eyes he had created it—blown, spun, flattened, trimmed and smoothed it. He had added handles, fashioned from thinly wrought pulls of his molten material, he had engraved it and signed it. I saw the Cup as he had held it that day in Blanche's shop. Then he set it down on the table between us, and it was nothing more than it had ever been—a plain, inexpensive, mass-produced wineglass.

"Try to imagine," he said, "the world without glass. No window glass—if you let in light you had to let in the weather. No eyeglasses, and genius would have raced against fading sight. No telescope for Galileo. No test tubes for Pasteur. No bulbs for Edison. No world as we know it. That's glass for you."

I stared at him, bemused. His voice and the movements of his hands had woven a kind of hypnotic spell for me.

"That," he said, "was what we talked about that night in Copenhagen—all kinds of visionary and foolish things. The

world of glass. We must have seemed very young that night.
It's no wonder, is it, that I was drunk on the memory for quite
a long time after."

He helped me on with my raincoat, and we went outside.
The night was calm and still. It was not raining, but moisture
dripped from the trees, and the sound of the rain-swollen stream
seemed louder than when I had sat beside it just yesterday.
The sky was beginning to lighten as the clouds broke. I slid into
the MG and turned on the ignition. Then Brendan's hand
reached across to mine as it rested on the gear stick, and halted
me.

"This is where she died—here, at the bridge."

"Yes, I know."

"It was raining." He spoke suddenly, quickly, as if there were
a compulsion now, having told me the beginning, that night in
Copenhagen, to take me through to its ending. "It had rained
for four days, and the stream was in flood. It's an old bridge
. . . it must have been weaker than any of us thought, and the
pressure of the water was too much for it. It went all of a sudden—just like that. The most terrible crash, and then the roar
of water again. I heard it go, and I ran outside to look at it. I
did what I could—I closed the gates and parked my car right
here where you are, and turned on the headlights so that they
shone through the gates and over on to the road—to warn anyone meaning to come to Castle Tyrell—like this—" He reached
past me and fumbled with the switches on the dash, and cruelly
the beam of the headlights cut the darkness, reaching across the
stream to the other bank, picking out the jumbled mass of stone
in its bed, the ragged edge where the bridge span abruptly
ended, the massive wooden barriers on the road. White water
swirled about the big slabs of tumbled stone.

"After I had done that I went and rang Meremount and rang
Castle Tyrell. But at Meremount I was too late.

"It was raining very hard, and she always drove too fast. She
must have seen the lights, but probably they blinded her. I was

in the house when I heard the skid and the crash as the car hit what was left of the parapet of the bridge. She drove a white Mercedes sports model—there was no mistaking it down there among the stones. But the water was much higher that night. The car was half under water and turned on its back. I got down there, but the door had burst open and the force of the water had carried her away. It almost took me too . . .

"We didn't find her for hours later, farther down the stream. Her poor beautiful face was horribly cut—by the glass from the windshield, and from being banged against the stones and boulders. Of course the water had washed all the blood away. But she wasn't killed by the first impact. The coroner's verdict was death by drowning."

He meant me to ask it; he meant me to know it all. He leaned against the door, quite close to me, waiting for the question.

"Why did you phone Meremount? Did you know she was going to Castle Tyrell?"

"She wasn't going to Tyrell—I was expecting her here. She was coming here—to me."

"Here . . ." I felt a kind of sickness within me. I knew better now the despairing rage of Connor's grief; the end of him and Lotti had brought the knowledge of unfaithfulness as well as death.

"I was making a trip to Copenhagen to try to sign up some experienced glassblowers for Sheridan. Lotti simply told me she would go too—a kind of jaunt for her, I suppose it was. A few days in Copenhagen, a few days in London, and she would tell Connor she had spent all the time in London. We were going to fly together that night. It wasn't the way I wanted it with Lotti— I wanted all of her, not the crumbs from the table. But that's what was offered, and—like most men would have—I took it.

"After the phone call to Meremount they knew—Connor and Praeger—that I was expecting her here. And they knew why. But at the inquest we all lied—Connor and Otto Praeger and I. Connor and Praeger both said she had been going to

Tyrell—that she was going to visit her father before catching a plane later that evening to London. Past this lodge is the shortest route from Meremount to Tyrell. And I—I said I just had time to warn them at Castle Tyrell. I said nothing about phoning Meremount. And Annie—she just said nothing at all. No one asked her, and she just said nothing. There was no one to prove anything different, and no one around here would want to. But Connor and Praeger and I—we're bound together by the lies we told to protect her and the Sheridans and Praeger from scandal. It would have served no purpose at all for everyone to know that truth."

"But you told me . . ."

"I had to. I seem to have made you some kind of scapegoat, someone to bear the consequences of what I helped to happen. When I said I owed a debt, that was what I meant. I thought perhaps I could give them back something through you. But I've dragged you back here and perhaps made things worse than they were before—and you're caught in the mess too. So you had to know." He added, "I'm sorry."

VI

Only one light showed in the windows of Meremount as the MG emerged from the avenue onto the weedy sweep of gravel before the house—the room next to the hall where Connor had his office. I took the flashlight from the car, but the front door was opened before I began to mount the steps. Connor stood there as if he had waited for some time.

"The front door of every country house in Ireland will be securely bolted at night, and every kitchen door will be on the latch," he said as I came close. "I thought I'd spare you the trouble of finding out."

"I'm sorry if I've kept you up." I moved past him into the crowded, darkened hall. The only light came from the open door to the office. I tried to move on, toward the staircase, but his hand was there at my elbow, urging me toward the office.

"You haven't kept me up," he said. "You're just in time. I'm finishing the brandy."

I halted. I could see the desk, the brandy bottle, two glasses, the sofa drawn up before the brightly leaping fire. But the image of Brendan was strong with me, the words he had said still repeated themselves. I couldn't face Connor, not face him now and still hide what I knew. I couldn't face the recollection of the brandy we had shared that morning when we had talked without restraint.

"I don't think so, thanks."

The pressure on my arm tightened. "Not very sociable tonight, are you?"

"It's late, Connor. I'm tired. The day began very early—remember?"

"Our day," he corrected.

Now the urging was a definite push. In the doorway of the office he swung me to face him. "Our day, Maura. It began as badly as you can imagine anything beginning—with the old lady having the attack. But after that there were some of the best hours I've ever spent in this house. We ate and we talked and I enjoyed myself. It was a sane, normal thing to do, wasn't it, to enjoy being with a beautiful girl? Is it so strange to want more of it? But I suppose time moves quickly for girls like you, doesn't it, Maura? I haven't been here all afternoon, so you hurry on to the next man available. Now you're tired, which means I'm to have no more of your company. Brendan has used up all the energy, has he?"

I felt my cheeks burning. "I don't know what that's supposed to mean. I had to see Brendan—did I need your permission for that? After all, Brendan's responsible for my being here. Naturally—"

"Naturally!" he broke in. "Naturally—yes! Everything comes naturally to Brendan. Women, children, dogs, money, even— God help us—a small slice of fame. There he is, the son of a farm laborer, sprung out of the bogs, but he's fortune's darling. Unscathed, untouched—"

"He isn't untouched. He's . . ." How could I tell Connor what Brendan was? To Connor, Brendan was only one thing. The single certainty I had about Brendan was that the passage of Lotti Praeger through his life had not left him untouched. But that I could never say to Connor.

"And always," Connor went on, "women to defend him, to help him." As I stood there rooted before him, he leaned his head back against the doorframe, stretching his neck as if to ease his weariness. Again I felt the danger of his appeal to both the sympathy and the senses of a woman. He had let go his hold of me, but still I remained, fascinated, compelled. He knew I would stay.

"I sound envious, don't I?—jealous. Yes, I'm that. Brendan is free now, free to go. He's free of the Sheridans and of Ireland, and I wish to God I were."

Suddenly, with a half-blind, instinctive movement his hands were upon me again, gripping my shoulders, pulling me to himself roughly. I was pinned against him, my face pressed against his sweater. The force of his embrace was frightening, as if I must be the one to bear the weight of his anguish and grief. I tried to pull back, but it was a useless, futile gesture. I felt myself begin to sink under the burden of what each of them here was trying to thrust upon me.

"Is he to have it all, then? Tell me, did you come here because of Brendan? Was he the reason? Not the Cup, not the Sheridans. Has he got you too?"

I was never meant to answer that. His hand had come under my chin, and he was lifting my face to his; the pressure of his lips on mine was painful, abrasive, burning, as if I were seared by his surge of loneliness, of desire, of regret, as if I must become the instrument of revenge against Brendan. I struggled for breath, no longer even fighting for freedom.

His lips moved against mine, and the words came. "Why

shouldn't I kiss you? Hasn't he?" His hand now moved up and down the length of my back, caressing, forcing.

"Why shouldn't I want the only thing that has grace and beauty in this dead house? You're . . ."

I managed to pull back my face a fraction from his. One word only came. "Lotti . . ."

His reaction was savage, as if the word had struck and clawed at him. He jerked me away from him violently, so that my head snapped back and struck the doorframe. The pain rocketed through me, and I knew it had been deliberately inflicted; he meant me to suffer with him, to experience some of the intensity of his own feeling.

"Damn you!" he said. "Lotti is dead, and you're alive. And so am I—so am I!"

He let go of me, and in the sudden release I nearly lost my balance. I think he wanted me to fall, and there would have been no help for me, no apologies. He didn't even look at me again, but turned and walked to the desk, standing with his back to me, leaning over it, his hands pressed down on it, waiting for me to go. It was as complete a dismissal as I would ever receive.

I stumbled twice on the stairs against the small objects that stood in my path; the only light came from the still-open door of the office. At the landing I looked back; his shadow was cast across the floor of the hall, unmoving. I clutched the banister for a moment, dizzy still, and wondering if the time would ever come when I would tell him how nearly I had gone to his arms, willingly, as he stood there hunched over the desk in that stance of despair and anger. And so I rode the wild seesaw of my feeling about Connor.

At my door Lotti's cat waited, and when I opened it she ran in and immediately sprang up on the bed, settling into the folds of the eiderdown. I found myself there beside her, face down, the throbbing in my head a physical mark that Connor had left upon me, fatigue and sheer wretchedness combining to make it worse. But in the way of her kind, the cat did not hold my misery against me; she just accepted my presence for what it was worth, young, female, reminding her of her lost mistress. She snuggled against me, and her purr was the cry of pleasure at the easing of her loneliness—as Connor's would have been.

CHAPTER 7

I

"It's half-eleven, Miss Maura," the voice said. I opened my eyes on Mrs. O'Shea's round starched form, cup of tea in hand, standing beside my bed. "I'd have told Annie to let you sleep longer but I thought you'd not be wanting to miss the day entirely, seeing that the sun's come out."

I sat up and gropingly took the tea from her. "That's very kind of you, Mrs. O'Shea. I should have been up long ago." My eyelids were sticky, though the brightness at the windows where she had drawn back the curtains confirmed what she had said about the day. It was a spring day, and half of it was gone. I took a long gulp of the hot, strong tea.

"Sure now, it's as well to be getting a little rest, and you on the go all the live-long day yesterday." She said nothing about the night, but I thought she had probably heard my return, the stumbling on the stairs. She had probably known that Connor had waited for me.

She stood expectantly at the end of the bed, and I knew she had come to say something, and it wasn't a complaint, or I would have heard it already.

"Well, it's not much of a fine spring day for me," she began, pulling her mouth down. "Didn't I get the news this morning that Great-uncle Pat has finally died—him that's been ready for it these past ten years, God rest his soul. The funeral's Friday, and a grand affair it'll be, with Uncle Pat been saving for it so that everyone could raise a glass or two to him in the next world. A very congenial man, my Great-uncle Pat is. Friday afternoon, and it's to Wexford I'd have to be going, and if I'm to join in any of the doings after, then I'd have to be spending the night. But there's Lady Maude, and I'm really only here to oblige Dr. Donnelly . . ."

Through my half-sleep I grasped what was required of me, and also the fact that I was expected to stay; that in their minds no one had set a time for my going. "I'm sure I could stay with her, Mrs. O'Shea . . . if you'd just show me what's to be done."

Her mouth lifted. "Nothing, and that's the truth of it. 'Tis me own opinion that the auld lady is as strong as a horse and will see many another in the grave. But Dr. Donnelly will not have her left to sleep quite alone this first week. All that would be to do would be just to sleep in my room and leave the doors open so you could hear if she needed anything. But I'd never let it be said that Molly O'Shea went off and left her patient in charge of a servant." She gave me a confidential smile as if to say we both understood what servants were; then she left me "to finish your tea in peace and get your eyes open," sounding as if I needed her permission for both.

But before I had finished the tea Bridget had come, sent by Annie to inquire if I would like her to start my bath running. "Annie says would ye be having it in Lady Maude's bathroom since there's a gas heater there." I couldn't imagine enjoying a bath that close to Lady Maude, so I declined and took it as usual, shivering, in the unheated bathroom on my own side of the hall. I noticed that there had been no move to offer me Lotti's bathroom. When I returned Annie had already arrived with the breakfast tray of sausage, bacon, and toast, all of it only slightly burned. "I thought you'd like to take it aisy now," and she fussed a little over my clothes while I ate. "I used to do a bit for Mrs. Sheridan—sure didn't she try having two lady's maids from Paris, and neither of them would stay for a minute. Not able to speak a word of English between them, ignorant creatures they were."

They were all paying too much attention to me, and it made

me nervous. I wondered if they had decided that I, and not Connor, was to be the new order of things; did they sense the old customs slipping and the new taking over? But if that was what they thought, I was convinced they were wrong when I paid a morning call on Lady Maude. I stood at the foot of the big fourposter, awkward, like a child, and she looked strong and almost well; her voice was firm when she spoke. "Tomorrow I shall not stay in bed."

I saw that a few of the things Molly O'Shea had ordered from the room had found their way back again, and somehow this small victory pleased me immensely. It was also the sign of Lady Maude's returning strength, and the beginning of my release.

Beyond my inquiry about her health, I had nothing to say. In desperation I offered to read the morning newspaper to her; she waved aside the suggestion. "I stopped being interested in what went on in the world when Winston Churchill retired. When he died, it was the end of an age. I don't care to know about the new one."

I swallowed, and commented on the beauty of the day.

"You must get out into the sun," she said. "You are pale— London pale." She spoke as if my paleness were a disease. "Do you ride—ah, but we keep no horses these days."

"I don't ride," I said.

"All ladies should learn to ride," she answered severely. Obviously, I was poorly educated.

It was oddly reassuring to be lectured by her, but I did not stay to try her tolerance too far; she now accepted my presence in the house, even demanded it, but the balance of feeling was delicate. I was her only grandchild, but I was also Blanche's daughter. I needed forgiveness for that, and she wasn't quite ready; for my part I wondered if I wanted to wait here at Mere-mount for the doubtful privilege of receiving it.

I went downstairs and cooked a lunch of breaded cutlets and fresh asparagus which Michael Sweeney's cousin had grown and sent for Lady Maude. She ate almost none of it; because of her diet, I had to send it without the hollandaise. Annie hovered over me during the cooking, but I was rewarded by the faint light of wonder at the results that dawned on her face, and the respectful silence that accompanied her eating it. Mrs. O'Shea condescended to come and eat at the kitchen table. "Sure Molly O'Shea had never been the one to stand on her dignity when there's no need for it."

When the dishes were washed I left the house by way of the kitchen garden. The sight of the empty, cleared beds depressed me; weeds were starting to come back, soon there would be no sign that any work had been done. Perhaps it would be easier for everyone when that happened. The cat was suddenly there on the brick walk ahead of me, long crinkly blue tail held high. She made her yowling talk as she skipped ahead of me toward the neglected herb garden. I sat for a while in the sun on the stone bench smoking a cigarette while she played hide and seek with herself among the tall lavender. I thought of Blanche as a girl among the herbs here, pinching, smelling, tasting, finding out the particular subtle alteration each could make in food. I wondered about my grandfather, Lady Maude's despised husband. He must have taught things to Blanche—like glass and herbs. Who had given her the urge to cook—perhaps that belonged to my own father. I had found a rusty garden fork thrust into the soil under the bench. I toyed with it as I smoked, and then found myself squatting before a clump of lavender, cigarette in mouth, working the soil, tentatively at first, then more boldly as confidence and enjoyment grew. The activity excited Sapphire; she dashed and made pounces on the fork, getting a little frenzied as if she had had no play for a long time. I must have stayed like that for a long time, the sun warm on my shoulders, the scent of the damp earth vaguely heady, before I paused to wonder what I was doing working Lotti Sheridan's garden and playing with her cat. It wasn't my garden; it never would be.

The cat called after me disconsolately as I tossed the fork under the bench and went back to the house to get the car keys.

II

Otto Praeger was at home; he must have heard my voice in the hall as I answered O'Keefe's detailed inquiries after Lady Maude, because he came out of his study, walking as quickly as his limp and cane would permit.

"So—you have come! It is good I am here. This week I do not go to Frankfurt after all. A holiday—because next week I am in New York. Come, come—you have had lunch?"

"Yes—I came to thank you for . . ."

"Ach! It is nothing." He took me by the arm. "All the food I have here no one could eat! Fräulein Schmidt and myself, we are both already too fat. But the food is here, nevertheless—needed or not. Hunger and war leave strange legacies, Miss D'Arcy. Come . . . come, I will show you."

I discovered then that Otto Praeger was shy and somewhat nervous when he had to do with something that was not business. This time I had nothing to ask of him, he could make no arrangements on my behalf, had no favor to give, no deal to make—and he didn't know what to do for lack of it. He toured me through the long rooms that faced the lake, each opening with immense double doors one into the other, at a pace that for him, with his disability, must have seemed like a gallop. Everywhere was the conventional furniture of a well-to-do country house—the chintz sofas and deep chairs set on Persian and sometimes a marvelous Aubusson rug; the modern parquet—I had to keep remembering that this had all been a burned-out shell—was polished, the windows framed in the usual formal brocades and silks and velvets. The effect was somewhat heavy and Germanic. The walls facing the windows, the fireplace wall in each room, were, by contrast, shockingly bare. Plain, white, untrimmed and unpaneled, on them in barbaric, unchallenged splendor, hung Otto Praeger's paintings.

"You know painting?" he said to me. "Sometimes the young know much about these things, and the old make themselves foolish with their explanations."

"I know a few names, a few typical examples—that's all. You can tell me anything you want to. I probably won't have heard it before."

But he said almost nothing. Just pointed his cane as he marched me past. "Léger . . . Monet . . . Rouault. You can come back alone and take your time to look if it interests you. De Kooning . . . Pollock . . . Kandinsky . . . Miro." He seemed afraid to thrust any of his enthusiasms on me; I wondered if he thought I would be bored and if it had been Lotti who had made him so afraid to trouble others with what lay close to his heart. As we moved through these long, quiet rooms I was struck again by how alone he seemed to be—there were no guests here, no children, no grandchildren; there was no one to meet and talk with at lunch or dinner unless he ate with his lumpy Fräulein. Perhaps he had no taste for company; did the crowding of the concentration camp leave one forever with the craving for space and solitude? But the rich were able to command guests for their own entertainment, and the spaces of this great house would absorb them without strain. There were always those who needed something from the rich and were prepared to pay the price by dancing attendance. Was it simply that Otto Praeger did not care to call the tune, so had no need to pay the piper?

"And this," he was saying, "is the real heart of Tyrell." We had reached the end of the long gallery rooms, and had come to an oak door, new but massive, fitted to a curved arch. "No one uses it—I was never able to achieve a satisfactory level of heat in here, and you will see why."

The door opened into a large, nearly square, stone hall, with three great fireplaces and a broad stone staircase without balustrade leading to higher floors that had long ago collapsed. A new beamed roof had had leaded glass set into it at intervals; the light filtered down to us, I guessed, a hundred feet. Electric sconces like flares had come to life on the walls as Praeger touched a switch. A few pieces of furniture stood about, oak tables and benches, two carved armchairs, leather stools. The walls were hung with tapestries and battle arms from antiquity. Praeger pointed out the narrow entrances to two spiral stair-cases within the thickness of the walls that led to the battle-ments. Neither the heat in the copper pipes along the floor, nor the warmth of the afternoon sun which shafted through the slit windows no wider than a bowman's arm required, did any-thing to warm the high, dim spaces; I shivered. Despite the reno-vation, there was the smell of age.

"O'Ruairc's Tower," Praeger said. "More ancient than mem-ory. Far older than the Tyrell family to whom it was given by grant of Queen Elizabeth the First. From the battlements the ancients watched for the beacon fires at Cloncath to warn them of the Viking raids, and then, later, of the English. Come," he added, "it is chilly here. You will come back, I think, and climb to the battlements and see the demesne of the Lords of Tyrell. I myself have never been able to do that."

He motioned me to the door and closed it carefully behind him. "No one uses it?" I said, more depressed than excited by what I had seen. "But you have restored it, and you maintain it."

He shrugged. "Why not? They say it is among the oldest structures in Ireland. Will I let it fall down?"

"But if no one sees it . . ."

"What use is it?" he finished for me. "Ah—for that they will have to wait. They must wait until I am dead before the coaches drive up, and they pay their two shillings. Then O'Ruairc's Tower will be returned to the keeping of the Irish people, and the house and the pictures will be my gift to them. Foreigners have plundered Ireland for too many centuries. It is time something was given back to them. Sometimes, I wonder, though, what they will make of the pictures. Come—it is time for tea."

✐   ✐   ✐   ✐

After Praeger had rung for tea, he led me to a small room that opened off the main hall—barely more than a large cupboard. The window had been darkened so that it needed the lighting within the display cabinets that lined its walls to reveal the collection of glass. "An old hobby of mine," he said. "Many generations ago my family were glassmakers—which is why I grew interested in optics when I was starting out. I lost the family glass collection, though, during the war. Some of these things here—the less costly ones—were the first little treasures I permitted myself to buy when there was some money that did not absolutely have to be spent on something more useful." He made his way heavily round the small room wearing a pleased little smile that his fabulous pictures had not been able to win from him. "Here"—pointing to a necklace—"one of my favorites—Egyptian, probably before fifteen hundred B.C. This—Alexandria. This cameo bowl—Roman, first century. And here, the Venetian glass. But of course this does not compare with Thomas Sheridan's collection of Venetian glass—so far as I know there is no collection to touch that one. But you have already seen it . . ."

"No—I haven't seen it. Is it in the house?"

"Ach, I had forgotten. Lotti made her little museum at the works with the Sheridan glass collection. You will see it. Come, I hear O'Keefe with the tray."

He switched off the light and closed the door. "But there are many other valuable things at Meremount. You must have noticed."

"I keep falling over furniture," I said. "There's so much of it there's no place to stand back and really look."

"You must look. It is worth it. Ach, what a sale it would make at Christie's! There are things that even Lady Maude has forgotten about—Lotti used to tell me. She was not an expert, but she had seen enough to know."

"Where did it all come from?"

"I am told Lady Maude began going to auctions very soon after she was married—that was after Tyrell and its contents had been burned in the fire. You understand, Maude Tyrell would have had the best connections in Ireland among people who had houses full of beautiful things. Times were bad, and people were leaving—the time of the Troubles, and then the depression years. Sometimes they sold off their best things privately —for the money and for fear they also would be burned. She already knew the best things in many of the houses, and she could make her price before the auction . . ."

"Aye, and pay dearly," O'Keefe said, chipping in with the assurance of a servant who knows his master's weakness. Ireland was Praeger's weakness, and any story that related to it. "Didn't herself run poor Mr. Sheridan into debt many a time to buy some load of stuff they didn't have use or room for?— even back in those days when the poor man was alive. After he died she went on at a merry old jig, and wasn't it the solicitors who had to get the money from the glassworks to pay for it. There wasn't ever much money, but what there was she spent —and more."

"Her mania," Praeger said, with surprising gentleness. "Everyone has their little madness."

"Aye, and that's the truth of it, sir," O'Keefe acknowledged. "With some it does be the horses, and with others the drink. But the Tyrells were always daft in a special way." And nodding, as if to urge us to eat, he left us.

"But think of it," Praeger said, and his tone was wistful. "Almost fifty years she's had of buying furniture and pictures and china—at times when prices had to have been very low. She is like the investor who bought stock after the crash of '29. There are a few minor masters among those pictures stacked against the walls which she doesn't even recognize—perhaps one or two that are more than minor. Strange things happen when a family who doesn't know the value of what they have sells at country auction. Lady Maude's eye is educated about furniture, but she is appallingly ignorant about market values. But then, she never thinks of reselling, so why should she care what it is worth?"

I told him about the shop in King's Road, and Blanche's skill in buying. "How often," he said, "she must have thought of what was stored at Meremount . . ."

I talked on, about Blanche, the shop, our lives, the personal disarray I had fallen into after her death. Finally I came to tell him of her own small collection of Sheridan Glass, and how Brendan had taken the Culloden Cup.

His eyes widened over the story of the Cup, but he did not want to talk about Brendan. "You have been led here by a twist of glass," he said softly.

Tea had been served in one of the rooms facing the lake. Today it was I who poured the tea, and he was free to make inroads on the large tray of sandwiches. It was a hard choice whether to look at the sunlight on the lake and the mass of azaleas beneath the windows, or to turn to the splurge of color of a huge Hans Hoffmann against the wall. "Take the sunshine," Praeger answered, when I said this to him. "In Ireland you must always take the sun when it offers; there are plenty of days when one would rather not look out the windows. Those are the days for the paintings."

He urged on me the scones and little cakes, and I tried to eat more to please him. He had his second cup of tea, and he said, "I see they have you working hard at Meremount." His eyes were on my hands. There hadn't been a brush at the kitchen sink where I washed, and the soil from the garden was under my nails.

I smiled. "I hoped you wouldn't notice, but it's pretty hard to eat with your nails tucked in." I began to tell him about the herb garden, about the prints on the stairs in King's Road, about Blanche's cooking, and the first night's dinner at Meremount.

"Ah, so." He nodded. "Things will not have improved since

Lotti was there . . . You know now about Lotti, of course. The other day I could not then tell you. One has these moments . . ."

I nodded. "Yes . . . I'm very sorry."

"Well, that is how things go." His small shrug was not of indifference, but a gesture to tell me that I could not be expected to bear his pain, to assume his sorrow. Unlike the young men, Connor and Brendan, he did not ask that I also carry the burden. He seemed to have lost the human knack—if he ever had had it—of being able to ask for something, of making an emotional demand. It was a dangerous policy; I had come to believe that those who ask for little get little.

"I got her out of Germany, you know, before they took me." He assumed, of course, that I had now been told his own story. "It was a hard thing to do—to send my only child out as the child of a Swiss woman returning to Switzerland. All through the war she lived there, and it eased those years for me to know that she was safe, and fed, and would survive, if I did not. I survived though—for a sight of her, I often think. When I did see her, she was already a person, and I had had no part of shaping her. Then it was necessary to work very hard to make some money—daughters in Swiss schools are expensive. That was my mistake. It would have been better to have taken her back into a collapsed Germany, have risked hunger and cold for her just to have kept her with me, to have her know that I wanted her with me. But I was preoccupied with getting back what I had lost, and I made the mistake of believing spending money will make up for not spending time. By the time she was twelve I had lost her. When I had both money and time, she was not there for me any more. She was not mine—but then she never had been. So . . . Lotti was here at Tyrell and Meremount briefly, and then I lost her again. Now that she is gone it is hardly different than it was before." I could not believe that; I was remembering the anguished cry that had woken me by the stream.

He gestured, "Do not distress yourself, Miss D'Arcy. The hold that parents have is, at best, tenuous. It is better if one does not deceive oneself. All I had from Lotti was the hope of a relationship in the future—when she was older and if I were yet alive. There was very little in the present."

"But, surely . . . with her married to Connor and here at Meremount so near you . . . ?"

"Ah!" He made a gesture of command toward the teapot and at once the indulgent gnome of my fancy was gone, and there was the authoritative man of business in his place. Quickly I refilled his cup.

"Lotti would never have stayed at Meremount."

"But Connor . . . ?"

"Nor stayed with Connor and the marriage. Lotti was not made that way. She was amused, intrigued . . . Women, I notice, find Connor very attractive. But you see, Miss D'Arcy, Connor, as they say these days, plays it straight. There are few mysteries in Connor's charm. He has looks and virility. It is just there—quite simple. Once Lotti discovered that she had to do no more to hold him, that there were to be no twists and turns to the marriage, she grew a little bored. It would have become worse, and it would have been the death of the marriage."

"But why did she begin it? Didn't she know?"

"She was mistaken. She came here in a moment of—what shall we say—of ennui, of dissatisfaction. Who can say what this glimpse of the simple life did to her, what fantasies she wove into it? Or perhaps she mistook this for one of the country playgrounds of the rich, and Connor and Meremount were her toys. Why else the wild plans for doing over the house? Why the weaving factory? Why the stables? And did she want to splurge on advertising for the new Sheridan Glass in all the expensive magazines in Europe to be able to say, 'I am Sheridan!' After the mass-produced commercialism of Otto Praeger, perhaps the idea of handblown crystal appealed to her. She was going to play with her toy estate, her toy horses, her toy glasshouse in the time when she wasn't doing what she had always done—which was simply to move about Europe looking for

where the most was happening. Perhaps Meremount was something to do in August when her kind of people are somewhat
at a loss to know what to do."

"But Connor . . ." I said again, feeling helpless before the
bluntness of his speech.

"You are right, Miss D'Arcy. You are right. Connor was not
a toy husband. He didn't know what the jet set did—he didn't
care. He was serious about something in life—the Sheridan glassworks, and perhaps that was part of his novelty for Lotti. It is
—what do they say—camp?—to be serious. I am serious, but then
I am German. I did not expect seriousness from Lotti, who was
a child of the war—with no roots but chaos. But Connor succeeded in keeping her here at Meremount for eight months,
except for little shopping trips—and that was longer than I
expected."

"You didn't want the marriage?"

"I was totally and utterly against the marriage. I knew there
was no chance it could succeed. I did not want to witness the
waste of emotion and energy that would go on before it was
finally ended. For Lotti it was playing a game, though she would
not admit it. For Connor it was desperately serious. I did not
see why these two had to go through their pitiful exercise only
to arrive at its inevitable conclusion. As it was"—his hand fumbled blindly for a scone, and he spilled half the strawberry jam
he had taken on a spoon—"the conclusion was unexpectedly
final."

*   *   *   *

We did not talk any more about Lotti while we finished tea;
we hardly spoke at all. But, when Otto Praeger came to see me
to the car, he said abruptly, "You will drive me a little way?
Today I have not yet had my walk."

"Of course."

He squeezed his bulk into the seat beside me; I would have

smiled at the sight of him, his earnestness, his importance, his sheer size in the little battered car, but his face did not permit it. His mouth was working strangely, his fingers gripped and ungripped the top of his cane.

As we crossed the bridge in front of the Castle, he said, pointing with one stubby finger, "To the North Lodge, if you would be so good—if you have time."

I almost checked the car in my surprise, but managed to say nothing. After all, why should Praeger not go to the North Lodge? It was there I had first encountered him; but this continual revisiting of the place where his daughter had met violent death seemed a strangely morbid quirk in a man so imminently pragmatic. But he was more aware of my reaction than I thought, aware that he seemed to be stepping out of character. "If I take my walk to the South Lodge I am expected to return by way of the farm workers' cottages. They are hurt if I do not. And today I have not the heart nor the energy for the children. They demand smiles, and some days I have no smiles in me."

The late afternoon sun filtered through the new green of the trees along the avenue, dappling the road before us, speckling Praeger's face with moving splashes of brightness. I slowed the car so that we seemed to glide through the green cavern of the arching boughs, but still the end of the avenue came too soon, the sight of the North Lodge and the gates barring our way. I braked gently to a halt, but Otto Praeger made no move to leave the car. So I reached and turned off the ignition. The rushing of the stream was suddenly loud.

"Brendan told me about himself and Lotti," I said. "I know about the night she died." I was compelled to say it. Praeger had shared with me things I believed he had given to no one else; he had turned and revealed the other side of the coin of Lotti. I could not keep back from him that I had this other knowledge as well.

"So . . ." The word was long-drawn out; he gave himself time before continuing. "You know Brendan Carroll well?"

"No . . . hardly at all. And yet I do, I suppose. Surprisingly well." It was true; he had revealed most, perhaps all, of himself to me. I knew what Brendan cared about; it was more than I had known for certain of any other man. "You see, he cared about Lotti. He cared very much about what he had caused to happen to all of you—Connor and you and Sheridan Glass—because of that night. He had the idea that my being here would make up in some way for Lotti. Of course, it can't be so, but he tried . . . he cared about it."

Praeger nodded gravely. "I do not doubt that he cares. But he is of less importance in this matter than he believes."

"What do you mean?"

"I mean that Brendan Carroll was only incidental in the whole happening of Lotti's death. That they intended to be together in Copenhagen would have been only a trifle to Lotti, although I suspect it was momentous for Brendan. Possibly for Lotti it would never have had a sequel, though I think Brendan imagined it was the beginning of a permanent, and, eventually, a licit relationship. Lotti, I swear, had no such thought. She was going through one of her periods of being bored with Mere-mount and Ireland—it had been raining for a week, and there was nothing to distract her. Why not say that she was going to London for a few days of shopping—and why not tell Brendan that she would go to Copenhagen with him? Brendan was being used—no less of a toy than any of the other things she had taken up here, and would eventually drop when she tired of them."

"Why are you telling me *this* about Lotti?" I cried. "This is . . . hateful. I had no need to know."

He turned and looked straight at me, his face stern. "Lotti is dead. You are very much alive, and now, very much involved in the situation she left behind her. I have known death too well not to cherish life, and to know that the dead must serve the living. I will not permit you the false picture of Lotti. I will not permit you the image of her that the people around here were given—the golden-haired princess, the Lady Bountiful. It simply amused Lotti to play that role for a time. It would not have lasted.

"Nor," he went on, "will I permit you to be forced into the role that Brendan's sense of guilt would have you take up. Neither Connor nor Brendan understood fully what Lotti was, though they would have come to it eventually. I am not saying they had no knowledge of women—that would be absurd. But neither of them comprehended the degree of selfishness she possessed, the urge to self-gratification, the lightness of her attitudes." He gestured. "Ah, but all the blame does not lie with her—I must assume a great part of it myself for the way I let her grow up. She opened her eyes on a world in chaos. There were no values except one's own survival. Nothing was sacred. You survived or you went under. Nobody cared. Lotti did not care then—she never learned to care.

"Connor or Brendan would never have been a match for her in sheer selfishness. In this case, it was Lotti who was the seductress!"

"I really can't believe all this," I said slowly. "Why did she marry Connor at all? The kind of girl you tell me Lotti was"—now I understood more fully Brendan's description of Lotti's kind of girl—"would just have had an affair with Connor which was ended when it suited her."

"Ah, yes. At any other time, yes. What no one knew was that Lotti was a very shaken young woman when she came to Tyrell that time. Why do you think she came flying back to her dull old father, in his dull Irish retreat? She had just been engaged in one of those international liaisons which make the gossip items in countries less innocent than Ireland. It had come to an end that was not her making. She was out of her class—I will not name his name, because you would know it—but the man was infinitely more experienced, infinitely more ruthless, even more selfish than Lotti. She had more than met her match, and her own world was sitting back and laughing at her. Connor was a salve to her pride. Her pride at that time demanded a marriage—a marriage to an aggressively masculine man. When

the pictures of them together appeared in the magazines—and
Lotti made sure that they did—her circle would know that she
had not picked up a weakling, or a homosexual, or any of these
half-males with which that world is peopled who can be bought
for mere money. Lotti Praeger had a man—a real man, and for
a time he satisfied her. But it was coming to an end—I knew the
signs. Brendan Carroll was incidental to all this—a means to
fight her boredom. I even saw her begin to practice her little,
charming wiles on the Reverend Stanton . . ."

"Oh!" I remembered the look of distaste that had crossed
Patrick Stanton's face when Lotti had been spoken of, how he
had talked, and I had not then understood, of the need that
house had for youth and enthusiasm. He had not used the
word innocence, but that was what he had meant. "You don't
need to tell me all this. You *shouldn't* have told me! I don't
need to know!"

"You do need to know." Suddenly a kind of passion broke
through his heavy earnestness. His hand gripped my wrist, and
the hold was fiercer, stronger than I would have thought the
pudgy hand capable of. "You *do* need to know. You stand now
between these two young men—as Lotti once did. You came
to Ireland because of Brendan. Perhaps you are staying because
of Connor. Whatever you do from this point on—whatever your
choices, and I suspect you will have to make choices—do not
be confused by the role Lotti played in their lives. With Lotti
it is all over. Neither of them now could love her, because they
know her. Do not forget it."

He began, slowly, to heave his bulk from the car. "I will
leave you now. But you will come again? I will not lose sight
of you now?"

All the way down the straight avenue I watched him in the
rear-view mirror—the kindly gnome, the man of business, the
anguished father who could not permit the lie to carry on. I
watched him until finally the trees seemed to close about his
tiny, diminishing figure.

III

I ate dinner with Annie and Mrs. O'Shea in the kitchen. "Mr. Connor rang through to say he'll not be back," Annie reported. I was glad he wasn't there; I didn't want to sit through a meal with him alone in the dining room with last night's encounter still looming large and unresolved. For dinner the three of us chose whatever pleased us from the prepared foods that Otto Praeger had sent—"Like a party," Annie said. That started Mrs. O'Shea happily speculating on Friday's funeral for her Great-uncle Pat; I could think my own thoughts and nod to let her know I was listening. What I was thinking was that by Saturday, with the funeral out of the way, Lady Maude making improvement and my task performed, I would leave. It was then that the telephone rang.

"I'll answer it, Annie—I'm finished supper, in any case."

"There's a darlin', Miss Maura."

I had to run to get to Connor's office before it stopped ringing. "A call from London for Miss Maura D'Arcy."

"Speaking."

"Go ahead, please." Claude's voice cut in almost before the operator was through. "Maura? Well, I've run you to earth at last. Listen, you bitch, you can't do this to me."

"Do what?" I answered him automatically, playing for a little time, wondering how he had found me, and knowing that somehow he would have got a lead to Sheridan Glass from Mary Hughes; a call to the Sheridan glassworks would have yielded the information about me he needed. Half of Claude's success lay in his persistence.

"Don't give me that!" he snapped back. I was aware of a sinking feeling; all that had been unsatisfactory, even wrong, with my London existence seemed to be contained in the very tone of that voice. "You know perfectly well what you've done. You've walked out on a commitment. You've failed to show up on a job. I'm furious with you, and Peter Hatch would be furious with you if you were important enough for him to bother with. I won't be treated this way, Maura . . ."

The voice ran on, shrill, tending to go off into a high-pitched shriek of real or pretended rage. I pictured Claude's face, white, round, the heavy tortoise-rimmed glasses giving it more authority than it truly possessed. Now he was indulging in a tantrum, but he would, in the future, use his grievances to browbeat me into doing things I didn't want to do, into taking jobs I didn't want. Claude could be very thrifty with his emotions, making them pay well. I was made more aware than I ever had been before of the kind of bondage my contract with a man like Claude placed me in. I had not questioned before that I could be screamed and shouted at, and was without the right to refuse to do what he told me; more than I knew, I had become Claude's creature. Suddenly I was glad of the gesture of independence I had made in coming here, even though its repercussions would last for a long time.

"I sent you a telegram, Claude." I tried to keep my voice even, not to reflect the hysteria which was part of doing business in Claude's world. "After all, I only knew about the job late on Friday. By early Monday morning *you* knew I wasn't able to accept the part in the film. It isn't such an important part that Peter Hatch won't have a dozen other girls who could do as well." I found the courage to add, "Don't browbeat me, Claude. I'm not in the mood for it."

The tone now grew silken. "Darling, I'm not browbeating you. I'm just pointing out that you could have missed a great opportunity. But I'm only ringing you to say that it still isn't too late. The second girl on Peter Hatch's list is in New York, so his agents are still asking for you. You can be on a plane from Dublin in the morning—you could be in Madrid tomorrow night. You do that, Maura, and I'll overlook your behavior this time."

"I'm sorry, Claude. I can't do it. I have obligations here." How extraordinary to hear myself say it; I had obligations that had not existed three days ago.

The scream of rage came back. "What obligations? Your obligations are to me. What the hell are you doing in Ireland, in
any case? There's *nothing* in Ireland, for God's sake!"

"There is for me, Claude." My own calmness surprised me.
"I'll give you a ring when I get back. I'll be ready for work
then."

For the first time in our association I was the one who ended
the conversation.

I didn't want to face the relentless curiosity of Mrs. O'Shea
and Annie, so I started up the stairs. Meremount was gloomy
in the twilight. The stairs creaked beneath my feet; I thought
of the sunshine of Spain that I had turned away from, the sunshine of California that I had refused. I wondered if my brief,
heady sense of independence was enough to compensate for
what I had portioned out to myself here—this large, dismal,
crowded house, too quiet in the twilight and yet filled with the
groans and creaks of age; an old woman, our contact established
too late to do either of us any good; Connor and Brendan, who
seemed to push and pull me between them as if I were Lotti
all over again. And now, this afternoon, I had taken onto myself some of the haunted memories, the self-accusations of Otto
Praeger. The price of independence, the choice of involvement,
seemed to come high.

Restless, vaguely unhappy, I continued on past the first-floor
corridor, where the great main staircase ended, to the smaller,
enclosed stairs leading to the next floor. I was glad of the creamy
shape of Sapphire that suddenly emerged from somewhere
among the furniture, going ahead of me up the stairs, seeming
to share the sense of venturing; she gave a low, encouraging cry,
and I could hear the gentle scrape of her claws on the bare
boards. I had never been up here; it was dusty—Annie's cleaning
would rarely get this far, not more than once or twice a year,
I guessed. This was the floor of the dormer windows, the floor
of the schoolrooms and nurseries that had housed governesses
and servants, in the days when there still had been governesses
and servants. The long corridor was narrower than the one be-

low, uncarpeted; my footsteps, though, did not echo in empty space. Here the furniture was crowded even more closely than on the lower floors. I prowled softly, conscious of the gathering dusk, and of the scampering of mice who sensed Sapphire's approach. I opened unfamiliar doors, seeing more and more furniture. Closest to the stairs and overlooking the garden, was the room where Annie slept—crowded, but showing her occupancy —lace mats on a whole row of dressing tables and writing tables, pictures of children in First Communion veils, faded Sodality pictures, a crudely colored print of Christ as the Good Shepherd above the bed, a crucifix with a piece of palm thrust behind it. A cot bed had been set up at the foot of Annie's bed—for Bridget, I imagined. With all the unoccupied rooms to use, Annie and Bridget slept together in this one; Bridget would not be accustomed yet to the noises of Meremount at night. I closed the door quickly. Next to it was a bathroom; a huge tub with claw feet and almost no enamel left, worn linoleum, threadbare towels, a water closet built into the dormer, and, conspicuously, a new gas fire. Lotti had been generous, then, and Annie's comfort had been remembered. I moved on—deserted, crammed rooms, one after the other—pictures stacked against the walls, mirrors, chests, commodes; sometimes I paused to marvel over the inlay work of one of the pieces; I saw a set of chairs that I felt reasonably sure had to be Chippendale; mice were nesting in their seats. I found the room where the rolls of Tyrell tweed were piled; most of it had been abandoned to the moths. It was in this room, also, that the china had been stored—whole dinner services, Spode, Wedgwood—even under the dust the marvelous crimson and blue glowed. There was a service of a distinct rose color I seemed to recognize. Gingerly I turned over one plate and saw the Sèvres mark. I wondered for what banquets for forty Lady Maude had laid it aside; had she seen such sights at Tyrell when she was a child and young woman—before the Edwardian twilight darkened forever into war abroad and rebellion here in Ireland? Had she expected such days to return? The prize of her garnering was the Chinese service; there would have been three hundred pieces of it laid out on the floor. In the last of the light I took a plate to the window to examine it more closely; it was a tobacco-brown pattern of great richness and depth; I was conscious of my ignorance—Blanche would have known at once what it was—but I did remember single plates of eighteenth-century Chinese porcelain that Blanche had had from time to time in the shop—how she had cherished them, how expensive they had been. Very gently I returned it to its place on the stack, being careful where I put my feet; I suspected the service was immensely valuable. As I groped my way downstairs in the near-darkness, Sapphire leaping ahead of me, Otto Praeger's words returned to tantalize. "What a sale it would make at Christie's."

On the first floor corridor there was visible one point of light. As if I had been a moth I was led toward it, and Sapphire was there before me. I heard the whispered voices before I reached the open door, Annie's slightly reverend, Mrs. O'Shea's disparaging, but impressed in spite of herself. I knew I should not go in, ought not to seek out what was not my business, but I couldn't help myself.

". . . Like something in the pictures," Annie was saying.

Mrs. O'Shea didn't quite acquiesce. "Well, she didn't stint herself, I'll say that. Then, why should she—with all that money?"

Blue had been Lotti's color, I thought, as I stood in the doorway. It probably had been the color of her eyes. The carpet that close-covered the huge room had the silver-blue sheen of pale water at sunrise; pale blue velvet covered the chairs and chaise-longue; deeper blue velvet hung as a frame to the windows, a waft of weblike silk, the color of blue ice covered the glass and blocked the sight of the dark tangled garden. The great bed was canopied in blue velvet; large embellished initials on the silk coverlet proclaimed the ownership of all this pale splendor—L.S. The blue-and-cream cat had leaped lightly onto the bed and settled herself against the bolster with an air of pleased familiarity.

Some of Lady Maude's most exquisite pieces had gone to furnish this room—a beautiful little inlaid marquetry dressing table
with a silver-gilt framed mirror set on it, a secretaire with
painted panels, a Louis XIV commode, a tall blue and white
Chinese prunus vase. Where pictures might have hung there
were mirrors, elaborately framed and gilded mirrors, but glass
that should have been age-spotted and dark had been renewed
so that the images were clear and sharp. I wondered that the
two women didn't glimpse me in one of the mirrors, but the
passage was in darkness, and they were absorbed in their talk.

"If you could have seen her here—with her blue-silk gown,
and those feathery slippers, and her hair like gold . . ."

"Oh, I *knew* her right enough," Mrs. O'Shea retorted.
"Many's the time I saw her in Cloncath."

"But here," Annie insisted. "If you could have seen her here
in her nightgowns and all the lacy things—that's why there's
all the heaters in here." She pointed to one of the five big electric storage units that stood about the room, spoiling its ele-
gance. "Sure she wore next to nothing. I used to blush for her
sometimes with Mr. Connor about—but then nakedness seems
to be the thing these days. And didn't he worship her. Sometimes in that bed . . ." She broke off, and the blush stained
even the skin at the back of her neck.

Annie was perpetuating the myth of Lotti and Connor, I
thought—and in the beginning, before Lotti grew bored, it must
have been the truth. Annie was recalling that time, living in
it, as she still lived in the promise of all the good things there
were to have been, and forgetting the telephone call from Brendan about the bridge that had betrayed their rendezvous and
had forecast the end. To talk only of the good times was her
way to guard the myth.

I took a few steps forward to announce to them both that I
was there, but as I did so, Annie moved quickly to the white
built-in cupboard that lined one side of the room. "Will you
look at this now . . ." She began folding back the doors to reveal
the long rack of hanging clothes. "Wasn't there a holy row with

Lady Maude about putting this in—said she was ruining the paneling. But wasn't it half done by then . . ."

Eagerly, greedily, Mrs. O'Shea's fingers flicked along the hangers, pulling out a garment here and there, letting it fall back among the others. "And here," Annie said, opening another part of the cupboard, "the drawers for her underwear and things —woolies, scarves, shelves for handbags. Feel this, will you, Mrs. O'Shea? Vicuna, she called it. And this—this is antelope. And the gloves—drawers full of them. It used to take me an hour sometimes to pick up and fold and put away what she had left around. Untidy, she was—but then wasn't it a pleasure to be doing things for her, and handling the like of what she wore. I'm tellin' you, the house was a different place in those days.

"Ah, but these are me favorites." She had reached the last section of the cupboard. "I just love to put me hands on these —four fur coats and five jackets. And don't be askin' me the names of them, because some of them I never heard of in me life before. Now look you— Ah, Holy Mother!"

I had been expecting to see the ocelot of Brendan's memory. Instead, there was nothing at all, just a row of empty hangers, swinging wildly as Annie's agitated fingers plucked at them as if to call back what was gone.

"Mother of God, where are they? Have they been stolen, do you think?—and me never knowing it. 'Tis weeks since I put me head in here."

"Or sold," Mrs. O'Shea offered dryly.

"Sold? Whoever would—" Annie spun on her heels. The expression of worried concern on her face was compounded by surprise. She looked at me, and then past me.

"Miss—Mr. Connor!"

"Have you shown enough, Annie?" I turned also; he was striving to hold himself in check, to keep anger below the surface of his cold inquiry. I had the feeling that he wanted to bundle all of us out of there, to close the gaping wardrobe, to shout his rage and slam the door on us. Annie had flinched visibly; it took her a moment to find words.

"I was just checking for the moth, you know, Mr. Connor. It does have to be done from time to time. And Mrs. O'Shea just stepped in, you might say . . ."

"And Miss Maura?" The question was asked of me directly.

"I wasn't invited," I said. "I just watched."

"None of you were invited, if it comes to that. All right, Annie—no more!" he added quickly, as she began further protestations. "We'll have done with it. No—leave it. I'll close them."

"But the furs, Mr. Connor, all those beautiful furs?"

"Are none of your business," he finished brutally. "Now if you'll all just get out . . . ?"

Mrs. O'Shea swept past me, and then past Connor, and her sniff was audible. After a second's hesitation Annie almost ran to catch her up, as if she feared to pass Connor at the doorway alone. Out in the passage Mrs. O'Shea's words came clearly back.

"Sold, of course. Some people have no reverence for the dead. Money is all they care about . . ."

It was my turn to go. I felt ashamed to have been there at all, but I tried not to lower my eyes as I came close to Connor. As I reached him, his hand shot out and caught my arm. His grip hurt, but I hadn't the power to protest it.

"I'm sorry," I said. "I shouldn't have been here."

His grip relaxed a little as if he were surer now that I would not run from him, sure the way he had been last night when he had kissed me. He drew me back into the room so that we were out of sight of Annie and Mrs. O'Shea if they had lingered in the passage.

"I'm glad you've seen it," he said. "This was Lotti—all of her. All that she was is in this room—selfish, vain, self-loving. She loved her own image." My gaze went around the room once more, as he meant it to, coming to rest, inevitably, on the bed, enormous, voluptuous, silken. "Yes, that too," he said. The grip became hard again. "Lotti was great in bed—but greedy.

It was her own gratification that counted. She didn't know what it was to love."

"I don't want to hear this," I said, "it isn't my business."

"It could be," he said, jerking me a little. "It could be—because it was my business. Haven't you been hearing about Lotti from other people?—from Brendan and from Praeger?"

I opened my mouth, but he didn't let me speak. "Oh, I hear things," he said. "I know about your afternoon with Praeger, the little drive to the bridge? Didn't you talk about Lotti there? Well, didn't you?" The demand was accompanied by a shake. "And didn't Brendan fill your ears with Lotti last night, so that that was all you could say to me when you came in? Well, now you know what Lotti was. What ought I to do—mourn her forever? She wasn't worth it. Brendan and Praeger know that —and you know it. You know all about Lotti."

I jerked back from him. "Don't any of you understand? I don't want to know about Lotti."

"You do—or you wouldn't have been in this room tonight. I want you to know about Lotti. So that it's over and done with. I want you to forget about Lotti. There's no mystery about her. All that's left of her is here, and that doesn't matter a damn."

I looked once more about this silken room; the mirrored images of ourselves were cast back at us, but also there, though the mirrors could give no precise definition to her, was Lotti— Lotti triumphant in the vast bed, Lotti combing her bright hair before the dressing table, Lotti laughing, flaunting, mocking, and Connor unable to withstand her, Connor saying that none of these memories mattered a damn, and still his eyes blazing in his head with love and hate and desire.

"But she's hard to forget, isn't she? Your Lotti is hard to forget."

He let me go without a word.

CHAPTER 8

I

The loud, angry tones—Connor's voice—reached down the stair-well to me. I had left Annie and Bridget in the kitchen, and passed Mrs. O'Shea on her way to have her morning coffee there; I knew it was toward none of them that Connor's anger was directed. That left just Lady Maude. I started to run. Half-way up the stairs I heard her voice—far too loud and forced. The hideous memory of the night when I had been wakened by these same two voices, and the memory of Lady Maude sprawled sideways in her bed when the shouting had stopped, didn't permit me any choice about not interfering. I couldn't pretend now that it wasn't my concern; the time of polite un-concern was long over. Words became distinguishable now.

". . . what rights I have! I've earned every right there is . . . sweated my guts out—"

Without knocking I threw open the door. The sounds stopped.

Connor stood at the end of the bed. There was the look of smothered fierceness in his very stance that now appeared to me too familiar; it was the everyday companion with whom Connor seemed to dwell.

"Well . . . ?" He had turned; his skin was drained of all color. There was left just the startling blackness of eyes and brows and hair.

I closed the door, taking my time about it, and making the action very definite and soft so that it would give them a mo-ment's pause. "You can't do this," I said. I kept my voice low but it wavered a little; I hadn't realized until now how frightened I was. "This is what started it last time—this shouting at one another."

". . . not your concern, Maura . . . I will handle this . . ." It was hard to recognize it as the voice of the woman I had heard raised in anger a minute ago. The words came in a half-whisper, strength deserting her suddenly. I sensed that what she said had been said automatically, out of the habit of command, not now from a desire to exercise it. With her hand she attempted an imitation of the peremptory gesture she used so often, but it came only as a feeble wave. I moved closer to the bed; her face was grayish, drawn. She had seemed so much better when I had visited her earlier that morning; abruptly the gain had been wiped out.

"It has to be my concern," I answered. "I can't stand by and let the same thing happen again. For as long as I'm here, whether you want it or not, I have to be concerned—to be responsible." As I spoke a strange expression had crossed the old lady's face; the features relaxed from their exhausted tautness; for an instant the eyelids fluttered closed, and her head seemed to settle back into the pillow. Then her eyes opened again, much wider, and she appeared to flash at Connor a look of triumph, as if to make sure that he marked that she had won a champion—however improbable I seemed in that role, and however little in need of one she seemed to be.

He had not missed it, this sudden unexpected closing of ranks. He had two adversaries instead of one; I felt my own courage restored by the fact that he took one single backward step, away from the bed.

"Lady Maude is right—it's not your concern. This is a purely family matter."

But at this moment he couldn't wedge us free of the unlikely bond that had been formed. The whisper came from the bed, more dominating than any shout. ". . . my granddaughter!"

They stared at each other for a moment, Lady Maude and Connor, and it was Connor who turned away. He shrugged. "As you wish . . ." I watched him go to the window and stand there staring out at nothing. He wanted to go, to leave the old lady to her victory, but he would not go and give possession to me. The silence was long, the room very still. I didn't know what to do; I wouldn't leave because I guessed that Connor might return to the argument I had interrupted, and yet I wasn't comfortable in this sudden intimacy with Lady Maude; I had joined forces with her because I had to, not because I wanted to. I walked over to where Mrs. O'Shea had left a Dublin morning newspaper on a chair, picked it up, and so gave Connor notice that I was prepared to stay.

The silence was ended by Annie's knock on the door. She put her head in, her expression apprehensive and excited. "There you are, Miss Maura. It's Mr. Praeger. He's come for you, miss."

I put down the newspaper, aware of the agitated flutter of Lady Maude's hands. "Come for me? Why?"

"To take you to the glassworks. That's what he said. 'Tell Miss D'Arcy I've come to take her to the glassworks.'" And then, as if to quieten Lady Maude, she added, "He wouldn't come in. He's sitting outside in his car."

"Well, blast him!" The anger was all to the surface again in Connor. "Who the hell does he think he is? If Miss D'Arcy cares to see the glassworks, *I'll* take her. Whose glassworks does he think they are?"

The whisper from the bed overpowered us all. "Not *your* glassworks, Connor—not yet!"

II

Long before I had got my coat and gone downstairs to Otto Praeger, I heard Connor's car leaving; the tires squealed and it bumped in the ruts of the avenue. Praeger climbed stiffly from the back of the big gray Mercedes to greet me; O'Keefe stood holding the door, his exaggerated chauffeur manner ruined by the wide grin on his face.

"I thought we should make a little expedition," Praeger said. He did not refer to Connor's departure. "I hear that Lady Maude is recovering, and that your presence is not required all the time." He was stowing me in the luxurious depths of the back seat, rather as if I had been a child, buttoning me up, nodding to O'Keefe through the glass partition that he could now start. It was Praeger in his authoritative role, with small sign of the gnome; I guessed that Lotti must often have revolted against the paternal assurance of rightness. It was a little shocking to find myself suddenly thinking with some understanding of a woman who had been dead before I ever heard her name. But I let Praeger have his way, not offering any revolt of my own, because I guessed that there was a grieving for Lotti in this man which could find no other expression than that of fussing over some other young woman who bore a chance resemblance to his daughter.

Cloncath was a gently mannered town with a clean river running through it, spanned by three picture-book bridges and, on the modest height above it, giving a view to the estuary, a superb Georgian crescent where the town's professional men now lived and worked. It was gray, as Irish towns generally are, but graced by the softness of the countryside, and by its own close relation to the human scale. Beyond the sea was Wales, and Praeger directed O'Keefe to drive up on the Crescent to give me a sight of its distant mountains. "But, as usual," Praeger said, "it cannot be seen." We paused and looked for a moment at the slope of the town beneath us, the chimneypots, the curls of smoke going idly into the still air, the shining river, the white ruffled sea. With his cane, Praeger indicated it all. "These people have known great tragedy—hunger and persecution, the dominance of foreign rulers. But they have not yet suffered the ugliness of the modern age. They will come to it, of course, as they grow more prosperous. Then they will no longer have salmon in the clean waters in the middle of their towns, and the trout will all die. But not yet—not yet, I hope."

It sounded strange to hear it spoken in his thick accent, the echo of the words Lady Maude had whispered. "Not yet." They were the old, holding back, and with some knowledge of what they did. Praeger added: "Next week I go to New York. As I look on the temple of money and materialism, I will know even better why I come here—why I hope for a time that this can survive. I am selfish. I would like it to last until I die." Then he rapped on the partition. "Come—we will go to the glass-works."

The Sheridan glassworks were in Glasshouse Lane, which opened off the main square. In the square was the courthouse-jail, built by the English and disguised as a Greek temple; there was a cinema, and the shops of the local merchants; from the looks of it cattle had recently passed through—not quite as tidy as an English town, and more individual. One of the streets from the square gave a glimpse down to the river and the quays, the small fleet of trawlers. At Tyrell and Meremount there was little sense of being so close to the sea, but Cloncath felt like a seacoast town; the smell of the sea was here, the smell of fish, the seagulls swooping overhead with the flash of white wings and their plaintive cries. "Sheridan settled here because there was easy access to the English ports for his glass," Praeger said as we turned in the big wooden gates marked *SHERIDAN GLASS*. "Waterford, of course, is by far the better port, but he couldn't set up under the nose of Waterford Glass." We were in a long, narrow yard, paved in brick, with old two-story buildings on each side. Connor's car was parked before a pre-fabricated building of light blue steel and glass; there were two entrances marked Museum and Office.

"This," Praeger said, indicating the modern building, "is as far as Lotti got with the new Sheridan Glass. There were plans to tear down all the old buildings—which I did not approve. There was a tendency to move too quickly . . ."

At the door of the museum, Connor waited for us. "Good morning, Mr. Praeger," he said. "How good of you to bring my cousin to see our humble little operation here."

Praeger gave an old-fashioned half-bow. "Entirely my pleasure, I assure you."

☙ ☙ ☙ ☙

The museum was too elegant for its surroundings, the floor covered in dark gray carpet, the walls in charcoal felt, the windows blocked out so that the only light came from the fixtures built into the showcases. Against the darkness, the crystal glowed like moonlit frost coating a bare winter field. There was a pretty young receptionist who greeted Praeger with awe and me with curiosity. She hurried to push forward for my inspection a big bound book whose first few pages were filled with press cuttings. "This was when we opened the museum last year, Miss D'Arcy." I saw the headline from the *Irish Times* of a long article A RENAISSANCE FOR SHERIDAN GLASS. The next page was photographs, obviously of a press reception of the museum. I caught a glimpse of Connor and Praeger, smiling unnaturally, and of a young woman, very blonde. Connor reached across and closed the book. "Miss D'Arcy can see that some other time, Daisy," he said.

"Come," Praeger said, "I will show you."

I was shown, and I saw, and afterward I could have recited only a very little of what I had been told. The encounter between Connor and Praeger at the door of the museum was the beginning of a tug-of-war between them that continued as long as the tour of the works, with myself in the middle. Praeger led me about the museum, less humble about his knowledge than he had been when he had shown me his own collection at Tyrell. He led me along the display cases that held Sheridan's own glass—pieces made by the master himself, beginning about 1720 when he finished his apprenticeship. There were pieces blown by his sons here at Cloncath, and some of his master glassblowers; there was one piece by a grandson, and more from blowers of his generation. "You see, about 1820 it all dwindles off," Praeger said. "The same pattern repeated and repeated, with nothing new attempted. The learned skills are not lost, but fewer care to learn them, and there is little inspiration. Sheridan Glass barely stays alive."

"But it did stay alive," Connor interrupted. "It did—and it will."

There was something ominous and a little malicious in Praeger's refusal to support what Connor had said; the silence carried its own damnation. To break the strain of that silence I moved ahead of them both to the display case at the end of the row; I guessed it had been intended as an extra space to hold the new designs that Lotti and Connor and Brendan had planned would come from Sheridan in the future. It was not empty, however. Side by side, as I saw them matched for the first time, were the two Culloden Cups.

"It's here!" I said. I turned back to Connor. "You brought it here!"

He shrugged. "Isn't it safer here? Would you have me put it with all the other things at Meremount—everything piled up, waiting to be broken. It *belongs* here."

"But I haven't given it—yet."

He shrugged again. "I didn't say you had. I merely said it's safer here."

Pressing my nose against the case I stared at the two goblets —the simple shape, the delicate, intricate stem, the symbolic pattern of the handles that now seemed burned into my memory. "Which is which?" I said. Badly now I wanted the reassurance of identifying the one that Blanche had discovered and cherished, the one that Brendan had handled with such knowledge and reverence. I felt a terrible sense of loss and frustration as I gazed at these two identical goblets.

"Don't worry." Connor's tone was faintly mocking, as if he guessed and enjoyed my fear. "You'll get your own one back. A glassmaker can tell the difference."

"I hope so," I said, as I responded to Praeger's tug on my arm and he led me across the room.

"On this side is Thomas Sheridan's own collection of glass.

In my opinion it is one of the finest collections of Venetian glass at its greatest period in the world. It has never been evaluated . . ." Here a quick look to Connor, somewhat accusing. I guessed that Praeger wanted very much to own the Sheridan collection. "Sheridan was not a rich man, you understand, but he was a famous and respected glassblower, and pieces came into his hands from other glassblowers, and so here . . ." He led me down the room, past the fragile, beautiful objects that were the mementos of Sheridan's own passion for his art—the goblets, plates, beakers, the dish that looked like a cake stand which Praeger told me was called a *tazza*—colored, gilded, diamond-point engraved, embellished, some of the goblets standing on the traditional dragon stem or the horse stem.

"Two of the most beautiful examples of *latticinio* I have ever seen," Praeger said, pointing to a covered goblet and a *tazza*, both with the woven white mesh captured within them which had always fascinated me, and which, I now realized, I had never bothered to inquire about from Blanche. She would have known how it was done, of course.

Praeger's instruction had gone on. "You see, they blew a gather of glass into a mold where the straight canes of white glass had already been set vertically. The vessel is then twisted, and the canes also twist, so . . . They build up the lacy texture by blowing the gather up farther in a second mold, also containing white canes. It required the most masterly craftsmanship . . ." He tapped the display case with his finger, and I sensed how he yearned to touch and fondle what he described. For a moment he had forgotten Connor and the need to show off to the younger man his knowledge of the technique and history of the art. "Observe, Miss D'Arcy, how a tiny air bubble is trapped in each of these diamond-shaped areas formed by the crossed canes." He gazed lovingly at the airy twisted stem of a goblet.

He lingered, but my own gaze was drawn to a large cabinet which stood alone; it held a long velvet-lined box of finely polished wood, open, turned on end and tilted to display its contents. I read the small label: *The Glassmaking Tools of Thomas Sheridan.* They were much used, they bore the marks of the intense heat of his trade. For some reason, not fully conscious or explored, I felt the prickling of tears in my eyes.

Connor came beside me; his tone fell softly, not mocking or bitter. "The great worked with the same tools as the humblest apprentice." He named them for me. "The blowing iron and the pontil—the pucellas, calipers, shears, and pincers. That scorched wooden thing there like a big butter patter was his battledor. You'll see the men using these same tools out in the works." As I continued to stand there looking at them he added, in a tone so low it was almost a whisper in my ear, a close and private thing offered to me alone, "It was Lotti's idea to have the case made for them. You see—quite often she had the right instincts . . ."

Praeger limped toward us, and the young receptionist was offering me the big leather-covered guest book. The first page was not yet filled. Connor closed it and turned it back to her. "No, Daisy. Sheridans do not sign the guest book at Sheridan Glass."

I felt the familiar surge of mistrust rise; Connor drew me in, included me, gave me place as often as he thrust me out.

The girl flushed and stammered with confusion. "I'm sorry, Mr. Connor. I just didn't think . . ." She returned the book to the desk. When Praeger came abreast of her she held out her hand.

"Mr. Praeger—I'd like to say good-bye. You don't come in here much, and it's probably the last time I'll be seeing you."

"Why, child . . ." He groped for her name, and didn't remember it. "Why, are you leaving us?"—the word "us" as though he had not given up all interest in Sheridan Glass.

"Well . . ." she moved uneasily, and looked at Connor. "I've got a job in Dublin starting in two weeks' time."

"Daisy isn't leaving us." Connor took up the explanation. "I've had to ask her to find another job. We can't afford a Daisy any more. As much as she decorates the place, and as little as we pay her, we still can't afford her any more."

"But—" Praeger's brow knit. His mind was obviously turned from Daisy and her job to the more important aspect, to him, of her leaving. "Who will be here to see that no damage is done when there are visitors? Umbrellas . . . children . . . it's unthinkable to leave the collection untended while the public is on the premises."

Connor shrugged as if to indicate the bad taste of discussing this before Daisy, who would relay it all about town; at the same time his gesture said that the town might as well know for certain what was guessed at already.

"The public won't be on the premises. I'm closing the museum. We just can't afford it. It's quite simple."

"What will you do with the collection?" I didn't know whether it was concern for those who would no longer have access to it that shook Praeger's voice, or the sudden hope that it might be for sale.

"What can I do with it? Leave it here. It's safer than at Meremount, as I've explained to Maura. As to what becomes of it eventually—who knows? It isn't mine to dispose of." He looked at his watch. "I think we should move along. The lunch whistle will go pretty soon, and the men are going to be very annoyed with me if they don't get a good look at the last of the Sheridans. Of course, if I'd been given a little notice that today would be the day of the visitation, I could have had the men working on their fanciest pieces. They'll not have the chance to show off as much as they'd like . . ." Impatiently he was holding the door open for us, in command now that the change from the museum to the glassworks was being made, now that we were leaving the area that Praeger money had touched and transformed, and stepping back into the world where, although impoverished and antiquated, the Sheridans were still in control.

Nothing Brendan or Connor or Praeger had said prepared me well enough for the sight of the glassblowers at work. We moved across the yard and into a long stone building, the walls mottled with smoke and age, ventilated by great hopperlike chimneys. It was as though we moved into a scene from a dark, medieval world. It was dim within the building—the only light seemed to come from the glow of the furnaces; their red hot mouths riveted and burned the eyes, their roar filled the air—that and the sound of breaking glass. In the dimness the figures of the workers appeared to move about in a confused, directless way; for a long time I could conceive no pattern or rhythm to it. I wanted to call to them to stop so that I could sort it out, try to remember what I had been told, try to listen coherently to the explanations that Connor poured into my ear, but the most unexpected thing of this whole strange scene was the speed of the movement. I began to understand that they all must work at a pace that held at bay the inexorable laws of gravity which will cause the gather on the end of the blowing iron or pontil to droop, must work against the speed with which molten glass will cool and so defy shaping by blowing and centrifugal force.

I felt myself shrinking against the solid forms of Praeger and Connor as the glowing hot gather came from the furnace. I did not want to move nearer the gaffer to watch him at work on his chair, revolving, trimming, clipping, measuring. Several teams of workers used the same glory hole, reheating time and again as long as the piece remained unfinished; these demonia-cal glowing balloons on the end of the irons swung through the air on each side of me, and I tried not to flinch at the heat and swiftness of their passage, tried not to close my eyes in panic. It was a precise, expert, and complex ballet, performed with intricate rhythm and timing; the outsider's eye could not see it all at once, only watch the miracle of the product that came from this interplay, this dance of dexterity and expertise—the transfer, as if they played with a ball of fire, between master and servitor, the passing of the gather from blowing iron to pontil, the precision of the sharp blow that freed the vase or bowl finally from its umbilical tool—a dance in medieval darkness, fearful, swift, wonderful.

One by one, as the pieces they were working on were completed, Connor called the gaffers and introduced them to me. There was a confusion of names, Irish faces with seared skins and eyes strained and faded from the years at the glory holes; they were reluctant to proffer dirty hands, but still not willing to forego the handshake. I could see their glances go from me to Connor to Praeger, and the instant speculation born, the hope springing, that there was still to be a new day for Sheridan Glass. Praeger represented money, and I—I suppose I was like a return of something they thought was dead. I was a Sheridan— the grandchild of the man who had apprenticed some of them, the bearer of the tradition; I think I was also Lotti, the strange young woman suddenly in their midst, the link between Connor and Praeger, the catalyst of a new era. Many of them must have remembered Lotti standing there between these same two men, but how much better that this young woman was of the house and line, not a foreigner, but one of their own. I thought of the talk that would run through the group while they ate their lunch, the talk at home that night, and how quickly it would all be over when they heard in a day or so that I had gone again.

The lunch whistle ended it. "You'll see the cutting and polishing some other time," Connor said. "I'll have to tell the men you'll be back."

Thankfully I walked into the cool release of the yard.

III

O'Keefe stood with the car door open, and Praeger's hand was on my arm. "Come," he said, "you will join me at Castle Tyrell for lunch?" It was hardly a question, as if there were no possibility of another choice. I felt reluctance, this time, to obey.

Connor broke in before I could frame an answer. "I think it's time, don't you, Mr. Praeger, that Maura saw something of the town, or the town saw something of her?" Turning to me,

"Wouldn't you like to have a bite at the local pub—not a gourmet's delight, but Guinness on draught is about the only thing Castle Tyrell doesn't have."

They disliked and respected each other, and perhaps it had pleased Lotti to be an object to be fought over; but I was weary of being Lotti for Praeger's benefit. I could not let myself be swallowed whole by him. I knew it would disappoint him, but I accepted Connor's invitation.

"As you wish," Praeger said stiffly. He held out his hand to me. "We will say good-bye then. On Sunday I go to New York."

"This is Thursday. May I come to Castle Tyrell again?"

"As you wish," he repeated. He didn't look at me again as he drove off, the heavy-jowled face mournful and unforgiving. But for me it felt good to join the stream of men crossing the yard toward the gate, to listen to their talk, to hear the quips tossed from one to the other, some of it, I thought, for my benefit. It was a strange sense of belonging to be here among them as if I had been accepted as always having been a part of Sheridan Glass.

Suddenly, at the gate, with a jolt of pleasure, I recognized the tall figure ahead of us. "Brendan!" The cry was out before I remembered Connor's presence at my side. The other man turned back, the slow, mischievous smile spreading, and I knew he had known we were there, and had waited to see if I would call, almost daring me to risk Connor's disapproval.

"It's herself, indeed," he said. "And hadn't I heard, of course, that you were at the works. Sure, you could hear the buzz of talk about it halfway across Cloncath. And how are you? And how is Lady Maude?"

"I'm well—she's improving."

He nodded. He was tall enough to look over my head at Connor; to him he said, "I was just picking up a few odds and ends I'd left behind in my desk. Saying a final farewell to a few of the men. Of course, it's the second time I've said good-bye, so they're beginning to make remarks about a prima donna's farewell."

"You're going?" Did I sound too forlorn?

"I am—again. Tomorrow. I've just made arrangements with some movers to get my things out of the lodge as soon as I've a place of my own in Bristol. Of course, the lease still has some time to run, but I doubt I'll be needing it." The information was more for Connor than myself; it seemed as if the two could communicate only through another person. Connor still was silent; no word of farewell, no wish for good luck. But then, I thought, why should he wish Brendan Carroll luck?—there could have been no word of goodwill between them since the night Lotti had died, no word at all that was not for the sake of appearances.

I felt a kind of desperation rise in me. He was going, and possibly I would never see him again. I clutched at the only thing I could to delay him a little longer, to keep a link between us. "Your check," I said. "I have to return your check."

"That was a part payment for the Culloden Cup."

"But I'm keeping it. I'm not leaving . . ." For the first time I felt sure about that.

He shrugged. "What you do with it is your choice. Perhaps you'll change your mind and decide to leave it. In either case, let's say I bought it and made a present of it to you."

"It's well to be those who can afford such gestures." Connor's tone mocked him.

"I thought you knew," Brendan drawled, "that those who can least afford extravagant gestures are most often given to making them. Allow me at least my own folly, man." Quickly, as if he had said more than he had intended, he held out his hand to me, and added, "I'll be saying good-bye then, and a safe journey back—that is, if you do go back." He turned, and without a word to Connor, he crossed the road and headed for the square. We watched him until he rounded the corner near the courthouse.

"Well, there he goes, and I hope I never see him again."

As he said it, Connor took my arm, something he had not done before in this way. We followed in the direction Brendan had taken. I felt an aching sense of loss, as if a prop had gone from my world; my feet seemed weighted, and the end of Glasshouse Lane a mile away. I was strangely glad of the comfort of Connor's hold.

IV

The Four Kingdoms was the only hotel in Cloncath, "The only place you can eat," Connor said as we crossed the square toward it. "It was once called The Tyrell Arms but after our glorious rebellion, it was changed in a hurry, they say."

"You sound as if you didn't believe in the glorious rebellion."

"I believe in whatever's most expedient—the pragmatic solution." He swung open the door of the bar. We were greeted by warmth and noise, and the gaze of many eyes. It was almost exclusively male—the town's professional men, a scattering of well-to-do farmers, a few who did nothing but go to the races, if their conversation was to be believed. Connor knew them all, and introduced me to most of them. "My cousin, Maura D'Arcy." He made the relationship seem much closer than it was, drew me into the fold as he had done at the glassworks, assumed a proprietary air over me. Among the older men I could almost read their thoughts as Connor pronounced my name—the story of Blanche Sheridan who had made the best match in the county, and the unknown man for whom she had ended it. Among those of Connor's age the story was something once heard and long forgotten, a story to this generation no longer either very shocking or scandalous. With them the first look was as it is with all young men, a frank appraisal of face and figure, and then the questions to see how well I could fit in. "I hope you'll be staying with us a good long time now that you've come," and "Will you be taking her to the Briggan races then, Connor?" No inquiries from this group about Lady Maude. To them she was already dead, if she had ever existed; they were the new Ireland, putting rebellion and the civil war behind them, wanting Ireland to move on, forget the past, grow prosperous. They plied me with questions and offered me drinks, and flirted in a way that was meant to be as much a compliment to Connor as to myself. Then came the moment when a hand fell too heavily on Connor's shoulder, and the voice slurred by whisky said, "Well, I have to hand it to you, Connor. You got two beauties, only this one looks Irish."

Without replying, or even looking at the speaker, Connor shrugged off the hand, put his drink on the bar, and took mine from me.

"We'll see if we can get some lunch." His hand was on my arm again, and he was leading me from the bar to the dining room. As he held the door for me, I looked into the corner near it. Brendan Carroll sat there, with two other men. I checked for a moment at the sight of him, and gravely he lifted his glass to me in a little salute. But his eyes and his mouth were laughing; he had witnessed the scene at the bar and all that had gone before it. For a second I saw it with his eyes, this ready inclusion in a small society, the recognition that a known name will bring, the instant sense of acceptance; he suspected that I had been beguiled by it, relaxed, charmed, warmed by it, and he was partly right. I heard again his words "if you do go back" and I knew now what he had been saying.

*   *   *   *

Brendan did not come into the dining room; I watched the door each time it opened. During lunch Connor and I hardly spoke to each other directly; there were many interruptions from other people who came to the table or who called across the room. I thought he welcomed them; Connor, with a predominating subject on his mind, had no small talk. A lot had happened since we had faced each other at the foot of Lady Maude's bed that morning but the memory and the traces remained. We couldn't, I thought, settle with each other. There in Lady Maude's room he had attempted to keep me on the outside, and had failed, throwing Lady Maude and myself into an unlikely alliance. But Praeger had injected himself, and since then Connor had done everything he could to make me feel that I belonged. I was wearied and bewildered by it, and in my own way I was grateful for those who interrupted, because I had not, just now, the strength to take on Connor.

When we had finished he led me through into the small lobby of the hotel. "If you want to wait here—or go and powder your nose—I'll get the car from the works. I'll drive you home."

In the way I had watched Brendan I also watched Connor walk across the square, wondering if he had made a slip, or if he had meant to say "I'll drive you home."

v

The careful, almost sedate pace of Connor's driving surprised me; I had expected something that matched the troubled rhythm of his moods, but this was smooth and effortless. Or had I been thinking of what Brendan had said about Lotti— "She always drove too fast."? Cloncath slipped behind us, and I scarcely noticed; we were among the stone walls of the countryside, and the leafing trees, and I let myself relax into the ease of our movement and the effect Connor's silence conveyed of his having all the time in the world to spend. The drink before lunch had made itself felt; I was drowsy, and I thought drowsily of Brendan, not believing, quite, that that had been the last I would see of him, and yet not knowing how it would be otherwise; but the drink had also given me a heightened sense of confidence. I would find whatever it was I had come searching for in Ireland, and I would handle whatever came my way.

I was jolted from my preoccupation when Connor turned the car in smoothly at the South Lodge of Castle Tyrell. "We're going to see Mr. Praeger?"

"I hope not," he replied casually. As he went by the lodge he waved to the woman who had come to the open doorway to check his arrival; I saw the kind of smile she returned to the wave, and knew that Connor, whatever his differences with Praeger himself, was quite sure of his authority and his welcome on Praeger's property.

"Then what?" I asked.

"Patience," he said. "You'll see."

"You're not notably possessed of patience yourself." I wished I didn't always so quickly respond to him when he was soft and gentle this way. I began to see how even someone like Lotti Praeger, experienced, discerning of the charm and masculine appeal of the men she had known, and perhaps a little bored with it, might have supposed herself enough taken with Connor to marry him, might even have believed that the marriage would last. It was possible that Connor knew all this himself, and used the knowledge well and skillfully. He kept me off my balance; he played the game of the sexes very well.

Before we reached the lake, he turned the car off at an unpaved road that eventually came to skirt the water itself on the shore opposite the Castle. Today the sun was not there to throw into violent color the banks of azaleas beneath the windows of the rooms where Otto Praeger's pictures hung; I wondered if today he would turn his face to the pictures rather than the lake while he ate his solitary tea.

Connor parked the car where the road ended at the ruin of a little temple-like pavilion which sat looking toward the Castle. Its roof had collapsed and the columns which had supported it were lost under a rank growth of ivy. "The story has it," Connor said as he opened the car, "that some of the servants at the Castle had stored arms and ammunition here during the Troubles, and Lady Maude's brother discovered and reported it. That night the local boys turned out and burned the place. I've never cared, though, to ask Lady Maude if that was the truth." He added, pointing to a footpath that wound beneath the trees, "We'll go this way. I think we'll not be seen unless Otto Praeger has his binoculars on us already. And if we are, the worst that can happen is an invitation to tea. I don't think he'd deny your right to be here—or mine, for that fact."

"I don't think so either—but then he's never tried, has he?"

He didn't reply, but I sensed from his silence that my small defense of Praeger hadn't much pleased him. I left him to his silence, not asking where we were going; I listened to the muffled sounds of our footsteps on the damp leaves of last autumn, the lap of the tiny waves at the rim of the lake. The path, almost lost at times in leaves and undergrowth, followed the curve of the lake, and I could see that it would end where the line of trees finished at the edge of the mown green slope fronting the Castle. A serene group of mallards kept pace with us as we walked, the vivid plumage of the male the single note of color on the gray-tinged water. We rounded the narrow end of the lake and the trees began to thin, gave way to an ivy ground cover, and finally to lawns. This brought us nearly directly in front of O'Ruairc's Tower, close enough to the line of the long buildings so that we could not be seen except by someone leaning from one of the windows. There was no one there, and Connor led the way unhurriedly across the smooth turf to a low door at the base of the tower. Over the centuries the structure had sunk and the turf had been built up, so that we had to step down to the doorway; Connor selected the key for the modern lock from the several he had on his ring.

"Do you have all the keys to Tyrell?" I asked. "Or do you only trespass in this part?"

He swung open the door and reached for the light switch, glancing back and smiling at my tone. "No trespass," he said. "I have a key, and then, in a way, I belong to the family, don't I?—Praeger's family? But you—you're a Tyrell. You have precedence here."

"Don't!" I said. "Don't try to wish Lady Maude's mania on me. Tyrell doesn't really exist any more—only in her own mind."

"It exists," he said. "It exists more than you think—the whole mythology of the Tyrells and their kind in Ireland. Even after fifty years the overtones are still here. And it will be a pity when they fade out of memory. Ireland won a war of moral independence long before independence was a fashionable word. It would be a pity if that were ever forgotten."

"I thought you regarded the rebellion as an expediency?"

"I do, but expediencies always have to have their heroes and their villains, their own folklore. It's easier for an Irishman to hate and fight someone he knows, like the Tyrells, than hate a whole amorphous mass called the English." With a return of his usual impatience he jerked his head for me to go in ahead of him. "Well, are we going to debate the Irish question, or shall we go up and see the view from the top?"

"Is that why we came?"

"Why else?"

It was trespass, and I had no real rights here, no more than he did; but as he had demonstrated to me, the myth of the Tyrells still had its own power to draw and to hold. I moved ahead of him and found my foot on the first of the steep worn stone steps that spiraled narrowly and dizzily above me in the thickness of the wall of O'Ruairc's Tower.

*   *   *   *

"The domain of the Tyrells." Connor's arm extended out beyond the parapet; his gesture took in the whole countryside. "To Cloncath, to Doylestown—as far as you could see, as Lady Maude is fond of telling me. It could very nearly be the truth, too. They once owned half the county, and what they didn't own outright, they controlled politically."

I looked where his gesture indicated; close about us the park of the Castle, beyond that the fields and meadows, small, neatly patterned, beyond that Cloncath and the gray glimmer of the sea; I could see Meremount and the two lodges. Mist was beginning to gather in the lower places, along the streams, wreathing into the trees that lined the roads—a gentle, intimate countryside with no hint of the violence of its history. I looked down the sheer drop of a hundred or more feet to the brilliant green turf and thought of the bowmen who had manned these walls, and the battles fought for the possession of these stones— of the last battle that, finally, the Tyrells had lost.

"What does it matter?" I said. I was growing weary of the subject. "What does it matter that it once belonged to the Tyrells? The Tyrells are finished . . . I said that before."

This time he didn't protest. "You're right," he said. "The power doesn't lie with what once was. And the future is still to be fought for. Over there," he added. He nodded his head toward the dark slate roof of Meremount set among its fields. "The Tyrells are finished, but there still could be a future for the Sheridans."

I waited. I wasn't going to help him, nor anticipate him.

"This morning . . ." he began, "this morning when you came into Lady Maude's room we were talking—"

"You were quarreling," I corrected him. "You were shouting —the way you were shouting that first night, the night she had her attack."

He looked at me, startled, his expression darkening. "How did you know?"

"I was wakened by it—why wouldn't I? It was enough to wake anyone. It almost killed her, didn't it? And since then everyone had thought that it was brought on by my coming so suddenly. I've been listening to you lying about it, and letting people go on believing that, and I've been waiting for you to tell me the truth yourself. But you would never have told me the truth, would you?"

He turned upon me, full face, and the man of the despairing rage was back again, the one I was familiar with, the one I knew better than the gentle charmer.

"No, by God, and why should I! If you've had to bear some of this trouble, then it was no more than your due. You came here, uninvited, unannounced—"

"Unwanted," I added.

"Yes—unwanted. You suddenly walked into what I've been building all this time. You just walked in, her granddaughter.

A Tyrell, not just a Sheridan, and she was ready to hand it all to you. So you were responsible—as much as if you had been in the room fighting it out with us."

"Is *that* what you said to her that night?—and this morning?"

"I did—I said it in as many words. You don't think I don't know the old witch? She's a Tyrell, and I've had enough time to find out exactly what that means—and of what she thinks it means, and the rights and privileges it confers. So I told her that if you were in, I was out—that I didn't intend to stay and become dog's body to the next generation of Tyrells."

"If I was in? . . . What did she say to that?"

"Nothing . . . nothing. She said nothing. She couldn't speak. That was when it happened."

"So you still don't know? You still don't know—what was it you said?—if I was in and you were out?"

"No, I don't know, and the old devil will do her best to try to keep it that way—to keep me on a string, and you too, if she can. As long as she's alive, no one will know."

"And that was what you were trying to find out again this morning, wasn't it? That was what the argument was about— the shouting?"

"Yes," he said, and his tone became quieter. "That was what it was about. This morning I heard Annie telephoning Swift and O'Neill. John O'Neill is coming down from Dublin on Monday, so she must have decided on changes in her will."

"Swift and O'Neill?" But I was remembering the name on the letter addressed to Blanche after I had been born.

"The Tyrell solicitors. So, there's going to be changes in the will. That means only one thing—you are in."

"It doesn't mean you are out."

"No, it doesn't necessarily mean that I'm out. But that's what she'll make sure neither of us will know. Not until the day of her funeral when John O'Neill comes to read the will. We'll be kept dangling until then."

"And you would rather she was dead now—before there can be any changes." It could not be left unsaid; it was forced out of me. "Was that what you were trying to do that first night—kill her? Did you try to do it again this morning?"

"Kill her?" The bitterness of tone was only a recognition of things as they were. "I wouldn't be human if I didn't want to at times. But killing isn't that easy. The deed is more difficult than the wish. But anyone who says he's never in his life wished another person dead is lying. Is that what you wanted to know? —did I try to kill her? Well, I didn't put my hands around her throat, and I didn't hit her with anything. But perhaps—yes, perhaps I tried to kill her. That's as much truth as I know. You asked for it. Now you have it."

I had it—or enough of the truth to make all of it sound like the truth. How skillful was he in manipulating the truth, and how much did he rely on its shock value to upset every calculation I had made of him?

"Suppose, just suppose Lady Maude does intend to change her will? To bring me in, but not to leave you out? What then?"

He shook his head. "It can't be done. There's nothing to divide. If you use all of what there is to one purpose—to put the glassworks on its feet, you just might make it. If you try to split it up, you'll destroy the whole."

"And suppose . . . suppose she doesn't intend it to be divided? Suppose the whole is for me?" I heard the cold injustice of what I was saying, but I was beginning to understand the depth of injustice of which the old lady was capable if it would satisfy her sense of what was due the Tyrells.

Connor's faint shrug acknowledged the possibility also, accepting that injustice existed and might be expected. He had already acknowledged the fact that he might have wanted to kill before the injustice could be made a legal fact.

"Then you're welcome to it. Because you'll lose the lot. What Sheridan Glass needs is a Sheridan. It can get along without a genius in glass, like Brendan, because it can continue to do what it has always done. But it needs a Sheridan's guts and sweat behind it. It needs a businessman, not an artist. It needs years of work and no profits taken. If it had just this much it could

struggle up from its knees. In time, Waterford could find its
rival. But it needs a Sheridan—it needs *me*. If you tried to do
it without me you'd go under. Even if you had Praeger money,
even if you had Brendan Carroll, I still think you'd lose it. It
needs a Sheridan."

"I'm a Sheridan."

"Exactly. And so am I. All right—I know I can't do more with
a piece of glass than break it, but no Sheridan since Thomas
himself has worked harder to make a go of the place. Why
waste the strength of that? Why dissipate what we both have?
Instead of dividing, we join strengths. The pragmatic solution."

"That means . . ." I marveled at the calmness of my own
voice ". . . that we would marry."

"Of course." He was sure and confident. "I've said I'd not
be dogs-body to another generation of Tyrells. But I'd work
like a dog for a wife—and if that wife were a Sheridan . . ."

"Is that all I am to you—a Sheridan?"

"You're joking! You don't believe that for a moment. You
don't have to go back to your mirror to be sure that finding a
husband will present no problem for you. You only have to know
the way men look at you—the way I look at you, and Brendan
looks at you, and every man you met today. The old and the
young—including Praeger. Finding a husband will not be your
problem, but choosing one. There are probably a dozen men in
London right now you could marry. Only up to this you've not
been sure enough that any of them is right for you—that Justin
man you told me about—him or anyone else."

"But you're sure you're right for me?"

"I'm sure. Look—I'm not saying I'm the only man you could
marry. I'm saying I'm the best man—given what you are, and
who you are. Given all the conditions that now exist—yes, I'm
sure."

What a game we played, I thought, with our voices held
down, our tones even and controlled, as though what we spoke
of was not an outrageous thing in an age when marriage was
never a contract, but an impulse acted upon. My seeming calm-

ness led him on, and I knew it; but I was fascinated and spell-bound by his ability to weave a future for us together when four days ago we had not laid eyes on each other.

"You're going to say it's all too quick—and what about love? Aren't people who marry supposed to be in love? But couldn't . . . Maura, couldn't we be a little in love right now? Couldn't we be much more in love if we let it happen? You see how it could be, don't you? You *know* how it could be between us. There are things working for us—things working between us already. You're more of a Sheridan than you'll admit or you'd never have come to Ireland in the first place. You're more interested in Sheridan Glass—or me, perhaps—than you'll admit, or you'd never have stayed on. Unless I miss my guess you're not at all sure you want to run back to London and all that modeling business—or you'd never have given up your chance in a film, or taken the risk of getting on the wrong side of all the people who can help you. You'd never have given up anything like that because of a mad old lady. If those kind of things were important to you, you'd have left here after the first hour —certainly after the first night. Why have you stayed? If it's Sheridan Glass you want, then I go with it."

"What about Lotti?"

He raised his eyebrows. "What about her?"

"She didn't stay."

"Lotti wasn't a Sheridan. She wouldn't have stayed here— with me or with any other man, for very long."

"You're so sure about me—couldn't you tell that about Lotti?"

"Lotti was . . ." For the first time he fumbled for a word. "Lotti was an education. I'm not stupid. I learn. I think I've learned the difference."

It had come to other minds, of course, this thought that Connor had dared so quickly to put into words. Other people besides him had seen the way we might go, the convenient arrangement, the pragmatic solution, as Connor called it. I had been too often compared to Lotti, and then the essential differences noted. I remembered the Reverend Patrick Stanton, and how, even in his naïve garrulity, he had happened almost on Connor's very words. "I know the difference" he had said. I had seen that thought flash into the minds of the men I had met in the bar at The Four Kingdoms; it had been plain in the way Brendan had raised his glass to me in his mocking little salute. It had been said in a drunken slur "—this one looks Irish." And then I thought that not even in the cool world of Claude, from which I had seemed to seek some kind of escape, could the sophisticated arrangement between two people have been bettered by what Connor proposed. It was as calculated as anything that other world could contrive.

I looked at the gentle intimacy of the scene below me, the soft fields bathed in the gray light, the marvelous green of the young leaves, the tender curls of gray smoke that came from the chimneys of Castle Tyrell. I saw from the smoke that rose from the chimney at the North Lodge that Brendan was there. One chimney only at Meremount gave sign of life. The mallards moved placidly on the lake, the waves were miniature and harmless. It was a scene of enormous serenity and peace, a scene of innocence. But it was capable of producing the same cool answers to the same questions one had to ask oneself in any place.

I turned and walked back to the narrow opening that gave access to the spiral stairs. Connor was sure enough of the power of his words that he hadn't needed to put his hands on me—not tried to kiss me or call me back. He would leave the coldness of reason to work for him, and that which he said was already working between us. His voice reached me just as I was about to disappear from his sight on the first twist of the spiral.

"You haven't said no."

That was the trouble—I hadn't. I felt my way down carefully in the alternating patches of darkness and light from the narrow slits in the walls; I made my way out of the tower and still Connor's footsteps did not sound behind me. I should have said no at once, but that would have been the square answer to the cool question.

I walked around the base of O'Ruairc's Tower to the front entrance to the Castle. It was already a familiar thing to walk up these steps and see O'Keefe come to the door, to see his acceptance of my being there, as if I had been there always and would be forever. There was no questioning, even by the lift of an eyebrow.

"Please tell Mr. Praeger that I have come to tea."

VI

O'Keefe drove me back to Meremount from Castle Tyrell leaving Otto Praeger with the feeling that he had won a victory. I had merely told him that I had climbed O'Ruairc's Tower, as he had invited me to do. He knew, of course, that I had been with Connor, but he did not question either my leaving him, or the fact that Connor still had a key to the tower. That I had come to him instead of returning with Connor seemed satisfaction enough. He did not press his victory, but was curiously quiet during the hour we spent together, urging tea on me, and showing me his rare books, scrupulous in his avoidance of anything personal; he did not even ask me to come again when I left, as if determined to prove how disciplined he could be. He merely said, "On Monday, I go to New York."

Connor was not at Meremount when I returned. "Himself rang through that he'd not be in this evening," was all Annie said. I spent an hour in Lady Maude's room reading to her. She had indicated a copy of *Country Life*. "There's a piece there about larks," she said. From the way she settled, the eyelids closed, her hands folded together as if in anticipation, I guessed she had read it already, and when it was done she asked me to read it again. I had gone on to a piece about white-tailed deer when Mrs. O'Shea returned.

A look of displeasure came at once to Lady Maude's face. "Tomorrow, Mrs. O'Shea, I'll speak to Dr. Donnelly. Having you here is quite unnecessary. An unnecessary expense . . . After all, my granddaughter is here."

"And I'll take my orders from Dr. Donnelly, thank you, Lady Maude," Mrs. O'Shea replied tartly. "I've no doubt you can do without me, but I'll go when Dr. Donnelly says I'm to go, and not before."

I left them, hearing again, with a sense of dread, the words "my granddaughter is here." It had been easier, if less comfortable, before I began to have this qualified approval from Lady Maude. The knot was pulling tighter.

I grilled chicken in herb butter with garlic for dinner. It was now an unspoken agreement that when Connor was not there, we ate together in the kitchen; then, to postpone the moment when the meal would be finished and the empty hours before bed still to be filled, I made zabaglione, using the last of Connor's cognac in place of marsala. "Sure, you'd never know the difference," Annie said, who had never tasted it either way before. Mrs. O'Shea spooned up the last of it with relish. "A grand beginning to tomorrow's doings," she said. "Great-uncle Patrick always loved his wee drop."

Meremount at night was an unfriendly place. I wandered through the huge, high-ceilinged rooms on the ground floor— the hall, dining room, morning room, drawing room, and library. The few lights that worked only dimly illuminated the vastness, no fires burned in the cold grates; the rooms had no purpose or function except to store the fruits of Lady Maude's garnering. Half-heartedly I looked at some pictures stacked one against the other—still life, hunting scenes—they had probably been bought in lots at auction, and I didn't know enough to pick the better ones that Otto Praeger said could be buried here. Connor's office would have provided a place to sit; a fire was laid ready for a match. But that, least of all, was the place I wanted Connor to find me when he came back. So I climbed the stairs; Lotti's cat went with me to the first landing; there she stayed, watching me, a single low plaintive yowl proclaiming the emptiness of that crowded house, the endless melancholy of her wait for the girl who did not come back.

Passing Lady Maude's door I caught the low tones of the two women inside, the latest phase of the unremitting battle they fought for supremacy. I was surprised by the strength and clarity of Lady Maude's tone.

Then late, but before I slept, there came the sound of Connor's car. He entered the house through the kitchen. It seemed a long time before the stairs creaked with his weight. Suddenly, in the quiet, was the cry of Lotti's cat, and the muffled admonition that followed it. Then the footsteps continued on their journey, up the stairs and along the passage, the tread soft, but the old house betraying it. Finally he reached my door, and stopped. I waited, and heard my own swift, hard intake of breath. I didn't know whether I wanted the door to open or not, and in that moment of waiting I seemed powerless either to invite or protest—perhaps I lacked the courage and the will for what I desired in my heart. But the decision was not mine. Very close at hand now there came, once more, the cry of the cat, and then the door trembled as if the cat's body had brushed against it. There followed Connor's breathy exclamation of annoyance, the stifled curse. Then he must have picked up the cat, because its cry was not repeated. I heard the footsteps move off along the hall in the direction of Connor's room. They did not return. I lay there wakeful for a long time, and I was feeling as I had felt that afternoon as I descended the tower steps and Connor's voice had cried after me "You didn't say no." But this time my body had been roused and he would have had a greater weapon than mere reason or persuasion. If he had come to me here in the darkness my senses might have made the answer he sought.

CHAPTER 9

I

The sound of the horn in the driveway came about ten in the morning; it was a gentle sound, but impudent, somehow gay. I guessed who it was, and I ran to the front door before Annie could get there. Brendan leaned against the iron balustrade of the steps.

"Good morning to you, *allanah*. I've been told by those who should know that it's very rude to honk for a lady, but I'll be damned if I can make the bell work. Is it the fairies have got to it, do you think, or just that Lady Maude doesn't want callers?"

I looked at him; he was smiling, relaxed; he looked back at me with untroubled eyes; there was no beginning of conflict here, no anger waiting to rise. I hadn't known until this moment how tense I was, waiting for something to happen, a little afraid, the fear centered in this house, centered in the highly charged involvement between Connor, Lady Maude, and myself.

I answered, saying quite simply, the truth. "It sounded like the trumpet of liberation to me. But you're going, aren't you? Isn't this the day you leave?"

"Well," he said, "that could depend on you. There's always more time to be leaving in, isn't there now?—always another plane, tomorrow or the next day. I was thinking I'd say my farewell to this Ireland of the legends in a fitting manner if I could persuade you to share the farewell with me. I'm of a mind to feast my eyes again on the Rock of Cashel—and it seemed

to me that I could do no better with my last day on the auld
sod than to introduce one of Ireland's chief glories to a new-
found Irishwoman. Will you come, then?"

Mrs. O'Shea had already departed, dressed in splendid black,
for the funeral of Great-uncle Patrick; I had just finished preparing poached salmon to be eaten cold for lunch. My turn in
the sickroom would not be until four o'clock. I was suddenly
free, and it had become a holiday.

"I'll come," I answered.

✓　✓　✓　✓

"Cashel of the Kings," he said. "The ancient seat of the Kings
of Munster—they do say that St. Patrick himself came here to
baptize one of them."

We had come upon it from the north, a great, dramatic outcropping of limestone rising two hundred feet out of the Plain
of Tipperary. More strongly here did one feel the past even than
in O'Ruairc's Tower—here, century piled on century. First the
great cross of St. Patrick, raised against a windswept sky, set in a
stone the legends said was the coronation stone of the Kings of
Munster; it had stood a thousand years with the black rooks
cawing above it and the Irish rains beating upon it, gradually
smoothing out its carved faces, while the building of a holy
and sacred place grew up about it.

"The Round Tower," Brendan said, "has been here since the
tenth century. Cormac's Chapel"—leading me into a gleaming
jewel of red sandstone—"is twelfth century. Built by Cormac
MacCarthy, King of Desmond. They say it's the best example of
Hiberno-Romanesque architecture anywhere in Ireland—but
then since the English didn't leave us too much of anything, I
suppose that isn't too great a distinction. Come, the cathedral
is very grand and big, but it won't move you the way Cormac's
Chapel does."

"You know it all very well."

"Someone brought me here when I was a kid—all my broth-

ers and sisters, too—and I went daft over the place. I used to
save up bus fare to come here when I started as an apprentice
with Sheridan Glass. Instead of taking out the prettiest girl
I knew, the first thing I did when I got my first car—a very old
car, mind you—was to drive here. I remember it was a Saturday, and pouring with rain, and I was here all alone. I climbed
up to the top of the Round Tower, and I felt as if I were the
King of Munster. People do tell me that one of my troubles is
that I occasionally act that way. Daft, you know."

We wandered within the open-skied vastness of the cathedral.
"Thirteenth century," Brendan said. "Unroofed in the eighteenth century by order of the Protestant Dean of Cashel, of
hated memory." Above the rooks wheeled and circled endlessly; they seemed eternal, like the Cross and the sky; we
climbed the ninety feet of the Round Tower and looked out
over the plain and to the ruinous Hore Abbey, half a mile from
the Rock. "I've always wanted to own a ruin," Brendan said.
"It's such a splendidly useless thing—and this is such a damn
practical world."

Outside the cathedral black-faced sheep grazed on the rich
grass clothing the burial ground; we walked among the tomb-
stones, the sheep moving only slightly to let us by, and I read
names and dates. The archbishops slept in their stony niches
within the walls of the cathedral; out here humbler people of
the countryside were buried. Some of the dates on the slabs
were recent.

"When I'm very old," Brendan said "—and mind you, I intend to live to a great old age, the Bomb or not—when I'm
very old and I feel death coming on me like a chill, then I'll
come to live near Cashel so that I can be buried up here, with
the sheep and the ruins and the rooks."

It began to rain, and the roofless spaces of the cathedral
were washed with opal mist; we came down off the Rock,
climbed over a gate and walked across a small field to the garden
of the Queen Anne mansion that had been the Palace of the
Archbishops of Cashel. "Them that took the roof off," Brendan

commented darkly. It had been turned into a small luxury hotel, and lunch was served in a room that reminded me of the dining room at Meremount, if the Meremount room had been cleared of furniture and its proportions had been visible.

As we drank coffee, I asked the question that had been on my lips almost since the beginning of the journey.

"Did you bring Lotti here?"

He looked up from his cup. "I did. It wasn't much of a success. Lotti wasn't the kind of girl for ruins."

"But you brought her here thinking she was?"

"Hoping she was, perhaps, but knowing that she came just for the hell of it—to get away from Meremount, perhaps to have something to throw at Connor when she complained that he never took her anywhere. But coming to see some ruins wasn't Lotti's idea of going anywhere at all. Going somewhere meant London or Paris—"

"Or Copenhagen?"

"Yes," he said. "Or Copenhagen."

"You're hard on her. But yet you loved her."

"I told you I fell in love with Lotti the first night I met her. Loving comes after falling in love. Sometimes it never comes."

"Did it with you?"

He shook his head. "It wasn't meant to. Love, for Lotti, would have been a burden too great to carry. She didn't understand it—well, who does, for that matter? But she didn't want it. She wanted to go to bed with a man she liked, and have fun with him. Nothing was meant to be serious. But Connor was serious—he was serious about a lot of things, particularly Sheridan Glass and marriage. She got bored—but more frightened, I think, than bored. She couldn't stand the responsibility of anyone being desperately serious about her—so she turned to me. What she never knew was that I, under all this nonsense I talk, was just as serious as Connor. She wanted a playmate, and I—well, I suppose I wanted to be loved. When I knew I wasn't going to get that I was ready to finish it."

"But you didn't finish it. You were on your way to Copenhagen with her. You would both have had your few days of fun, and Connor was never to know. Wasn't that the way it was?"

Again he shook his head. "No, that wasn't the way it was. Yes, I went along with the plan for her to come to Copenhagen and say she was going to London—I agreed, because it was very hard to say no to Lotti. But then I wanted to call it off. I could imagine how it would be in Copenhagen—yes, that part of it any man would have wanted with a girl like Lotti. But it was what it would have been like afterward that I couldn't either imagine or face. Back at Cloncath, working with Connor, seeing Lotti at the works almost every day and carrying on as if that was all I saw of her. I can lie with the best of them if I have to. But a sustained lie, a lie that I had to carry on, not for the love of a woman but only for the sake of possessing her—well, I just didn't think I could stand it. I was out of my depth. Lotti was too much for me, and at last I got enough sense to admit it."

"But you still were going to Copenhagen?" I hoped I sounded skeptical. The truth was that Brendan had touched a part of me that no man had ever found before, the deep need in me to know that some man had wanted love as much as I had, and did; had understood enough of it to know that what was offered was not the real thing, who had refused to give more when he knew that what he was paid back was false coin. He had wanted the responsibility of loving, had sought the burden of it, the obligation. I felt strangely envious of Lotti as I listened, envious and sadly wondrous at what she had rejected. Of all the things she had been given in her life, she hadn't known how to take the one thing of value. She had cast away the thing I hadn't yet found—she had been offered love, and she had wanted only pleasure.

"There would have been no trip to Copenhagen," Brendan said. "At least, not with me. I was going to tell her when she came that night that it wouldn't work. I was going to tell her that she would take her plane to London, just as she had told

Connor she was taking it. And I would go to Copenhagen and do the job I was supposed to do. And I would look around for someone to take my place at Sheridan Glass. Yes—I was running from her. I was running for my life. But I took too long to understand that it had to be that way. I didn't tell her in time. I waited until that night, and then it was too late. The bridge came down, and I was too late to stop her coming. And they knew—Connor and Praeger—that I was the one she was coming to."

"You didn't tell them . . . about you deciding it was all over . . . calling off the Copenhagen trip?"

His lips twisted. "And deny Lotti when she was dead? She wasn't the kind of girl you did that to, either. We were both as guilty as hell, whether Copenhagen was part of the story or not. I had almost loved Lotti, and I wasn't going to take that away from her after she was dead. God knows, few enough people loved her then—not the ones who should have."

And then he beckoned the waiter and paid the bill. It rained all the way back to Meremount; we didn't talk and we both smoked too much.

*   *   *   *

Brendan halted the car when we were halfway down the avenue to Meremount. The rain was coming down heavily now, the rapid swish of the windshield wipers was like a knell to the day.

"Would you ever," he said, "give an Irishman a kiss on his last day on his native soil? He that took you to Cashel of the Kings, don't forget?"

I leaned toward him; there was sweetness and some heartbreak in our kiss. He held me for a long time close against him, his fingers stroking my neck, twining in my hair. He said, very softly, as he released me, "Will I ever, I wonder, see you again . . . ?"

I had no answer; I was not meant to answer, then.

He drew the car in close to the steps at Meremount; the rain poured down solidly. But some prickling sixth sense made me glance upward as I ran up the wet steps to the front door. Connor was at the window of the upstairs room at the end of the house on the right. The window was curtainless, the room used for nothing but the storage of furniture. He did not attempt to move back to avoid my gaze, but met it with the same calm assurance, akin to arrogance, he had always shown. He would have seen that the car had stopped before it had drawn up to the steps; probably he guessed what had happened then.

When I closed the door I went to a side window and watched as Brendan turned the car, and it started up the avenue and then vanished. I wanted to call him back; the sense of foreboding that this house possessed so strongly reached and gripped me. I felt a sense of menace in it. The rain-dark afternoon deepened the shadows of the hall and the staircase. I waited for the door of the room from which Connor had watched to open when I reached the bedroom floor, but it remained closed, the silence more threatening somehow, than if it had opened with a crash. Connor had a way of making his displeasure felt. For the first time I began to wonder if there had not been more reason than sheer self-indulgence in Lotti's flight from Connor.

II

After I had changed I went to take my turn in Lady Maude's room. Annie brought tea for us both, announcing that Connor had been and gone again, and that he wouldn't be in to dinner.

"Very restless, Mr. Connor is these days—all this coming and going. He's as bad as when—"

Lady Maude cut her short. "Annie, don't gossip."

I marveled that she had never learned that no one in these times could speak in that fashion to servants and expect them to stay—but Annie seemed not to have learned either. She took the rebuke meekly. "Yes, m'lady." The Tyrells did not count any more, except with those for whom they still counted very much.

The evening dragged slowly by. I asked if Lady Maude had any sewing for me to do; her gesture of reply was impatient, almost contemptuous. "Sewing? No. Annie puts a stitch in anything that needs doing. I have no time for fuss or feathers." I thought of the cobbled darns in the worn damask napkins we used, and knew the extent of Annie's needlework. Lady Maude indicated an article on wood anemones that I was to read aloud, and when that was done she had me sift through a stack of ancient *National Geographic* for a favorite piece on the high Himalayas. The description of the snows and the solitude seemed to soothe her; when she spoke again her tone was softer.

"Tomorrow we will begin Churchill's *Life of Marlborough*." She indicated a row of volumes on the mantelshelf. Going closer I saw that they were all Churchill works, from his account of the Boer War right through World War II. I had a sudden frightful vision of myself trapped in this house reading Churchill and the *National Geographic* to an old woman who refused to die.

When Lady Maude was settled for the night, after Annie had brought the last cup of tea and herself gone upstairs, I took my bath in the room adjoining hers; it was a quick business because the water was tepid and the place was stamped with the grimness that most of Meremount wore. I was a little intimidated, perhaps, by the sight of Lady Maude's toothbrushes, the worn facecloth and sponge, the few toilet articles that lay about, bespeaking the austerity of her life. As I splashed hurriedly in the bath I heard Connor come in; I heard his voice in the hall outside as he spoke to Sapphire, then the quiet of the night fell completely on Meremount. Then I lay in bed—Mrs. O'Shea's bed—with my feet on Annie's hot water bottles and pondered the slow twilight of this aristocrat, who had long ago given up concern with the world about her, neglected by that world, supremely indifferent to the neglect, her imagination feasting on such things as white-tailed deer and wood anemones, and the snowbound reaches of the high Himalayas. And as I had previously thought of myself trapped in that existence I now thought of Connor.

III

"For God's sake will you wake up, miss? Wake up!" For the second time since I had come to Meremount I was shaken out of sleep, but this time with rough, purposeful hands. "There—gather yourself up and run downstairs and get Dr. Donnelly on the phone. Tell him he's needed out here."

The only light came from Lady Maude's room—the two connecting doors were open, and Mrs. O'Shea's figure was outlined by it. She wore her hat and coat still, and the gloved hands with which she had shaken me were damp with rain. I struggled out of sleep, sitting up slowly.

"What's the matter?" My head ached; with great effort I held my eyelids open.

"Gas!—that's what's the matter. The gas fire in the bathroom left turned on and the flame out, and God alone knows what it will have done to my patient. Hurry now, tell Dr. Donnelly I don't know the damage, but he'd be best to come. And he'd better telephone for the ambulance."

Then Mrs. O'Shea's body stiffened as a call came from the bedroom. "Maura—Maura, are you there?"

"It's her—and praise God she sounds all right. No, don't waste time going in to her. I'll attend to that." Mrs. O'Shea called this after her as she hurried through the bathroom. "Ring through to Dr. Donnelly. But I don't think we need the ambulance . . ."

Then I heard her voice, authoritative as ever, showing none of the alarm it had betrayed when she had shaken me from

sleep. "Well, now, Lady Maude, what's all this? A fine scare
you've given me, and me just back this minute from a funeral.
Now, just let me look at you—well, I had to open the windows
to get a bit of fresh air. Very stuffy it was in here. A fine night
it's going to be after all. The rain'll be done in no time at all,
so it will."

I found slippers and gown and ran for the phone in Connor's
office. Only the light from the upstairs passage illuminated the
stairs. On the way down I brushed against a pile of brass fire
tools stacked on one of the treads. They went hurtling before
me, taking a whole mountain of small pieces with them. At
the bottom in the darkness I heard Lotti's cat give a howl of
fear, and then I heard, but could not see, her terrified scamper
through the hall.

I got through to Dr. Donnelly at once. "I don't understand
what it's all about. Mrs. O'Shea's just come back and wakened
me. Something about a gas fire being on without being lighted,
and she thinks Lady Maude may have been affected. But I heard
her talk—she seems all right."

"I'll come at once," he said.

I switched on whatever lights in the hall were working, and
the main light on the staircase, and picked up the worst of the
debris of my encounter with the fire tools. A Chinese vase was
broken; I wondered if it was valuable, but I didn't much care,
since I could have been broken along with it. I was aware of an
anger rising in me, that gradually came to take over from my
fright. Damn it, where was Connor?

He was in Lady Maude's bathroom. I came through Mrs.
O'Shea's room, picking up my cigarettes and lighter on the way.
The smell of gas was present, but not strongly. The windows
in the bathroom and Lady Maude's room were open. Connor was
bending to pick up something from behind the door. When he
straightened I saw what it was. He held a bath mat in his hand
which he tossed away from him when he saw me. The gesture
was elaborately casual; he aimed for the rim of the bathtub,

where the mat usually hung, and missed. It fell to the floor with a soft thud.

"I wouldn't do that if I were you," he said, pointing toward the cigarettes and lighter in my hand. "You might blow us all sky-high."

I thrust them into the pocket of my gown. Over his pajamas Connor was wearing a dark blue robe that seemed superlatively luxurious by contrast to the rest of his clothes—cashmere or vicuna, I guessed. It had probably been a gift from Lotti; it bore her stamp, even to the color. Somehow the sight of it, of Connor himself so collected and casual, made me angrier.

"How did it all happen?" I demanded. "I didn't leave the gas fire on." I went to the door of Lady Maude's room where both Annie and Mrs. O'Shea were now hovering over the old lady. I could tell from the way they spoke and acted that Lady Maude was all right. I could hear the thin old voice querulously demanding a cup of tea, and an explanation for the whole household being in her bedroom at this hour. "Two o'clock in the morning," she said.

"And none of it would have happened if I'd have been here," Mrs. O'Shea said, looking darkly at me. "As it was, it was a great mercy I decided to come back when I did—had my nephew Rory drop me off here. Sure the funeral was a washout. One of those new parish priests in charge down there who doesn't believe"—here she mocked his tone—"in turning a funeral into a party! So it broke up early and I decided to ride back with Rory. I'll not be able to face Dr. Donnelly and tell him I've let an inexperienced young girl—"

"Will you hold your tongue, woman!" The demand burst from Lady Maude. "There is no harm done. I am perfectly well. I wish everyone to leave me alone, and I want some tea, Annie."

"You almost weren't perfectly well, Lady Maude." Connor came to stand beside me. "I assume that Maura left the gas fire burning when she finished in the bathroom last night—but of course that would have just gone on burning until the tanks were used up. The trouble was in the gas pipe itself. A connection's broken—a bad solder job, I suppose. If you'd had too many hours of it, it could have made you very sick."

"Might have finished her off," came from Mrs. O'Shea, too disturbed to mind her words. "I always sleep with my bedroom door open and the door of this room open so that I can hear what is happening to my patient. I would have smelled the gas —but then, the young sleep heavily."

"That infernal gadget!" Lady Maude plucked at the sheets angrily. "I wish you to have it removed in the morning, Connor. I hold you responsible for its installation, remember. When these things are done behind my back there's bound to be trouble. If you have to sneak in to do a job like that in a few hours, what can you expect but poor workmanship?"

Connor shrugged, as if he didn't care how she criticized him. "What I'd better do right now is go down and shut off the tank. There's no way to stop the flow of gas here because the copper tubing's come apart. You must have kicked it, or something, last night, Maura. An accident, of course, but unfortunate." And then, coolly, he turned and walked out through the bathroom, leaving us four women to stare at one another, or at least the three of them to stare at me, their eyes accusing me of criminal carelessness.

Even against the force of my boiling anger I managed to keep my mouth closed on the words that wanted to come spilling out at Connor. I wanted to run out into the passage and scream after him that it had not been my doing, that I had not even lighted the fire, and had left the door of my room open as Mrs. O'Shea had instructed me. I wanted to demand to know, right there and then, why Connor had been picking up the bath mat which I distinctly remembered having folded over the rim of the tub. I knew, from the position he had been in when he stooped to get it, that it had been bunched up behind the door—that in her haste Mrs. O'Shea had not noticed it there, had simply swept it aside in the dark as she opened my door and called to me.

I wanted, to his face and before Lady Maude, to accuse him

of having closed my door and laid the bath mat along the crack at the bottom. The gas then would flow only one way—into Lady Maude's bedroom. Given enough hours of even that small amount of gas, she might have suffered another attack from lack of oxygen and the increasing struggle for breath. By early morning Connor could have removed the mat and opened my door again. It was a crude and hastily improvised plan, possibly conceived at the moment when he had passed the bathroom and heard my movements, the splashing in the tub. But it might have been fatally effective. Mrs. O'Shea's early return had not been part of the plan.

But I held back on the accusation. I had learned enough to know that if I said these words now, they would have traveled by Mrs. O'Shea's tongue to the four corners of Cloncath by tomorrow night. I needed time to think, and I was learning the kind of evil compact that one makes against scandal—the kind that Brendan and Praeger and Connor had made over the death of Lotti. I wasn't sure then what I would do. I could cry "murder," and pull down the pillars of this house about our heads. Or by my silence I could shore up the outer structure while it continued to rot within. By remaining silent even in these minutes I took the first step into the compact of lies.

IV

"I've given her something so that she will sleep." Dr. Donnelly slumped a little in the chair at Connor's desk as he drank his tea. "It's impossible to determine what damage, if any, has been done without tests. And that means hospital. Lady Maude has never been in hospital in her life. It seems to me more risky to subject her to that"—he gestured, and no more words were necessary because all of us could imagine that determined old woman expending the last of her strength in battles with nurses and hospital routine—"than to let her remain here. When she is more rested I will have to take the chance. She could be in and out of hospital in a few days, and then I would know better how to treat her. In the meantime she is to rest. Try not to let anything disturb or worry her."

He looked around us—Connor, Mrs. O'Shea, Annie, and myself—and his gentle gaze was vaguely accusatory, as if demanding to know how we could have let that night's episode occur. None of us, not even Mrs. O'Shea, had any defense to offer, or we were ashamed to try.

"With rest . . . with devoted care, she may recover almost entirely. She could have many years yet." Then he shook his head. "But the Tyrells are not a strong line, and she is already old . . ." He began writing on his prescription pad. "Now, Mrs. O'Shea, I want you to send into Cloncath for these, and administer . . ."

While they engaged in their professional talk my own gaze stayed on Connor. I had been watching him as Dr. Donnelly had said that there might be years yet for Lady Maude; he had made a supreme effort for control, but knowing his face as I had come to know it, I saw that already he was experiencing the long agony of his wait, the years when his youth went from him, but the power to do, to direct and order as he wanted, still denied him. He had longed for the chance to work for Sheridan Glass with all his skill and strength, but as its master, not as the servant of an old woman. I believed that this night he had taken a desperate risk to win that freedom, and he had failed. The knowledge of failure and of what he must endure in the future seemed written on his face for me to read.

CHAPTER 10

I

The few hours until the dawn were slow; after Dr. Donnelly had left all of us went back to our rooms—Mrs. O'Shea, though, I imagined, would be the only one to sleep. This morning there could be no companionable dawn breakfast for Connor and me. I dressed, and I paced the room to keep warm, and at six o'clock, as quietly as I could, I left the house. The engine of the MG was cold—it took long, noisy minutes to get it started. Connor must have heard it in that time, but he made no attempt to come and find out where I was going.

Already the countryside was beginning to stir. I met farm lorries with livestock on the way to market; the herds had been milked and were back in their fields, in the farm laborers' cottages men got in an hour's work on their vegetable gardens before it was time to go to work. I was comforted by the sense of the people about me, by the friendly lifting of a finger to acknowledge me, although I was a stranger. The hours since Dr. Donnelly's departure had been the loneliest I had ever lived through; I drew the friendly presence of these people about me like a warm robe to ease my hurt and fear.

The woman at the South Lodge of Castle Tyrell recognized me. "You're early this morning, miss," she said as she came to open the gates. "But sure isn't Mr. Praeger an early riser too."

At the Castle, though, I did not cross the bridge, but continued on along the avenue to the North Lodge. The barricades at the remains of the bridge were an ugly reminder of that first conspiracy of silence.

Brendan heard the car and came to the door.

"You're early this morning, *allanah*." Almost the words the woman at the lodge had used, but the tone was of concern, not surprise. "What troubles you?"

"I wish I were sure." The living room was stripped. Roped-up boxes stood piled together ready for the movers. Brendan's bags were packed and waiting near the door. I was aware of a terrible sense of desolation at the sight of them; he was going, and I would be left alone. I had no certainty now, as I had had two days ago, that I could handle whatever came my way.

"You look terrible," he said candidly. "Wait a minute . . ." The kettle was on the boil, and he went and put instant coffee into two mugs, mixed it with thick cream and sugared it heavily. He carried one mug to me, and I took a sip, winced at the sweetness, but savored its warmth. He gave me a cigarette and grasped my wrist to steady its trembling as he held the lighter. Then he brought his own mug of coffee and sat down on the sofa beside me.

"Now tell me," he said.

With as much clarity and detachment as I could, I told him what had happened at Meremount in the early hours of that morning. He listened to the end without interrupting.

"You're certain you left both doors open?"

"As certain as anyone can be—it's confusing when everyone tells you something different, and you begin to ask yourself could you have been mistaken."

"And the gas fire—you turned it off?"

"That's just the point. I never lit it. I was in such a hurry to be done with my bath that I didn't take time to let the room warm up—you know, Lady Maude is right next door, and I'm sure she'd think it was frivolous to stay in a bath a second more than was necessary."

"And the bath mat?"

"I *know* I put it across the bath." Suddenly my weariness and the doubts that the intervening hours had allowed to creep in seemed too much for me. I put down the mug and held my hand across my eyes. "I'm so afraid now," I said. "I'm afraid of what all this means. I'm afraid to stay, and yet I can't leave her alone with him. If I speak out the scandal and fuss may kill her, and I'm not sure anything can be proved. When Mrs. O'Shea goes she'll be alone with him . . ."

I heard his movement as he left my side, and then the burr of the telephone dial.

"Good morning . . . O'Keefe? This is Brendan Carroll. Is Mr. Praeger awake? . . . Good. Would you tell him, please, that I am bringing Miss D'Arcy to the Castle. We'll be there in about five minutes. Thank you."

He hung up and turned to me. "Come on," he said. "We'll both drive. We might need the two cars."

"Why are we going to see him?"

He slipped on a sweater over his open-necked shirt. "It's time someone spoke up around here."

✓ ✓ ✓ ✓

O'Keefe met us as we came up the steps. "Good morning, Miss D'Arcy. Good morning, Mr. Carroll."

"How are you, Kevin?" Brendan answered.

"Grand, sir—just grand, Bren." A look of a kind of amused acceptance passed between them. I wondered about it, and then realized that they were about the same age; they had probably sat in the same schoolroom together. It was likely that O'Keefe remembered Brendan as his own description of himself—little Bren Carroll slogging up the lane in his brother's gumboots. It was hard to realize how far-reaching were the ties of this country life, how long were the memories when the threads were not broken by the pace and changes of a city, or of a land upset by war. It helped to explain how Lady Maude, without power, without money, without friends almost, still commanded respect and obedience.

O'Keefe had coffee and a dish of toast kept hot under a silver cover for us. The cups were huge, and we gratefully drank the half and half mixture of coffee and hot milk. "How in the world," Brendan murmured, crunching into the toast, "does Otto Praeger manage to get anyone to make coffee like this in Ireland?" The decision, whatever had formed it, to come to Otto Praeger seemed to have released him. He did not appear anxious or worried as he sipped his coffee and gazed out over the lake; there was an early, pale sun, and the dew glazed the lawn like frost. But he was watching me also; as I put a cigarette into my mouth I felt his hand gently again on my wrist.

"Not another one—not yet. You'll smoke too many before the day's out, I'll guarantee you."

It didn't seem hard to put it away when his concern urged it.

We heard Otto Praeger's step and his cane on the stairs. He came toward us slowly, no sign of curiosity at our presence, carefully shaved and dressed, smelling of bay rum.

"Good morning," he said. His accent seemed heavier than I remembered, as if his tongue had not had enough practice with English this early in the day. He gestured to me and to the coffeepot. "Would you please? Ah, thank you . . . Now, Mr. Carroll?"

Brendan repeated, more succinctly, what I had told him. It made odd telling—a few facts and more uncertainty. What it wasn't able to convey was the feeling of fear that had grown upon me, the sense of menace, the conviction that my own will became weaker as Connor's dominance grew. What it lacked, because Brendan did not know of it, was the monstrous coolness of the proposition Connor had made to me in O'Ruairc's Tower, the kind of strength it had carried because of Connor's own conviction of the rightness of his claim.

"There's much more than that . . ." I heard myself saying when Brendan had finished. "Things have mounted up . . . oh, I can't tell you them all, but enough to make me believe—"

"Yes, enough." Praeger waved his hand to finish for me. His face, always pale, seemed now like a flaccid mass of dough; I wondered if he were feeling ill. He raised his head and looked at Brendan.

"She must be told—yes, yes, I understand why you have come. We each gave an undertaking of silence. But that undertaking did not include the possibility of harm to another person—harm now to Maura through her involvement here. But she will not hear only what we have to say—she will hear all sides of the story. Come, we will go to Meremount."

II

Annie went upstairs to tell Connor that we were there, and I led Praeger and Brendan to Connor's office. Annie's face worked strangely when she saw who it was with me, a nervous twitching of the lips, a swift plucking at her apron.

"Right away, Miss Maura—I'll tell him right away."

Praeger stood for a moment in the door of the office looking back into the hall. I wondered what it was that absorbed him, and it was a shock to realize how, in less than a week, my own eyes had ceased to be amazed at the sight of the tiers of furniture, had come to take it all for granted; I was even slightly offended by the shake of his head and the click of his tongue.

"Ach!—it does not change, this place—only more of it!" Then he added, "What a prize—what a prize it is!"

He came and sat heavily in the armchair before the ashes of yesterday's fire. It was chilly in the room; I wondered if Praeger felt it after the perfectly maintained warmth of Castle Tyrell. I said, tentatively, because I wasn't sure it could be managed, "Would you like a fire? There's turf in the basket there, and I could get some kindling from the kitchen. The only thing"—now I looked at Brendan for help—"is that I haven't got the knack yet of lighting a peat fire."

Brendan shook his head. "I hear Connor coming."

There was a low-toned exchange of words on the stairs, a glimpse of Annie as she passed the door of the office with a quick, nervous jerk of her head, and then Connor himself stood in the doorway.

"Well, we are all assembled, I see. Good morning, Mr. Praeger—Meremount hasn't been honored with your presence for quite some time. Maura . . . Brendan . . . It's very early in the day, isn't it, for all this activity? What's the occasion?"

I felt the thrust once more of his sureness, and of my own doubts. He moved into the room and even the presence of Praeger was made a little less important. He seemed to make his own pace; Brendan waited until Connor had picked up a pack of cigarettes from the mantel, offered one to me, which I refused, and then lighted his own, before he spoke.

"Maura came to see me this morning, Connor—"

"So I gathered. And woke all of us getting out of here, too."

"Blast it, man, will you shut up and listen! She came to tell me what happened here last night."

"Last night? Oh yes, we had quite an eventful night. Nothing serious, though. Could have been. I'm thinking of suing Leo Dougherty for the bad job his men did in installing that gas fire. Of course, it was done in half an hour, more or less, but still . . . I suppose I should have noticed the state of it myself, but I never go into that bathroom, and every other thing in the house is falling apart . . ."

For the first time Praeger spoke, and the thick, heavy voice seemed to dispel the lightness that somehow Connor had managed to convey. "Maura does not think last night was an accident, Connor."

His black eyebrows shot up. "She doesn't? What was it then?"

Brendan answered, "She thinks—"

I cut him short. "I'll say this for myself, Brendan. If it's going to be said, I'll say it. I think, Connor, that you broke the joint in the pipe yourself. That you closed the door to my room and stuffed the bath mat along the bottom of it so that I wouldn't smell the gas. It was meant for Lady Maude, wasn't it? —in the hope that if she just got enough of it it might bring on another attack. Mrs. O'Shea didn't notice the mat in her hurry, but you were picking it up when I came in—the one thing I'm sure about is that I put it across the tub—"

"Of course you're sure about it, because that's where I found it."

"Then what were you—?"

He cut in, "How do you suppose I got the window open? I don't think anyone's raised that sash in ten years. I had to pound at it with my fists to get it to budge. I simply used the mat as a pad for my hands. If I happened to drop it just where it suited your suspicions to see it. . . ."

I felt the questioning gaze of both Praeger and Brendan on me, and the doubt was established more strongly than before. Connor had had time, of course, to find an explanation for the mat. At the same time it sounded like the truth. But I didn't believe him.

He took my silence for uncertainty. "Do you seriously think," he said, "I would be capable of anything—"

"Yes, I do," I burst out. "I do think you'd be capable of it. I think you meant her to die!"

"You haven't let me finish," he said, and his calmness was an unnerving contrast to my growing agitation. "I was going to say that it would be an incredibly clumsy effort, wouldn't it?— and I should be credited with a better try. And why should I do it? Lady Maude is old—in her own time she will die. I've endured this situation quite some time now—I can last a little longer."

"No," I said. "You forget—you forget that you told me you knew the solicitor was coming on Monday. You think you could lose it, after all—all the work, all the waiting. You may lose it because I have come and Lady Maude may make a new will."

He shrugged. "I hadn't forgotten. But let me stir your memory a little more. I also said that anyone who says that he's never wished another soul dead in his whole life is a liar. And then I said the wish is not the deed. There's a very long step between one and the other. I haven't taken that step yet."

"But you didn't need to the last time, did you?" It was Brendan who spoke. "The other time the deed was done for you. You had the wish and all you had to do was to wait and let the deed happen. No one else had to do the deed—Lotti did it herself."

Finally, something had reached to Connor. I thought that his face had altered and taken on that "black look" of my own fancy. It was startling to discover how well I had come to know him, to anticipate the change of expression, the passage from cold to hot—in the way I had come to know the whole strange world of Meremount and to accept it. The danger lay in the acceptance.

"For God's sake why bring Lotti into this? Lotti is dead—and it's all done with."

"That's what we thought then." Brendan's words now were not a challenge to Connor, but a recollection; they were thoughtful and slow. "We thought, the three of us, that when we had made our compact all to do with Lotti was finished. There was no point in raking over the coals. We agreed to preserve of her what there was left, which was the way people felt about her. We agreed, you and I, Connor, to preserve some tranquillity for Mr. Praeger and Lady Maude, even if there could be none for ourselves. It made no sense to tell what no one needed to know." He lifted his hands, including the other two men. "So we said then."

"And so I say now." Connor's face had resumed its familiar look of rigid control; his voice was tighter. "Nothing has changed."

"Something has changed. Maura is here—she has changed it. Her whole involvement in this house, with all of us, has changed it."

"What the hell has this to do with last night?" Connor demanded. "You're talking wildly—you're saying things you've no business to say."

"Things that have to be said now. Maura might walk out of here tomorrow. Then again, she might stay—"

"No!"

He paid no attention to my protest. "It's her right to stay, if she wants to. Then again, perhaps you've persuaded her to stay —who knows? You're not the only one, Connor, who can see the advantages of that. If she stays—if she even thinks of staying, she has to know."

"I don't agree. This is nothing to do with Maura."

"You think, Connor, that I would permit Maura to be drawn closely into the family without telling her." Praeger was very sparing in his participation, but when he spoke it was decisive. "She may decide yes or no—but she must be allowed to decide knowing all that we know. Now, I think we had better call in the woman—Annie?"

"Tell her, then," Connor said roughly. "But for pity's sake don't drag Annie back into it. At least we can be spared the tears and the lamentations."

"If she hears it from Annie she will hear it as we did. Nothing will have been added or taken away . . ."

"No, nothing added except the hysteria and whatever fancies she had embroidered into the tale since last November—"

"Call her," Praeger commanded, cutting Connor off.

Brendan went out into the hall. "Annie . . . ? Will she be in the kitchen, Maura?" But Annie had hovered near the dining-room door, apparently expecting the summons. She appeared in view, her apron twisting in her hands, her shoulders assuming a defensive hunch.

"You called, sir?" She was not quite sure to whom to address the question; positions in this room had undergone a change, authority was uncertain. Praeger decided to assume it.

"Yes, Annie, come in. Close the door, please."

She was slow in doing it, and when she turned her face had registered a frank reluctance, a kind of dread. "Oh, sir, it's not going to start all over again, is it? I mean, sure I try not to think about it, the way you said, but I can't help it. I've barely had a decent night's sleep since it all happened, and that's the truth of it . . ."

Connor flung out his arms, his teeth clenching in exaspera-
tion. "Is this going to go on . . . ?"

"Annie," Brendan said gently, "we know it's hard, but if you
didn't keep quiet, Lady Maude would have been through a
dreadful time, wouldn't she? And you wouldn't have let that
happen to her, when there was no way to bring Mrs. Sheridan
back?"

"No, sir, and I stick by it. But I wisht . . . ah, well, I made a
promise, and I'll keep it."

"Well, now, Annie, we're asking that you tell just one other
person." He gestured toward me. "Miss Maura has to know what
happened that night. It's best all around if she does. It's hard
to explain . . ."

Momentarily the demeanor of fear and nervousness was replaced by a bite of shrewd sensibility. "I think I know why, sir.
Ignorant I may be, but a fool I've never been. I see what's before my eyes, same as anyone—even if there are those who
think I don't." She permitted herself only the merest glance at
Connor, but he turned away from it, leaning back against the
mantel and staring toward the window, as if what would happen here was no concern of his.

"Annie, the night of Mrs. Sheridan's accident—"

"Yes, sir," she said, speaking now with far less reluctance.

"You remember I telephoned here?"

Instead of answering Brendan, she spoke directly to me. "Mr.
Carroll telephoned here, and I took the message, and I went
upstairs to tell Mrs. Sheridan, and that's God's truth."

I wheeled to Brendan. "Lotti was still *here?* You told me she
had already left. You said you got through too late!"

He motioned me to silence. "Did you deliver the message,
Annie?"

"I did not, Mr. Carroll. When I went upstairs wasn't Lady
Maude herself in the passage outside Mrs. Sheridan's bedroom.
She said I wasn't to go in. So I told her what Mr. Carroll had
said, and then she sent me back downstairs."

"Why weren't you allowed to go in?" Then, as Annie's look

of doubt reappeared, he urged her. "Go on, Annie. Half the truth isn't going to mean anything."

She turned to Praeger. "Am I to tell it all, then, sir? All about Mrs. Sheridan and Mr. Connor?"

He nodded; he looked desperately weary, as though he had already lived again the events of a long and tormented night. The tight grip on his cane never relaxed.

Annie took up the recital again, more slowly. "Well—it was because of the row that was going on. That's why she wouldn't let me go in. Sure you could hear it—every bit of it—as plain as daylight. Mrs. Sheridan never minded who heard anything. It had been going on ever since I brought up the first message, and I suppose it was what brought Lady Maude out of her room. She could never stand to hear Mrs. Sheridan carrying on." Annie shot an apologetic look at Praeger. "But sure it was only because Mrs. Sheridan was young, and spoiled like—there seemed no harm in her. It was only high spirits, that is, until this business with Mr.—"

"Miss Maura knows about that, Annie—but you tell her about the first message, and what happened after you went up to give it to Mrs. Sheridan."

"Well, it had come about half an hour before that. Miss Lotti was upstairs packing for her trip, and she'd sent me to bring up a bottle of champagne. She and Mr. Connor were having it together—they often did that. When I brought it up they were having a little argument, you might call it. Oh, nothing serious, mind you—he was sitting there watching her put her things together and complaining because she wouldn't let him drive her to Dublin to get the plane, seeing it was such a bad evening, an' all. And she was saying that she liked to have her own car waitin' at the airport in case she took it into her head to come home early. And of course he was lettin' her, because she loved to drive about in that little car of hers, and be her own mistress, so to speak. She always said she didn't like people keepin' reins on her—and Mr. Connor, he was trying hard not to do it. There weren't many men in Ireland, I'm tellin' you, that would have stood for her flyin' about here and there—but then, I suppose there weren't many young ladies like Mrs. Sheridan, either."

"Oh, for God's sake!" The words burst from Connor. "Let's get to the point, can't we, and have done with all this gossip!"

"I was only sayin' what happened, Mr. Connor."

"Then get on with it!"

"Well, I knocked and came in and told Mrs. Sheridan that there had been a telephone message from the airline people. They said to tell Mrs. Sheridan that there was a two-hour delay in the time the plane would leave, on account of it being delayed in the last place by bad weather—sure it was terrible weather all over at that time, I do remember. I said to them both—Mrs. Sheridan and Mr. Connor—that I'd told the airline people that there was no one here goin' to Copenhagen, like they said. Mrs. Sheridan was goin' to London. But they would have it that she was booked to Copenhagen, so there was nothing for it but to give her the message and leave her to straighten it out. But, of course, if I'd have thought for a moment . . . well, I never should have said it before Mr. Connor. That was the terrible mistake—*that's* when I was the fool, right enough. But I never thought for a moment—they had their words, mind you, like any married pair, but I never thought . . ."

This time it was Praeger who stopped her. "Please, Annie, just say what happened."

"Well, Mr. Connor sat there listenin' to what I said about Copenhagen, and there was a mistake, an' all. Then he said, right out in front of me, mind you, as if I wasn't there at all, he says 'There isn't a mistake, is there, Lotti? This is the night Brendan flies to Copenhagen.'

"Mrs. Sheridan didn't deny it at all. She just laughed. 'A little detour, Connor' was what I think she said. He leans over and takes her ticket from her handbag—it was all open there on the dressing table where she'd been collecting her things. He takes it and opens it, and he reads it aloud. 'Dublin, Copenhagen, London, Dublin—a nice little round trip, Lotti,' he says.

And right there in front of me eyes he picks up the bottle of champagne and pours it over her two packed suitcases—over all the lovely things she had. 'Well, here's a little send-off,' he says. And that started it! They started shoutin' at each other—terrible things Mr. Connor called her. And she shoutin' back at him that she wasn't goin' to be held down in a dull old place like this, shoutin' about his glassworks and all the rest. I ran, I'm tellin' you. But all the way down the stairs you could hear it, and even down here. Oh, sure I know they didn't mean the half of it, and they would have come to their senses, but they were like two mad people then. I put my hands over my ears and was praying for them—that they'd stop sayin' those terrible things, and it would blow over but I had my doubts since the Copenhagen business—and her not even sorry about being found out. 'I'm glad!' she kept screamin' at him. 'I'm glad—glad. Now you know and I don't have to pretend any more. And I don't have to play this stupid game of being a country lady in tweeds . . . Oh, it makes me sick,' she says, 'and I'm glad I'll be gone.'"

Connor had turned his back and rested his arms along the mantelshelf. I was thankful I couldn't see his face. Annie's tone had grown louder and fuller as she had warmed to the recital; the love of drama that lies in all the Irish had come out in the telling, as the memory grew more vivid, and her tongue found again the hot words. I could hear the echoes of that battle even in Annie's broad brogue, Lotti's faint accent, the lightness of her laugh, the dark rumble of Connor's fury and hurt. Annie's body swayed as she related the scene, seeming to swing from one role to the other, her own interjections a rough Greek chorus.

"Then," she said, and the pitch of her voice fell. "The telephone rang again, and it was Mr. Carroll tellin' me about the bridge being down. So I went right back up to tell Miss Lotti and that's when I met Lady Maude, and she said she would give the message. Well . . . I had to leave it that way, since that was what Lady Maude said I was to do, but then I thought for sure Miss Lotti would never go, now that Mr. Connor knew all about it . . . I thought he'd make her stay behind, the way any other husband would have. So I went back to the kitchen, sayin' a few Hail Marys for those two poor young creatures that they'd end their quarrel peacefully. Upstairs I heard a door bang a couple of times, as if they were going in and out of their rooms. Then a few minutes later I heard the racket on the stairs, a lot of the wee things fallin' the way they do if you're not mindin' yourself when you go down. The next thing I heard the front door slam; I ran out into the hall and to the door, prayin' it would be Mr. Connor, but it was Miss Lotti's little car that started up. I ran out into the rain callin' to her, and wavin', but she didn't stop. She must have seen me, for sure, because I remember the headlights swept right across me. But she didn't stop. It was then I began to worry that she had the message.

"I wasn't sure what to do—I didn't dare go back to Mr. Connor—him in that black rage an' all. So I took it on meself to ring through to Mr. Carroll. Sure it wasn't any use pretendin' I didn't know that that was where Miss Lotti had meant to go—that the pair of them were goin' together to Copenhagen. It would have been all right so long as Miss Lotti knew about the bridge —she could have gone the long way round. But I was worried, you know. I meant to tell him to watch out for her, just in case. But the line was engaged. I waited and I tried again. But you know it's only a few minutes from here to the North Lodge. This time the phone rang and rang, and no one answered. Every few minutes I'd try again, and no one answered. I began to think that maybe, after all, they made the arrangement to meet in Dublin, but I kept tryin', all the same.

"Finally, someone answered. It wasn't Mr. Carroll. I said I was callin' from Meremount, careful like, not knowin' how much to let out about Miss Lotti. 'Meremount, is it?' the man said. 'Then you'd better tell Mr. Sheridan to get on over here. Mrs. Sheridan's car's in the river, and we can't find her.'

"I ran upstairs to Miss Lotti's bedroom, but no one was there —the lights were on, and her bags just as they'd been when Mr.

Connor poured the champagne over them. Only the little dressin' case was gone. There was no sign of Lady Maude. I went along and looked in Mr. Connor's room, not really expectin' to see him, because somehow I was beginnin' to feel that maybe he'd gone after her, and I'd missed him in all the fuss. But he was there, right enough. Just sittin' in a chair, starin' at the wall, like a man who was never going to get up out of it again. I told him about Mrs. Sheridan's car. He didn't seem to take it in for a while. God help me, I was so upset I went and shook him. 'Surely to God,' I said, 'you or Lady Maude told her about the bridge being washed away? You couldn't have let her go knowin' that . . . ?' He just looked at me, very calm-like, and said, 'I don't know what you're talkin' about.' Then he got up and started downstairs, not in a hurry, as if he already knew that she was dead.

"And dead she was. She left here not knowin' about the bridge, and ever since that night haven't I blamed myself that I didn't make sure that she knew. If I had just been able to stop her—or to get through to Mr. Carroll in those few minutes . . . Well, it wasn't meant to be, and I've had a death on my conscience ever since."

Brendan turned to me. "When Annie was trying to get through to me, I was phoning Castle Tyrell. As I finished the call I heard the crash."

Annie had begun to weep noisily; she held the hem of her apron to her eyes, and rocked back and forth. "And haven't I held my tongue about who was responsible, and not able to go to confession since? I'd not want to bring scandal and grief to Lady Maude, she that was good to me family in the past. If I'd said what I knew about Mr. Connor, sure there would have been murder to account for."

Connor spun round to face. "*Now* listen to her! She knows nothing more than what she told you. The rest is fancy . . ."

Praeger stirred himself. "Annie—I thank you. You have been a brave woman, and you have done your duty. Lady Maude is well served. Will you wait now outside for a time . . . ? You have no more to worry about. You have done your duty."

The apron came away from her eyes momentarily while she looked at Praeger. "Thank you, sir." Her head bent again, but she was reassured by his words about duty. They had their effect on Annie; to a younger woman they would have had little meaning. We waited until the door had closed behind her.

Connor spoke first. "Well, now we've been through the whole bloody wretched business again, and what has it proved? No more than it did last time, or will ever. It didn't prove, either, that I was responsible for what happened last night."

"We prove nothing," Praeger said, shrugging. "We do not try. When Maura came with her story of what she believes happened last night, I knew that it was also necessary that she be told what else happened on the night Lotti died. She has become too closely involved now to be denied the whole story."

They all looked at me as if they expected some kind of answer, some decision. There was none. I felt myself shaking.

"You let Lotti go . . ." I said to Connor.

His hand cleaved the air with a gesture of denial. "Why does everyone assume that it was I who let her go? Until the moment Annie stood there in front of me in the room shaking me and telling me there'd been some accident, I hadn't the least idea that there was any danger to Lotti. I didn't *know* the bridge was down! You—all of you—seem conveniently blind to the fact that Annie keeps saying she told Lady Maude. She just assumes that Lady Maude gave me the message and that, knowing it, I let Lotti go. The truth is I didn't even see Lady Maude at that time. I left Lotti's room and went through the bathroom to my own room. I was letting her go, because nothing would have held Lotti, and I was sickened by the spectacle we were making of ourselves. But I wasn't letting her go to her death. You all keep passing over the fact that it was Lady Maude who was told about the bridge—not I. Why am I guilty? Why not she?"

Praeger answered him. "Lotti has just flaunted her infidelity

before you—held up to scorn everything you thought worth-
while . . ."

"Mr. Praeger, no one kills these days because of infidelity. I
knew I had lost Lotti . . . she would go. It hardly even mattered that the immediate cause was Brendan, because he was
even less able to handle her than I was. I knew it wouldn't be
with him she would finally go. I had lost her—killing her wasn't
necessary."

Praeger sighed; he passed his hand wearily over the folds of
flesh at his jowls. "I did not want to go through all of this
again. But I cannot have Maura listen to the argument, and not
hear its answer. Let us not forget that money was involved
here, and money has a way of changing everything it touches.
Lotti was my only child, and I am a rich man. I put no bones
upon it. You were not only losing a wife, but the chance of a
fortune."

"Then why—if you want to put no bones on it—why would
I kill the goose that laid the golden egg? I'm not stupid, Mr.
Praeger. I'm not stupid even when I'm angry and hurt and sick
as I was then."

"Because—" Praeger's finger wagged in a sudden gesture of
Teutonic authoritativeness. "Because you did not know then
that none of the money belonged to Lotti in her own right. If
she had simply left you—divorced you—you had no claim. As
the husband of a dead woman—a rich woman, you thought—
you had a very strong claim."

Connor seemed to struggle for the words to frame his reply.
There was something in that slowness, in the faint sigh which
preceded it that conveyed the impression that he did not expect
Praeger either to understand or believe him, that Praeger could
never understand any value except money. "Mr. Praeger . . ." he
began. And then again, "Mr. Praeger—yes, I like money. Yes,
I would like money so that the glassworks could amount to
something. Yes, I'm ambitious—six times as ambitious as most
men you'll ever encounter. But no—I have never wanted money

badly enough to kill for it. As I've said freely to Maura, there is a long step between the wish and the deed."

It was appallingly effective. He told half-truths so well. I didn't believe him, but I was almost compelled to believe him. How could anyone as reasonable as this, as cognizant of his own failings, also possess the capacity for such violence? But I couldn't let myself be swayed once again.

"Then if not you," I said, "why Lady Maude? Why should she possibly want Lotti dead?"

He treated me to almost the same look, the same gesture of weary patience that had accompanied his answers to Praeger. "You know Lady Maude," he said. "Now you know her. It isn't difficult, surely, to imagine what it was like for her to have Lotti in this house. It often occurred to me that Lotti must have been the strongest competition Lady Maude had encountered since she was a young girl. Don't you see it? The household began to revolve about Lotti, all the plans were to be Lotti's, the money appeared"—he mocked Praeger with his emphasis on the words "to be Lotti's." "Lady Maude saw the control slipping from her hands, and she couldn't endure it. If any of you could have known what additional loads of furniture came in those months Lotti lived here. Lady Maude went to auctions she would never have dreamed of attending before as beneath her notice—and paid far more than she had ever paid before for pretty worthless things. All the bills came to the glassworks for settlement, of course, and I had somehow to pay them. It was her way of asserting herself, and a way to inflict annoyance on Lotti and myself. Can you imagine how Lotti reacted the day she came home and found Lady Maude moving a new load of furniture into the room she had just redecorated for herself? And the row that went on before we were able to get it out again? Can you imagine what Lotti said when Lady Maude threatened to sell off the farm rather than let Lotti have it for pasture for her horses? Lotti wasn't exactly tactful about whose money would be spent on Meremount and the glassworks— whose money would provide a future for the Sheridans. And she wasn't very tactful, either"—here a nod to Praeger—"about whose money had bought the Tyrells' past. Lotti was a constant thorn in Lady Maude's side. Too many people were coming to Lotti for their orders and passing over Lady Maude. It had never happened to her before in her life. Even Annie—yes, even devoted Annie—upset her because she just couldn't stop talking about and quoting Lotti—"

"One does not kill for such reasons," Praeger interrupted.

Connor turned swiftly. "What? One only kills for money, Mr. Praeger? Is that it? Well, don't forget that if I was ignorant of Lotti's financial position, so was Lady Maude. Can you think that she might have seen a future at Meremount, without Lotti, but with Praeger money? She knew, of course, that if I had money, it would have gone into the glassworks. She had tested me for a long time, and she could be very sure of that. Perhaps, in her sick brain, she even thought that with money within her control it would be possible to have Tyrell back again. You yourself, Mr. Praeger, have often described the nature of her mania. Don't you think that it's possible for an old woman, lost in her dreams of the past, to let slip into death someone who seems to thwart those dreams? Brendan said—didn't he?—that I had to do no deed that night, but only let it happen. Why couldn't it have been Lady Maude who let it happen?"

If only he didn't make it so plausible, I thought. All the uncertainties came creeping in upon me, urging me to listen and to believe. "Has anyone ever asked Lady Maude that question?" I spoke to them all.

"Ach!—ask Lady Maude?" Praeger dismissed the idea. "She answers nothing she does not want to answer. Naturally that question was asked. After Lotti was killed I sat in this room and I asked all these questions. But other people's laws and other people's rules are not for her. She declined to answer me—should I have tried to force her to answer a coroner?—and finally a judge and a jury? One or other of these two people let Lotti go to her death that night—either deliberately, because they withheld the information, or accidentally, because she left too quickly. I seriously doubted that the law would have given me a more satisfactory answer than the open one I found for myself that day. So between us all we made our contract of silence. We have lived with it, in our various ways, ever since. Nothing is changed, except that now you also are included. I know"—he held up his hand to forestall my protest—"I know you did not ask for it. But then who does ask for whatever happens to them in life? Not often are we permitted to choose."

He began to stir himself, as if he were preparing to leave. "And now, what have we accomplished this time? Not very much. The same doubts, the same lack of answers to the same questions. Maura thinks that Connor tried to end Lady Maude's life last night. And all we can say to her is 'Beware—he may have taken another life.' Beyond that we do not go. Things will not be arranged in a tidy way for us, no matter what we—"

The door opened. Praeger was the only one facing it, and it was he who first saw her. The sight brought him, struggling, to his feet.

"Lady Maude!"

She was oddly regal in the faded purple dressing gown and the worn embroidered slippers, the silver braids like a coronet above her handsome, wasted face. It was surprising, again, to see how tall she was. Even bent somewhat over the stick she held, she overshadowed Annie who stood beside her, her arm extended as if she had just aided her down the stairs. Annie looked fearfully at Praeger, and it was she who spoke before anyone else could.

"I'm sorry, Mr. Praeger. Didn't her ladyship send Bridget to bring me up to ask who was down here so early—she heard the cars and all the commotion, and when she saw that I was upset an' all . . ."

"Annie, be silent!"

"I'm sorry, m'lady, but I promised Mr. Praeger—well, sir, she would have it all out of me about what was going on down here."

"Annie, you have no business making promises to anyone but me. Now be silent and leave us—"

"Oh, m'lady, and you hardly able to stand . . ."

"—at once!"

Annie backed away. There was supreme confidence in her servant's long habit of obedience in the way Lady Maude stood with her back to the hall, looking in turn at all of us, not speaking, until the click of the dining-room door announced to us that Annie was gone. Somehow, the waiting had held us all, too, because it wasn't until then that Praeger spoke again.

"Lady Maude, please—a seat. You have been in bed . . ."

"Herr Praeger, I am not accustomed to being offered a seat in my own home. This house is still mine, regardless of what rights you think your money bought you here—you and your daughter."

Praeger gave a half-bow. "A courtesy gesture only, Lady Maude. I assure you I assumed no proprietary rights."

"And none were ever granted." The tone was clipped and sure. "And now"—the hand holding the cane was raised and its sweep indicated all of us, though the other hand, to compensate, had to come up to grasp the doorframe—"I have to ask what all of you are doing here. I do not recall having invited you."

"This was not intended as a social visit, Lady Maude." It was wrong to leave it all to Praeger, I thought, but they had been protagonists before any of us had known Lady Maude or Meremount. They squared off as natural fighters, though I knew at once that Praeger himself was not entirely free of the old woman's dominance. "We had come here because . . ." His words faded out. He did not want to begin on it again; there were no new answers to be had from her; she did not hear questions she did not want to answer; her rules were her own, her standards set by her own measures. "There were some questions . . ."

"Questions? You have no questions for me. Herr Praeger— or for anyone else in my household. There is nothing to answer.

You have come, as you did last time, to make impertinent charges, to accuse, to slander—to lie."

"No, Lady Maude, you mistake me. My visit had nothing to do with you. It was for Maura—"

"Maura!—*my* granddaughter, Herr Praeger. She is already your creature, isn't she? Coming when you say, doing as she is bidden. You are a despoiler, Herr Praeger—you despoil and devour, you believe you can buy whatever your greedy gaze falls upon. Corruption follows you—you and your kind. You and your daughter have brought more harm to this house than your money can ever repay. But money is your only coin. You have no other way to repay. I know why you come here—to steal my granddaughter, to torment my servant, to make her believe tales which her simple mind could never have devised, to make her repeat them so that my granddaughter is turned against me—"

"Lady Maude, this time you go too far! This time you have said more than courtesy can endure! What your servant spoke —this morning and on the night my Lotti died—was the truth she saw with her own eyes. She herself was witness to it."

"Lies! All of it lies! Your daughter died because she deserved to die. The fruits of her corruption were already sprouting in these two young men standing here. Before she would have been finished with us all here, this house would have been a muck-heap. It was better that she died, but the damage was done, and the corruption did not die with her. Here is another"—the stick was raised and pointed at me—"that the corruption has reached through these same two men, and through yourself, Herr Praeger. Somehow you have won her to your side, so that she believes the lies you have fabricated. She has sold herself for flattery and promises and, for all I know, bribes. The vulgar rich have their way, and it shames me that any Tyrell could be so seduced. When she came to me I thought my long wait was ended, that now there would be someone to whom I could entrust what was left. She was my own flesh and blood, but now I see that between all of you you have made a stranger of her—"

"No!" I said. "*That* is the lie! All the years that I have been a stranger were your doing, Lady Maude—they need not have been. You had twenty-three years to make a granddaughter of me. You chose not to do it."

"Your mother betrayed me. Do you think I wanted you while her influence was there to destroy and corrupt what good I would do? Yes, *corrupt*—Blanche was no better than this other one, your daughter, Herr Praeger. Blanche betrayed me and the whole future of the Tyrells for a man. Then this other one came and not only betrayed what was good here, but tried to steal it from me. And now my granddaughter—but she already belonged to your kind. She hardly had to hear the lies before she believed . . . I was wrong to hope. I was wrong to think that because she was a Tyrell she would be different from her mother, different from all the stupid, corrupt, selfish young women who inhabit the world these days."

She brought both hands to rest on the stick. It was a man's cane, long, but still not too long for her height, surmounted by the silver head of a lion. The leonine head and the old woman seemed to belong together, fierce and proud, and dying hard.

"Well, I will hope no more. I have received my last betrayal. Where there is no hope, there is at least peace."

Her old frame gathered in to itself, as if she were tensing every muscle so that she might stand alone.

"I will have each of you out of here—*all* of you! You, Connor, and you, Maura, also. Out of my sight and my life. You have no claims on me, no rights but those I granted you. Now I withdraw them. You gave me nothing. I owe you nothing. That is all."

She drew herself up and I saw the willful effort to straighten fully, to resume the erectness of her youth; she turned her back and carefully made her way to the foot of the stairs. None of us moved or spoke. There was a terrible sadness in the sight of her slow ascent of the stairs, and yet it was a wonderful sight, also. I thought, as I stood there, not daring to go to her help, knowing that I would instantly meet her scorn and contempt, her final rejection, that this would be the last sight I would have of her, this demented old woman, living as an aristocrat still when the whole code—all that she lived by and for—had been eroded to nothing by the wash of this century. I felt, also, a sadness for myself, a vague sense of loss, but yet it was a loss of something I had never known. She had been right. I had given her nothing; she owed me nothing. The loss was on her side, too. As we watched her move higher until all but the hem of the purple robe and the ancient embroidered slippers with their tiny frayed silken heels had vanished, I thought that if that letter from Blanche, twenty-three years ago, had not been dismissed, both of us, Lady Maude and myself, might have had a better balance sheet to show at this moment.

Perhaps she relaxed her effort a little when she reached the topmost step and knew she was out of our sight; perhaps the effort itself had been quite beyond her strength; perhaps, though, it was the final weakening of one of the sharp little heels on the old slippers that twisted her ankle and sent her plunging; it could have been the hazard all of us in that house had suffered from—the stacks of small objects piled on the stairs and landing. When she fell a whole cascade of them came down with her— vases, stools, lanterns, a chiming clock, a lacquer tray. The noise was deafening, and we never knew if she cried out.

The heap of her body at the bottom of the stairs was grotesque and without dignity. Absurdly, a lady's fan of yellowed, tattered lace lay across her chest where it had fallen like some totally frivolous comment. Connor was with her first, kneeling beside her, bending to her, touching her face.

"Lady Maude . . . ?" I had never heard his tone so tender.

Praeger pushed past us. "Let me, please. I have dealt with many sick people . . ." Clumsily, he also lowered himself to his knees, accepting help from Brendan without demur. I thought of all the people, sick and dead, that he must have handled in the years in the concentration camp when I saw the way his fingers reached expertly for the pulse, the way he bent to listen for breath, the way he pulled the purple robe aside and laid his ear against the thin old chest in its shrunken flannel gown. I was glad that he did not open the neck of the gown; for Lady Maude that would have been the ultimate indignity.

At last he straightened and raised his head. He twisted until he looked, not at Connor, but at me.

"I believe," he said, "that Lady Maude is dead."

It was Connor, then, whose fingers stroked the eyelids closed. He looked at the face for a time, unsoftened still in death, as if even in that final moment, she had never been able to let go; then he also looked up at me.

"If this had happened a week ago you need never have had to go through all this. You need not have been dragged into all that you saw and heard today. But now she's dead, and maybe she's almost the last of her kind. Perhaps it wasn't a bad thing, after all, to have known her." From the way he spoke it could have been possible to believe that he was sorry she was gone.

Then he added: "She was a mad old woman—madder than any of us knew until the night Lotti died. She never did tell me, you know, about the bridge."

He was safe. The dead lips would not move to deny what he had said. He was the only person who knew with certainty, now, what was the truth.

CHAPTER 11

I

Mrs. O'Shea was wakened, and Dr. Donnelly arrived and confirmed what Otto Praeger had said.

"Impossible to say which came first—the fall or the heart failure. She has no serious injuries so I can safely write the certificate for heart failure, and you'll have no trouble about an autopsy. Well, it had to come, didn't it? She'll be missed around here. No one ever saw much of her, except at auctions, and even then she didn't mix very much—but she was someone to point out and talk about. Ah, well, the world's getting to be a terribly dull place with all the real characters leaving us. Will you be staying on now, Miss D'Arcy?"

"No, I won't be staying."

"You'll be closing the glassworks, then?"

"I have nothing to do with the glassworks, Dr. Donnelly. They don't belong to me."

He shook his head, and I saw that he didn't believe me.

The last moment of comparative calm that day came when Connor had carried Lady Maude's body back to her bed, and left her to Mrs. O'Shea's ministrations. Until then, Otto Praeger had sat quietly in Connor's office, waiting for Dr. Donnelly to be finished with the formalities, being served abominable coffee by Annie who was weeping with a kind of hiccuping sob, but who refused to give up her tasks.

"You'll not be sendin' me to me room, Miss Maura?—sure that would be hard. I'll sit with her ladyship for a while when Mrs. O'Shea has her ready, and say a Rosary for her, although she'd not thank me for such Popish practices, as she used to call them. But I've served Tyrells all me life, and I'm of more help down here than up in my room lamentin'.' "

After Dr. Donnelly had left, Praeger settled at the telephone, and from then on there was little time for anyone to sit alone, or to weep. "You will let me help you?" he asked, more of me than of Connor. "We had many differences, Lady Maude and I, but an old enemy is almost as well known as an old friend. My generation is perhaps better attuned to the ritual of death than yours."

"Of course, whatever you want to do . . . and Connor thinks best. But will there be so much formality?"

"Many people will come—older people who will expect certain things. Do you not agree with that, Connor?"

He shrugged. "There'll be a lot of curiosity—especially since Maura is here. And there'll be a few who are genuinely sorry—not about Lady Maude, because she had no friends that I knew of, only people who were afraid of her. But for some of them her going will really mean the very last of the old days gone too, and they'll be sorry about that. For herself—" He shrugged again. "Yes, I suppose it might please her if the formalities were observed."

Praeger now regarded himself as being in charge. He sent to Castle Tyrell for Fräulein Schmidt and O'Keefe. They conferred together in Connor's office, and then O'Keefe left again, a list from Fräulein Schmidt in his hand. Already the first of the farm workers from Castle Tyrell were arriving. They came and spoke to myself and Connor, caps in hand, before going to Praeger. "I'm sorry for your trouble," they said. "God rest her soul." And then they listened to Praeger's instructions; it was Saturday, and a free day for many of them, but the planned trip to town did not compare with the interest of having a hand in the preparations for the funeral of Lady Maude Sheridan. "It's going to be a decent old-fashioned send-off, so it is," I heard one of them say approvingly. There was a kind of stunned wonder among them at the piles of furniture in the hall and the dining room, which they had had to walk through to go to see Praeger, and then a kind of antic enjoyment in carrying most of it out to the lorries that were coming from Praeger's estate and from a mover in Cloncath whom he had already engaged. "Just so there will be a little space," Praeger pleaded. "Everything will be returned immediately after the funeral. See, Fräulein Schmidt is taking an inventory as each piece leaves. We will try to create a little order before the first callers arrive."

"Just so long as the glassworks doesn't get the bill," Connor said. Praeger nodded briefly, and went off to check what was being done in the dining room.

"Isn't this a little too much?" I said to Connor. "Lady Maude wouldn't have liked all this fuss, I think."

"She wouldn't have liked the expense of it—but yes, I think she might have liked the fuss. Befitting a Tyrell would have been her sentiment, I think. But, of course, she couldn't have expected to command the services of a genius at organization, as Praeger undoubtedly is. Let him have his way—whatever he does will be superbly done, and done three times as efficiently as anyone else could manage it. After a fashion, I suppose he's enjoying himself. He'll organize a funeral for Lady Maude that he'd like to have for himself—except that when he dies he won't have four hundred years of history to follow him to the grave."

By late afternoon, Praeger was very tired; I could see it in the slowness of his movements, the efforts to stem the fatigue with the endless cups of coffee that O'Keefe now made and brought to him. He still talked on the telephone, and he still gave his orders crisply. And he had wrought a transformation.

Six gardeners from Tyrell had weeded the gravel sweep before the house, mown the grass and tidied the beds; pot plants had been brought to place at the bottom of the steps, the long grass on the sides of the avenue had been scythed to make more space for parking. The hall was almost empty of furniture, except those chairs in the best state of repair. For the first time I saw revealed the splendid proportions of the room, the beauty of the Adam mantels, the long empty sweep to the staircase. The

Sheridan chandeliers had been taken down and washed, and four electricians were attempting to make as many of the lights work as possible. It seemed to me that the whole staff from Tyrell was there. O'Keefe presided over a strangely bare dining room —the four sideboards had remained, and one long table; the chairs were set in groups about the rooms. The tables and buffets were laid with fine white damask, and shining silver—Meremount's or Castle Tyrell's I didn't know. The coffee and tea urns waited, and out in Lotti's unfinished kitchen, the cases of whisky and sherry were unpacked.

"How can you let him?" I said to Connor. "If he weren't here to provide all these things, would you do it?"

"Of course not. Lady Maude's estate can't afford it—nor can I. But he can, and he wants to. I have no false pride, Maura. I leave that to the Tyrells. If you want to stop it, you do it. After all, you're the closest relative."

I didn't stop it, though. It had taken on a momentum of its own, and Connor had touched the heart of it in saying that Praeger was doing it for himself. Somehow I also had been caught up in Praeger's idea; I didn't want the house, with its strange jumble of contents to be exclaimed and laughed over; I didn't want to hear the sharp-pointed comments which came so readily to these tongues; I did not want Lady Maude to go meanly, without notice.

Finally, the hothouses of Castle Tyrell were emptied to deck the drawing room where the simple coffin now stood. Praeger's staff now withdrew, all save those who were to help in the kitchen; Lotti's bedroom and bath had been opened for the ladies, and the stairs were at last clear of their accumulation of hazards. Revealed now, throughout the house, were the threadbare carpets, the peeling paint, the long cracks in the walls, but all of it softened by Praeger's flowers. With the departure of the Tyrell staff, the house was strangely quiet; it was bare and beautiful. Praeger walked at last through the empty quiet rooms with me, pridefully. "Ach, how it can look, this house! The old lady does not go off unworthily. Look, already the first cars come . . . I will go home. I will come on Monday."

"Monday? Why won't you be here tomorrow? After all you have done for us you should . . ."

"Tomorrow is for the Tyrells and the Sheridans—and the Irish. Not for foreigners. O'Keefe has instructions to send for anything further he requires. On Monday I will be at the funeral. You have O'Keefe to help you—and Connor."

The emptiness had been more than just the strange new bareness of the house. "Where is Brendan?"

"Brendan? Brendan left a few hours ago—to get a plane to Manchester. He goes to Bristol, I think. You were upstairs. He asked me to say good-bye."

Praeger watched my face for a few seconds; I didn't know what it showed him; I didn't know what I felt. O'Keefe appeared to see Praeger to his car, and Connor joined me in the hall, wearing a dark suit. I had on the black skirt and sweater that Praeger had telephoned for from Cloncath, the tucks in the skirt hastily sewn by Mrs. O'Shea, who had welcomed the excuse to stay a few hours longer; the hem of the skirt decently came to mid-knee. We were as ready as Praeger's genius and money could make us in a few hours. Connor pronounced the names of the first people to arrive to me, and in their gaze, as they made their formal condolences, I could already see the speculations grow.

I heard it spoken plainly enough when I went upstairs later for a few minutes break from the flow of people. The voice that came from Lotti's bedroom was clear and carrying. "Which one, do you think, did the old lady leave everything to? But perhaps, then, Connor is clever enough to snare the second one—keep it in the family, you might say."

And Brendan—Brendan had left me to it. As I stood before the mirror in my room to put fresh powder on my face I saw the sudden welling of tears that had nothing to do with Lady Maude.

II

All day on Sunday the people came and went. I fell into the rhythm of it; the names spoken by Connor, or, because they belonged to Lady Maude's early years and were unknown to him, speaking their own names—so many of them, and only a few was I ever after able to recall along with the face; the acceptance of the condolences "Sad—and you so recently here"; the appraisals "So you are Blanche's girl . . . ?" From a few I received disapproval, the sense that Blanche had done the unforgivable and that I must forever share the blame—as from the old man, thin as a rail and taller still than most men present, who peered at me but didn't offer his hand. "It's a damn shame," he said, "that you left it so late to come—Maude Tyrell has spent too many years alone." His name was John Carew, and afterward I remembered his face very well. I accepted the burden of blame from him and those who thought as he did, though it wasn't mine; it was something I did now for Blanche with more will and understanding than I would have been capable of a week ago. I was haunted by the memory of Lady Maude's slow ascent of the stairs, the infinite loneliness of the action, with her words still hanging on the air, "You gave me nothing. I owe you nothing." I was now a little frantic to begin to make some deposit against my own future.

The hall and dining room were filled with the low murmur of voices, the discreet clinking of tea cups and glasses. People paused briefly in the drawing room; there was the heavy smell of too many flowers, and the smell of rain-damp clothes, for it rained all day. A fire burned in the dining room and in the two fireplaces in the hall. A fire burned also in the drawing room, but neither it nor the masses of flowers did much to relieve the deep sense of austerity and aloofness conveyed by that plain coffin in the midst of the luxuries Praeger had provided. Through the long day his staff attended to what had to be done with

astonishing smoothness—only one ripple disturbed the afternoon—at the moment when Lotti's Sapphire, perched on the
mantel in the dining room, reached out with an inquisitive paw
toward a shining ornament on a woman's hat. There was a
shriek and a glass was dropped, but even that excitement
dropped back quickly into the general low-level murmur. Annie,
wearing her good black dress, but insisting on retaining her
apron—"I know my place, Miss Maura"—had nothing to do but
sit in a corner of the drawing room, counting the people as they
came and went, the Rosary slipping endlessly through her fingers. And through the whole day Connor was there beside me,
speaking names, smoothing my way, insisting that I come into
the office occasionally to sit by the fire there, pouring me a
brandy or bringing me tea and guarding the door so that I could
have a few minutes of quiet. I wished that I could have drawn
some comfort from him, but I didn't. It was a lonely and be-
wildering place I dwelt in that day.

They went at last, all the people whose names and faces I
never would remember, leaving me with the numbness that
was as much of spirit as of body, the feeling that I was partici-
pating in a ritual as a stand-in for someone else—not for
Blanche, because Blanche had rejected the role—but for the
person I might have been, and the person Lady Maude might
have been to me, if I had come to this many years ago. But I
was not the beloved granddaughter to whom the proffered sympathy would have been appropriate, but the stranger of her accusation. That it had not been of my choice seemed to make
little difference. We had been strangers, alien, and, in the end,
hostile. It was for this fact, not for death, that I grieved.

Almost the last one to leave was the Reverend Patrick Stanton; he had not shaken my first instinctive liking for him by
offering any of the conventional phrases; rather, during the afternoon, he had helped me out sometimes when talk became difficult, knowing and easing my ignorance of things local and
Irish. Now he said simply, "So I shall be seeing you in church

after all. But the Lord has chosen a hard way to bring you there."

Most of the lights were out, the fires dying; O'Keefe and the rest of Praeger's people had left. Annie wanted to sit up in the drawing room with Bridget to keep her company. "Sure, I'll not sleep in any case, Miss Maura." As I went up the stairs Sapphire brushed against my ankle, giving her low, keening cry; I gathered the cat up in my arms. Then, as I reached the first landing, Connor's voice came from below.

"Good-night, Maura." He stood with one hand on the newel post, making no move to come up; he did not show the strain of the long day, nor of the waiting he had to endure. John O'Neill, Lady Maude's solicitor, had spoken to us today; tomorrow, after the funeral, he would open and read to us Lady Maude's will.

"Good-night," I replied, faintly, and turned to start up the next flight.

"Maura?"

I looked back. He was darkly handsome, a strong man who did not reveal his strain, and who did not lose sight of his desires, his purpose. "Yes?"

"You did very well, today. Far better than anyone could have expected. You see, it isn't so difficult to fit in—not such a bad thing to be a Sheridan, and a Tyrell."

The cat moved restively in my arms. "It's too late, Connor," I said. "It's far too late."

III

It was a joyous spring day, and the somber black of the people who came to Meremount seemed out of place; warm sun bathed the sparkling green of the fields and the trees, the song of a hundred birds was a loud and exultant anthem as the coffin was carried from the house between the two rows of people who clustered on the steps and out on the gravel circle. Somewhere

Praeger had found a horse-drawn hearse; it waited now behind a pair of matched blacks, black-plumed, their coats the glossy hue of a raven in the sunlight. Most of the people who had gathered at Meremount, Connor and I among them, walked the mile to the village of Fermoyle; here was the parish church of the Tyrells, the church which Tyrell money had built too big and too grand. Sheridan Glass was closed for the day, and there was no work on Praeger's estate; I saw many of the faces I remembered from the works among the crowd, and every last one of Praeger's people had turned out. Women came from the cottages along the way, blessing themselves; the murmur "God rest her soul" ran like a refrain from one cottage to another. In Fermoyle the shops were shuttered as the procession moved through; the doorways and windows were filled with faces, some sympathetic, some merely curious. At the church many more people waited; the churchyard and side streets of the village were filled with cars. At the church itself the ancient division of Ireland became apparent. The Catholics remained outside. But for once Mr. Stanton had his church filled. They were mostly of Lady Maude's generation, old people, the remnants of the Protestant Ascendancy, people who no longer mattered very much in Irish life except as a reminder of what used to be. Many of them had come, Connor whispered to me, halfway across Ireland to see Maude Tyrell buried. In death she went back to the Tyrells, where she had always belonged. The Sheridans, Connor said, were mostly buried in Cloncath.

Across the grave, as Mr. Stanton read the prayers, looking up I was shocked by the intensity of the gaze of an elderly woman, a stare both devouring and hostile; as our eyes met she turned her head with great deliberation, her lips set in a tight line of anger and old bitterness. I leaned close to Connor and whispered, "Who is . . . ?" He had seen the exchange. "Mrs. Geraldine Findlay—the mother of the man Blanche Sheridan was married to. I think she and Lady Maude used to be close friends before it happened . . ."

As we moved away from the grave the unforgiving back of

the old woman was turned on me, and she left the churchyard ahead of everyone else.

✠   ✠   ✠   ✠

The scene of the day before was repeated at Meremount as people came to refresh themselves before the drive home. But now they were freed of the restraint imposed by the presence of the dead woman. The talk was louder, livelier, and there were more requests to O'Keefe for Scotch than for tea. Today, Otto Praeger was present, keeping in the background, yet knowing that for many, now that I had been thoroughly examined, he was the center of interest. Gossip had reached those who had come to the funeral of Praeger's activities beforehand; the presence of O'Keefe and the Castle Tyrell staff confirmed it. As people judged the quality of the Scotch, the lavishness of the buffet, they knew that Maude Sheridan's estate was not paying for this part of the day's business. As they asked each other why, the glances swung between Connor and Praeger and myself. It seemed that in their minds I had fallen heir to all that Lotti had not fulfilled.

Then it was over. The people were gone, the cars maneuvered out of their parking places, the dining room stripped of its linen and silver and big urns. Annie was back in the kitchen. Even the twilight of that incongruously joyous spring day was rosy, the evensong of the birds seemed to have lost none of its exultant quality. Now the Reverend Stanton left, and even Otto Praeger must go. He had to go, because etiquette demanded it, with the most important question still unanswered.

We knew soon enough what the answer was. We withdrew with John O'Neill to our seats before the newly lighted fire in Connor's office. The document was spare and tight, and more realistic than the will of a supposedly demented old woman had any right to be. There was a bequest to Annie, and the residue of the estate was left to Connor "who has served me well."

When the reading came to an end, the solicitor peered at me over his glasses, saying immediately, as if to forestall an objection. "That is Lady Maude's will as she revised and amended it two years ago. As perhaps you know, I had an appointment to see her here on this very day, if she had lived. I don't know if it was her intention to make any changes. But this"—he tapped the stiff legal sheets—"is her last will and testament, legally executed. In my opinion, this is what the law will uphold."

Then he too left, and we were alone in what now seemed a huge and empty house. As he closed the door on the radiance of that spring twilight, Connor said quietly, "The old bitch . . . Even when she formally gives me what I have already earned, she treats me as her servant."

CHAPTER 12

1

I stayed in my room the next morning until I heard the front door slam and Connor's footsteps on the gravel below. His car and mine were now the only ones parked on the drive where yesterday there had been so many. From the window I watched him as he crossed toward them. He was wearing the tweed jacket he usually wore to the glassworks, and there was a kind of lightness, an eagerness, in his step that betrayed him. The slam of the car door was not the kind of moody gesture of displeasure I had seen in him, but a youthful impatience to be on the way. Well, the way was his now; from this day on he worked for no one but himself.

Almost at once Annie's knock sounded on the door; she came in balancing a tray. "Himself's just gone," she announced, "and I thought you'd be likin' a wee bite, Miss Maura—but I see you're up an' all." She laid the tray on one of the many tables in the room and brought a chair up to it. "There now—I tried to do it to suit your fancy." The tray was set carefully with a starched cloth that didn't yet wear Meremount's look of defeat, the silver shone, the china breakfast set was matching and complete, the toast was not burned. "I hope it's to your likin'."

I cracked the top of the boiled egg as she watched me anxiously. "Perfect—thank you."

Her smile of pleasure faded though, when, her effort approved, she took time to look around the room, and her eyes fell on the open suitcase on the bed.

"You're never leaving, Miss Maura?" It was a wail of protest.

"I have to leave some time, Annie. It might just as well be now. What's there to stay for?"

"Well, sure there's . . . Ah, don't go, Miss Maura. What ever will we do without you?"

"Just as you did before, Annie." I said it as gently as I could, but still she winced.

"Before there was Lady Maude . . . now that she's gone, I've no one to tend—nothin' to do."

"Mr. Connor will need you."

"Ah, him? No, he'll not need me. *That* one needs nobody. And are you thinkin' for a minute he'll keep on this great house just for a single man? He'll sell it if he can, and all that's in it, now that it's his."

"There's nothing to stop him doing that, Annie. Things change. You're quite right." I broke a piece of toast and buttered it. "What would he need with a big house like this?"

"Unless . . . unless you were to stay, Miss Maura. Unless you and Mr. Connor . . . ?"

I bit violently into the toast. "No, Annie. It is not going to be. Now you just put it out of your head."

"Well, sure it'd be no worse than many a marriage I know of, and better than some. He's a worker, I'll say that for him, and Miss Lotti fancied him enough to marry him . . . You could go a long way and do worse."

"Annie!"

She sighed. "I'm sorry, Miss Maura. I'm speakin' out of turn. Sure, your mother made that kind of match, and it didn't work out for her. And Mr. Lawrence was a gentler kind of man than Mr. Connor is or ever will be."

"No . . ." I agreed. I nibbled slowly now on a crust. "No, Connor is not a gentle kind of man, at all, is he, Annie?" Then I looked right at her, and said, hard and fast, "Do you think he did it, Annie? Do you think he was the one who didn't tell Mrs. Sheridan about the bridge being down?"

She started away from the question. "Honest to God I don't know, Miss Maura. I don't know atall."

"You must know, Annie. You were so close to both of them. You have to feel it about one more than the other."

"Ah, now you're tryin' to catch me, Miss Maura, and I'll not be caught, for I don't know, and that's God's truth. If it wasn't Mr. Connor, then it had to be Lady Maude, and that I'll never believe."

I had reached the same impasse that Praeger had come to long ago. I could go no further. I poured tea, and said slowly, as I stirred, "Annie, why is it that you've done so much for Lady Maude? You must know that other servants these days have an easier time of it—far less work and better conditions. Why did you stay all these years—coping with this all by yourself?"

"Lady Maude was good to me," she answered evasively.

"Lady Maude didn't know how to be 'good' to anyone in that way, Annie. She wasn't a soft woman, or even a reasonable one. She demanded services of you as if there were six others to help you. And finally—finally, you did more for her than anyone had the right to expect. You took a fearful risk for her, Annie. You might have gone to jail—you know that, don't you?"

"I know it, right enough. But I owed it to her. It would have been a terrible thing to do to her to have dragged that whole business before the police and all the rest of it. A terrible thing. And what good would it have done, atall?"

"No good, Annie," I said. "No good."

"And yet she never asked it of me, mind you. I don't think it ever occurred to her that the police would come into it, or any of that kind of thing. She used to think in an old-fashioned kind of way, you know. That you kept these things inside the family. She knew I would never speak out against her—or Mr. Connor. Of course, Mr. Praeger thought I did it because I was fond of Mrs. Sheridan—and sure I was that. But Lady Maude was the only one I would have done that for—the only one."

"Yes, Annie, I know," I said, waiting. She had begun to talk, and she would finish.

"It's as well for you to be knowing a wee bit about what your grandmother was like. Sure you thought she was a cranky

auld body, fond of her own way, and gettin' it, too. Not carin'
much for people. Well, it's best you know what she did for me
—an' you the last Tyrell there is. For me and me mother. Me
mother was in service at Castle Tyrell—lady's maid to your
grandmother, she was. Well, it's the auld story. She got in the
family way, and wasn't the young fella not goin' to do anything
about it. He was bound for America, and didn't want a wife
and child to hold him down. Lady Maude found out, and didn't
she go and get him, and tell the priest about it, and arrange
the marriage and herself was witness to it. You'll not be knowin'
what it was in those days for a Protestant—an' the daughter of
an earl—to stand up as witness for a poor young country girl
in a Catholic church. But she did it, and she only a young girl
herself, and the devil to pay when her father found out. But
I had me father's name, though he did take off right after. I
could hold me head up, and me mother too, because of what
she did. What was her own, she took care of. So when her turn
came, I took care of her, though she'd never be admittin' she
had need of anyone's help, much less the help of the likes of
meself. She bore a lot, Lady Maude did, with her father sort of
daft-like, and her brother a wild one—him that was killed the
night Tyrell burned. Sure she hadn't much left over to give to
her poor husband, and maybe less to give to her only child. It
was all used up, you might say. It's as well to be rememberin'
all this when you think about Lady Maude, Miss Maura. I could
never forget it—me mother neither—so that's why I've stayed.
Now it's come to the end of the line in you, and I thought it
was surely a miracle when you appeared the way you did. And
so I was hopin' . . ."

"Don't hope, Annie." I heard myself echoing something Otto
Praeger had said to me. "Life doesn't tidy up the ends the way
we wish it would."

"I suppose not, Miss Maura. And what's not worked out here
will be settled in the hereafter. Well, she's there now, God rest
her soul. I'll pray for her, and you too, miss. God go with you."

The words followed me, more than any wishes of good luck

or good journey would have, as I drove away from Meremount, and Annie's figure, planted squarely in the middle of the perfect symmetry of the house, diminished in the rear-view mirror, and finally the trees closed in, and it was ended.

II

O'Keefe showed me into Praeger's study immediately, without inquiring first if he should do that, as if he already knew what Praeger's answer would be, and didn't waste time asking the question. Praeger was working; the desk was covered with orderly piles of papers; Fräulein Schmidt sat on the straight-backed chair near him with a stenographer's notebook balanced on her plump knee. As he rose to greet me, Praeger jerked a quick nod in her direction, and she left at once.

"So—you come! I was going to telephone Meremount when I thought you would be up. Tonight I fly to New York—I thought you might give me the pleasure of having a little lunch . . ."

"I came to say good-bye, Mr. Praeger. I'm going back to London. I'm planning to get either the sea or air car-ferry—whichever can take me."

"So . . . !" He waved me into a chair opposite, and himself dropped back heavily into his own. For a moment he was like a man winded, and struggling for breath. "This is very quick," he said. "You could not stay a little longer? You must rush off? —everyone is in such a hurry."

"I can't stay at Meremount," I said. "You know that."

He shrugged. "Meremount is not the only place. Castle Tyrell also has a few spare rooms." He leaned forward, suddenly spilling out his eagerness. "You could stay here while I make my journey to New York. Have your holiday—lie in bed late, give O'Keefe someone to look after, and Mrs. Sullivan someone to cook for . . ." He stopped, because I was shaking my head.

"I can't stay." The temptation was almost more than I could

withstand—just to relax into Praeger's organized luxury, to let him take care of everything, to do nothing myself, to look at his pictures and walk in his gardens, read his books and eat his food, not to see Connor and to try not to think about Brendan. But it could not be; one other thing that Lady Maude had said haunted me: "She has sold herself . . . the rich have their ways . . ." I could lose myself in all this luxury. "I have so much to see to in London . . ."

"So . . . ?" He shrugged unbelievingly. "Is it that you don't want to stay because you are hurt a little—disappointed that the will was not different?"

My head snapped back. "No! I wanted nothing! How could I? A week ago I didn't know any of this existed! What is there to want?"

"Does it need a week to want something? You'll forgive me if I say you are naïve, Maura. It needs only the instant of first beholding."

"Perhaps," I said. "But I don't want it. And how did you know about the will?"

"You'll forgive me again," he answered. "But I had to know. I was leaving for New York and I had to know so that I could start in motion the means to help if it was needed. I sent O'Keefe to see Annie last night. So you see, I know. That was why I was going to ask you to come before I left. I have telephoned my Dublin solicitors . . ."

"Wait!" I stared at him, staggered at what had already gone through his mind, what had already been done. "*Why* have you done all this?"

"Because, naturally, you must contest the will. And the machinery should be set in motion at once. A delay could be quite fatal."

I slumped down in my chair, wondering for a moment how I could put across to Praeger what apparently was a new idea for him. "I don't want it," was all I could say. "I *don't want it!*"

"What has wanting to do with it? I am certain Lady Maude meant to change that will—once you came she knew where the inheritance belonged. It is your duty to see that her wishes are carried out."

"But we don't *know* that those were her wishes. She made a legal will recognizing Connor's rights—"

"He has no rights! You remember what she said at the end? 'You have no rights but those I granted you. Now I withdraw them.' What could be plainer?"

"But we were both rejected, Mr. Praeger. If you remember that so well, you must also remember what she said to me. 'You gave me nothing. I owe you nothing.'"

He took a deep breath. "Well, then—you are equal. In spirit, if not in fact, Lady Maude died intestate. If she had reached the top of those stairs she would most probably have lived to let a new will speak her decision. But being without it, the one with the closest blood relationship has the stronger claim."

"Connor would fight it—unless we tell in court what really happened that morning, made Annie and Brendan tell it. And Connor knows we won't do that. So, it is still her signed will against the fact that I am her grandchild."

"What would Connor fight us with? He has no money, and we can tie up the estate so that he can get no money from that source."

"And what would I fight with? I have no money, either!"

He dismissed the thought with a wave of his hand. "The finest solicitors in Ireland are on a retainer from me. Let them work at something."

"Supposing they succeeded—and a court ruled that I did have a claim? But that Connor's work, and his expectations were also a claim? They would split Sheridan Glass down the middle—and it's almost dead now. It couldn't survive."

"Connor would not survive!" His voice was growing thunderous as his mind played with all the possibilities. "He would be bankrupt from the legal fight, and we could force him to sell out. He would not exist. He would be wiped out!"

He hated Connor—was it because he believed that Connor had let Lotti die, or because first Connor had taken Lotti from him? His anger and hate had swept away all the reasonableness with which he had made himself speak of Connor before I had known the full story. Now he seemed not to care that I knew he would like to destroy the other man if he could. And he would use me to do it.

I went back to my first defense, less confidently now. "I wish you would try to understand. I don't *want* any of the inheritance."

He sat for a time, fingers pressed together, eyes half-closed; he looked as if he were trying to gather patience. "You are saying this because you are young. The young think freedom is everything. But let me tell you that there is no such thing as freedom. The most you can have is the freedom to choose which will be your prison."

"But doesn't one also need the freedom to find that out?"

"So . . . you start to be clever with the old man, eh? But let me tell you also that if you should let this go now, you can never have it back again. It is no use ten years from now deciding that after all it would not have been such a bad thing to have owned Sheridan Glass, to have Meremount, to be a Sheridan and a Tyrell."

Amazement made me edge forward in my seat. "You expect me to *run* Sheridan Glass? To live at Meremount?—not to sell it?"

He shrugged. "You could not run Sheridan Glass alone—at least, not in the beginning. But these things can be arranged. Good management can be bought for good money."

"And where would the money come from?"

"There are ways of borrowing money. If you have the right guarantees, and I would see that you did."

"There weren't any guarantees for Connor and Lotti. When Lotti died there was no more help for the glassworks then."

The heavy jowls trembled. "When Lotti died I had no interest in helping Connor Sheridan. The arrangements Lotti made for Sheridan Glass were her own. They ended with her."

"But for me it would be different?"

"It would be different—yes."

He wanted Lotti back, of course. He had been wishing Lotti back into existence from the moment that he had first caught a glimpse of a blond-haired girl stretched out on the bank of the stream. But it was an idealized Lotti he saw in me, the little girl that the war years had taken from him forever. He thought he could yet teach me, train me in the things that he held important—money, Ireland, even being a Tyrell. This would be a different Lotti, obedient, stay-at-home, cherishing what her father cherished—but with the added virtue that my real fathers had already had four hundred years in the country to which Praeger craved to belong, wholly and completely. I was reminded again of the atmosphere, the feeling I had sensed when Connor had taken me to The Four Kingdoms in Cloncath, and how one man had said it, "this one looked Irish." Praeger wanted that—wanted it so badly that he could not see that he had created his own image of me. For him I had to be what he imagined me to be. It left no room for what I really was, or might become.

I stood up. "Thank you, Mr. Praeger. It's very good of you to offer all this help. But I'm not going to fight Connor. I really don't think I'm suited to Sheridan Glass or Meremount, or any of these things. But of course I have to find out. And as you said, if I've made a mistake, by then it will be too late to do anything about it. But that's just a risk I'll have to take."

The hand he gave me was limp, and it seemed to cost him an effort to raise it. I said, "I'll leave my London address with Fräulein Schmidt. I'm sure you must often be in London . . . if you can spare the time I would like to cook a meal for you."

He nodded, but didn't speak—or couldn't.

III

I asked Daisy, the receptionist at the Sheridan Museum, to ring through to Connor's office and say that I would like to see him. He came at once, nodding briefly to the girl as he came through the door. "Thanks, Daisy—just skip across to the canteen and have yourself a cuppa, will you?—there's a good girl." She went, reluctant to miss what might happen, and Connor walked slowly down to where I stood before the showcase containing the two Culloden Cups; he was fumbling for cigarettes, and held the pack toward me. "You'll notice it's strictly forbidden to smoke in here," he said, smiling.

"What's the use of being boss if you can't break the rules?"

He took his time lighting both cigarettes, and he waited before he spoke again. "Do you mind my being boss here—finally being boss instead of dog's-body?"

I shrugged. Inside I still shook from the encounter with Praeger; I had resisted him, fought him against his desire to take me over, to shape me into a more satisfactory Lotti. Connor wasn't to know it, but I didn't have the strength left to engage him also. I would have to seem indifferent and cool, and just hope that enough was left in me to get me through this last interview and on the road away from Cloncath.

"You can be anything you want, Connor. A week ago we'd never heard of each other, so it makes no difference what the other was or did. A week can't change things so much . . ." Why was I trying to prove to him what Praeger had already shown me was not the truth?

Connor pointed the cigarette at me. "I'm tempted to say rude things like 'Come off it!' You're talking a lot of rubbish and you know it. Everything has changed this week. You have made it change."

"I didn't do anything. I was just here."

"Being here was all that was needed."

I pushed my hair away from my forehead with a sudden movement of distraction and impatience. "Oh, don't start! Don't *you* start! All right—perhaps some things did happen because I came. But if I hadn't come here, it's just as likely that the end of the week would have shown the very same results. Lady

Maude is dead—but one day she had to die. And you have Sheridan Glass. That's what you worked for—what you wanted. Now you have it. It's nothing to do with me. I'm going, and all I want is my own property to take back with me. I came to get the Culloden Cup."

"Wait . . ." he said, drawling the word. "Just wait a minute. Why are you running off like this? Why the hurry?"

"I'm not running off. It just happens to be the time to go. You can't want me to stay now."

"I asked you to stay—do you remember that? I once asked you to marry me."

"Remember? How do you forget things like that? But that was before you knew you had the glassworks. That was before you knew—how did you put it?—if I was in and you were out. What was said before Lady Maude died doesn't count."

I saw the frustration begin in him, the tightening of the mouth, the striving to hold the words in check. "Oh, to hell with you! What do you expect—do you want me to start all over again? Do we have to pretend that what has been didn't happen? Do I have to start to woo you? Well, it's too late for that. I'm too old to play the romantic boy, and too many things have happened to me. I haven't time to jump through all the hoops again. If we married, we'd know what we were doing. It wouldn't be love's young dream, but it could be a good thing —a damn good thing!"

"You wanted a business partner . . . wasn't that it?"

"Damn you! I want a wife! I want *you!*"

They were terrible, long seconds while he plucked the cigarette from my fingers and put it out, a long, long time while he kissed me in which to begin to doubt again everything I had decided about him. It didn't seem possible that the urgency and warmth of his lips could have been calculated, that the grace note of tenderness in the way his hand supported my head as he tilted it backward could have been feigned. It was more real than when he had kissed me before, as though we had

known each other a lifetime in between, had known and understood and forgiven. We seemed already old in what we felt, as
if we were past any possibility of deception. "I could be a husband . . . I could be a lover," he said softly, and I knew why
Lotti had made her marriage; if she had sought a man to flaunt
before her world she had found him. The first rare tastes might
have dulled as the long-established patterns of variety and
change which was her life had reasserted themselves; but for
a time, I thought, she would have had more from Connor than
most women could dream of. It was there, and it was real, and
it could be mine if I wanted to take the chance on withstanding
the wearing force of the rest that I knew about him—or, more
truthfully, what I had been told about him.

At last I drew away from him, my breath coming a little hard.
"It won't do," I said. "It never would do . . . it would be just
too much of a good thing. You said the other night that I fitted
in well. That's the trouble—I fit in a sight too well. All any of
you can see is the outward part—the part that's Sheridan and
Tyrell, the part that's Irish and that belongs. And none of you
give a damn about the rest of me, the person that's Eugene
D'Arcy's daughter as well as Blanche Sheridan's. All of you—
every one of you—are doing your reckoning about me, but not
with me. Everyone's told me what I should do, but no one's
asked me what I want to do."

"You're talking nonsense again," he said, his tone growing
thick and angry. Strangely, I wasn't as afraid of his anger as I
thought I would be; perhaps that also was part of the change.
"You're talking romantic nonsense, and it's got nothing to do
with what you really think. Are you afraid—is that it? Have
you believed that stupid tale—that I let Lotti die? Have you let
yourself believe something that you imagined at two o'clock in
the morning because you saw me pick up a bloody bath mat?
They've been at you again, haven't they?—Annie and Praeger?"

"No one's been *at* me. And I'll never know if you let Lotti
die—I'll never really be sure if I was mistaken about you that

night when I thought you tried to kill Lady Maude. Annie and Praeger will never convince me, either—because they believe two different things about you."

"Two . . . ?"

"Praeger thinks you let Lotti die—but he believes it mostly because he resents and dislikes you—perhaps he hates you, and it suits him to believe it. Annie . . . in her heart Annie believes Lady Maude was responsible. And that's why she's kept silent. She never would have done that for *you*. So you see . . . between the two of them, they cancel each other out."

"And you? What do you believe?"

"I've told you—I don't know. I'll never know. Only two people knew for sure, and one of them is dead. Which leaves four of us—Praeger, Annie, Brendan, and myself—to wonder for the rest of our lives. And that's what you have to live with for the rest of *your* life, Connor. Four of us know—or don't know. Praeger is getting old—he hasn't so many years left. Annie has longer. But Brendan and I—well, I will probably outlast you. Someone will always know. Perhaps you got away with murder, but success in murder is like an edge of glass, Connor—it's both smooth and sharp."

⁂

I was on the Dublin road, almost ten miles out of Cloncath, when the thought came. Beside me, on the other bucket seat, was the wooden box in which the Culloden Cup was packed—it was traveling back to London in far greater security than the way it had come here, probably in Brendan's coat pocket. I glanced sideways at the box often, feeling glad that I had made no claim on Connor except for what had already been mine. I thought of the Cup as I had grown to know it—I could now visualize it intimately and in part, the marvelous, delicate intricacy of it, the beauty of its lines, the supreme display of the glassmaker's art as Thomas Sheridan had shown it to his world, and to those who came after him, his heirs, either by name and blood, or by the claim of their own skill. It was then I knew what else it was I wanted that Thomas Sheridan had left behind him. I wanted it very badly, and if Connor would not give it willingly, this was something I would fight him for.

So once again I turned the car back to Cloncath.

CHAPTER 13

I

After the car was taken off the ferry in Liverpool, I had a long, late breakfast at a hotel, smoking too many cigarettes with coffee, and making a show of reading a newspaper so that I would be left in peace by the waiters. They were closing the dining room before I had made up my mind. I put through the call to Claude from the hotel lobby and waited nervously, knowing that it had to be done before I was back in London, before the pull of the old values reasserted themselves.

His tone was affable when he answered. "Claude? This is Maura. I'm in Liverpool."

The tone changed to a kind of peevish snarl. "Well, darling, as far as I'm concerned, you can stay right there. You've let me down—you've made me look a fool! This is going to take a lot of forgiving, Maura . . ."

"Claude, please listen quietly, and don't explode. It's just that there's nothing else I can do. I've thought about it all and I've decided . . ."

"Sweetie, get to the point, will you? I haven't all morning."

"Claude, it's about the photos—the ones Max took that you were going to use for the Wild campaign."

"Yes . . . ?" The tone was ominous. "What about them?"

"Well, Claude, I don't want you to use them. In fact, I have to have them back. You see, they're—"

"What! Have them back? You're out of your mind! You can't do that to me, you little bitch! Listen, you dumb bunny, I *sold* you on the strength of those pictures. And it isn't that you're so great, but Max is an inspired photographer. They're sold, I tell you. You can't have them back. It's too late—they'll never have time to get new ones ready for the autumn campaign for Wild."

"Claude, I *have* to have them back. I'm telling you that and I mean it! Those photographs belong to me, and I didn't give you permission to sell them. They're my property, and I mean to have them back. If necessary I'll sue for recovery of them." I couldn't believe what I heard myself saying; a kind of mad exultation was surging through me at the sound of my own voice telling Claude what he could not do with my life.

"You *can't!* You'll wreck the whole deal. If you withdraw those photos the Wild people will back down on the whole deal." The voice had dropped its note of peevish ill-humor. He sensed that I meant what I was saying, and he was summoning the force of threats and cold logic to beat me; he grew deadly earnest. "Maura, I promise you this—if you carry through this crazy idea you'll be black-listed by every agency in London. You'll never work again. No one will touch you with a forty-foot pole. And I, personally, will see that they don't!"

"Claude, it's no use threatening me. Whatever happens will happen. I can't help it. Those photos were never meant for publication. They never belonged to me—or to Max, either. They were my mother's private property. I had no right ever to let them out of my hands. They are just not meant for commercial exploitation—and that's that!"

"I'm listening to you, Maura, and I don't believe that someone can be saying good-bye deliberately to a promising and possibly a very lucrative career." The silken, menacing drawl was back; he hoped to paint the other side of the picture, the side I would be missing; he hoped to ridicule me out of my determination. "Just by way of curiosity, darling, tell me what brought on this sudden change? It would be quite refreshing if it weren't so stupid."

"No business of yours, Claude. I just happened to have discovered that everything in life is not for sale. That's a good enough reason."

"How perfectly nineteenth-century of you, darling! How delightfully eccentric! I wonder how long this pose will last? Are you going back to nature in the Irish bogs? Such a pity—you had quite a potential. You might easily have been big-time. But of course you know that you're finished. From the minute I make that phone call to the Wild people, you're finished in modeling. You know that, don't you, Maura? Just that one phone call, and you're finished. Are you listening, Maura . . . ?"

"I've been listening, Claude, and I've heard enough." Very carefully I replaced the receiver.

I had to sit in the lounge and have some more coffee, smoke two more cigarettes, and wait to grow calmer. My blouse was wet with sweat, and my hands still shook slightly when I went and placed a second call to London, to Max Arnott.

"Max? It's Maura."

"I've been expecting you." The deep slow voice was calm, reassuring. "Claude's been screaming at me for twenty minutes."

"I'm awfully sorry, Max. I just had to do it. It doesn't really make any difference to you, does it? I mean, they'd be delighted if you'd agree to do the whole series whether I'm the model or not."

"I suppose so . . . It doesn't matter, Maura. I'm not much interested in doing the series unless it's for you. But I'm glad —I'm glad we're not using Blanche's pictures."

"You're sure?"

"I'm sure. And I'm glad you realized it in time. You can't sell what was in those pictures and ever pretend you're going to capture it again. They were for a special time—it was a very personal thing. I didn't think you were old enough to understand that—and I didn't like to spoil your chance . . ."

"I'm a good bit older than I was ten days ago." My voice was starting to shake. "I have to go, Max. I'll see you and Susie soon."

When I was able to, I put in the final call, to the shop in

King's Road. It was odd to hear Mary Hughes' voice answer with my mother's name. "Blanche D'Arcy."

"Mary? It's Maura. I'm in Liverpool—I'm driving to London today. I'll be in some time tonight."

"Well, thank goodness for that! I've been worried about you —that sudden change of plans. I didn't know what to think. You might have sent me a card."

I had a wild vision of a colored postcard with Castle Tyrell or Meremount, in its better days, on it—*wish you were here*. "There wasn't time even for that, Mary. It's been—mad, and terrible. My grandmother . . ." I couldn't begin on it now.

"Grandmother! I didn't know you had one. It all sounds very Irish, dear."

"It is! I'll tell you all about it." Of course I wouldn't tell her all about it; only four of us would ever know all about it, as I had said to Connor. "Mary, I just rang to let you know that I was coming back—and would you be an angel and leave some bread and milk in the flat for me?"

"Well, I'll wait for you, of course."

"No, don't do that. I'll probably be quite late—the morning's gone already, and I expect traffic will be heavy. I'll probably have dinner somewhere on the road, to have a break. I'll see you in the morning."

"Maura—just one other thing."

The voice of the operator cut in, with a demand for more money. "Mary, it'll have to wait. I've used up all my change. See you in the morning."

I brought the car from its parking place to the front of the hotel, and watched my bag and the two boxes being stowed in the back. "I took good care of them for you, miss," the porter said, pointing at the boxes. "Didn't take my eyes off them." He got more of a tip than he expected, but then he didn't know what was in the boxes.

I eased the car into the traffic, and settled down for the tedious drive. I would be sandwiched between heavy lorries all the way, bound for London and the Southern counties; there would be many hours to think about what had happened, what I had done, and what had changed. The past was gone, Claude and perhaps the whole existence I had known in London; Lloyd Justin was gone; the future that had opened up had come and gone —Connor, Meremount, Sheridan Glass, Praeger, Brendan, all gone. I had not become the Wild girl, I had not become Lotti, nor the owner of Sheridan Glass; I had not become the young wife living the American dream. In place of all these alternatives a kind of frightening emptiness waited for me—frightening, because it occurred to me that in the end I might do nothing that was worth doing with whatever identity I had won.

II

It was late, as I thought it would be, when I got into London, and I was able to park in front of the shop in King's Road. The lights were on upstairs in the flat and on the stairs. I had brought in my bag and the two boxes—the second one big and awkward to carry—before I saw the envelope on the little hall table. It was addressed in Mary's loose scrawl—*Maura*. As I ripped it open I was conscious of the smell that floated down the stairs to me, a rich mingled smell of onion and garlic and wine, and the faint odor of burning. With the note in my hand I started up the stairs, and then stopped as I read the first sentence.

Maura, dear—I really don't know if I've done a foolish thing —whether I should have let him in or called the police. My knees felt weak, and I held onto the rail as I skimmed the remainder. *But he's most persuasive, and I couldn't help believing him. I don't quite understand what it's all about, but he's been here Monday and Tuesday and again this morning asking if there was word from you. He said he didn't know whether you would come back from Ireland, but if you did, he meant to be waiting for you. So I let him wait.*

I stood in the living-room door and looked at him, asleep, crumpled on the sofa that was too short for him, and I knew that I would see his sleeping face many times again, that I would know every expression of it, see my own moods mirrored there; I would love him, and at times believe that I almost hated him, I would laugh with him, and have him comfort me, I would grow bored with him, and angry, and long for him, as I had done since the moment he had left me. I knew, as I looked at him, why it was that I had turned back to Cloncath yesterday and demanded from Connor the glassmaking tools that had belonged to Thomas Sheridan. Connor had given them without protest, and I think he also had known for whom they were intended.

He slept heavily. I bent over and touched his cheek with my hand, and that too I knew I would do a thousand times.

"Brendan!—the stew's burning."

CHAPTER 14

We do not live romantically above the glassworks in Bristol, as I once pictured Brendan doing, but near enough so that I walk over there in the afternoons and do some bookkeeping, and type letters, slowly and carefully, because I am still learning. The old stone warehouse that we rent from the family of Tim Henderson, who is Brendan's partner, looks out on the river, and I spend more time than I should watching the river traffic, and even more time watching the work around the furnaces, the fantastic dance of skill and grace that I had seen first at Sheridan Glass. I am not afraid of it any more, I do not blink and draw back as the glowing molten glass flashes by me on pontil or blowing iron. I am attuned now to the rhythms and patterns of the dance, and I love to watch it—and, as Brendan said, it's warm around the furnaces in winter. There are only two glory holes, and it is doubtful that Brendan and Tim will want many more, even when the demand calls for them. They have six apprentices, and two servitors and another master glassblower; expansion would mean the end of the individual quality of the pieces they blow. In the spring they will give their first exhibition in London and Stockholm, but already the orders are coming in —for glass screens, for abstract glass sculpture, for bowls and vases. "We'll have to watch out," Brendan says to Tim, "that we don't get too successful and start repeating ourselves. Then we're dead." Success is with us already, but it is not the kind of success one grows rich on.

As Claude had threatened me, for a while there was no modeling work for me in London; probably I will never work again for a high-fashion magazine—Claude will see to that, as well as the fact that I have gained the fatal extra pounds that stop me from photographing gaunt and hungry-eyed. But there is enough of the other kind of work, cake mixes and Marsh's chocolates, and modeling the sweaters that go with the knitting instructions in the women's magazines. It is gentler work, almost dull, and it does not clutch at me and make me sharp and bad-tempered and exhausted, as the other used to. I commute to London when I am needed, like any businessman, and I am anxious to get home again. Letting go can be a sweet relief.

We do not talk about Meremount or Tyrell or Connor—not because the subject brings pain, but because we have said all we want to say about it. I know that for Brendan I am not a substitute for Lotti, and that is all I need to know. In *The Times* we read about the auction of Meremount's contents at Southby's; there were some New York buyers, and so bidding was brisk and prices high. They did uncover the small treasures, the minor masterpieces that Praeger had predicted; some of the special pieces I could remember having seen—the sets of Chippendale chairs, the matching commodes, the eighteenth-century Sèvres dinner service stacked on the floor, the Chinese service. Mary Hughes attended each day of the three-day sale, and sent me a catalogue with the prices jotted down. I could feel her chagrin come through the scrawled figures—she knew about Meremount now, and her pain was for Blanche and what Blanche had missed. For myself I didn't care. The only time I was touched with anger and hurt was when a woman journalist, on holiday in Ireland, caught the scent of the Meremount story, and wrote it up in the *Sunday Express* before the auction: RARE TREASURES IN MANSION OF ECCENTRIC RECLUSE. Parts of the truth were there—Lady Maude, Sheridan Glass, a rehash of the tragedy of Lotti's death, Otto Praeger's wealth. It was vulgarized and overdone, and part of the truth being there made the falsity worse.

Mary Hughes still hangs on to the shop—will do it, probably, until the lease runs out, so Blanche's name is still high above the King's Road. I drive out sometimes to the auctions in the countryside around Bristol, and I've made a few purchases for Mary, tentatively, with no great confidence that they are the right buys. But the dealers who always appear at each auction were Blanche's friends, and they make a little game about teaching me the business. I have a sense that they loved Blanche, and miss her.

Otto Praeger has bought Meremount, and at last has been able to buy Thomas Sheridan's own collection of Venetian glass —and so both are off Connor's hands. That and the Southby sale have given him enough capital to let him borrow more, and to begin the process of pulling Sheridan Glass into a competitive position. He will not do as much as he could have done if the Praeger money had backed him, but unless things go very wrong, it seems certain that Sheridan Glass will not disappear. For that I am glad; Connor I try not to think about.

Praeger does not let us go—Brendan and I. Three times he has been to Bristol and we begin to dread his visits, and yet lack the sternness to turn him away. He is lonely; he talks much of Meremount, but not of Connor. Meremount is being restored, and Praeger's chief pleasure is sending his agents to scour England and the Continent for the furniture and paintings that will decorate it as the perfect eighteenth-century house. He paid Connor inflated prices for the privilege of picking over Meremount's contents for what would best suit the house. The Hogarths, Gainsboroughs, Romneys, and Reynoldses are coming in, and Praeger is paying the prices a collector must when he is in a hurry. "Meremount is to be a museum of eighteenth-century arts—paintings, furnishings, ceramics, silver, glass, rugs, landscape gardening . . . It will be presented to the Irish people. President de Valera will come to open it." His eyes mist over as he says it; he dreams he is buying a birthright.

With Brendan and I the attempt to buy is more subtle. He inspects the glasshouse, and says, "With a little capital you could double your output in a year." Brendan tries to explain, with great patience, that all Tim and he want is just to sell the products of their own making—that a dozen master glassblowers would make a dozen different things, all needing their own market. Praeger shakes his head. "You could institute design control—look at Steuben in America." But Brendan doesn't want to see the same piece ten thousand times. "We don't want to be Sheridan Glass, or Steuben, or Kosta. We have to stay a studio workshop. The big boys will copy our designs, but we will have done them first." So Praeger shakes his head, and the offer to lend or give money is bitten back.

But he keeps reaching to us in other ways. He is waiting for my first child to be born as a grandfather would; when it comes he will be harder to restrain. He keeps urging us to come to Tyrell. "The North Lodge is still empty," he says. "I have never rented it. You could be quite private and on your own." He doesn't understand how marvelously private we are now, because we live in each other. He will keep reaching for us, and it will grow harder and harder to keep him out. He wants to give us things—I am afraid he wants to give us everything. We know, Brendan and I, that if he takes away from us the opportunities to give to each other, if money should take away the need to work for each other, to work physically and in all the other ways that love demands, then we are already beginning to lose.

So we hold him off for as long as we can; but we don't yet know who will win.